Fallback

Planetfall

Book II

L.E. Howel

L.E. Howel

DEDICATION

TO MY SON
WE ALMOST LOST YOU
I CAN'T IMAGINE LIFE WITHOUT YOU
I DON'T WANT TO

L.E. Howel

"SOLAMEN MISERIS SOCIOS HABUISSE DOLORIS"

L.E. Howel

Fallback

Planetfall
Book II

L.E. Howel

ONE

A finger of smoke traced across the empty sky. From below it was a miraculous wonder, like the dawning of a new age. Nothing like it had been seen in living memory. Blanched faces looked up, blinked into the sunlight, and wondered. The gasps of awe and fear from those that now watched the phenomenon was the only audible sound as the distant ship streaked up into space, leaving only the trail of its spent fuel behind.

Normality returned as quickly as it had gone. A few persistent individuals continued to watch as the vapor slowly dispersed into the atmosphere, but most had already forgotten its significance and were hurrying on with their lives. Soon even this ethereal trail would be lost, and no one would remember.

From within the hurtling craft, the perspective was quite different. G-forces had pushed the five occupants deeper into their seats and contorted their faces into determined grimaces. The ship shook, and Birch's hands tightly clasped the controls as they raced through the air toward the vacuum of space.

Already they were fast approaching the first barrier to their escape, the debris field. Realistically Birch knew the chances of making it through were slim. There had been no time to plot the course, and they couldn't wait. It was suicide, but he knew that even now the guidance field that had saved them on their arrival all those months ago would now be seeking them out to pull them back down to Earth. They had to rush for freedom and hope.

It was hopeless. Those million metal fragments surrounding this world represented the broken dreams and promises of space exploration, and now they probably meant certain death to this last escape. It was stupid to try, but he feared his own annihilation much less than what he had found in this place. There were some things worse than death.

The familiar blue of the sky faded toward the alien darkness of space. Birch imagined he could already see the chunks of forgotten metal swarming toward them, protecting this fragile planet like a host of hornets buzzing around their nest. This ship was an enemy of this world and their escape would be blocked. Even their own history was against them.

"Major," Jane's voice interrupted his thoughts, "the ship's laid out a course through the field." Her voice was even, but her face betrayed both her relief and surprise.

Birch blinked and looked down at his own screen. She was right. Without any prompting, the ship had independently calculated the path of every fragment in the wretched sky. No computer he knew could make the calculations that quickly, but there it was, a way out. This tenuous red thread, a computer generated path through the field, represented the sum of their hopes. Now all he could do was follow it.

He altered their course, taking them into line with the coordinates set out by the computer.

It wasn't his imagination now; he could see the floating debris as the sunlight glinted off the jagged bits of metal that swirled ominously in the darkness. As always, this was going to be tough. The computer had plotted a course, but he would have to navigate it. There were just too many variables for a computer to handle. It took human instinct.

Birch was steeling himself for the ordeal when he felt a sudden shift in the controls that sent the ship plunging forward toward the floating wreckage. In the next instant, they would be in the middle of it and he had lost control.

"What are you doing?" Birch growled, glaring accusingly across at Jane in the copilot's seat. His hands were fighting against the turn of the stick, but he couldn't regain control.

"It's not me," she barked back. "It's the ship! It's veering off on its own. It looks like the thing's set its own course, and now it's going to take us through."

"No," Birch muttered furiously as he wrestled again for control. No system, no computer, no automation of any kind could get them through. He knew that. The debris field was just too much. It needed human input- human control. He had to stop it.

The ship plunged into the field, and the fact that they were still alive didn't stifle his logic. He knew it couldn't happen, and so he continued to fight against it.

The struggle was useless. Perhaps with a better knowledge of the ship he fought against he might have known what to do, or what not to do. Instead, he fumbled ignorantly at the controls that seemed so familiar, yet strangely wrong. Everything had all the marks of NASA technology, and he performed all the set procedures that should have returned the ship to his control, but it didn't work. Nothing he did worked. As his frustration grew, so his actions became increasingly violent. He pounded at the panel. Still, nothing changed. Panic had him by the throat; they were locked out of the controls and they were being blasted into the center of the field.

It was the course display that proved his fears. It wasn't easy to see in the data, but when you looked for it the evidence was plain. They were going to die, and this computer was going to kill them. It had laid out a course straight into one of the millions of floating fragments. It was small enough to be missed on the display but big enough to finish them. He could imagine why. A thousand possible answers came to mind in that single instant. Perhaps this was the last revenge of a forlorn NASA base. They might have left this ship as a last strike at their enemies, as a booby trap to destroy any who would use it. That was possible, or perhaps this was just another malfunctioning relic from the age of space exploration. Whatever it was, this computer had set a course to destruction and now it was leading them to it by the nose.

"I want all terminals shut down," Birch barked at Jane. "Get that computer offline now!"

She blinked dumbly and looked up. In the pale light of her screen Birch caught the look of disbelief. The display was flashing alerts that winked on and off, casting her face alternately from darkness into light and back into darkness. She shook her head.

"I can't do that," she responded gruffly. "We're right in the middle of the field now. If we lose the computer we lose all guidance. We'd be flying blind. That's suicide!"

"Do it!" Birch growled menacingly. He didn't have time to explain. She had to obey, but her flinty eyes met his and did not falter. She was uncowed by his bluster and merely shook her head again to emphasize her resistance. She trusted the computer more than him and nothing he could say would change that.

He had to act. Furiously he snatched at the buckle of his restraints and hauled himself from his seat toward Jane's control panel. She raised her hands defensively, covering it as though protecting a defenseless child from an aggressor, but Birch flung her aside and started pounding at the keys. The result was the same. Nothing happened. It was as though all the flashing buttons, and all the buzzing panels, and all the humming computer displays were nothing more than a beautiful mock-up. They didn't control anything.

Suddenly the ship lurched and rolled, sending Birch skidding across the floor. A scraping clang from the hull indicated a glancing blow, but the ship hurtled on, weaving and twisting at amazing velocity through the debris, until a moment later when the ship came to an abrupt, complete stop.

They were through! They had cleared the debris field.

The lights went out.

Birch felt himself rise, floating off the floor. They had lost gravity.

"The computer's down," Jane's voice rasped in the darkness. "It's taken everything with it: engines, oxygen, gravity, total power loss. Everything's dead. Give it a day or so and we'll be dead too. That's about how much air we've got."

Birch sighed. Sometimes there was no fate worse than getting what you wanted. He had been sure they couldn't trust the computer, that it was flying them to destruction. He had seen the collision coming on the flight path. It was deliberate, the computer had planned it, but it had only been a small hit, one they had survived. Maybe that had been the plan all along, the only way, their only chance to make it through. The speed of their launch had left no time for anything else. It had been an ugly escape, a dangerous escape. The computer had calculated that; it had taken that chance and saved their lives. He couldn't have done it. By instinct, he would have tried to avoid that smaller fragment and hit something bigger. He would have gotten them killed. The computer had been right. He hated to admit it.

Now that computer was out it had taken all the other systems down with it. Without it they were dead. He had to fix it, fast.

A sudden trace of light passed across the cockpit window.

"Incoming!" Jane hissed.

A moment later the ship shook as a blinding explosion burst around them.

"Missiles!" Jane shouted, clutching habitually at her inoperative console, "More on the way," she added as glowing trails of crimson light crossed paths in the ebony sky. Instantly a magnificent conflagration erupted, engulfing the convulsing ship in its fiery grip. Somehow they survived.

"They won't let you go," Edwards observed grimly. As an unwilling part of this crew, he was still seeking a way back to earth. "They could have killed you already. They're looking to disable the ship, then they'll bring you back down. You can count on it."

"Not alive they won't," Birch spat back bitterly.

Pushing his feet against the bulkhead, Birch performed a less than graceful approximation of a swimmer's plunge and dove for the control panel. A moment later he had a flashlight from the emergency kit and the hatch pulled aside to reveal the wiring to the computer. It was intact but dead. No power was getting this far. The problem went deeper.

"Looks like I'll have to get to the source. Any idea where the computer mainframe might be housed, Gray?"

Jane shook her head. "It looks like a pretty complex system. With everything it controls, it may be somewhere near the propulsion unit, or maybe it has its own auxiliary station. I couldn't really say for sure. Whatever it is, you'd better find it fast. Much more damage and this ship'll be crippled for good, with or without a computer!"

Birch nodded, trying to make up his mind where to start. Another round of explosions pummeled the ship, proving the urgency of the decision.

"Okay," Birch grunted, "I'm heading below to see what I can find. I'm taking Edwards with me." He collared the reluctant astronaut, pulling him to the door with him. "If anyone can understand this modern technology it'll be him. Besides, I want to keep an eye on him. You be ready to get us out of here as soon as I get everything back online." Without waiting for a reply Birch pushed Edwards through the door and followed him out into the darkened corridor.

Birch's flashlight cast a pallid glow on their surroundings. In its meager light, the stark corridor stretched gloomily into darkness. This wasn't going to be easy. He followed his instinct, seeking a path down, always descending in the belief that what he was looking for would be somewhere deep in the heart of the ship.

Floating clumsily from level to level, fighting their weightless bodies, they clambered down narrow crawl spaces, ever deeper into the darkness.

The dulled thud of continued explosions sounded through the bulkhead. The ship shook.

"Major," Jane's voice crackled over Birch's radio.

"Yeah, what?" He answered tersely. He didn't really want to hear from her right now. He didn't need any more bad news about the condition of the ship.

"It's that animal you insisted on picking up, the Ares kid. Better watch your back. He snuck off during the last attack. He's running loose on the ship."

Birch shuddered. The kid had been so quiet since their departure he had almost forgotten him. That little beast, the cruel animal that had killed Karla, Birch knew he should have killed him when he had the chance, but something had stopped him. He had looked into that face and seen something there, something he almost recognized. On a whim, he had saved him. Now he was on the loose, on the prowl again, and probably looking to kill them all.

Birch sighed. "Yeah, I'll be watching."

TWO

Another explosion sent a heaving shudder through the ship. It was close, the closest one yet, and the echo thundered through the empty corridors. Birch and Edwards tumbled helplessly in the surrounding tumult, smashing into a nearby wall.

"We better find that computer system soon," Birch muttered darkly as he steadied himself. He had never enjoyed the weightless experience, it left him feeling weak and helpless, but this constant pummeling, being thrown about like a worthless piece of driftwood, was almost too much. Angrily he pulled himself to the access hatch and climbed clumsily to the next level.

Birch's mind buzzed with frustrated energy. Everywhere trouble surrounded him, and yet there seemed so little he could do about it. Room after room of emptiness was all he found. Now the thin light of Birch's flashlight seemed to be dimming. The shadows around them seemed to grow darker and more encroaching, and the thought of that wild Ares kid running around down here was less than comforting.

Perhaps it was his imagination, but it seemed to be getting harder to breathe. The air shouldn't have been running short yet unless maybe the hull had been breached somewhere and they were leaking oxygen out into space. He briefly considered the possibility of going in search of an EVA suit, of telling the others to do the same, to prolong their lives a few hours, but what was the point. If they didn't get that computer online soon they were dead anyway. No time to waste, he had to get to the central system now.

A sudden, sharp electrical whine pierced the stale air and a whooshing gust of oxygen hit them like an exhaled breath. The power was back on. In that moment, Birch and Edwards felt the immediate effect of gravity. They toppled, plummeting headfirst to the floor. Landing hard, Birch wheezed painfully, the breath knocked from his lungs.

In that same instant, the lights came on. Birch blinked, squinting in the new light. The return of power was so unexpected, so sudden, that for a moment he hardly knew what to think. He quickly recovered. Snatching up the radio he barked the order to Jane.

"Get us out of here, full power, now!"

"Already on it," Jane replied coolly. "Actually, we've cleared Mars' orbital circuit. We came out of earth's range less than half a second after I hit the button, and we weren't even up to full speed! I had to stop almost as fast as we started, or who knows where we'd have ended up."

"How's that possible?" Birch's mind was trying to calculate the numbers, to figure out just how fast they had to go to make that happen. He couldn't manage it. It was too fast.

Breaking the light barrier had been NASA's boldest dream and brightest achievement. It had opened up the possibility of deep space travel and made the Hypnos missions happen, but this went far beyond that. This wasn't breaking the light barrier. This was smashing it, pulverizing it- obliterating it altogether, then casting the shattered remnants of their limited knowledge to the wind. Now they could go places!

Birch shook his head. It just didn't seem possible.

"I know it seems impossible," Jane's voice echoed his doubts, "but here we are."

Birch glanced over at Edwards, wondering if he knew any more about this technology, but his expression was as bewildered as his own. This was something beyond either of their experiences.

"Well, I'm just glad you finally got it together up there," Birch admitted. "I don't know how you fixed it, but we owe you one. We were getting nowhere down here."

An awkward silence followed.

"We didn't fix it," Jane finally answered. Her voice sounded confused through the radio static. "We thought it was you."

Birch and Edwards looked at each other again, trying to process this new information. Edwards' face suddenly went ashen. Something had occurred to him. He grabbed Birch's radio and shouted into it.

"Shut the door! Shut it now! Seal off the cockpit!"

Jane's reply was crackling through the radio when an unearthly scream screeched through the receiver. A mighty clang sounded on the other end, and the radio went dead.

Edwards was already running up the corridor, back the way they had come. "We have to get to the cockpit before it's too late!" he shouted over his shoulder.

Birch gave up his fruitless attempt to regain contact with Jane and followed. Almost immediately he overtook Edwards in a mad dash for the control room. That scream had been chillingly familiar. He had heard it before, and he knew what it meant. Jane and Lauren were in danger and he had to get up there now.

The lights went out again. It wasn't a complete power loss this time. Gravity was still engaged, but as they approached the elevator to the flight deck Birch knew they weren't going to get there that way. The panel was dead, and there was no response to anything he tried.

Birch sighed. There was no way around it. They were back to climbing the access shaft. There was no other way up. He opened the hatch and shone his light up into the darkness. It was a long way up. It had been bad enough getting down when they had been weightless, but getting up like this was going to take some time. They didn't have any time.

"Let's go", he muttered, and with grunting effort flung himself at the ladder. He climbed. Weariness gnawed at his muscles. His arms ached and burned as he mechanically lifted arm-after-arm, ascending into the darkness, his small flashlight clutched between his teeth to give him some sight of the smooth, metal rungs as they climbed endlessly upward.

Twenty minutes passed in silence. His progress was steady but not fast enough for the purpose of saving Jane and Lauren. He could hear Edwards puffing somewhere beneath him. He must have been finding the ascent even harder than he was.

"You alright down there?" Birch called, pausing to shine his light down the shaft. Edwards was laboring some thirty feet below. He gave no immediate answer, but his upturned face was gaunt and shone with perspiration. His faltering, jerking movements answered Birch's question far better than any words could.

"Oh yeah, just great," Edwards finally managed to gasp. "Keep going. I'll catch you in a minute."

Birch turned and climbed again. Quickly he got into a rhythm. His body ached, but his mind was possessed by the one single thought. He had to save his crew.

His boots clanged swiftly on the metal rungs. Their reverberation was his only company in the shadowy semidarkness. Edwards had fallen further behind again and couldn't be seen or heard. If there had been time Birch might have paused to worry about that, to wonder where Edwards was, to consider the possibility of danger. He might even have begun to wonder where that Ares kid had gotten to, but he didn't. He was busy. He had to get to the top.

Then he saw it. In his haste he almost missed it. He had already missed it on the way down, but then he had been sure that the vitals of a complex vessel like this would be housed on the lower decks, far from the main body of the ship. He hadn't really been looking for it here. But here it was. Power conduits. Not much to look at, a few extra wires, thick ones, running off the shaft into the bulkhead, but that was enough. It was the sort of clue he should have been looking for. It was the sort of clue he should have seen. More power to this floor could mean only one thing- more equipment. That was it! The auxiliary station would be here.

"Edwards," Birch called down into the darkness. "Edwards, I've found it, the auxiliary station! Look for the wires running into the wall. When you get up here, see if you can find the computer and get things under control. I'm going on up to the flight deck and I'll be back down as soon as I've got Jane and Lauren."

No answer.

"Edwards!" Birch shouted again. No answer. He trained the thin beam of light down into the inky maw below. There was nothing. He took a few steps down, leaned out from the ladder and searched again with his flashlight, piercing the darkness, but exposing nothing more than the empty rungs stretching out into the shaft beneath him. Birch shivered. Edwards was gone.

THREE

Suddenly Birch was alone. Jane and Lauren were silent; the radio was dead. Edwards had gone altogether. The only person Birch was certain he would see again was the Ares kid, but that was no comfort. That was going to be a fight if he got the chance. More likely the ubiquitous little demon was going to jump him from behind and slit his throat. He would have to watch himself.

He watched. Shining his flashlight up and down the shaft he took in his surroundings with newly cautious eyes. There was still nothing- nothing to be seen except for the bare steel walls and the empty rungs- and nothing to be heard but the ragged rasp of his own panting breath. Whatever had happened to Edwards had happened silently and quickly. He needed to get out of here fast before the same thing happened to him.

Birch paused; he had a decision to make. He could either continue climbing up to see what happened to Jane and Lauren, or go down and look for Edwards. The choice was an easy one in the end. It was all a question of math, really, two people at the top, one down below. It was that simple. He would go with the numbers and continue up to the flight deck to save the two, then come back down for the one. Besides, Birch knew enough about the Ares to expect a trap if he went blundering down there looking for Edwards. He was going to be smart for once. He was going to wait and find the Ares when *he* was ready- when he would have the advantage, when the little monster wasn't expecting him. Until then he would continue with the original plan and save Jane and Lauren if he could.

Birch thumped up the last rungs of the ladder. Only another five or six levels remained and he quickly reached the top. He pushed the hatch aside, heaving it open with a heavy clang, and tumbled wearily out into the darkened corridor.

The pulsating squeal of an alarm was enough to warn him that things were as bad as he had feared. A muffled computerized voice told of an impending doom that he couldn't quite understand amidst the din of claxon signals.

He rushed for the cockpit door. It was locked. He banged on it, calling for Jane and Lauren, but there was no answer. The door wouldn't budge. Its control panel was dead and everything he tried had no effect. The only perceivable change was an increase in the volume of the computer's voice.

"Cabin depressurization in the cockpit," it warned flatly. "Critical level achieved in thirty-five minutes."

Birch panicked, instinctively throwing himself at the door, trying to bring it down with brute force, but the effort was wasted. It was too strong. He fumbled at the control panel again, trying to override the locking mechanism, but with no effect. It wasn't getting any power.

He gave up the direct approach; the door wasn't opening that way and stormed back up the corridor. Flinging himself back into the access shaft he half-slid, half-fell the six levels back down to the conduits. He was sure they would lead him to the auxiliary station.

He almost came off twice. In his hurry his sweaty hands slipped, leaving him dangling, just catching himself before he fell to a certain death below. He didn't care. He had people to save and he was going to save them, whether it killed him or not.

He leaped off the ladder at the seventh level and passed through the hatch into another darkened passageway. There was nothing here to encourage any better hope of finding what he sought, but his gut told him he was right. He was sure the auxiliary station was near.

It took a few minutes before he found it. The door was located at the far end of the corridor. It looked very much like the others, except that attached to it was a simple metal sign that read, "AUXILIARY CONTROL".

Birch ran to the door, but it didn't open. It was locked or jammed. Either way, he wasn't getting in. He pushed hard against the metal frame, but it proved just as immovable as the cockpit door had been.

Time was running out. He had to get through. He opened the control panel in the wall, but again, like the one to the flight deck, it didn't offer much hope. No power was getting to it. Still, he fumbled desperately with the wires, seeking a change he knew wasn't possible. He couldn't think of anything else to do.

And then it opened. A green light flashed on the powerless panel and the door slid aside. He went in.

The room was almost completely dark, but not quite. Faint points of light flashed from control panels, casting a strangely cheery glow, like the festive lights of a youthful Christmas celebration. They provided more atmosphere than illumination and Birch shone his flashlight around the large hall to take in his surroundings.

Stark machines lined the gray walls. Empty workstations sat in dusty neglect, untouched by humanity for centuries. Apart from that, the room was empty. Birch pause to take it all in for only a moment before hurrying to the nearest terminal.

He quickly got to work. The display was already up. In fact, the computer was engaged in a countdown, tracking the depressurization level of the cockpit. There was now less than fifteen minutes left to critical level.

Birch's head snapped back as realization crackled painfully

through his brain. Someone must have used this computer recently, and they must have let him in here, it was the only way he could have gotten through that door, and now they were watching him, waiting to pounce and finish him off.

With deliberate nonchalance, Birch reached for the flashlight. Grabbing it, he swiftly spun in his chair, flashing the beam around him. The room was empty. There wasn't anything to be seen except the machines with their winking lights and unused consoles. He traced the outline of the floor and the walls with his light, covering every inch, but the lingering examination confirmed his first impression- this place was empty and there was nowhere to hide.

Birch chuckled nervously to himself and turned again to the computer. He was too jittery. Of course, the ship's computer would track the situation in the cockpit, he reasoned. It would be working on it now, trying to fix it through automated response procedures. No one was here.

He tapped furiously at the keys, looking for the source of the problem. He almost had it. He was sure he had found the code that had shut off the air, all he had to do now was figure out how to override it.

His hands flew at the controls, seeking out the answer, when he knocked the flashlight, sending it clattering to the floor. The sound echoed gloomily off the lofty ceiling. Muttering, Birch leaned over to pick it up.

The screen's display flashed in the darkness. Less than ten minutes to go. He could feel the pressure of the ebbing time weighing on his chest, making it hard to breathe. He had to hurry. He was almost there. He could do it.

Concentration wasn't coming easily. Other things were crowding his mind. Suddenly one thought struck him like a jolt of electricity. The echo, the ceiling that sounded so far away, what was up there? A vast darkness seemed to open above him as he imagined what it might conceal.

His eyes moved slowly upward. Lifting the flashlight, he sent a thin shaft of light above his head, exposing the ceiling to his worried gaze. The light flickered, making the shadows dance and creating the illusion of movement, but he couldn't see anything definite. He looked back at the screen. Eight minutes left.

A sudden screech pierced the air, followed by a brief impression of matted hair and flashing teeth, and then Birch was on the floor, rolling and fighting for his life.

FOUR

From a perch, nearly twenty feet up the Ares had launched himself at Birch. Somehow the little savage had managed to cling to the smooth walls and avoid detection until just the right moment, the moment when Jane and Lauren had needed help the most. Now Birch's only thought was for his own survival as he fought with the screaming beast.

In the struggle, the flashlight hit the floor. It bounced and rolled, sending its circular beam of light spinning across the room, before coming to rest some distance away.

Now in darkness, Birch couldn't see the Ares clearly. Only his faint outline was visible, framed in the light of the computer screen. Knowing where he was wasn't a problem, though. He was at his throat.

The hard, thin fingers squeezed his windpipe with expert ease. Birch felt himself swooning. Like his first encounter with the Areas on earth all those months ago, he felt powerless to stop the onslaught. He couldn't breathe. He couldn't think. He was losing consciousness and soon he would be gone. Everyone would be gone. He was the last one, and he had failed.

This single reality brought him back. Volcanic rage surged through his veins. He had not come this far to have the life squeezed out him by some rabid delinquent youth that he had been stupid enough to save. He might fail, but not this way.

In desperation Birch writhed and bucked, but the boy still had him pinned. Birch sent a thudding punch to the side of the Ares' head. That dislodged him for a moment, but the lithe youth was quick to regain his footing and came back at him with doubled aggression. Birch was ready this time and gave him a hard kick to the stomach that sent him skidding back across the floor.

Already the little animal was on his feet again, coming back, undaunted. But then he stopped and, seemingly thinking better of it, turned and ran to the computer.

For a moment Birch was relieved at the respite until he realized the motive. The Ares youth was putting the finishing touches to Jane and Lauren, the coup de grace. He was making sure they never made it out, that the computer couldn't correct the problem he had created.

Birch took advantage of the distraction and staggered to his feet. Grabbing the flashlight from the floor, he took five quick steps and brought it crashing down on his foe's head. The young man should have collapsed under the force of such a blow, but instead, he swiftly turned from the computer, eyes aglow with rage. With one hand still at the keyboard, he struck out at Birch, smacking him hard in the stomach.

Birch gasped, winded. Roughly, he pulled the kid off the computer, fighting him to the floor. The two rolled, kicking and hitting each other. Those hard little hands were at his throat again, trying to squeeze him dead, but before they could get a solid grip Birch had pulled him away and landed punch after punch to his body. Birch was fighting for his life, for all of their lives, and he was going to win.

Finally, the Ares went limp. Birch pushed his attacker aside and lunged for the computer. The screen display was not encouraging. Less than a minute remained on the countdown. He gulped down air, struggling to breathe, fighting to concentrate. Luckily the kid had coded into the network already, preparing to work whatever final mischief he had planned. Now Birch could start where he had left off and reverse the process, getting the door open and the air back on.

Swiftly Birch tapped in the last few lines of data, sending the override codes. The screen flashed green and the number display froze at seventeen seconds. Birch sighed and slumped over the computer. He had done it.

For a time all he could do was breathe. The exhaustion of relief left him struggling, even for that most basic necessity of life. Finally, he lifted his head, blinked dully at the computer's flickering display, and started working to get the ship fully operational.

It didn't take long. Following the same path that had led him to the cockpit's problems, Birch was able to easily restore full function to the ship.

The lights flickered and came on, and for a moment Birch hesitated, considering what to do next. Of course, he needed to get to Jane and Lauren and make sure they were okay, but he needed to deal with the Ares kid first.

Leaving him lying there unattended would be a stupid move. Even tying him up didn't seem like a good option. He had far too much respect for the Ares' capacity for mayhem to expect anything but trouble if he took his eyes off him, even for a second. He had to get him on ice, literally, before he could do anything else.

Grabbing the youth by the scruff of the neck, Birch pulled him onto his shoulders and ran down the long corridor to the now-functioning elevator. Sensing his presence, the doors slid aside, and Birch stepped in. After the briefest of moments, the lift shot down to the level he had selected. Birch stepped out.

This floor was not a narrow, door lined corridor like all the others. Instead, it opened out into a vast, expansive chamber, lined with row-after-row of rectangular boxes. Like the markers of a well-ordered cemetery, the boxes formed a pattern of geometric uniformity. Unlike a cemetery, however, these boxes were unoccupied.

This was the cryogenic chamber he had discovered earlier in his search of this vast ship. Whatever great strides of technology had been made to make this ship possible, one thing was clear. Space was just too big, too formidable, too much to be taken on without cryogenics. Whatever incredible speed this ship could manage, it was clear that one lifetime was still too short a blip in eternity to ever get you anywhere truly important.

Birch paused at a box along the far wall and began typing on its attached keyboard. The lid lifted and he shoved the Ares into the empty compartment. Swiftly attaching the necessary equipment he slammed the lid down and watched with satisfaction as the glass window fogged and iced during the dramatic first stage of cryogenic freezing. Soon the ice cleared and the frosty-still face of the boy could be seen. Birch smiled grimly. Even an Ares couldn't get out of that one. They were safe.

Now Birch's thoughts turned to Jane and Lauren. He ran to the elevator, punched the button, and hurtled back up to the flight deck. Moments later he was in the corridor, staring at the same door he had struggled with earlier. It remained obstinately shut. Instead of sliding aside as he approached, it buzzed angrily and would not admit him.

The control panel was getting power now. Birch reached for it but was jolted back by a massive shock that sent him flying into the nearby wall. He shook his head groggily and stumbled back to his feet. Jane must have rigged the door to juice anyone who tried to use it.

The course of events now seemed clear in Birch's mind. The Ares kid had wanted control of the ship and had tried to get into the cockpit; Birch had heard that over the radio. Jane must have kept him out by wiring the door. With no way to get in, the Ares must have gone down to auxiliary control and monkied around with the ship's systems. He could have shut off the air and other power grids as a way to force Jane and Lauren out of the cockpit, or maybe he just planned to kill them and get in after they had suffocated.

And in the middle of all this, the kid still had time to nab Edwards and had almost gotten him too. In the end, Birch himself had been the sole barrier to this plan to seize control of the ship and, no doubt, take it back to the Ares for use in their war against President Michaels.

Birch shivered. It was a bold scheme and one that had almost worked. The Ares were dangerous enemies and he was glad to have the kid out of the way.

But now Birch faced the same problem he had begun with. He had to get into the cockpit. Without being able to touch the door his options were limited. He thought briefly about going back down to auxiliary control and trying to override it there, but if the kid hadn't managed it, he doubted he could. Eventually, he decided on the simplest, most direct approach.

"Major Gray, Jane! Lauren! It's Major Birch." he shouted at the door. If anyone was alive and cognizant of their surroundings in there they would hear him through the speaker.

"Are you alright in there?" he shouted again.

He could hear something from inside. It was faint, but most certainly there. He shouted again.

"Jane!" he called, "Lauren! Open the door!" The response grew louder, more defined. He heard a muffled voice and a retching, hacking cough. A moment later the door slid aside and Jane fell at his feet.

Birch stooped down, catching her up in his arms. Her eyes fluttered and she coughed in his face. Birch winced as her dry breath covered him.

"You okay?' he asked anxiously. She nodded between gasping breaths and gestured weakly behind her to where Lauren lay slumped over her console. Birch dropped Jane and ran to her.

Lauren was unconscious, but even as he kneeled to examine her he could see that her breathing was becoming more regular, more pronounced. Her eyes blinked open and she slowly lifted her head to meet his gaze. For a moment a flicker of a smile passed her lips before the "Lauren mask" descended again.

They were going to be okay. Birch stood up and walked to the door. "I've got to go," he announced quickly. "Edwards is still out there somewhere. The Ares kid got to him. I have to find him."

Without waiting for a response Birch ran down the corridor to the elevator and punched the key for floor twenty. That would be the best place to start. It was somewhere around there that Edwards had disappeared, and Birch hoped that he would find him nearby. The Ares hadn't had time to take him too far.

It wasn't as easy as he had hoped, however. An hour's searching produced no result. Everywhere he checked was empty and silent. His sense of foreboding grew as the hour stretched into two and still, no sign of Edwards could be found. Then, as he stepped out of the elevator onto the seventeenth floor, he was startled as a strange, guttural grunting sound met his ears. He feared what it meant. Perhaps Edwards was injured, bleeding to death from the Ares' attack.

Birch rushed through a nearby door to the source of the noise. What met his gaze as he entered was hardly what he had expected. There was Edwards, trussed up like a common fowl ready for cooking, trying with all his might to cross the floor caterpillar-fashion to get to the door. Apparently, his efforts had been ineffective, for he was still some distance from the exit even now.

Birch laughed. "Well, well. Look at what happened to you," he sniggered. "Our zookeeper went and got caught by his own specimen. Now, isn't that funny?"

Edwards' face, already red from struggling to escape, went crimson. Sweat streamed from his brow and his hair was matted, plastered to the side of his head. Now, at the sight of Birch, he writhed and kicked all the more, trying to free himself. He grunted and spat what he thought of Birch's humor through a makeshift cloth gag, but it was impossible to tell what he said.

"Okay," Birch soothed coolly. "Calm down. You know, unlike your own 'enlightened' culture, we 'savages' don't believe in trapping people and imprisoning them for our own purposes. I'm going to let you go, but I want to tell you something. The Ares that did this to you is down in the icebox right now, cryogenically frozen. I won't be letting him out anytime soon. If you try anything I'll do the same to you, and by the time you get out they'll be scraping the freezer burn off your brain. Got that?"

Edwards nodded mutely, his eyes wide and rolling with apprehension.

"Good," Birch muttered as he started working on the tight little knots, "because creating all these immortal memories seems to be earning me nothing but trouble so far. Maybe she was wrong..."

Edwards couldn't answer that. His mouth was still gagged, and the words meant nothing to him anyway. For the first time, he stopped struggling and went limp as he let Birch work on his bonds.

Soon Edwards was free. He rubbed his aching wrists and struggled wearily to his feet.

"Okay," Birch muttered. "Let's go. It's time to get this ship moving."

"Where exactly are we going?" Edwards asked.

"Yeah," Birch answered thoughtfully, "that's the question, isn't it. Where?"

FIVE

It wasn't until a few days later that they were ready to make a decision, or at least try to make a decision on where they should go. It was strange. A whole universe had opened up before them, an existence beyond their knowing. They were free to go anywhere, and yet there didn't seem to be anywhere to go.

If he'd had any idea, any inkling of where they should go, Birch would have happily made the decision. He had done it before. When the colony project had failed he had made the decision. His path then had been clear. He had taken them back home, back to Earth where they had started, but now he was lost. With failure before them and failure behind them, he didn't know where to turn.

And so he had given everyone free rein, a chance to study the computer records, to find out what they could, to think of where they might go.

His own efforts had proven fruitless. Every door he could imagine had been barred. Every hope he had considered had been baseless. Every chance he sought seemed hopeless. He had to face it, for all their fight and struggle to earn their freedom, they had gained nothing. There was nothing for them now but an empty universe.

When the time of the meeting came, Birch reluctantly made

his way to the conference room. He hated going with nothing, with no ideas and no solution. He felt weak and helpless in his own inability to see the path forward, and now he had to depend on the judgment of others. That wasn't coming easily.

He scuffed his feet along the hall, delaying, trying to come up with anything. He was reaching for something he couldn't quite grasp, for a memory or something that would tell him what to do. He just couldn't get it.

Finally, he entered the room. He had started early enough so that he should have been the first to arrive, even with the delay, but to his dismay Jane was already there, seated with her eyes closed and hands folded, a perfect picture of control-led serenity.

Birch sweated. Something about the way she looked made him uncomfortable. She was a little too calm, a little too ready for this meeting. He wondered what was going on in her mind. Somehow he knew he wouldn't like it.

"Hello Jane," Birch muttered awkwardly and slid into his seat at the head on the table.

"Good afternoon, Major," Jane replied. Apart from this simple greeting, she barely acknowledged his presence at all. Her eyes remained closed. She didn't move.

Birch couldn't figure Jane out. In the immediate aftermath of the cockpit rescue things had almost seemed back to normal between them, back to the way it been before- before every-thing had gone wrong all those years ago. He had just saved her life; she had saved his before that when they had made their final escape from Earth. Everything was even, the score was settled, but then she had pulled away.

They had been researching, trawling the database for any-thing to help them find where to go next. They had worked separately, it doubled their chances of success, and at first it had felt like they had worked to a common goal, but that soon changed. The old walls went up. The longer they worked the further she drifted from him. He had lost her again; he knew that. It wasn't his old friend Jane who sat opposite him today.

It was the Jane who hated him. The foe who had opposed him at every turn, who had sought to undermine him, who had fought him every step of the way- that was the Jane that was here today, and clearly she had something on her mind.

Birch fidgeted uncomfortably in his seat. The silence remained undisturbed until Lauren and Edwards came in together a few minutes later. Their voices, already muted, died away in the icy atmosphere of the meeting room.

Birch cleared his throat as the two found their seats at the table.

"Well," Birch began uncertainly. "I guess we've all had a few days to look into the options. It's a big decision and I'm sure we all have our ideas. That's why I wanted to get us together like this… to see what we've all come up with."

"What's he doing here?" Jane asked sharply, pointing at Edwards. "Your other little friend nearly killed us all. Do you really think it's wise to include this one in all our plans? I'm not saying you have bad judgment or anything, but I'm not really ready to trust anyone you chose to bring along on this little trip."

Birch sighed. The fight was on.

"Look," he answered grumpily, "he was a part of the government system down there. Maybe he has some insight you might miss. There's a chance he knows more about this than any of us. I say he stays, so he stays."

"Fine," Jane smiled icily. "Just watch your throat."

"Yeah, sure. Let's get started. Why don't you tell us what you came up with then, Jane," Birch added with false indifference. He'd had enough of Jane's games. She was up to something, and whatever she was planning to drop on him, he would rather she just dropped it now. The waiting was killing him. He would rather know.

"Nothing," she answered simply. "Go on to someone else."

Birch's eyes narrowed. "Nothing? Really?"

"Nothing."

"I've never known you to have nothing."

"There's a first time for everything."

"Sure," Birch let it drop. He wasn't going to get anything out of her that way. He might as well wait. She would be certain to make whatever it was known at a moment of her own choosing, at a moment most inconvenient to him.

"What about you, Lauren," he asked his junior officer. She didn't immediately answer, but looked blankly at him, her face expressionless.

Birch missed Karla and DeSante. He would have given anything just then for a crewmember with either a brain or a heart. Right now there seemed to be a short supply of both.

"It looks pretty bad for us," Lauren finally answered grimly. "Earth is obviously out and Base Two on Mars is dead so that rules out anything close.

"The rest is pretty murky from there. I didn't find anything we didn't know about before. From the records we know that Hypnos I and II failed, they got nowhere. Everything after that isn't on record. There were at least another ten missions, but no written account remains. We have no way of knowing where they went, if they were successful, or whether any possible colony remains there today. Basically, it's a hit-and-miss guessing game as far as I can see. We can study the star charts and try and figure out where they might have gone. We'll have to take a chance and see where we end up, and that's all I could come up with."

Birch shook his head. Lauren's plan was about the best he had been able to come up with himself, but it was unacceptable. The idea of tramping around the galaxy hoping to stumble upon something or someone was stupid. It would take an eternity, even with an advanced ship like this, and the likelihood was that they would still get nowhere. No, they needed a better option.

"Thanks," Birch responded tersely. "What about you, Edwards, got any input on this?"

"Sure," Edwards answered flatly. "You need to go back to Earth. We're going to die out here. There's nothing out here.

It's empty out here. Let's go home. It's the only way we can survive. You know it's true. Let's go back!"

Jane laughed. "You were right," she chuckled sharply, "Edwards does have a different perspective on things. It's a good thing you brought him along to share it. We would never have thought of it without him!"

"Yeah, yeah," Birch barked impatiently. "Forget it, Edwards. We're never going back. If that means we're going to die out here then okay, we die.

"And you, Jane, if you find it so funny then why don't you tell us what your great idea is? We're all listening."

"Nothing," Jane responded as before, "but what I really want to hear, though," she continued, "I mean, what I think would really help us all, would be your idea. You know, after all, you were the one who had this great idea about abandoning our mission, abandoning everything, and coming back to Earth. And since that worked out so well, I was hoping you could guide us on this next stage of our grand adventure."

Birch could feel the blood pulsing in his temple. A throbbing, pounding anger was trying to break loose and he was trying to stop it.

"What is your idea?" Jane taunted. She seemed to sense his hesitancy, to know that he didn't have any idea at all.

"I'm working on it still," Birch finally stammered. He was looking down at the table.

"Well," Jane responded with an assured smile, "while you 'work on it' some more, I can tell you exactly what we're going to do."

"What?" Birch didn't look up. The blow was about to fall, and he didn't want to see it coming.

"It's simple really. The only option we've had all along."

"What?"

"I'm surprised you didn't think of it yourself." She was drawing it out. Torturing him, and enjoying every minute of it.

"Just tell me what it is, Jane."

"R67.3," she responded simply.

Birch's head jerked up at that. Even Lauren's usually placid face wore a look of disbelief. Only Edwards showed no reaction to this cryptic statement.

"No!" Birch thundered. "No, no, no, no, no. That's the stupidest thing I ever heard. What would be the point? What could we possibly gain from that?"

"What is 'R67.3'?" Edwards tried to interrupt.

"You know it's all we've got, Major," Jane reasoned. "It's the only place that established a colony. It's the only place we know to start. Where else can we look?"

Birch fell silent.

"What is 'R67.3'?" Edwards tried again.

"It's our world," Lauren finally answered. "The world we tried to terraform, but we abandoned it to return to Earth."

"It was more accurately know as 'The Rock'," Birch remarked bitterly. "And a more barren, windswept lump of inanimate granite you couldn't hope to find. But that's the place Ratliff choose. The place that almost killed us last time. I can't see any reason to go back there."

"Except," Jane answered coolly, "that it was the only place to have successfully established a colony. Except for the fact that it's the only place we know where people lived more than five minutes out here." She pushed a button on the panel beside her and a shimmering blue holographic map of the known galaxy filled the tabletop. Their ship's location was marked by a flashing green dot. A great distance away, across the far side of the table, blinking red was the location of R67.3, The Rock.

"It's the only place," Jane continued. "I programmed the computer with our circumstances, with everything we know from the records, and this map represents the result of that. It's the only place.

"But no," Birch snapped. "We can't go back. Anywhere would be better than that."

"You're not afraid of ghosts, are you, Major?" Jane asked meaningfully. "You're not worried about what we'll find there are you?"

"Well, no..." Birch's face flushed "but nothing has been heard from that colony for hundreds of years. It's dead. Why go back?"

"Because," Jane's hand passed over the sea of blue, holographic emptiness, a vast expanse of barren space stretching out to a single flashing red dot. "Because it's all we've got."

Birch shook his head, but he knew she was right. R67.3... R67.3... R67.3... R67.3... R67.3... The ID code flashed red on the blue holographic background. The crimson dot of the planet faded in and out, winking at him knowingly. The one place he never wanted to see again, and now it looked like he had no other option. He was going back.

SIX

It took a few days to get everything ready. Birch wasn't in any hurry. He was still hoping that something else would turn up, that maybe an alternative could be found. He didn't just idly hope; he searched. Every spare moment he poured over the records, looking for anything, even the smallest possible clue to another location or a settlement, but there was nothing. At least there was nothing that he could find in the short length of time he had to look. And so the day came.

Birch shuffled to the elevator and reluctantly began the swift descent to the lower floors. Soon they would be on their way, and this new ship would take them back to their old destination more quickly than he had ever imagined possible.

There was no doubt about it- this was a remarkable ship. Powered by the Dark Drive, that harnessed previously theoretical matter, it created a field around the craft that challenged its very state of existence. In effect, the ship almost ceased to belong to the physical universe. Like the old dreamed theory of hyperspace, the Dark Drive took them almost completely out of the natural realm of space, to travel speeds beyond comprehension.

Birch had learned all of this with wide-eyed wonder. The minds that could have imagined and built such things were extraordinary. If the Hypnos missions had developed this sort of ability he couldn't see how they could have failed. And yet they did, completely.

Now Birch and his crew were the sole beneficiaries of this lost technology, and with it, their journey would be drastically shortened. Yet, for all that, space was still space. It was still immense. Journeys that once took centuries would now take years. But years were still years and not to be wasted, keeping vigil on a ship traveling through the dead wasteland of space. Even at this speed, it would take a little over two years to reach R67.3. They would sleep until then.

Birch arrived on the cryogenic level. The doors slid open and he stepped out into the wide chamber. The others were already there, standing in an awkward little knot by the main console. If Karla had been here the place would have been abuzz with lively laughter and conversation. The room was silent.

A large screen above the console displayed the status of every chamber in the room. Only one was occupied; the screen blinked blue in the place where the Ares boy remained in his unwilling repose.

Edwards wanted to say something and quickly moved to Birch's side, but the Major dismissively waved him away.

"Forget it, Edwards," Birch barked. "I know what you're going to say. You've said it a hundred times. You know my answer, too. Yes, you do have to go through with this. No, you don't have any choice. In fact, let's start with you right now and get it over with."

He led Edwards to the nearest freezing chamber and pushed him in almost as roughly as he had the Ares kid. He hooked him up, ready for stasis.

Edwards said nothing, but his eyes betrayed the fear inside. He was breathing hard. His chest heaved erratically. He was hyperventilating.

"Calm down," Birch muttered. "Do you want the machine to pop your lungs like a balloon?"

"Is that possible?" Edwards stammered.

"Nah," Birch laughed. Despite his continued resentment of Edwards' part in trying to make them a permanent part of President Michaels' zoo exhibit back on earth, Birch simply couldn't hate him.

"It's safe enough," Birch added almost soothingly. "Modern cryogenics has a very low fail rate, maybe 0.003%. That makes it safer than eating Brie cheese."

Edwards seem unconvinced.

"Anyway, see you in two years," Birch concluded swiftly and shut the lid with a click before Edwards could protest. The glass fogged and the machine hissed as the freezing process commenced.

"Well," Birch remarked with false good humor, "anybody else ready to get frozen?"

Lauren was already in her compartment and almost answered Birch's question with the click and hiss of her own chamber sealing her in. That just left Birch and Jane.

"I guess it's just you and me, kid," Birch drawled.

Jane eyed him suspiciously.

"So, the computer's all set, course programmed in, and everything is good to go," Birch added.

"Yeah, I know," Jane answered evenly. "I checked," she added, gesturing to the computer behind her.

"I thought you would," Birch smiled crookedly. "Well, I guess we should get to bed. We'll have a long day ahead of us in a couple years, you know."

"Yeah," Jane answered, walking toward her own chamber. She hesitated. They both hesitated as if waiting for the other to go first.

Neither moved. Finally, the delay became uncomfortable. Birch sighed and strapped himself into his machine.

"I guess I'll go first," he muttered. "See you in two years," he added, pulling the lid down on himself, leaving Jane alone in the perfect stillness of the cryogenic hall.

SEVEN

Of course, he had lied. Not in the strictest sense of the word, because what he said was essentially true, but in the actual meaning behind the words there was a lie. If everything went according to plan then it would, indeed, be two years, possibly more, before he talked to Jane again, but it would not be two years before he saw her.

It was a dangerous plan, perhaps even a stupid one, but it was the only one he could think of. Fooling Jane was never easy. Thus, two weeks later, when one of the five markers displaying the status of the cryogenic chambers changed from its customary cool, blue to a pulsating red warning signal, everything was going to plan. When, a few minutes later, smoke started spewing from the malfunctioning stasis chamber, everything was not.

'Warning,' the computer intoned, 'cryogenic breach in progress: critical malfunction.'

Birch, of course, knew nothing of this. His first conscious thought was that of anyone waking from cryogenic sleep. He was profoundly sick. His mind was fuzzy, and the white haze that fogged his eyes registered as little more than an aftereffect of the freezing process.

He quickly realized something was wrong. The whooshing blast in his ears was the first indication that there was a problem. More compelling evidence was provided by the tingling, icy fingers of pain that clawed at his skin and gouged his flesh.

Birch writhed, struggling to free himself from the machine. A flurry of ice engulfed him. He pushed at the lid, but it wouldn't move. He kicked out at the metal casing but found that equally ineffective. In the confined space he shifted, turning to the internal panel, trying to key in the emergency override, but he was locked out. The codes didn't work.

He pounded on the chamber's glass window. It was no good. It was too thick. He could never break it, and no one would ever hear him. The glass was frosted over, but he knew that no one was there. Everyone else was in stasis. No help was coming. He was trapped in his living tomb, like a typical character from a famous story by Poe. Panic clawed at his throat, but he wasn't ready to give in to the madness and start scraping his fingers to bloody stumps against the sarcophagus lid. He had one last chance.

Muttering angrily to himself, Birch tried his final option. Pulling the cushioned padding aside he revealed a panel that he quickly opened to expose the chamber's wiring.

With blue, shivering fingers he fumbled at the wires. If the design of these chambers hadn't changed much since his days then he might have a chance. Maybe he could get out. If he was really lucky he might even get out alive.

He found the wires he was looking for, at least the ones that would be right if things were the same. He cut them with a piece of metal he broke from the panel and started stripping them down, exposing the filament. Finally, he was ready. "Here goes," he muttered grimly and pushed the wires together.

In the next instant, a number of things happened in quick succession. The chamber howled a piercing screech as Birch's modifications took immediate effect. The electrical surge sent a quick blast of power to the chamber that flung the door, Birch, and half the wiring out into the room.

Birch landed in a sodden lump, skidding across the floor, finally coming to rest some twenty feet from the chamber. He looked dead. Frosty crystals melted in his hair and trickled down his face. He lay, scarcely able to breathe, until finally he pulled himself onto his side; blinking at the damage he had caused.

It certainly was a display. A tornado of ice was blowing out of the unit, falling as misplaced snow that melted as soon as the flakes touched the ground. Soon flames began licking up from the chamber, devouring the ice in sizzling gulps. In his dizzily abstracted mind, Birch wondered which would win: fire or ice. Two equal foes pitted against each other, only one could prevail. The flames leaped up, quickly growing, answering Birch's question and snapping him out of his semi-conscious reverie.

With determined effort, Birch grunted and clambered to his feet. The ship was already responding to the emergency. Directed sprinklers were targeting the fire. Birch grabbed an extinguisher and added his effort in an attempt to suppress the flames. Soon the fire was out, leaving only a gutted, smoking shell where his cryogenic chamber had once stood.

Luckily, none of the other units were damaged. The fire had been extinguished in time. Birch hobbled around them, checking their glass windows to be sure. They were all okay.

Birch smiled bitterly to himself. He was alive, and nothing could have surprised him more. Wearily he fell into a chair at the main console. His head slumped over onto the panel. From here he could see the four blue icons, testifying to the safety of his crew. He didn't feel comforted. His own light had winked out, there was nothing there.

Birch shook his head. This had been the plan, after all. He was awake and alone, but something had gone terribly wrong. The defect he had programmed into his cryogenic chamber was a little too effective, or perhaps a little too defective, either way, it had almost killed him. He couldn't understand how he could have gotten it so wrong.

At least he was free. For the longest time, even going back before the Hypnos mission, he had been bound by circumstances, by people, by life. He hadn't been free; at least he thought he hadn't. Now was his chance to set that straight. No one was here to tell him otherwise, and there was nothing left to stop him doing whatever he wanted to do, if only he could figure out what that was.

That was a question for later. For now, Birch had other things to attend to, like the wounds he had accumulated in his escape from the cryogenic chamber.

He limped to the elevator. Soon he was shooting up to the medical deck. He leaned heavily against the metal wall, trying to keep the pressure off his throbbing feet. The doors slid open and he stumbled out. The stark, empty corridors barely registered in his thoughts. Pain was coursing through his body like the blood in his veins, and he could think of nothing else.

He entered the emergency center. Three automated medical chambers lined the far wall, but Birch avoided them. They could have diagnosed his every medical need. They would have treated every problem with the utmost care and with all the procedural knowledge of a hundred doctors combined. They would have done a better job of healing him than any living doctor ever could, but Birch didn't trust them. His time in the icy embrace of the cryogenic chamber had left him feeling more than a little wary of any automated devices. He wasn't ready to place himself back in the care of the very same computerized hands that had almost killed him.

Birch stooped over the examination table. The ship's computer, sensing his presence, switched on the light, covering him with piercing illumination. In its sterile glow, he examined the damage. His shivering hands were blue- the early stages of frostbite he guessed by the look of them, painful enough, but nothing permanent if he treated them quickly. His feet probably looked the same, but he hadn't removed his boots yet. Apart from that his wounds were limited to a few scrapes, minor cuts, and a big purple bruise that covered his left thigh. He had been lucky.

Birch peeled off his wet clothes, dried himself, and put on a gown he found in a nearby closet. Still shivering, he ran some warm water and bathed his feet and hands. They were starting to swell and white blisters had formed on the skin.

For a time all he could do was sit huddled in a painful stupor. As the feeling came throbbing back to his fingers and toes he winced angrily and bit hard against the pain. Having bundled his hands and feet as well as he could, he lay on the examination table and shivered miserably, drifting in and out of consciousness.

The next few hours passed fitfully. Birch's mind was a jumble of plans and memories, mixed up in a mental muddle that made his memories the future and his future the past. In his mind, he knew that the ship had already returned to planet R67.3. It was the door to heaven. Karla was there, not dead on the plains where he had left her, but alive and smiling. He hadn't failed her. She bent over and her blonde curls brushed his face. He could smell her hair, smell the very life in her that drew him in.

"Welcome back," she whispered in his ear, but the voice wasn't her own. It was a man's voice, familiar, yet out of place. The tone wasn't angry, but neither was it friendly. It was the voice of someone declaring the inevitable, telling him what he already knew. It was a voice of judgment.

Instinctively Birch pulled back, looking up into the face he knew so well. Her clear, blue eyes met his, and he almost felt better, but something was missing. Her piercing gaze looked through him, looking for something he didn't want her to see. Finally, she smiled, but it was a cool smile of knowledge, not of warmth and friendship. As he watched he eyes clouded and a single tear brimmed and fell down onto his face. Then, slowly, her eyes changed. Red veins crept across the sclera, flowing like a tide over the iris, even reaching the pupil as if to engulf it. Karla gasped, blinked hard, and disappeared.

Birch jolted awake. He was sweating. His hands and his

feet still hurt, but he barely gave that a thought. He was breathing hard. Glancing about, he almost expected to see Karla, but he was alone. No one was there.

He sighed. Pulling himself up, he shuffled painfully to the edge of the examination table and gently placed his bandaged feet on the floor. He could manage. He knew enough about frostbite to know he should stay off his feet, but he couldn't wait any longer. He had to get started.

Birch grabbed his uniform from the chair where he had left it. It was still damp, but it would do. He pulled it on and shuffled to the supply cupboard. There he found some crutches and a bottle of mild painkillers he could use to keep himself going. Stubbornly he refused to take anything stronger, despite the almost debilitating pain. Somehow instinctively he felt vulnerable here. He was alone, the only one awake in this strange, convenient ship. He wanted to stay sharp.

Using the crutches, he swung around and hobbled slowly through the doorway, down the corridor, and to the elevator doors.

It was time to get this ship turned around, time to get it going in the right direction. Destination: Anywhere but R67.3.

EIGHT

If only it had been that easy. Sadly, Birch had to acknow-ledge the wisdom of Jane's conclusion- heading for the silent colony of R67.3 was preferable to shooting off into unknown space with no destination. Following a course for R67.3 would get him where he didn't want to go, but aimlessly wandering through space would get him nowhere at all, and so he had decided to allow the ship to persist on its course, but only until he could find a better alternative.

He had two years to find something, two years before they arrived, but Birch didn't hesitate. He started right away, beginning a thorough search of the ship's database.

Line-by-line, item-by-item, he examined the records. In some ways, they were surprisingly complete, in other ways they were frustratingly lacking. There was a lot to take in, but as the weeks passed he began to see the pattern. There was a lot written, but not much was said.

Technical data was plentiful. Schematics for all the Hypnos ships were stored here. There were some gradual improve-ments over the course of the program, but this vessel, the one they flew in now, represented a huge leap in a whole new direction. This was a prototype, the beginning of a new hoped for future that never came. If this technology had been avail-able from the very beginning then perhaps the Hypnos missions might have succeeded, but it had never gotten off the ground. Instead of being the foundation of their future it had become a monument to their failure, a dusty relic of their forgotten dreams, left to decay deep beneath the surface of a monstrously altered Washington DC.

But now all of this had changed, Birch told himself. He had brought this ship up from its forgotten tomb. He had raised it to the life that its stillborn invention had denied. The people who had created this craft were all gone, but their hopes lived on in his mission. The spirit of humanity would continue.

In every respect, this ship was a wonder. This nameless craft, that Birch had somewhat nostalgically dubbed the *Hypnos III-A*, astounded him. As he learned more, so his respect for the society that had built it deepened. Everything about it testified to the desperate measures of a world in conflict, of a genius born out of adversity.

The Dark Drive, miraculous enough because of its speed, was equally remarkable for its efficiency. Its fuel consumption was minimal, and as such it changed the design of the vessel drastically. While a standard craft, like their old ship the *Hypnos III*, had consisted of a ninety-five percent engine and fuel storage ratio, with only a remaining five percent for serviceable crew space, the new *Hypnos III-A* reversed those figures. This ship could house a crew of hundreds, far beyond the mere five that Birch now led.

The way this ship had been built under Washington was surprising too. Traditionally NASA would never complete construction of such a large craft on Earth. It would have been built in pieces and assembled in space later. Ground launches were inefficient with larger vessels, where huge amounts of energy had to be devoted to achieving escape velocity. Instead, a small shuttle would use rockets to launch into space, where it would rendezvous with its fuel cells and deep probe engines. Once coupled together, the long-range exploration would begin.

The fact that they had abandoned this perfectly sensible

measure with the *Hypnos III-A* indicated two things. Firstly, that the Dark Drive was immensely powerful, producing enough energy from its small engines to push this great ship to escape velocity with minimal fuel loss. Secondly, it demonstrated just how bad things had gotten for NASA in those last days. They couldn't count on a space dock. They couldn't risk any knowledge of their final plans. It was one last bolt for freedom. The records showed the lengths they had gone to in order to make it happen, all the effort they had poured into this last desperate hope. They had sought a way out, and they had almost made it. They had done their best. It was a noble end to the NASA dream, but noble or not, it was still the end.

Birch learned all of this in his first few weeks of research. He had tried to limit himself to studying the Hypnos missions. His single objective was to find the clue to another colony, any possible destination besides R67.3, but he kept wandering back to the wider picture. Little clues in the text lead him to other accounts, other documents, and he would follow their trail, uncovering the last pitiful cries of a dying civilization.

It was clear that they hadn't understood what had happened to them. It was all so quick. The Ares were the enemy-that much was clear. At least it started out that way. The Ares had destroyed cities and harvested resources in a way that Birch couldn't understand. The Ares he had encountered on Earth were a wild, dangerous enemy, but hardly capable of systematically dismantling a society. Perhaps, Birch reasoned, in the years after these events the Ares' own culture had deteriorated, their savagery had overcome their reason, and they had descended into the brutes they were today.

The final accounts of the end of NASA and the civilian government that had sustained it was little more than a confused mess. Things deteriorated badly. People blamed each other. They tore themselves apart from within, even as the enemy approached from without. Whatever happened after that, and how President Michaels came to oppose the Ares was unclear. The records simply ended, as in fact their society had ended, in simple, futile shock and raging. *How could they lose? Good always won, and they were good. They couldn't lose.* And yet they did lose. The calm assurance that every Hitler would meet his Stalingrad, and that every Napoleon would face his Waterloo was shattered. They were good and they were losing, and that realization, more than anything else, had defeated them. They had given up.

The more Birch found out the less he liked, but he had to keep looking. Days passed with little physical activity beyond stumbling from his bed to the computer, and then back to bed twenty hours later. He ate sporadically, he slept fitfully, and he worked feverishly, but his efforts produced no tangible results. Beginning with the Hypnos I mission he had read every detail, considered every possibility, and followed every lead, but it seemed to be a short and fruitless trail.

For some time Birch didn't learn anything he hadn't already known. On earth, before their launch, he and Jane had hacked into the Hypnos mainframe, and what they had found there was exactly what he was finding here- very little. Hypnos I and II were failures, but the details were sketchy. His mission, the Hypnos III, was inexplicably listed as a success and a phantom colony was established on planet R67.3, but Birch knew it couldn't be true. Their mission had failed and they had left R67.3 as cold and lifeless as they had found it. No terraforming had begun, no base had been established. No groundwork had been laid. Their supplies had all been destroyed in the storms that almost killed them all. They barely had enough to get back home. There was just no way that a colony could make it there, and yet it had.

He didn't like it. Everything was wrong with the whole R67.3 situation, and if he could have found any alternative he would gladly have taken it, but there wasn't one.

Another ten missions had followed after Hypnos III, but the details were sparse. Paranoia seemed to have gripped the Space Agency, and no one trusted anyone to keep a secret. Locks and counter-locks blocked any information on these last missions. He couldn't get through. Even the computer he was using now seemed to be fighting him, slowing him down-diverting him away from the truth that he sought.

The Hypnos I had been destroyed, that much was clear. It hadn't made it that far out of the solar system when it inexplicably exploded, killing all on board. Birch gulped at that. This all must have happened long before the launch of the Hypnos III, but they hadn't been told. NASA had covered it up and kept the Hypnos missions going, despite the fatal flaws.

For some time that was all Birch could find. No record existed to clear things up, to show how NASA had responded or what they had concluded. The only thing Birch had been able to uncover was a simple classification code buried deep in one of the few documents he had been able to access, *Hypnos I: Code-Uriah*. Birch puzzled over that, but couldn't come up with anything. It didn't match any of the codes he had known from that time. For now, it seemed that the cause of Hypnos I's demise was an impenetrable mystery.

The fate of the Hypnos II was even less clear. It wasn't listed as destroyed, but there was no indication of what had happened to it. It had simply disappeared. Birch could at least tell the general direction it had been sent. Before the Hypnos missions, NASA had developed a coordinate system, dividing the vastness of unknown space into gridded sections. The Hypnos III had been sent to sector R. In subsection 67 they had discovered planet 3 as a possible colonization site. Thus publicly the planet would become known as R67.3. In NASA documentation it would be coded as R/III/67.3, denoting the fact that it was the Hypnos III that had logged the discovery. If the missions had continued at the pace they had envisioned the clerical trick would have simplified the record keeping for them. As it was, as far as Birch could tell, R67.3 was the only suitable planet ever discovered.

The Hypnos II had been sent out to sector D. Nothing was heard from them after that. Maybe that meant that they were still out there, that their ship hadn't found anywhere suitable and that they were still cryogenically frozen, waiting to awaken to some great discovery. Birch doubted it. He figured they were dead.

The pace of things had picked up after Hypnos III. Before that it had been a slow, considered process, picking out suitable locations, making sure everything was right. It had been four years between Hypnos I and II, and another three years later when the Hypnos III had been launched. By the time of the Hypnos XIII mission, the delay had shortened to a few months. They were desperate to get away, but Birch couldn't find where any of them had gone. No records remained.

He had hit a dead end. There was only one planet and one possible destination, R67.3. Like the map Jane had used at the meeting, the dot of that insignificant planet flashed in his mind, red and foreboding. He was caught in its gravitational pull and it seemed he couldn't escape.

NINE

Birch wasn't ready to give up yet. He didn't have much choice. He wasn't about to step back into the cryogenic system that had almost killed him, he didn't trust it, so he was stuck with another year and a half of waiting for their scheduled arrival at R67.3. He decided to use the time wisely. He was going to continue his research. Maybe he might still find another colony, or at least get a few answers. There were too many unanswered questions rattling around in his brain- questions about the world and their mission and how it all fit together. He was going to get some answers.

He reapplied himself to his studies, but everywhere he looked those same walls impeded him. As much as he tried, he could only gain open access to the records of the first three Hypnos missions, and he investigated each of these thoroughly.

The picture of the three crews flashed up on the screen, group shots with smiling men and women in their flight suits, helmets tucked under their arms, and a starry field printed in the background. They could have been anyone. The shots were the same, only the faces changed.

It was strange to think that they were all dead. He didn't know anyone from Hypnos I, they were a bit before his time, but he knew most of the Hypnos II crew. Lana Smith had been in command. Birch had served with her a couple of times on the Bread Run to Base Two on Mars. She had been a good pilot and a good leader. It seemed a shame to waste her on such a futile mission. They had all been wasted.

He glanced indifferently at the personnel bios. The brave and the good, they all had earned their place on Hypnos.

Then he came to their own mission, the Hypnos III crew. It seemed just like the others- the same formulaic crew picture, the same flight suits, the same practiced smiles, the same starry background, and to a large extent the same result-failure.

He took a longer look at these bios, even though he knew them well. This was, after all, where it had all started, where things had really gone wrong. Running from one crisis had landed him in something far worse, and he still couldn't figure it out. It was the mission. A dark cloud had descended on his mind, and it hadn't lifted since. Could he trust anyone? That was the question he hadn't figured out. He hadn't given himself time to figure it out. All he did was all that he had ever done. He ran.

Birch squinted at the screen. The first file up was Lt. Colonel John Ratliff. The original commander of the mission, he had an exemplary record. The list of commendations and citations was long. He was a highly decorated, highly competent officer. In the picture, his white teeth formed a perfect box-like smile. His skin tanned, his lacquered, black hair neatly arranged, his square jaw set, he was the perfect picture of a perfect commanding officer. Birch winced at the memory and clicked on.

His own file was next. His picture was a poor comparison to Ratliff's. His sallow skin, tousled graying black hair, and the furtive shiftiness in the eyes all gave his picture the look of a criminal mug shot, rather than of a promotional photograph for a high profile NASA mission. Still, that had been fitting enough. Birch had been a fugitive, running from his own life when the picture had been taken.

That was his hidden shame. Only the top officials in NASA

had discovered Birch's true story. He had been running from his wife, Sarah, and the terminal cancer diagnosis that she had received. She had looked to him for comfort, but when he had looked inside himself he had found nothing. And so he ran. He volunteered for the Hypnos mission and never saw Sarah again.

He had known it was wrong. Of course, it was wrong, but he had never felt it. He had never felt anything. He had never loved anything except because of what it could do for him. As people loved ice cream, or a favorite piece of music, or a new car- that is how he had loved people, because of what they did for him. It was only later that he truly understood what he had done. He had finally *felt* it, and so now, as he looked at this photograph, and into his own hollow, shifty eyes, he hated himself. He could never change that.

Birch clicked again and Jane's picture flashed up. Major Jane Gray: cocky and resolute, her long black hair spilled casually over her shoulders. In the picture, her hands were on her hips and she smiled crookedly at the camera. Her grey-blue eyes sparkled. This was the Jane he had once known. They had been friends, but the mission had pulled them apart. He had been forced to take command, and she had hated him for it. From that time she had opposed him openly, every step of the way. If one of them didn't kill the other by the end of the mission it would surprise everyone, including themselves.

The next picture up was Lauren's, but there wasn't much information to go with it. She was an Industry employee contracted to NASA for her expertise in terra-forming. As such, her life was a mystery. The Industry never released personnel files, even to NASA. They were a law unto themselves and nobody liked it, but the Agency needed the money and the politicians needed the support, so nobody ever asked too many questions of The Industry.

Lauren was a typical Industry operative- aloof, alert, and highly efficient. Her work was good, but she seemed barely human. Her social interaction was minimal, but again that was pretty standard for Industry workers.

You couldn't join The Industry. They wouldn't give you a job. Some said The Industry didn't employ workers- they grew them, and to a great extent that was true. It had been Industry policy to adopt unwanted children at a young age and bring them up in their profession. 'Bring up a child,' the company slogan stated, 'and they will not depart from you,' and that was apparently true. No one ever heard of an Industry worker leaving the company. It was a lot like the old apprenticeship program, except it started at the very beginning of life. It was all a highly efficient and mutually equitable setup. The Industry got a ready supply of new train- ees to shape as they saw fit, the government got rid of the fin- ancial burden of children and families struggling in poverty. Everyone was happy. Nobody complained.

Birch shook his head and moved on. He had never liked Industry workers. He didn't trust them.

Next up was Lieutenant Carlos DeSante. Smiling and wide- eyed, his picture brought a sting of regret to Birch's mind. He had lost the young officer in the mountains back on Earth. The kid had trusted him, and that had probably gotten him killed. DeSante had always been the one he could count on. He had never doubted Birch, never questioned his right to command, even as Jane had railed against him and done her best to raise up a mutiny on the Hypnos III, DeSante had stood firmly by his side. Birch missed him.

The worst was yet to come. Birch's finger hovered over the button, dreading the next click. It was Karla. Truth be told, he wanted to see her again, but he dreaded it. Her face already haunted his fitful dreams. Seeing her again, even if only in a photograph, would just reopen the wounds. Maybe he wanted them reopened.

He clicked. DeSante's face faded and was replaced with Karla's, but Birch didn't see her. His head was in his hands. Finally, he glanced up, peering through his fingers.

If DeSante's picture brought Birch painful memories then

Karla's rammed a massive jolt of sorrow straight into his brain. She had died in his arms, and he knew that it was his fault. The Ares kid had done it, but he was to blame. He couldn't escape that. He couldn't escape anything. Recent experience had proven that to him.

In her picture, Karla was smiling as usual. It was the same infectious smile she always had, not a posed effect for a photograph, but a true reflection of what was inside her. She was happy, and not because things were easy for her, as Birch had once supposed, but because she had chosen to be happy. That was something he had never managed. She had more power than him; she was stronger than him, and he had never known it until it was too late.

Her golden, clipped curls, her shining blue eyes, the faint freckles on her cheeks, every detail was etched in his memory, but as he drank in the wonderful normality of the picture it began to change. Altering slowly at first, it darkened and swirled. Her eyes became pained, and a deep red pool formed in the corner of her mouth. The lips closed and then reopened in a ghastly crimson smile. This was how Karla looked when she had died when he had held her all night as her life had slipped away.

She looked at him, reached out to him, and in a deeper voice not her own, called to him.

"You left," she gasped raggedly.

Birch stifled a sob. Leaping from his chair, he flung the screen aside, trying to escape the image, but it wasn't really there. When he looked again it was just Karla as she had always been- happy, vibrant, and alive.

Birch collapsed back into his chair, breathing heavily. He wiped his eyes with the back of his hand, sniffing loudly. He was cracking up. He had another year and a half of this solitary existence ahead before they reached R67.3, and he began to doubt that he would ever make it.

TEN

Imagined or real, Karla was haunting him. As the slow months dragged on his mind seemed to wander back to that single subject, like a moth to a flame. He tried to think of other things, and often he seemed to succeed. He studied other things, worried about other things, and did other things, but always he came back to Karla.

The ship rang emptily with his echoing footsteps as he passed restlessly up and down its blank corridors, seeking something; he didn't know what. Most of the time, the ship was in darkness. Only Birch's location remained lit. The computer had an economical habit of turning lights on in anticipation of his future location and extinguishing them as he left. Its timing was impeccable. Sometimes, out of curiosity, Birch would look back to the room he had just left, but everything was still illuminated. Other times he would change his mind, and suddenly enter a room he hadn't originally intended, but the lights were always on there too. It was almost as if the computer could read his mind. After a while, that bugged him. Was he so predictable?

He tried to outsmart the computer, to see if he could catch it with the lights off for once. He never did. It was like a kid trying to open the refrigerator quickly enough to see if the light stayed on when the door was closed. It was impossible to catch. Perhaps it was a childish whim or just the result of spending too much time alone, but for whatever reason, he wanted to do it just once. It seemed important.

Birch's wanderings through the ship changed over time. At first, in the early months, he had paced the corridors. Caged in this craft, escaping to a place he didn't want to go, his energies had been channeled into this useless effort. He was trying to outrun his memories, and he hoped the activity would help. In the end, however, he couldn't escape. The memories came. They came whispering to him in the empty rooms and in every silent passageway. They crept into his dreams, and in those wakeful moments when he couldn't sleep. They were there when he ate and when he was hungry, when he thought and when he didn't think- when he did things, and when he did nothing. It didn't make any difference. They were always there.

He took to traveling down to the lower decks, down to the cryogenic level. He could rest there. Life was there. He could look through the frosted glass and see real, living people, and in the hum of the machinery, he could almost imagine that he heard the gentle thump of their almost-still hearts.

Sometimes he watched Jane. Her long black hair, tinted frosty-white in the chamber, was frozen in mid-flow about her shoulders. Her icy lips, slightly parted, wore the old cocky grin of the woman who had once been his friend. What had she been thinking? Something about the way she looked made him uneasy, like she had a plan he knew nothing about. Even in stasis, it seemed, she was plotting something.

Birch occasionally glanced into Lauren and Edwards' chambers, but the other main focus of his interest had been the Ares kid. It was the face of a killer he saw there, but it hardly looked the part. In his quiet repose, the features were smooth, untroubled by the world around him. It was the same look he had worn when Birch had shoved his unconscious body into the freezer months ago. It didn't fool Birch, though. He still saw the killer.

When he wasn't pacing the halls or keeping company with his cryogenic crewmates Birch was engaged in other, less wholesome pursuits. For a long time after his nightmarish vision of Karla he had avoided looking at the crew records altogether. Later, as a gnawing yearning ate into his mind, he came cautiously back. Slowly at first, nibbling away at the edges of what he wanted to see. He looked at the crew's picture, at them all standing before the starry backdrop, but it was Karla his eye was drawn to. He would glance at her, half fearing those smiling, blue eyes would redden, that the pool of blood would form again at the corner of her mouth, but it didn't happen, and as time passed his confidence grew.

Eventually, after weeks of faltering, he clicked on her profile. She was still there, still smiling and unchanged. Her open smile and her clear eyes were as they had always been. Funny how he had never taken the time to notice before, like the sunlight you took for granted until you had spent a lifetime in the darkness of space. He missed them.

There were other records, personal postings, candid shots taken by the crew, things used to promote the missions and the astronauts in NASA's publicity campaign. Birch poured over them all, wallowing in a past he hated, but Karla was there.

He saw a picture; it was one that he had taken himself. In it, everyone was looking down at a control panel. Ratliff was pushing some buttons and everyone else was suitably engrossed, except for Karla. She was looking up at him, a delicate smile turning up the corners of her lips. Her eyes were lifted to meet him. She was looking at him, and now as he looked at her he saw her for the first time. It smote him like a blow to the chest, but he came back for it again and again.

He tried to understand. He dove into the picture. Moving in closer, magnified a hundred times, until her pupil alone filled the screen, but he knew nothing more. In the inky blackness at the center of her eye, he could see his own reflection, taking the picture, but he could not see her thoughts. He could not glimpse her soul. All he could see was darkness.

It wasn't healthy. He knew that. He should stop, but somehow he couldn't make himself stop. It was all he had.

At the same time, Birch's obsession with the Ares boy grew. With Karla's face fresh in his memory, he would walk down to the cryogenic deck and watch the kid. There was a certain grim satisfaction in seeing him that way, weak and helpless. Even now Birch wondered why he had saved him. Once Birch had almost killed him with his bare hands, but something about him had reminded him of Karla, and so he had stopped. He couldn't see it now. He couldn't remember what it was that had stopped him. Maybe this, after all, was why he had brought the kid along. Not to save him, but to give himself a better chance to do what he what he hadn't done before, to finish the job.

He was in a dangerous mood. Sometimes as he watched the boy Birch would finger the wires that powered his chamber. It would have been a simple thing to rip them out, to send the system into a critical shutdown, skipping the correct thawing procedure, and dooming its occupant to an agonized death. Birch wanted it. He could feel the power of it throbbing in his hands, like a pulse so easily stopped, but he still couldn't do it. He hated the Ares boy, but as much as he despised him, he couldn't make himself do it. Karla wouldn't want him to. With that realization, he always stumbled away, off into the ship until the next time the urge brought him back.

The one place he could find peace was on the observation deck. Like most of the ship, it had no windows. The ability to see outside came not through glass, but from external cameras that projected an image of the ship's surroundings onto the walls, floor, and ceiling of the compartment. Transparent benches in the center of the room provided seating without obscuring the view.

Birch would come here for hours. He would lie back on the bench and watch the stars. Despite the ship's velocity, their position seemed constant. It was the distance that made it look that way. They were moving, but it was imperceptible. It was like watching the minute hand of a clock. If you observed it closely nothing seemed to happen, but if you looked away, when you looked back you could see the difference.

It was after many months that these observations began to disturb him. He could almost lose himself here in the sensation of floating among the stars. They surrounded him, and their positions were never the same. Constellations slowly formed, stretched, and collapsed about him as the ship hurtled on to its destination. It was fascinating to watch and to imagine the shapes they made. They drifted by like cloud patterns on a warm summer's day.

The one constant was change. Only it wasn't. *Almost* everything changed. The stars were all impermanent features on this landscape, but there was one thing that didn't alter, a dim, winking light directly behind them that was always there. He hadn't noticed it at first, but as he returned, again and again, it finally registered. Like an unlikely Northern Star, its position in space remained fixed.

That tiny point of light troubled him. Perhaps it was only a distant star that because of its position didn't seem to move as the others did. He doubted it, though. It should have disappeared in the distance long ago. It had to be something else. Soon his mind was in a whirl of speculation about what it could be.

His first thought was that someone was following the ship, but then he couldn't imagine who. The Ares were a primitive, feral species at best. Once, perhaps, they may have been more than that, but like the ancient Romans they had forgotten their knowledge. They were stupid brutes. It couldn't be them.

President Michaels' people seemed a more likely prospect, but the more Birch thought about it, the less he believed it. Michaels' men were barely able to deal with the Ares' threat on their own world, much less embark on a galactic mission chasing him across the stars. The speed alone made that impossible. The new Hypnos III had been hidden far beneath Michaels' capital city and it had been a prototype, the only one NASA had ever produced. Michaels had nothing that could match it for speed, Birch was sure of that. If they did they would have used it against the Ares and found a way to end their bloody stalemate. No, it couldn't have been Michaels either.

That left Birch with an uncomfortable third option- someone else, someone he knew nothing about, was following them. He couldn't imagine who it might be. He tried everything he could to find out, but that wasn't much. He tried magnifying the image, but only managed to increase the small dot to a larger, fuzzier dot. He tried the direct approach and sent a message requesting ship identification. There was no response. He scanned for any telltale sign of spent fuel but found nothing. He even searched the ship's records again in the slight hope of finding any clue about the identity of this new threat, but with no success.

Whatever he tried had no effect. He powered down the Dark Drive and let the ship drift for a time, but the dot drifted too, keeping the same distance as before. In final reckless desperation Birch turned the ship about and plunged full speed at their pursuer, but no sooner had he turned than the blip vanished, appearing again the same distance behind them.

Birch gave up. Perhaps he was chasing shadows. He remembered a story about an Apollo 11 astronaut who thought he saw something similar through the window on the outward journey to the moon. Some people believed that he had seen a UFO, but the man himself dismissed it as nothing more than a reflection from their own ship. Maybe that was all he was seeing now, nothing but a shining illusion.

Sighing, Birch turned the ship around, resuming their course for R67.3. He didn't look forward to getting there, but it needed to happen soon. He was cracking up.

ELEVEN

Paranoia was quickly becoming Birch's second vernacular. When he wasn't fretting over unexplained blips, fleeing the haunting echoes of Karla, or hovering over the Ares kid like a living pestilence, he was at war with the very ship that sustained him.

It had all started with the lights. Perhaps that was just the most visible manifestation of his slow descent into madness, or maybe he was right. Either way, he didn't trust those lights or the computer that controlled them. There were other things too. Mostly small insignificant niggles at first, like the way the food dispensers got his orders wrong or the way the doors often jammed, denying him access to certain parts of the ship. The computers were glitchy too. Sometimes they were smooth and quick, running at optimal speed. At other times, inexplicably, they slowed right down or stopped altogether. Systems froze and denied him access. Was it his imagination that this only happened when he seemed to be getting close to something important? He watched all the episodes of *Gilligan's Island* he could stomach, and the streaming was free and clear, but if he strayed off onto a more serious topic, if he tried to find out any important information, then the console slowed to glacial speed or stopped altogether.

If these had been the only problems Birch might not have worried so much, but as time went on the incidents increased in frequency and magnitude. More critical malfunctions were occurring daily.

The first real indication of a serious problem came unexpectedly and almost proved fatal. Birch had been working on the flight deck, adjusting the instruments and checking the interminable red line showing their progress toward R67.3. It had all been routine stuff, and he had done it automatically, almost without thinking. His mind had been on other things. He was considering that mysterious point of light again, the star that seemed to be following them. He was going to go down and have another look after he finished. He knew it would still be there, it always was, but he kept going back anyway, just to see.

After completing the routine Birch had shuffled down the hall, pressed the elevator button, and waited. A sudden sound nearby set him whirling around, his eyes darting fearfully up and down the corridor. It was a sigh, the quiet but distinct sound of a woman's breath. It sounded like Karla.

In his dreams, Karla often appeared. It had never been a pleasant experience. It always began happily enough. She was her old, lively self, darting around, joking and laughing, until that inevitable spot of red appeared in the corner of her mouth. She wouldn't notice. She would laugh and talk the same as always while the blood oozed, forming a pool, small at first but quickly gushing and flowing into a crimson stream down her chin and neck, covering her clothes until it spilled onto the floor. Then, suddenly, realization would come. She would wince and double up with pain. Her arms would reach for him, seeking solace, but he couldn't do it. He would step back instinctively, recoiled by the blood and reality of it all.

Birch dreaded those dreams, and he had no desire to live them out in reality. As the doors hissed open behind him he edged backward toward the safety of the elevator. Only, it wasn't there.

Birch's foot stepped back into nothingness. He quickly lost his balance and toppled into the gaping shaft behind him. He plunged into the darkness. Instinctively reaching out, he found the elevator cable and grabbed hold. His momentum pulled him down anyway, and he howled painfully as the sliding steel cut into his fingers. He slipped another fifty feet down with the cable snaking through his bloodied hands.

Finally, he stopped. Gasping painfully, he coiled his arm around the stiff wire to take some of the weight off his injured hands while he looked for a way out. He couldn't see much. The door he had fallen through was still open, and for once he was glad for the computer's habit of keeping the lights on in any area nearby. The thin glow from above was just enough to allow him to make out the dim outline of a hatch a few feet below. That would get him into the access shaft. If he could just ease himself down that far and jump over to it he might get out of here alive.

It wasn't easy. After slowly edging down the cable he still had to get across. The width was a little too much to jump comfortably, and he tried swinging toward it, but that wasn't any easier. The cable was bulky and stiff, and his sweaty bloodied hands couldn't get much of a grip. Somehow he managed to get enough momentum, though, and he made the leap. He landed safely, but only just. His hand caught the railing and he hung there, dangling, a tenuous finger-hold from death, before hauling himself up, through the hatch to safety.

Birch had learned an important lesson about the ship that day. Trust nothing. After this, the incidents came more frequently. There was the time that a surge of electricity in the console jolted him badly. He was fortunate to get away with a few minor burns that time. Or there was the night when he awoke gagging, gasping for air. Karla had been there, in his dreams. She leaned in to kiss him, but her lips were ice cold and she was sucking the life out of him. The air... his air... came out of him and he couldn't breathe. She was killing him in his dreams, but when he awoke the danger was real.

Somehow the air filter in his cabin had malfunctioned and shut off the oxygen. He was suffocating, and when he tried to get out, the door had jammed. He trashed the room, desperately seeking a way out before his oxygen starved brain finally came up with a solution. Ripping the metal rail out of his closet he used it as a wedge, prizing the door open and saving his life.

This was more than paranoia. Obviously, something was very wrong, and in one of his rare moments of clarity Birch had reasoned it out. There were only three possible explanations. The first was that he had gone insane. Perhaps the loneliness of deep space travel had gotten to him. He was hearing voices and seeing things he knew couldn't be real, so maybe that was it, but he didn't think so.

The second possibility was that Karla really was haunting him, but he couldn't accept that. He didn't believe in any of that stuff, and besides, Karla was good. She wouldn't be haunting him, pushing him down elevator shafts, or suffocating him in his sleep. That wasn't her. But still, his visions seemed so real and hadn't she once said something about people never really dying. Maybe she meant more by that than he had ever imagined.

The final possibility was the only one he could do anything about and it was the only one he was willing to accept. It was simple, really. Maybe he was just thinking too much, reading too much into things. Everything that had happened could be easily explained by something as simple as a computer malfunction. The ship had spent so many years stored secretly underground. In that length of time, any number of problems could have developed. System degradation was almost inevitable under those circumstances.

He knew that was it. He had known all along that something wasn't right with the computer. The only thing he couldn't figure out was why Karla had been such a central part in all these dangerous malfunctions. In the end he concluded that her presence was just a physical manifestation of the danger, something his mind had created in its loneliness to give meaning to what was happening to him. That explained everything. At least it explained everything well enough to calm Birch's raging fears. This was something real. This was something he could do something about.

And that's what he did. His first thought had been to disable all but the most basic computer functions, but that was impossible. The Ares kid had managed it though the auxiliary station, but Birch couldn't even get on the same floor as the station anymore. The elevator wouldn't stop there, and when he tried to get in through the access shaft an electrical buzz had warned him of the foolishness of attempting to open the hatch at that level. Of course, that hadn't stopped him. He tried anyway and was rewarded with a sharp electrical shock before his hand had even touched the handle. That was lucky for him. Most likely he would have died instantly if he had made contact with the metal.

Birch was coming to see the computer as a living organism, as a dangerous foe to be outwitted. The thing had learned from the way the Ares kid had switched it off, and it was defending itself. That demonstrated an intelligence and Birch didn't trust it at all.

He tried everything he could think of, but in the end, he was forced to acknowledge that there wasn't any way to stop the computer directly. It was just too well protected for that. Outwitting it was the only option left to him, and that was going to take subtlety, not direct force.

To achieve this he had two immediate goals. The first was to gain some sort of localized control over the ship's systems. He couldn't get the computer offline, and he couldn't get total control of the ship. He had tried that and failed, but he did find that he could juggle things around to form temporary safe zones and emergency overrides if he needed it. He was sure he was going to need it. It looked like the computer had been testing things out- building up to something bigger, and soon it was going to finish the job.

He had many fears, but what worried him most was a repeat of what had happened in his cabin. The loss of air, that most basic necessity of life, had almost killed him. Could it happen again, only this time across the whole ship? With a computer system gone wacky anything was possible, even a complete environmental shutdown across the ship, and he had to be ready for that. He prepared as best he could.

The other goal Birch set himself was to get off the computer's tracking grid. The lights that followed him everywhere were a very visible indication that the ship knew his every move. He couldn't escape it.

It took a while, but Birch finally figured it out. He was able to cobble together an emitter with parts he scavenged from nonessential equipment that the computer wouldn't miss. He used it to fool the computer in two ways. Firstly it jammed the signal he was giving off, essentially erasing him from both video and tracking devices. The downside was that this left a hole in the reading where he should have been, thereby making it easy for the computer to detect his location. That was where the second feature of Birch's gizmo came in. It took readings from the surroundings- selecting some nondescript section, a blank wall or an empty piece of floor, and transmitted that in place of the hole that his absence had made. Thus wherever he was, the computer only sensed a blank corridor identical to a part further along.

The true mark of the success of this deception was demonstrated in the darkness that now engulfed him. The ship had lost him. It had no sense of his presence, and so it no longer illuminated his way.

This was how Birch lived for most of the last six months of the journey. He was in darkness, save for the little red points of illumination provided by the emergency lighting that lined the floor. He didn't get his food from the dispensers anymore. He raided the ship's stores, gathering up all the prepackaged food he could and depositing it in little stashes throughout the ship. He stopped using the elevators, using only the emergency access shaft to move between floors. He limited his access to the computer. Using a seclusion field he had programmed into the mainframe before disappearing, he was able to get limited updates on the ship's status and their progress toward R67.3. He didn't dare do much more than that.

He reverted to animal instinct, tramping the halls, staying on the move, avoiding detection, staying alive. Sometimes he still felt the whisper of Karla's presence, but it wasn't as clear as it had been before, except in his dreams. She was still in his dreams.

Finally, the day arrived. Birch had been expecting it. Little things had been happening all week. Random depressurization on different levels, rolling electrical surges, and roaming camera searches all pointed to something bigger. The com-puter was preparing to flex its muscle.

And then it happened. His first indication came through the emitter's display. He had rigged it to warn him of danger and it was flashing red now. Depressurization- the computer had made its final move. It was venting the atmosphere and within minutes the whole ship would be airless.

Birch was ready. He ran full tilt down the corridor. The sound of escaping oxygen whooshed around him and he gasped as his pumping lungs struggled for air in the thinning atmosphere. Racing for a storage cupboard, he flung the door open with a bang. Inside was an EVA suit he had prepared. He had done the same throughout the ship, placing suits in strategic locations, ready for just such an emergency as this.

Swiftly he put it on. It was getting hard to breathe and it was a relief when he finally clicked his helmet in place and felt the cool, sweet air of the suit sweep over him. Hungrily he gulped it down, struggling against the instinct to hyperventilate, to grasp and claw at every particle of air that sustained him.

Finally, his breathing returned to normal. He was ready. He had planned for this; he had plotted it all out, and now he was ready to act.

With the swiftness of certainty, he strode down the corridor, opened the hatch and began his quick descent down the access shaft to the lower decks. He knew where he was going and how long it would take to get there. Hand-by-hand, rung-by-rung, he moved with rhythmic certainty down to his destination.

Finally, he reached the level he was seeking. He pushed the hatch aside and emerged out onto the hangar deck.

Two little pod craft sat ready in the quiet darkness. They were tiny ships, the space version of an economy family car and not much bigger or more impressive than that from the outside. Inside they weren't much better. They could easily seat four. At a pinch, you might get five in, but it wouldn't be comfortable or safe.

Without pause, Birch strode over to the nearest pod and punched in a code on the keypad. The door opened and he got in. A few seconds later he had begun the launch sequence. The engines roared. Birch pushed a few more buttons, brought up a plot map, and with one swift motion leaped from the pod and shut the door behind him.

He ran. With all his might he ran and flung himself behind the heat resistant launch screen just in time to see the bay doors opening behind him. A moment later there was a boom as the little craft's engines geared up to full power and launched through the doors into open space.

Birch waited. It didn't take long. It was barely noticeable, except that he had been waiting for it. A slight jostling of the ship, the faintest shift in their location was all it took to tell Birch that he had been right. The pod had exploded, and if he had been on board he would have been dead.

The computer had destroyed the pod, and to it, he was now dead. Birch was certain of that, and he knew that if he wanted to stay alive that impression had to remain. He had to be cautious.

Slowly oxygen returned to the ship. There were important

instruments and systems on board that were not designed to work in an airless environment, and it was probably this feature more than anything else that had stopped the computer from just flushing him out in the first place. It had tried a more controlled response at first. It had sought to kill him in a less drastic way in order to avoid possible damage to the ship, but when that had failed it had gone for this last option.

Birch had seen it coming. He was right; the computer had been trying to kill him. When he had disappeared it hadn't been fooled. It had no reason to believe he was anywhere else but on the ship and, like a proud homeowner with a roach infestation, it wasn't going to rest until it knew its house was clean. Well, now Birch had given it that. As far as it knew its house was clean. It thought he was gone.

Birch was both surprised and delighted at his success. His plan had worked out remarkably well. He had programmed a false life sign into the pod, creating the impression that he was on board when he engaged the system. Everything was pre-set, all he had had to do in the end was get down to the hangar when the computer made its final play, start up the pod, and launch it into space.

And now he could rest.

For a time that was all he could do. His struggle against the ship had drained him. All he could manage for now was mere existence. He breathed, he slept, and he ate. He was at peace. Even his dreams were clear and free. He went to sleep in darkness. He woke up in darkness, and no voices oppressed him.

Finally thought returned. He began planning again, thinking about what he would do when he arrived at R67.3. How he would get off the ship alive. He watched the red course line plotting their progress as they drew ever nearer to their destination.

As the weeks passed he could almost taste the freedom he sought. For now, he was still left scurrying in the darkness, hiding from a crazed computer, but soon he would stand tall again. Soon he would walk in the light, and when he did he was going to kick the circuits out of that computer. For now, though, he had to be careful.

And then it happened. With a month left to the destination point, Birch was awakened by the throbbing red warning pulse of his emitter.

It was too early. He had checked the chambers himself a few weeks ago. They weren't due for another three weeks. Still, there it was. The emitter display made it clear. Someone, or something, was moving down in the cryogenic hall.

TWELVE

Birch ran for the access shaft. It didn't take long for him to tumble down the ladder and emerge in the corridor outside the cryogenic hall.

The lights were on. Birch winced against the glare. His eyes had grown accustomed to the darkness over the last few months and the sudden revelation of light was an uncomfortable one.

He edged closer to the cryogenic room. Peering through the doorway he saw the shadow of a form hunched over his burned out chamber. Birch crept closer. Still, the form didn't move. Whoever it was, they didn't notice him. They seemed engrossed in the devastation. Their back was to him, but Birch could see a piece of debris in their hand. The fingers gently turned and stroked the jagged chunk of metal, as though caressing a treasured relic of a distant era.

Birch crept closer.

The figure froze, sensing his presence; then spun swiftly around. It was Jane, and for just a moment Birch thought he caught the glisten of a tear in her eye.

"Jane," Birch rasped. His voice was rough and gravelly. He hadn't spoken for so long that words came with difficulty and their sound startled him.

Jane seemed no more soothed by his voice than he was. Her hands went up in a defensive posture and her eyes narrowed as she surveyed his disheveled form. Birch hadn't thought of it, but in the months since his war with the computer had begun he hadn't shaved, bathed, or changed his clothes. He had been too absorbed with the single purpose of survival and had avoided anything that might have drawn the computer's attention to him, even the basic necessities of good hygiene. Now his hair was long, his beard shaggy, and his eyes wild with the look of a hunted prey. His uniform was dirty and torn and Jane looked at him now as a young Jim Hawkins must have looked upon Ben Gunn on his Treasure Island. That was fitting enough. He had lived like a castaway all these months, except that he had been a castaway on his own ship.

"It's me, Jane." Birch tried to make his voice sound natural. "I... um, I woke up a little early," he added simply.

"Major? Major Birch?" For a moment she seemed confused. She blinked a few times then smiled, letting her arms fall limply to her side. She laughed. Quietly at first, but soon she was doubled over in convulsive fits. Every time she seemed about to calm down she looked up at Birch and began again.

Birch eyed her sourly. He had almost begun to warm to the idea of Jane when she was frozen, but now she was out again his feelings were cooling already. He didn't see how his problems and his struggles over the last year-and-a-half could be remotely funny.

Finally, Jane stopped. "So, what happened?" she asked. Her eyes still twinkled merrily from her amusement at his appearance, but her voice showed concern.

"Like I said, I woke up a little early," Birch's reply was purposefully vague on that point. "The chamber wouldn't let me out. It almost killed me. After that, things seemed okay for a while, but then about five or six months ago the computer seemed to go nuts and has been trying to kill me ever since."

Jane's eyes narrowed. She should have been worried about the dangers of a ship controlled by a psychotic computer, but he could tell that she was far more struck by something else he had said.

"Five or six months?" her voice barely veiled her incredulity. "Just how long were you out of stasis without us?"

"A while," Birch muttered. "I wasn't going to trust them again," he gestured to his burned out chamber. "But why are you out of stasis so early, Jane? What are you doing?"

"I'm checking on you," she hissed. "I knew I couldn't trust you. I just knew it! I was supposed to wake up ahead of you and make sure everything was locked in and secure before we got there, to make sure you couldn't make up some excuse, some technical glitch or something for why we couldn't stop at R67.3, but it looks like you beat me to it. So what have you done? Where are we?"

Jane was striding toward the computer console, bringing up the course display showing their destination.

"Nothing," Birch answered simply, gesturing to the pulsing red line on the screen that marked their course. "I didn't do anything. We'll be at R67.3 in a few weeks."

Jane seemed confused. She typed and retyped on the console, checking to see if what he was saying was true. It seemed to be. Birch wasn't lying. They were approaching R67.3, and soon they would be there.

"Okay," Jane responded cautiously. For a moment she simply stared at the screen, watching the line as though witnessing some great personal achievement, something she mustn't miss in the slightest, not even to blink. Birch cleared his throat impatiently, and her eyes finally snapped back to him.

"So, the computer's been trying to kill you?" By the tone of her voice, Birch could tell she wasn't taking him seriously.

"Yeah," Birch snapped, "and you better watch yourself. It'll be after you now."

"What happened?" Jane still didn't seem to believe it, but at least she was listening now.

Birch explained the events of the last year-and-a-half, how

he had almost died in stasis, the creeping incursion of the computer into his daily life, the malfunctions that had nearly killed him, and the final battle of wits that he had won through his deception with the false life sign in the pod. Jane listened to all of this without expression. When he finally finished she nodded.

"Are you sure you didn't just get a bit spacey?" she asked bluntly.

"I'm sure!" Birch fumed. He was beginning to wish he was alone again.

"Only," she paused, measuring her words this time, "you remember what happened back on Earth? How they put us in those enviro-domes when we first got back, and yours went wrong. It was supposed to send us to a paradise of our mind's own making, but they said something about your mind being wrong for it, not being able to do it. Maybe this is the same. Maybe you just couldn't handle the solitude over that length of time. I mean, I've heard of computers malfunctioning. That can happen anytime, but computers trying to kill you? That's not reality, Major. Computers go wrong; they don't go crazy and become homicidal. That just doesn't happen."

Birch gritted his teeth but answered as calmly as he could manage.

"I'm not saying the computer had some kind of nervous breakdown, Jane. I'm saying that someone messed with it, trying to kill us all. I only just figured it out myself recently." He pointed to the cryogenic chamber at the far end of the hall that contained the dormant body of the Ares boy.

"Do you really think the only thing that kid did to the computer was to lock a few doors and shut off the lights? He had plenty of time to do something while he was in auxiliary control, and I think that's what he did. He set the computer against us, to kill us and get control of the ship."

Jane's eyes were wide now. Finally what Birch was saying made some sense to her.

"Okay, so what can we do about it?"

Birch shrugged. "Maybe not much, I'm not sure, but with two of us maybe something is possible. We need to try and get back onto the auxiliary deck."

Jane agreed, and soon they were in the hallway heading for Auxiliary Control. Birch opened the hatch to the access shaft, but rather than follow him Jane continued to the elevator and pushed the button.

"What are you doing?" Birch hissed. "I told you, the elevator's not safe, and besides, it won't even stop at the auxiliary floor."

"You try your way; I'll try mine." She smiled and passed through the now open doors into the waiting elevator. She disappeared behind the closing doors and Birch turned again to his hatch. Climbing through, he looked up into the long expanse of inky darkness towering above him and sighed.

"Fine," Birch muttered gloomily, "get yourself killed." He could tell by the look on her face and her willingness to take the elevator that there was still a large part of Jane that didn't believe his story. Soon she would see. If she was lucky she wouldn't die finding out.

It was a long, arduous ascent. By the time he reached the level of the auxiliary floor his hands were sweating and his arms ached. For a moment he rested his head on a rung of the ladder and waited. He had hoped to see Jane here, having climbed down from whatever level the elevator had taken her to, but she wasn't here yet.

He waited. She didn't come. She had been stupid to try it. There wasn't any telling what had happened to her. Perhaps the elevator had gotten stuck, or maybe the computer had waited until she was in that tiny, enclosed space and sealed the doors, then pulled the oxygen, leaving her to suffocate. Birch sighed morosely. He had just resigned himself to a long search for Jane's body when the nearby hatch opened and her face appeared.

"Are you ever coming out of there?" She smiled triumphantly down at him. "I've been waiting here for a long time, come on!"

For a moment Birch could only stare up at her in wonder. She wasn't dead, and she was *on* the auxiliary floor. It hadn't occurred to him before, but now that he thought about it the electrical hum of power flowing through the hatch hadn't been there as he had waited. Whatever defense the computer had erected against him was gone now.

He climbed out. They walked silently down the corridor and, arriving at the auxiliary chamber door, they found it unlocked. The room itself was unremarkable in its normalcy. No red-eyed-monster computers or dangerous electronic booby traps were present, just a well-lit, functional room lined with all the equipment and computer displays associated with the running of the ship.

Birch and Jane quickly got to work at the consoles, trying to find any sign of sabotage or malfunction, but nothing came up. Everything seemed to be running smoothly, at optimal speed and performance. For Birch, it almost seemed too good, like when you took a used car out for a test drive and somehow the mechanic coaxed one good ride out of the thing before you bought it and ended up with a lemon.

Jane quit first. She shrugged and turned away from the display. "I don't think we're going to find anything here," She smiled, a little too widely for Birch's liking. "Everything is coming up clean, almost perfect, in fact."

"I know," Birch grumbled. "I don't like it."

"I don't suppose you do," Jane got up and walked to the door, "but that's the way it is. Anyway, I've got other things to get on with right now. Let me know if any computers come at you with a kitchen knife and I'll come running." She left without giving him a chance to answer.

Birch was left alone. He glanced up at the lights and panels that surrounded him. He almost expected the computer to laugh or say something malevolent now that Jane had gone, but that could never be. NASA had learned that lesson long ago. People preferred their computers mute and subservient.

No one liked a smart-mouthed console that knew your job better than you. Events had proven that such computers were dangerous, and so, perhaps for the first time in human history, they had chosen not built something simply because we could. In later years no NASA computer could ever talk back, much less plan anything without human assistance. They were designed that way, and that was what made this computer's actions so surprising. Birch doubted it was as dumb as it was supposed to be. It had learned, it had adapted, and it had fooled Jane. He knew that. He was completely certain that all of this hadn't been in his mind, as Jane thought. This computer had tried to kill him, and he wasn't going to trust it.

***

For the remaining weeks, Birch and Jane busied themselves with final preparations for their arrival. They took inventory and tested equipment. They searched the records and studied layout plans, gleaning for any last fragment of information about the colony of R67.3, but there was nothing new, and they were left unsure of exactly what to expect. A basic blueprint of the standard base construction was all they could find. As for the rest, they would just have to wait and see when they got there.

Birch stayed busy. He never relaxed. Partly through his determination to get them to safety, and partly because of his distrust of the computer, he found himself unable to do anything but work and vigilantly watch their progress. In those last three weeks, he slept rarely and fitfully. Slumped over his console, he would awake with a start as Jane entered the control room, tutting over him having spent another night at the controls.

She was far more trusting- far more convinced that there was no danger here. She fully believed that Birch's problems were solely the result of an imbalance in his fevered brain. And why shouldn't she? There was no physical evidence of his fight, save for the missing transport pod that Jane thought he had wastefully destroyed in a fit of delusion. Everything else had vanished like the fears of the night in the daylight. There was nothing to show Jane. Even the star that seemed to follow them couldn't be seen anymore. So, of course, Jane hadn't believed him. Birch didn't care. He knew he was right.

Time passed slowly, but finally, the day came. The line marking their course had changed from its customary red to green and the words, "Destination Achieved", were written on the screen. They had arrived.

THIRTEEN

The *Hypnos III-A* winked into existence, born into the universe of reality as the Dark Drive disengaged. The silvered craft arced gracefully and slipped into a silent orbit above R67.3.

The great, gray world glowed dully beneath them. The atmosphere swirled and heaved darkly, barely penetrated by the crimson light of the giant red sun that should have fed and nourished it. The planet was too distant from its light to be counted in the "Goldilocks Zone", the perfect distance for the natural promotion of life, but it had been close enough to be workable. Terra-forming could fix it, just as it had done with Mars. That had been the plan anyway. Judging by the way things looked here it didn't seem as though that plan had gotten very far.

Birch was soon down in the cryogenic hall, tapping away on the computer, beginning the reanimation process. He watched everything closely, making sure nothing went wrong. Jane watched too, but less intently, she still trusted the computer. She still thought all his experiences with it were nothing more than the product of his imagination, and so far the computer had done nothing to prove her wrong. Everything had been normal since she woke up.

Over a hundred cryogenic chambers filled the hall, but only two were now opening. Jane shot a glance over at Birch, but he was too busy keying in codes to notice. He was making sure the computer did what it was told, or more importantly, that it wasn't doing what it hadn't been told. So far everything seemed to be working out as planned. Lauren and Edwards' chambers were opening, while the lid to the Ares boy's compartment remained firmly shut.

Birch planned to keep it that way. He put double coding on the override and set the controls to manual. If the kid had been messing with the computer, Birch was going to make sure that there was no chance of it getting him out.

It took a little while, but finally, Edwards and Lauren began showing signs of life. They moved. Birch and Jane didn't help them. It was always better to leave the newly awakened to themselves for a while. Even the most placid, reasonable personality was strained by the reanimation process. Anyone trying to help at this early stage was more likely to get a fist in the face or a kick to the gut than any thanks.

Finally, Lauren lifted herself out. On unsteady legs she walked to Birch's console, checking the readings for their location. She smiled thinly, nodding to herself. They were here.

Edwards took longer. His first experience of cryogenics, apparently, had been rough. It usually was. No one enjoyed their first time in The Freezer. He would get over it.

Birch was impatient to get going, to get this final stage of their approach underway, but he understood cryogenics well enough not to rush things. Edwards would be ready when he was ready. It didn't look like that was going to be anytime soon.

"I'll be up top," Birch finally said, striding for the door. "Jane, bring Edwards up whenever he's ready. You come with me, Lauren. We can't wait forever. "

A moment later Lauren and Birch were in the elevator, hurtling to the flight deck and to answer that one vital question- Was there anyone on R67.3? Soon the silent planet would answer.

They entered the cockpit and sat in their old accustomed

positions. Birch liked being back at the controls again, back in familiar territory. A place like this, with all its flashing buttons and displays, was comforting to him. It put life at his fingertips. There was no other place where Birch felt so comfortable. Everything was here. He had control. Life and death were here, at the push of a button or the flick of the stick, success and failure were in his hands. Everywhere else was troubled and unknown. The choices were never so clear as they were at the controls in a cockpit.

Birch barely had time to start up planetary procedures before Jane walked in with a gaunt looking Edwards in tow.

"Ah," Birch looked up as they entered, "just in time. Jane, I need you to finish prepping the probe for launch. Lauren's been trying to figure out how far they got in the terra-forming process, but we need more data."

She nodded and walked to her station. Birch turned his attention to Edwards. "I need you to start signaling the surface," he barked. "Auto-communication has tried to reach them, but we're getting no response. They may be following NASA protocol- no live transmissions to auto-messages, so that's not unexpected."

Edwards nodded but looked uncertainly down at his panel. Lauren was soon at his side, efficiently showing him the steps he had to perform to make that happen.

Birch studied his own screen, trying to figure out possible landing sites based on the sketchy information provided in the records. At last report, it seemed there were two main outposts, the original landing base, set up (supposedly) by the seeding crew of the Hypnos III. The second, larger base was established by a later colonizing crew. There were a few other isolated outposts listed, but these two larger establishments were just a few miles apart. He would land near them.

"Probe launched," Jane announced. "It'll be a few minutes before we get anything."

He nodded mutely. Edward's faltering voice had started through the base communication codes and Major Birch was more interested in listening for a response.

"*Hypnos III-A*, calling R/III/67.3, code ECHO 4-7-7-7, Omega Phase, over." The words came awkwardly from Edwards parched lips. He licked them and began again.

"*Hypnos III-A*, calling R/III/67.3, code ECHO 4-7-7-7, Omega Phase, respond please, over." He parroted what Lauren had told him to say, but still there was no answer, no sound at all, just the silence of dead radio waves.

"This begins to look familiar," Birch remarked sourly. Edwards was tuning the instruments, trying different settings, but nothing changed the silence.

"Initial data coming in from the probe, Major," Jane announced. "Just patching it through to Lauren's computer."

"Well?" Birch didn't take his eyes off Edwards.

Lauren shifted uncomfortably in her seat. Staring down at the screen, her brows knit as she squinted into the display. "Atmospheric data- not all that different from when we left. Nitrogen, carbon dioxide, oxygen's ticked up a little, it's still not enough, maybe five percent, somewhere around that level. It looks like there's been some attempt at terra-forming, but they failed."

Birch's breath hissed through his teeth.

"*Hypnos III-A*, calling R/III/67.3, code ECHO 4-7-7-7, Omega Phase, over," Edward's voice was droning on robotically. Their hope was fading.

"Visual coming through." Jane's voice was flat, no glimmer of hope there either. Whatever she saw hadn't inspired optimism. "Bringing it up now." She pushed a couple of buttons and their view of the planet through the window dissolved into the probe's camera display.

Gray dust blew across the lens. The wind whipped the swirling particles into the sky, across the land, everywhere. The heavens were gray. The ground was gray. Everything was gray. It was just as he remembered. The wind roared and ripped at the iron earth, churning it up into the atmosphere, choking, blinding, darkening the world.

It wasn't always like this. There were periods of calm. He remembered good days when the winds had died and the sun had almost managed to break through, giving a reddish glow to the leaden sky, but those days were rare. There was something about the way the Red Giant heated R67.3, the unevenness of it through the atmosphere, that constantly created these howling winds, and whatever the colony here had tried to do about it, this natural feature of the planet had remained unchanged.

"Colony coming into view," Jane's voice cracked.

Grainy, dark shapes could just be made out in the distance. Birch squinted at the screen.

"Can you get a better image than that?" Birch barked.

"It's already maxed out," Jane replied. "That's as good as it gets. Give it a minute. It's closing in."

The image shifted, turning with the slant of the probe correcting course against the howling gale. The spike of a solitary thin, black tower came into view, shaking, braced against the gusting wind.

"That's the newer base, *Colony I*," Jane breathed. "No indication of any activity there yet, but the fact we're seeing anything at all is a good sign. With all this wind the place should be buried under a hundred feet of dirt by now if nothing was being done to keep it up."

The camera swerved again, taking in the roof of the large building complex. From this position, it reminded Birch of a misplaced shopping mall, launched into the desolation of deep space. With all of its little component cells housed under one protective roof, the comparison was not unfitting.

Jane scowled, tapping furiously at her computer before lifting her head to look at Birch. "No power," she murmured, "negligible trace levels anyway. The base is dead. I'm getting no energy readings- heat, electricity, oxygen: all off."

"What?" Birch was out of his seat and glowering over Jane's shoulder. She pointed to the display. She was right. Everything was down. The place was dead.

"But how does that fit with the lack of dirt accumulation around the base? That must show some activity there."

Jane shrugged. "I don't know, but the probe's moving on to *Primary Base*, the earliest settlement, now. Maybe we'll get some answers there."

Birch and Jane silently watched the screen, seeking the first sign of *Primary Base* amidst the blowing dust.

"*Hypnos III-A*, calling R/III/67.3, code ECHO 4-7-7-7, Omega Phase, over. Respond, please. Respond, please." Edward's mantra continued unnoticed in the background, muffled, almost apologetic for intruding on the silence of this somber place. He was giving up hope. He would stop soon.

A sudden shrill screech of jumbled noise ripped through the cockpit. The ship convulsed in the aftershock, knocking Birch to the floor. Edwards squealed, ripping the headphones off his head before collapsing onto the panel before him. Birch was quickly at his side.

"What was it, Edwards?" Birch was pulling him up, but while the man's eyes were open they were glazed and uncomprehending.

"Primary Base, Major," Jane announced. Birch gently lay Edward's head back on the counter and turned to the screen.

A black dome came into view. He recognized it. It was the structure they were supposed to build, the first outpost on a colonizing mission. They hadn't built it. They couldn't have built it. All the supplies had been destroyed in that first terrible month on this barren rock. That had been the start of it all- his decision to abandon the mission and to go back to Earth. But now here it was, this impossible structure was here on the surface of R67.3.

"Voices... voices... VOICES... voices! Stop, stop... STOP!" Edwards was shouting deliriously. Birch glanced back at him, then back at the screen.

"Anything yet, Jane?"

"Not yet."

Birch turned back to Edwards. "What was it; what did you

hear?"

Edward's eyes rolled, unable to focus. "Voices," he mumbled, "thousands... millions of voices. All stuck... all at once. I couldn't understand. I couldn't help. They need help." Edwards' eyes closed as he drifted back into semi-consciousness.

Birch laid Edwards' head back on the control panel and turned to Lauren. "Get him down to the med deck. See what you can do for him." He turned to Jane.

"Anything yet?"

Jane nodded grimly. "Yes, *Primary Base* is dead, just like *Colony I*. No power, no oxygen, nothing. But again, like *Colony I*, there is no evidence of deposit buildup outside. If these places have been abandoned for any time at all they should have disappeared into the ground, but here they are."

Birch sighed. He watched the probe's camera sway, hurtling through the blowing gray dust, taking in the black arc of the dome. "Well, I guess it looks like we have ourselves a mystery."

FOURTEEN

The words 'I told you so' were as natural as breathing, but he didn't whisper them, not even to himself. Their flavor was on his tongue, and he could imagine their triumph, but still he kept quiet. Jane had been as wrong about the prospects for R67.3 as he had been about their return to Earth, but there was little satisfaction in that. All they could do now was all they had ever done, pick up the shattered pieces of their dreams and run for the fallback position- survival. That's all it ever came down to in the end. For all their great dreams and grand designs, it all came down to that one simple objective in the end.

R67.3 was as bad as he had feared. Subsequent probes had given a more detailed account, but none of it changed the basic reality. Both stations were dead and any attempt to make a life on the planet below was going to be difficult. Still, he wasn't sure what alternative they had. For now, at least it seemed that R67.3 was their new home.

Birch and Jane worked together on the plan for their descent. It had been a long time since they had worked together on anything. Jane had been against him since he had assumed command, but now, finally, they had a common goal. And yet strangely, even in this new-found commonality, there was still a difference.

Birch took on the task with a grudging determination. He was diligent and efficient, but there was no joy in his work. He did what was needed to make the landing possible, and that was as far as his thinking went. They would get down, get the bases' systems running again, and see where life took them from there. Any other hopes or concerns were just too much for him right now. It was all about survival.

Jane, on the other hand, was strangely buoyed by their arrival. Any expectation Birch had of her falling into despondency or despair at the dissolving of their hopes was quickly proven wrong. She was resilient. She had been as troubled as the rest of them at the first initial news of the dead bases, but she had recovered more quickly than the rest of them. It was as though it didn't really matter. To everyone else the revelation had been a devastating blow to their hopes, but to her it seemed little more than an inconvenience, something that made things harder, but it didn't directly affect her.

And so they worked toward their shared goal. Like earth and sky they met at a common horizon, but like those two elements, they shared little in common. Jane was light and passed airily through every obstacle. Nothing could stop her. Birch found everything hard. His work was slow, methodical, and precise. Base schematics and the collected data from the probes were poured over as he tried to work out what had gone wrong and what they could do to fix it. In the end, the results were inconclusive. All he could do was pack the transport pod with spares and equipment for the most likely contingencies and hope that would be enough.

Finally, the day of departure arrived. Birch was nervous. What they were getting into and what they were leaving behind both troubled him equally. The decision had been made early on that they would all go down to the surface. That wasn't protocol, of course, someone should have remained on the ship, but with a crew as sparse as his, he didn't have any choice. He couldn't leave Edwards or Lauren alone onboard.

Lauren was Industry and not to be trusted. Edwards was an unwilling conscript to the crew and to be trusted even less. Both of them needed watching. That only left Jane or himself as the remaining options to stay aboard, but they would both be needed to get things running down there. So there was no choice. They would all have to go, and fortunately Jane, usually a stickler for doing things 'the right way', seemed willing to ignore this infraction of the rules for once.

At last, they were ready. Birch took a final look around the cockpit, checking panels and settings before their departure. Everything seemed okay, but he still didn't like it. He hated leaving the ship unmanned like this. The way the computer had been acting earlier left him with serious doubts about the wisdom of even attempting it, but there wasn't any choice. He had at least gained access to the mainframe from auxiliary control. Once inside he had found a few obvious things that the Ares kid had done, but he couldn't be sure he had gotten it all. If he had missed anything they might all get down to the surface, only to find that the ship had left without them.

He sighed. Long streams of data scrolled down the screen. His eyes focused there one last time, searching for more rogue input, but he couldn't see anything. The light from the display cast a sickly glow on his skin as he blinked against the illumination. Finally, he turned away. Leaving the empty cockpit humming softly behind him, he descended to the hangar deck where the others were already waiting. He put on his helmet and they were all suited and ready to go.

It was a tight squeeze in the pod. Birch and Jane took the controls at the front, Lauren and Edwards, as passengers, were wedged in the back seat. Something about it reminded Birch of a bizarre family outing, an interplanetary road trip on their way to some grand adventure or exciting holiday. Of course, this was neither grand nor exciting. The work ahead was difficult, dangerous, and potentially deadly. Whatever had happened down there had been enough to wipe out a whole colony, and Birch wasn't optimistic about the chances of their little band overcoming the odds that had destroyed them.

"Engine startup commenced," Jane announced as the pod's hatch sealed. She glanced down at her screen. "It doesn't look good down there."

"It never does," Birch muttered.

"Yeah, well it hasn't gotten any better."

They had been tracking the weather for days. R67.3 was never balmy. Its chances of ever becoming a resort destination were remote. During their original mission Birch remembered very few good days. More often the winds howled and blew the dry dirt into your face. Storms like this could last for days, weeks, or even months. These were the prevailing conditions and this was what it was like at the base right now. It hadn't changed since their arrival, and Birch didn't see the point in waiting any longer. It wasn't going to get any better. He could handle it. The landing wouldn't be easy, but he had managed worse before, so he had decided to go for it, and to his surprise, Jane had agreed.

"Bay doors open. Launch ready," Jane added as she clicked another few buttons. The dark emptiness of space opened up before them.

"Launching," Birch responded as the engines roared. He pulled gently back on the stick, easing the pod through the bay doors and into the vacuum beyond.

The tiny pod arced, for a moment, taking in the complete aspect of the Hypnos III-A's silvered hull before turning again to the gray planet below.

"I'll be setting down at *Primary Base* first," Birch announced, eying his instruments before looking up at Jane. "I'll drop you and Edwards there to see what you can make of the situation at that site. Lauren and I will work at *Colony I* and see what we can do there. From the base plans, it looks like we'll need to get both sections running to last long. They're co-dependent.

"Oxygen supply in the suits should be sufficient for a full

day, but we're not taking any chances. I'll be picking you up in exactly eighteen hours. We'll head back to the Hypnos and compare what we find there.

"I want you to keep communications open at all times. If the slightest problem or concern comes up then I want you to radio me right away. I don't care what it is. Let's just be safe down there. Call me at your first worry and we can abort and head back up immediately. Got that?"

Jane nodded, but Edwards was leaning forward from the back seat. "You two should really stick together," he remarked acidly. Edwards still chaffed at his presence here. Already a piece of flotsam adrift on the current of his own life, his abduction from Earth had thrust him into a world he didn't understand and didn't want to acknowledge. Clearly, he wanted no part of this mission.

"You two shut us out of every decision anyway, and the way you've spent so much time together recently, maybe you like each other's company." He paused, letting the innuendo sink in. "Lauren and I wouldn't want to break up your happy pairing," he added, apparently trying to gain an ally in the enigmatic officer. Lauren was an outsider like him. He must have sensed that. "If you two want to stay together you should leave us on the ship and then go exploring your pretty little planet together. You don't need to risk us down there."

In a perfect echo of exasperated parents on an interminable road trip, Birch and Jane turned quickly in their seats to glare at the unruly 'children' in the back, but the effect was marred by a miscalculation, and their helmets clanged together painfully.

"No!" Jane spluttered, shaking her head more in pain than denial. "We'll stay as we planned, and your childish insinuation is ignorant. Even if I was that desperate, I wouldn't want him; it's against regulations. It would never be allowed!"

That was true enough. The Hypnos missions were a little like the priesthood in that respect. It wasn't as though there was a literal 'vow of chastity', but it was a part of the written agreement that there would be no relationships between crew members. They were supposed to be above all that, and at the time this had only added to the myth and mystique of the Hypnos astronauts.

It hadn't always been that way. The practice had really begun during the early colonization period. Things had gotten out of hand during those formative years on Mars. Before establishing Base Two, when space travel was slow and dangerous, relationships between NASA personnel had been pretty common. It was an open secret that no one worried too much about. It was one of the few comforts afforded them in their dangerous existence, but that soon changed.

As Base Two became more established and travel became easier existence on Mars also became more mundane. The media tended to concentrate less on the technology or the heroism of the missions and more on the 'personal aspect'. For the respectable press, this meant day-in-the-life documentaries and personal biographies of the men and women who worked in space. For the less respectable press, it meant gossip.

Soon reports were finding their way back to Earth revealing all the personal details of the lives of the astronauts, and it wasn't pretty. Somehow heroes have always been expected to be something more than ourselves, something better than us, and these reports exposed the men and women of NASA for what they really were- human. Mars was quickly becoming an interplanetary soap opera, with all the subtlety of an average daytime drama. NASA couldn't tolerate it. It wasn't the scandal that bothered them as much as the laughter. The sniggering sneers of the late night comedians with their catchy punch lines about the 'astro-naughties', and the lewd wordplay about future plans for trips to Venus, Uranus, and the Galactic Bulge at the center of the galaxy did little to improve the mood in the Agency. In the comedy skits, their boldest achievements had become little more than an interplanetary version of The Love Boat.

They had to do something. Their most valued asset had never been their equipment, their bases, or even their scientists- instead, it was the idea of who they were and what they were achieving. Their reputation, like their rockets, had soared high above the heavens, but the news from Mars was bringing it down with a crash.

NASA brought an abrupt halt to the debauched debacle. With immediate effect, they demanded that all such activities cease. Any refusal to comply would result in a loss of position to something menial and inconsequential within the organization, where the offender's activities could no longer harm the Agency's reputation.

It hadn't taken long for that message to hit home. A few spectacular demotions soon alerted everyone that NASA was serious. A new wind of Victorian Values had swept through the Agency, and anyone who didn't want to get swept away with it had to tow the line. By the time of the Hypnos missions, the policy had become so ingrained that no one questioned it. It was understood that any infraction meant a loss of status and, more importantly, a loss of financial support for those you left behind. Breaking the rules risked too much, and very few ever tried it, at least not when they thought there was any chance of getting caught.

Even so, regulations weren't the most compelling reason for avoiding a relationship with Jane, but Birch wasn't going to get into that with Edwards.

"Shut-up, Edwards," he muttered as he squinted down at his screen. They were descending into the upper atmosphere. Entry, at this level at least, was easier than Earth. There was no debris to contend with, and with Birch's deft handling the pod quickly slipped into the gray stratosphere of R67.3.

Things quickly got harder. Already the monochrome dust was flying across the cockpit window like the static on a TV. Visibility was poor. He kept adjusting their angle to stop the engines getting clogged with dirt and cutting out. Even with his best efforts they coughed and sputtered, almost dying as the ship weaved and turned, buffeted by the howling gale.

"Watch the engines!" Jane snapped.

"I've got it," Birch answered evenly. He chewed his lower lip, concentrating on the ship, feeling his way down to the surface. "Primary Base is just ahead. We should get a visual on it pretty soon."

Jane strained to see it, but the blowing dust was just too thick. They could be right on top of it and they wouldn't see it.

Suddenly a solid green blade of light cut through the darkness. Its reverberating boom shook the little pod off course. Birch pulled up, saving them from a fatal crash.

"What was that?" Edwards hissed.

"Trouble," Birch answered, but his attention was on the ship. He weaved again, trying to anticipate the next shot, but he guessed wrong. Another bolt of green energy leaped up, this time passing through the pod's left wing with a thundering crash.

Alarms sounded and red lights flashed. Birch wrestled with the controls, sending the ship limping away from *Primary Base*, the source of the destructive beam.

Another shot leaped up, hitting them again. Smoke filled the cabin as Birch pulled at the unresponsive control stick. The pod took a steep dive.

"Prepare for a hard landing!" he shouted over the sounding alarms. "We're going down!"

FIFTEEN

There wasn't much time to react. It didn't matter anyway; the condition of the ship didn't give Birch a chance to do anything. He had already lowered the landing pads in preparation for their arrival at *Primary Base*, but now he was trying to retract them, to give the pod a better chance at a smoother, controlled hard landing, but it didn't work. None of the controls were responding.

The pod hit the ground sideways. One stubby wing broke off and the impact rolled the ship, bringing it down on the landing gear. At that speed the result was disastrous. The pad buckled, pulling the ship forward onto its nose before flipping it over three times and sending it skidding upside-down along the planet's sandy surface.

It was probably the sand that saved them. A hard landing on rocky ground would have smashed them to pieces. As it was, for the first time in his life Birch was thankful for the sand and dust of R67.3, at least he would be once he could make sense of anything. At that moment the world was a jumble of flashing warnings, screaming alarms, and crashing destruction. The lights flickered intermittently, creating an abstract stop-motion effect. Snapshots of reality flashed before his eyes. The control panels, warning lights ablaze- Jane's face, her eyes glowing, her teeth strangely prominent as she shouted uselessly, unheard amidst the tumult- the cockpit window with its turning, rolling landscape and flying dust- all merged into one disjointed reality.

The pod skidded to a halt. The lights flickered again and went out for good. A voice moaned in the darkness; it sounded like Edwards. Then there was silence.

"Another textbook landing, Major," Jane finally coughed from her seat beside him.

Birch couldn't see anything, but he could sense her movement nearby. Only a thin stream of light trickled through the window. Half the glass was buried in the dirt, but both sides were equally dark. It was daytime outside, but the storm made it hard to tell.

Birch tried to move. His eyes rolled into his head. He was about to lose consciousness. The blood was rushing to his head, and suddenly he realized that he was hanging upside down, suspended by his restraints. He fumbled with the clasp, trying to release himself, but he couldn't get out. He was stuck.

"Is everyone okay?" he called to the back. No answer came, save for the sound of his own respiration and a continued rustle of movement from Jane. An instant later their four internal helmet lights flickered on in reaction to the darkness. A soft glow bathed their faces, but from his seat, Birch couldn't tell if Lauren and Edwards were alive or dead.

He took a second attempt at the belt and managed to release the mechanism, sending himself plummeting from his chair, falling quickly down onto the upturned ceiling. It was his second painful encounter with gravity in a short time, and he lay for a moment, panting. His legs were tangled in the restraints and he couldn't get up.

"Whoa there, Major- next time maybe you should take the slow way down!" Jane's voice called. She had already freed herself from her seat and was crawling to assist him.

"Not me, them!" Birch was gesturing back to Lauren and Edwards, whose suits had remained ominously still, but Jane ignored his instruction, pulling him free so he could help with them.

Despite a giddy sickness that made movement difficult, Birch was quickly up and helped Jane get Lauren and Edwards down. There was a flicker of movement from Lauren, it looked like she was going to be okay, but Edwards was unresponsive. Birch had him on the floor, quickly attaching his EVA suit directly into the pod's respirator, but no power was getting through, the ship was completely dead. Even the backup systems were down.

"We've got no power!" Birch shouted. "Only what's in the suits!" He quickly pulled Edwards toward him, preparing to perform CPR in the most difficult circumstances, but it wasn't necessary. Unknown to Birch, these new suits were highly automated. Already it was increasing the oxygen flow to Edwards' helmet and putting pressure on his abdominals. He was choking and the suit, having recognized this, took action, pushing the obstruction free.

It worked. Edwards' eyes fluttered open. He grabbed his stomach, wretched, and vomited. For a moment his face disappeared amid an oozing flow of his half-digested breakfast. Birch winced. Edwards' visor was coated, but the EVA suit was working on that already, suctioning away the liquid and cleaning the glass. By the time Birch could see him again Edwards was breathing normally, and while it would have been an exaggeration to say he looked well, at least he looked better.

"We need to get out of here!" Jane shouted, grabbing a fire extinguisher and dousing a sparking, fizzling panel with foam. "This won't hold it much longer. There's enough oxygen and fuel left in this ship to make a big impression. We've got to get out of here, now!"

Birch nodded. She was right, but they couldn't get through the hatch. It was blocked, pushed against the ground because of the angle of their landing. That left one option. It meant the complete certainty that they could not use the pod to get back up to the Hypnos. Looking at the wreckage around him it was already clear that this pod was going nowhere. He had nothing to lose.

"Prepare for atmosphere breech," Birch barked. "We're getting out the hard way." He reached up, typed the command code, and hit the emergency escape button. A long crack appeared in the cockpit's main window. In geometric patterns, the lines grew and spread across the glass, like threads spun by a predatory spider. Finally, the shape had expanded to its full potential and collapsed in on them in a shower of tiny glass pebbles.

Uninvited, the raging wind of R67.3 burst in, sucking the flying dust and dirt in with it. Visibility immediately dropped to zero. In the light of his helmet, all Birch could see was the reflected glimmer of the dust as it blew around him, but he remembered enough to know where Edwards was. He grabbed him, pulling him toward the cockpit window.

The broken windshield hadn't left a very large gap, half of it was blocked with dirt, but it was enough. Already Jane had urged Lauren through, and it was only a moment later that she also disappeared.

Birch half-dragged, half-coaxed a barely conscious Edwards toward the exit. Already he could see the flames licking hungrily at the control panel. It was a race now, a race between the oxygen in the cabin and the sterile atmosphere of R67.3. Would the fire ignite and explode the fuel before this alien environment could smother it? Birch didn't want to hang around to find out. He pushed Edwards through the hole and then clambered out after him.

It was a bleak, confusing world they entered. Dust blew everywhere and one direction looked much like another. He couldn't see Jane or Lauren. Edwards still lay prostrate where he had fallen, and Birch lifted him up, pulling him forward.

"Move it, Edwards!" Birch shouted. "The pod's about to blow!" Edwards nodded mutely and started a faltering run from the crash site.

Birch grabbed his arm, pulling him along. They ran. Unconcerned about direction, only distance, they moved as quickly as Birch could coax a hobbling Edwards to go. It wasn't quick enough, and moments later a loud explosion shook the ground, sending them both tumbling into the dirt.

Dust and debris flew into the air. Chunks of metal zoomed by. Edwards gasped as a wall of crimson flame leaped out at them, but the explosion devoured the last of the pod's oxygen, and as quickly as it appeared, the fire vanished.

They had survived. Birch got up, dusted himself off and, after checking on Edwards, trudged back to the smoking wreckage to see what was left. He found what he had expected- a mess. The fire had been brief but intense. Everything was gone. The pod, their equipment, everything that would have helped them survive on this barren world had been reduced to a pile of charred debris.

Birch sighed and kicked the wreckage. Things had just gotten a lot harder.

Edwards limped to his side. "What are we going to do now?" He asked, his voice cracked with emotion. He was asking for hope, and Birch didn't know if he could give him any.

"We find Jane and Lauren, and then we get into the *Colony I* Base and get things back online there." Birch didn't look up. It was easier to lie that way. "We'll see where we take things after we get done with that."

"What happens if we can't get *Colony I* online?"

Birch looked up. "We die."

Edwards flinched. "Couldn't we contact the ship, get some help from there or something?"

"No," Birch had turned his attention to the display on the wrist monitor attached to his suit. He could see there that Jane and Lauren were approaching. "You can forget that. We used the last pod, and the Hypnos could never get through the atmosphere on computer control alone, so we can't get up and nothing's getting down."

Lauren and Jane emerged from the swirling darkness. Jane was looking down at her own monitor, following their signal.

She looked up at Birch.

"I've got a fix on *Colony I*, Major," she announced without pausing for any greeting. She was almost shouting to be heard over the howling gale. "It's a couple of miles south of here." She looked back down at her screen. "Pretty even terrain, but in this weather, it'll be hard going. As it is right now we've probably only got about another twenty-two hours of air and power left in these suits, and it will take us at least an hour, maybe longer to get there, so we need to get moving."

Birch nodded. She was right. He had been about to say the same thing himself, firstly because it was true, and secondly to forestall the berating he expected from Jane for the crash, but again she surprised him. She had said nothing about it.

Already she was striding out, pulled almost magnetically toward the abandoned base. She wasn't waiting for anyone. Birch and the others hurried after her, but keeping pace with her hurried steps wasn't easy. Soon they had lost sight of her in the choking dust. Birch was left trying to help Edwards. In the end, their languid pace was too slow even for Lauren, and she also vanished into the storm. That left Birch to pull Edwards along as best he could.

There wasn't any danger of losing the others, he could see their location on the sensor, and it probably made sense for them to go ahead and try and to get started on things at the base rather than wait for them, but that didn't lessen Birch's frustration at being left to play nursemaid to Edwards.

"Come on," Birch snapped as Edwards paused again, panting hard with his hands resting on his knees. Edwards wasn't injured, just slow. His previous life as a zoo-keeper hadn't exactly prepared him for this. It wasn't that he had been an inveterate sluggard before- Edwards had been active enough, it was that the demands made on him now were just too much. Major Birch and his crew were astronauts and were trained for this sort of thing. Edwards was way out of his depth. Months of cryogenic sleep, their horrific crash landing, and now this storm beset trek across an alien planet in an unaccustomed, cumbersome EVA suit had him stretched to breaking point.

They trudged on through the bullying blast of the storm. Edwards did improve. He didn't give up, and eventually, he was lifting one leaden foot after another at a consistent pace. It still wasn't fast enough for Birch, but finally after an hour-and-a-half they were nearing the base.

The storm was getting worse now. It was little wonder that they didn't see the dark, ominous outline of *Colony I* as they approached. Their world had been reduced to the space of eighteen inches in front of their face. It was a world of sand, and it was everywhere. It caked their visors, building up and obscuring their view until they had to brush it off to see at all. They could feel it in the grainy grinding in the joints of their suits as they moved. It clung heavily to their boots, sinking them down into it as they fought for every step, but finally, they won. They had reached *Colony I*.

It was only the sensor that saved Birch from walking blindly into the base's wall. A bleeping sound warned him of its proximity, but it was only as he reached out his hand that he had felt the solid reality of it. He hadn't seen it until he touched it.

"It's here," Birch shouted back to Edwards, his voice muffled by the wind.

Edwards pushed forward, raising both arms as if to embrace the one immutable object in this world of shifting sand. In a strange way, he seemed happy. *Colony I* didn't represent hope for him, but it did offer stability. If they were going to die on this planet at least they would do it in a human place, in a place they had built with technology, and furniture, and dignity. These little things seemed to matter a great deal. They would die, not as alien objects on some foreign world, but as humans.

Birch's reaction was very different. He was just as pessimistic about their chances, but *Colony I* wasn't a place to die, it was a long shot, a last slim chance to live.

"Where do we get in?" Edwards was moving along the wall, feeling for an entryway.

Birch looked down at his display. "It's another couple of hundred meters that way." He gestured into the distance, beyond the point where the wall disappeared into the gloom. "There's an airlock up that way. We'll get in there."

They trudged on, Birch softly tapping the wall to keep track of it in the darkness. He looked down at his display again. He had lost Jane and Lauren's signal. Their position didn't register. He tried radioing them, but only got static in response. That was a troubling development, but tracking was notoriously difficult in an alien environment, and there was probably a simple explanation. Perhaps they had made it inside and were getting interference from the building, or maybe the storm was breaking up the signal. Birch knew there could be any number of causes.

There shouldn't have been any reason for worry. The probes had covered the planet's surface and their reports had been clear. There was no life here, and no potential threat beyond the natural ones presented by a hostile alien environment, but then that was before *Primary Base* had shot them out of the sky. There were dangers here that the probes hadn't warned them about, and Birch couldn't help worrying that this was the true cause of Jane and Lauren's silence. Perhaps whoever had shot them down had gotten to them too. For now, though, there wasn't anything he could do about it. He had to get Edwards and himself inside.

Soon they found the door. Birch might have missed the airlock altogether if he hadn't been running his figures along the wall. Only the slightest indentation indicated its presence.

"Here it is," he shouted, turning to the access panel. He pushed the entry button, but nothing happened. "Yeah, I expected that", he muttered. "No power." He rubbed his fingers again along the side of the panel, searching for a gap in the smooth surface. Finding it, he clicked a compartment on his EVA suit, releasing a small tool that he inserted into the slot.

The manual mechanism engaged, dropping the crank. Birch grabbed it, pulling the metal bar toward him, but it was stiff, seized up with age and decay. A few hard shoves finally got it moving, but it took a number of turns before there was any perceivable movement of the door.

This first tiny opening in the airlock sent a stream of white mist spurting through the crack. Birch paused, startled by the effect.

Edwards instinctively stepped back. "What was that?" he gasped, his eyes wide as the strange apparition faded and dispersed into the blowing storm.

"Old air," Birch answered as he got back to work at the crank. "No telling how long it's been since that door's been opened, maybe a hundred years. It certainly doesn't look like Jane or Lauren got in this way."

"Where do you think they are?" Edwards glanced around as he asked the question, as though he was hoping for them to appear before him now.

Birch shrugged and kept working the crank. "Let's figure out where we are first," he puffed between turns. "Most likely they got in through another airlock. We'll check later, but I'm more worried about getting us in right now. Jane and Lauren can take care of themselves."

By now the door was half open. That was enough to get through. Birch stopped.

"Go ahead." He pointed to the opening.

Edwards peered into the darkness, then back at the storm, as though weighing up the lesser of the two evils. After a moment's hesitation, he stepped through. Birch followed.

The sandy air followed them inside. In the dim light cast by their helmets the airlock appeared as a stark metal chamber, featureless save for a single panel to operate the doors and regulate the flow of air into the compartment. Birch was quickly to work, releasing the mechanism and slamming the door shut behind them.

The dust floating around them fell to the ground in clumps as the howling rage of the tempest was shut out.

It was silent. Birch's ears rang in the soundlessness. For a moment all either of them could do was stand, panting, trying to catch their breath. Edwards, exhausted from his exertions, finally succumbed to his body's demand for rest and collapsed, sliding down the wall into a squatting fetal position.

Birch moved over to the control panel. As he had expected there was no power, but he was already busily engaging the manual override. A few minutes later he was turning the crank and the internal door, like the outer one moments ago, slowly opened. It creaked noisily to one side, and the sound echoed in the stillness of the chamber and off into the cavernous darkness stretching out behind it.

Finally, with the door less than half open Birch paused, took another couple of turns of the crank, then straightened up. He glanced down at Edwards, then back at the beckoning darkness of the doorway. It was just enough for them to squeeze through.

"Well, I guess this is it," he bent down to help Edwards to his feet. "You ready?"

Edwards nodded, but once standing he shivered visibly and swayed, almost toppling over again onto the floor. Birch held him up. He wasn't sure if it was exhaustion or terror. Either way, it was a problem. He put his hand on Edwards' shoulder and looked him in the eye.

"Let's do this," he said simply and turned to the now open doorway.

Birch stepped cautiously into the darkness of *Colony I*, and Edwards followed.

SIXTEEN

A gray corridor stretched out before them. Birch could only just make out the dim outline of doors and walls in the thin illumination of his helmet light, but he couldn't see much more than that. He resisted the temptation to increase the lighting level; power was too precious to be wasted on such luxuries. They only had perhaps another twenty hours left, and he was going to need every minute to get things running down here before they died.

"So far, so good," Edwards commented, glancing up and down the empty passageway. He seemed reassured by the quiet nothingness that greeted them.

"What were you expecting, an attack of the space zombies?" Birch asked sourly.

"No," Edwards replied, still looking around. "I figured it would be the mind-warping, brain-sucking, alien slime worms bent on our destruction."

Birch laughed despite himself. Edwards looked as sick and as worried as ever, but at least he was trying to lighten the mood.

"Nah," Birch called back as he started up the passageway. "Not likely. Alien slime worms only come out on a full moon, so I think we've missed them."

They came to a closed portal at the end of the corridor.

Birch sighed. It was going to be another drawn out job, like the airlock. With no power getting through to the controls it meant another manual override and that meant more time and sweat wasted in the simple operation of getting through a door.

Birch got to work. "You'll find," he puffed through turns of the crank, "that space exploration is a lot more like this. It's not the alien slime worms, laser battles, or interstellar conflict you have to worry about. It's the banal that'll kill you, the things that back on Earth wouldn't warrant a second thought. Something as stupid as a sealed door like this one could kill us, and if this one doesn't, then maybe one of the next ten or twelve on the way to the Central Control will. All it takes is one simple thing going wrong, some rusted out bolt or a mis-placed spring in a vital system, and we could be locked out of our only path to survival. That's all it would take."

"Who knew bolts and springs could be so scary." Edwards laughed hollowly. "Well, that's really put my mind at ease. At least we don't have to worry about the monsters."

"Oh, I never said that," Birch answered darkly. "We bring plenty of our own monsters along with us."

The door had finally rolled aside enough to admit them. Birch let go of the crank and hurried through into a passage identical to the one they had left.

The same silent emptiness greeted them. There was nothing here, no signs of distress or destruction at all. Everything was ordered and in place. Whatever had happened to the colony, it hadn't led to panic, at least not here. Maybe that would change as they got further in, but Birch had expected to see some sign by now.

They hurried on to the next obstacle. Their boots clanged heavily on the metal floor, and the empty echoes reverberated around the walls, increasing the sense of intrusion. They were aliens in this quiet world.

Lines of closed doors faced them on both sides, but Birch wasn't concerned with their secrets, at least not yet. The base's control center was still a good way off and getting through the next obstruction was the only thing on his mind.

"I'll get this one," Edwards offered as they approached another sealed door.

"Be my guest," Birch answered wearily. Sweat was sticking to his skin from the exertion and, despite his suit's cooling systems, he was becoming increasingly uncomfortable.

After a somewhat clumsy beginning Edwards got into a good rhythm, and in the end, he had the portal open almost as quickly as Birch could have managed. The work seemed to do Edwards some good. Something about the reality of a physical task strengthened him. This was something he could do, and he did it.

Together Birch and Edwards worked their way through the corridors and passages of the base. They took turns with the doors, and their pace improved. All the while Birch was trying to raise Jane or Lauren, but static was still the only response. He couldn't get a fix on their location at all and it was starting to worry him.

Finally, they climbed a narrow flight of concrete steps that led them to the last door- the door to *Colony I*'s central command.

"Is this it?" Edwards gasped, panting for breath after their long climb. It was a blank metal door with nothing to indicate its importance.

"This is it," Birch answered, searching for the mechanism to engage the manual override, "and it *only* took us a couple of hours to get here. That probably leaves us with a little more than eighteen hours to get things going. We better find a way to get the base back online from here or things are going to get tricky. We've got no time to go exploring for other options right now."

"You think we've got a pretty good chance, though, right?"

"Maybe not," Birch sighed. "I'm not finding a manual port here." His fingers had searched the entire panel and now he was leaning over, trying to get a better look. He examined the door and its mechanism from all sides.

"Nope," he muttered, "no manual override. It must be part of the security system, keeping unwanted visitors out." He rubbed the panel again with his fingers. "Well, I think maybe we've found that 'rusted out bolt' I warned you about. This could be the ruining of us."

"There's got to be a way," Edwards' voice sounded less confident than his words. "We can't have gone all this way to be stopped at the last door. We haven't gotten this far for nothing!"

"Yeah, that's what I used to think, but experience teaches you something different. Sometimes it seems like the further you go, and the harder you try, the bigger the nothing you find when you finally get there."

Edwards nodded. Something in Birch's words seemed to resonate within him, but somehow he wasn't ready to give up. Perhaps he had expected to die already, but now that he had gotten this close he wasn't ready to quit. He wanted to live. "Come on! What can we do?" he cajoled.

Birch was still rubbing his fingers along the panel, thinking. An idea came to him, though he wasn't sure he liked it. He hesitated. "Yeah, there is one thing we could try," he finally answered. "It's stupid, dangerous, and might get us both killed, but I guess in the circumstances it's worth a try."

Edwards looked worried. "You don't happen to have any ideas that don't involve stupidity or death, do you?"

"None that'll work. You might want to stand back a bit." Birch had already removed the first bolt from the door's control panel and was working on the next one. "It's a simple idea. I can jump start the door by sending a shot of power from my suit directly into the unit. That should be enough to get the mechanism to release. If everything goes right we'll be in there in ten seconds."

"And if everything goes wrong?"

"Just stand back. An old mechanism like this might take a charge, or it might blow up. We'll see."

"You're right, Major," Edwards shook his head, "that sounds like a stupid plan. I mean, even if it doesn't kill you, won't it drain your suit? Can you afford to lose that much power? We don't know how long it'll take to get things working, even if we do get in? You can't just eat up your energy like that. It's too risky."

"You know, the really wonderful thing about everything you've just said is that I totally agree with you." Birch had the panel off. He released an attachment wire in his EVA suit and held it poised over door's exposed battery. "Who knows what'll happen, but the one thing I do know is that we don't have time to wander around this base wrestling with every door in the hope of finding a better answer. Main Control is the hub; it's the center of everything that went on here. We have to get in."

Birch leaned in closer to the door. "Step back," he warned. "Now, let's see what happens." He put the wire to the battery.

The keypad flickered briefly then went dark again. Birch made some adjustments to the output and tried again. The pad's lights came on and this time and stayed on. Instantly a red beam shot out, locking into his eye, scanning for retinal identification. It was working. Birch smiled, but it didn't last.

Sparks flew out, crackling wildly, blue at first, but intensifying into a shower of white electricity, spurting up, engulfing Birch. Edwards lost sight of him. For his part, Birch knew little about it. A quick impression of white, an electrical magnetism that he couldn't escape, and then everything went black.

SEVENTEEN

The next thing Birch knew something was hitting him hard in the chest. A fist came down, again and again, blurring into an indefinite line of motion. Birch choked a breath, convulsed, and set into a fit of coughing. The punching stopped. Birch tried to lift himself up into a sitting position, failed, and slumped back to the floor.

"I told you that was stupid," Edwards shaking voice was chastising from somewhere nearby, but Birch couldn't see him. He couldn't see anything except the flashing glare of imagined electrical stars flying past him. He shook his head, trying to clear his vision, and Edwards' scowling face came into fuzzy focus. A moment later his eyes had cleared enough to see the control room door, now open behind him.

"No," Birch finally wheezed, trying again to get to his feet. "I'm the one who said it was stupid, but I also said it would get us in, so it looks like I was right both times."

"Well, you also said it could kill you, and it almost did. Lucky for you I paid attention in all those safety procedure protocol talks you and Major Gray made me sit through, otherwise you'd be dead right now. That power surge shut your suit down. I had to do an emergency restart to get you breathing again."

"Thanks," Birch muttered, rubbing his sore chest. "Next time maybe try the button override before doing a punch start, though. That's supposed to be a last resort."

He shuffled unsteadily to the door. He needed to leave. It wasn't that he was ungrateful, or even that he didn't understand his debt to Edwards, but for Birch, it was always difficult. He hated owing anything to anyone. He would happily help others. He would do anything for anyone without any expectation of reward or gratitude, but when others helped him he didn't know what to do. Needing help was an admission of failure and he hated it; he hated himself for needing it.

"Let's get going," he growled.

The control room was a large oval, laid out very much like the bridge of a ship with various control centers and display panels. Metal ladders around the room led to a second level with more stations and more panels circling the wall above. Birch couldn't see any further up in the dim light provided by his helmet, but he had the impression of a high ceiling sitting somewhere above it all.

At first glance, the control room had the same appearance of quiet abandonment seen through the rest of the base. There was no obvious sign of struggle or of any cataclysmic conflict that could have snuffed out the life of this colony. It was just another empty room in an abandoned outpost.

Birch was quickly working at one of the stations, pulling off the panel and crawling underneath checking for problems.

"Wow," Edwards whistled as his light caught the control center's thirty-foot screen in its beam. "What is that?"

Birch sighed, looking up from his work. "What is what?"

"That." Edwards gestured back to the screen.

Birch pulled himself up, looking where Edwards was standing. He stifled a gasp as his own light illuminated the cause of Edwards' concern. Written in towering, dripping red capital letters across the massive screen was one single word. The word was 'EVIL'.

"What does that mean?" Edwards whispered.

"Nothing good," Birch responded curtly. He looked around again, taking in his surroundings with a new sense of concern. Until now everything had seemed so normal, so quiet. He had almost lulled himself into believing that nothing bad could have happened here. The simple fact that a whole colony's population had disappeared had somehow been lost in his preoccupation with his own troubles, but now this very visible evidence of their struggle brought it immediately back to mind. Something bad had happened here, and if his crew lived long enough they also might have to contend with whatever had destroyed them. It wasn't a comforting thought.

Birch turned his attention back to the station he had been working on. There wasn't much else he could do right now.

"Keep an eye out for anything else," he ordered Edwards. "Let me know if you see anything unusual. I need to work on this."

Edwards nodded and walked away.

For a time Birch struggled with wiring and circuits. It was confusing. There didn't really seem to be much wrong here. Everything should have been working, but it wasn't.

Garbled static sounded in his headset. Birch tapped his ear, trying to make sense of the noise. It sounded like Jane's voice, but he couldn't make anything out. Checking his wrist display there were two additional readings, dots fading in and out. Whatever had been interfering with their signal was clearing up. It looked like Jane and Lauren were somewhere inside the base.

"frst… stndz… main comlutz sesst… zkc…" Birch couldn't distinguish the words.

"Jane? You're breaking up. Repeat, over."

"Major… Major Birch," Jane's voice came through sounding tinny and hollow, but finally, he could understand her.

"Yes," Birch spoke loudly to be heard above the static. "Where are you?"

"We're at the main computer station on the lower level, on

the far side of the base. I think I've worked out part of the problem with the power, but I'll need help from your end. I'm sending the information over now."

Birch looked down at his wrist display. Jane's instructions were coming through. To his surprise, there wasn't anything immensely technical about them. There were a few adjustments to make, some switches to flip, all very rudimentary stuff, not at all what he would have expected to be needed to get a base like this back online after a major power failure.

"Let me get this straight," Birch said dryly, "you're asking me to turn stuff on."

"Yeah, that's pretty much it," Jane's voice came back lightly. "I don't quite understand it myself, but I'm not finding anything actually wrong down here. I just went through the start up process and everything's ready for your part now. Just go through the startup procedure I sent you and we should be back online."

"That makes no sense." Birch was already up, making the changes Jane instructed him to make. It apparently was a process expected to involve a number of officers, and Birch and Edwards were both kept busy running from one station to another, from one floor to another, setting things in motion. "Why would they turn everything off?"

"I'm not sure about that myself," Jane's voice crackled in Birch's headset. "It looks like it was complete chaos here at the end; they left as fast as they could and just turned everything off at the end."

"What do you mean, 'chaos'?"

"You know- 'pandemonium, a lack of tranquility, a descent into general disorder.' Look around, it's pretty obvious that something bad went down here and they cleared out as fast as they could."

"It's not obvious from here," Birch snapped back. "Everything we've seen so far has been orderly and quiet. It's like they never left, and there's certainly no sign at all of any struggle or general panic."

Jane didn't answer for a moment.

"That is weird," she finally responded. "Everything's torn up down here, like they were in panic and couldn't get away fast enough. Well, whatever happened it's obvious they switched the systems off themselves. There isn't any damage here. It just like I said, it's all been turned off."

Birch shook his head. "That still doesn't make any sense. You're saying they were in a panic, falling over themselves to get away, and they stopped long enough to switch everything off. It's like they said- 'could the last one off the planet please remember to switch off the lights'."

"Yeah, pretty much. That's how it looks anyway."

Birch shook his head again. "You know, it's not that easy to shut down a facility like this, all the safety protocols and everything. I just don't see why they would do that."

"It is what it is, Major" Jane's voice took on an exasperated tone. "I can't explain it any more than you, but at least it's an easy fix. Once you're done we simply turn it on."

"Well, we're almost finished here," Birch answered. As he spoke Edwards ran to his last console, turned the knob, and gave the thumbs up, indicating he was ready. Birch adjusted his last setting and they were done. "Okay, we're ready."

"Alright, be ready just in case something goes wrong. This system's been shut down for a long time. No telling how it will react. I've tested it as best I could, but you never know."

Birch shuddered at that. The memory of the door's reaction to his electrical charge was a little too fresh in his mind to dismiss that warning lightly.

"Commencing power up in 5...4...3...2...1... Powering up now."

Birch felt a shudder in the floor beneath his feet as the lights flickered and came on. The screens about them came to life, and he heard the whining hum of the life systems pumping oxygen into the base. It worked! To his surprise, it seemed that they were going to live after all.

"YES!" Jane shouted over the radio, deafening them all.

"Let there be light, and it was good!"

Indeed the light was good, but it wasn't the warm, welcoming light Birch had expected- the sort of light that mimicked sunlight and had been specially developed by the space program to stave off the effects of life in the darkness of space. That light was a way to make the astronaut feel welcome and at home, but this light wasn't welcoming at all. It was a warning. It was red.

A muffled voice was saying something urgent that he couldn't quite understand. At first, he thought it was Jane, telling him something about what was happening down in the computer room, but it wasn't her.

The garbled voice was becoming louder. Birch looked up at the large screen. Behind the word EVIL he could just make out some sort of movement, it was showing something, but the letters got in the way. He couldn't see what it was.

"Jane, what's going on down there?" Birch asked, but there was no answer.

The unidentified voice grew in intensity, and the pitch changed from a deep baritone to soprano as the computer struggled to function. Birch still couldn't understand it

"Are you getting anything, Edwards?" Birch bellowed, but the man shrugged. The systems were alien to him, and he couldn't make anything of it.

Finally, the computer seemed to catch its rhythm and a calm, clear female voice could finally be heard.

"Self destruct in five minutes, forty-seven seconds."

EIGHTEEN

"Jane, Jane!" What's going on down there?"

It was a moment before her harried voice responded. "I'm trying to disable the autodestruct. I don't think I can do it."

"Oh, great news."

"Wait, though," Birch could hear her tapping furiously at a keyboard before she continued. "I don't know how to reverse the autodestruct, and obviously I don't have time to work on it just now, it's too complicated, but we could shut the power off again. That would have the same effect. We have clearance to do that, so all we have to do is reverse the process we went through to get it on."

"It took us twenty minutes to get this thing running," Birch snapped. "How are we going to undo it in five?"

"I suggest you learn, otherwise we're dead! I'm doing all I can here, but we need you to finish it off!"

Birch was already running for the ladder to the second level. "Edwards!" he shouted as he clambered up, two rungs at a time. "We need to get the power off, NOW! Get over to the last station you worked on and undo whatever you did. We have to go through this whole thing in exact reverse order in less than five minutes or we're dead."

Edwards was already sprinting to the console, but once

there he paused. "I can't remember exactly what I did. How can we ever get this done in time? I just can't remember."

"Oh, just shut up and listen!" Birch barked, looking down at the instructions on his wrist display. "I'll trace back your moves and mine, just do what I tell you each time, and do it fast! Now, two clicks right to 0.75!"

"Two clicks," Edwards mumbled as he turned the dial. Birch was already at his next station on the second level by the time he had finished. "Station five," he shouted down to Edwards as he quickly reversed the changes he had made only moments ago. "Three clicks left to 1.39!"

Birch and Edwards ran quickly between consoles. Birch was always one step ahead, leading Edwards, guiding him to his next task.

"Three minutes, forty-two seconds," the computer announced evenly.

"There's no way we'll make it," Edwards shouted.

"Shut up and run! Station seven, two clicks left to 0.67!" Edwards was probably right. Their chances were slim at best. Birch was acutely aware of his own feet as he flung himself from station to station. The slightest stumble would finish them. There was no time for mistakes.

"Two minutes, thirty-seven seconds."

"It's useless," Edwards lamented.

Birch wanted to tell him to shut up, to save his energy for trying, not crying, but even that was a luxury he couldn't afford. All he had time for was the next instruction.

"Station 6, ten clicks right to 7.90!"

"One minute, ten seconds," the computer's soulless voice informed them.

"Four to go between us!" Birch shouted. "Station two, one click left to 5.39! I'm on my next one already, then just one more each!"

"Forty-seven seconds."

"Okay, last one for you Edwards- station eleven, three clicks left to 9.31, then it's me."

Edwards ran, turned his final dial, and slumped over, exhausted. Through his fingers, he glanced up to watch Birch's progress.

Birch was running full speed around the curve of the steel walkway surrounding level two. His legs were heavy, tired, and his breath came in ragged gasps. He flung himself the last few steps to the station.

"Nineteen seconds."

Birch glanced down at the last instruction on his display. Seven clicks right to 8.43. He grabbed the knob, wrenching it to the right. 1-2-3-4-5-6-7. He wondered if he had miscounted. He had done it so quickly, did he get it right? Did he count the clicks correctly? Yes, the display read 8.43.

"Eleven seconds."

"Go, Jane!" Birch shouted into his mouthpiece. "Go, go, go. We're done, we're done!"

"Eight, seven, six…"

Edwards was still watching Birch through his fingers. Birch glanced at the large screen covering the far wall. Somewhere beneath the 'EVIL', he could just catch the impression of the numbers ticking by. The screen flashed red and warning klaxons sounded. Their world was falling apart around them.

Then it went dark.

For a time Birch wasn't really sure what had happened. Had they been in time? Was this death? He didn't know. All he did know was that he was here, wherever here was.

Their helmet lights came on, reacting to the darkness. Across the room, he could see Edwards pulling himself to his feet.

"Jane," Birch's voice cracked dryly. "Jane, are you there?" For a time no answer came.

"Yeah," she finally replied shakily. "We made it and had a whole three seconds left over after that. Easy."

They both fell silent again, taking in the weight of those three seconds. There wasn't much more they could say. The moment was too heavy for words.

"Okay," Jane finally spoke. "We've got to figure out a way to get the power back on without blowing ourselves up, and we're running out of time. Maybe we should meet up, put our heads together, and see what we can come up with."

"Don't bother," Birch answered, "I've been looking at the schematics of the base and there's at least ten sealed doors between us. We don't have time for that. Just tell me what you're thinking and we'll see what we can do."

"Okay, that makes sense. Well, the way I see it we've only got one possible option, and I'm not sure how it'll work exactly. Not yet anyway.

"I need to disarm the autodestruct. That's pretty obvious, but the trouble is- in order to disarm it I need power to use the computers, but as soon as I turn on the power to do that we'll have three seconds before the base blows up. "

"Yeah, that's quite a problem," Birch muttered.

"I think I could isolate one computer from the mainframe and attack the destruct coding from there, but I would need an independent power source to do that. Anything that brought power to the rest of the network would take us back to that three-second countdown and destroy us all."

"Well, that's it then," Birch shook his head. "All we need is a power source, and that's the one thing we clearly don't have."

"What about our EVA suits?" Lauren chimed in for the first time. "Couldn't we siphon off some of their power and use that to work the computer. If wouldn't matter if we lost some of our energy because we wouldn't need it once environmental control was working again."

"I wouldn't recommend it," Birch answered grimly. "I tried to do the same thing to get here into Central Control and it almost killed me. It may still kill me. The power drain sucked away more than half of my reserve. I've only got probably another six hours left before my suit shuts down."

For a while no one said anything. Six hours wasn't very long. The rest of them still had fourteen hours left, and that was the number they had built their hopes on. Fourteen hours sounded like a chunk of time, a long enough period to achieve something, but six hours just wasn't enough.

"Well, couldn't we just use the same principle between our suits?" Lauren persisted. "If we each shared an hour or so worth of power we could even things up, give you longer to work with, Major."

"No," Birch snapped. He was becoming exasperated with time being wasted uselessly. "That won't work. My connecting port got fried when I used it to open the door. I can't take a charge. The only answer for me is to get this base online as soon as we can. So, what's this plan of yours Jane, how are you going to save us then?"

There was an uncomfortable silence before Jane's voice finally came through. A half-formed plan with fourteen hours left to perfect it was one thing, but that same plan now looked very weak from the perspective of a six-hour deadline.

"Well, it's not exactly a full-blown plan as such, just an idea really. Obviously, we need a power source to give us a chance. I did think of one possibility, but I'm not sure we can get at it very easily." Jane paused again.

"Yes, well?" Birch could feel the minutes ticking by.

"It's the probes, the ones we send out to the planets to observe and send back information. Those things are stuffed with useful technology, including energy cells that I could use to run a computer off the grid. I think I should be able to get one launched using my wrist computer. I could even set its course from here. The only problem is, it won't land. They're not designed for that. It won't come any lower than fifty feet, and if I try and bring it down any lower the safety mechanism will engage and send the probe right back up to the ship.

"We'll only have one chance at it too. If we don't bring it down successfully the first time around, if we bungle it, the computer will wise up and refuse to respond to any more of my control commands. Of course, the only problem is figuring out how to get it to land, and that's as far as my thinking has gotten so far."

Birch knitted his brows, deep in thought. "Yes, that's good as far as it goes, but 'a miss is as good as a mile', as the old saying goes. Having all that power hovering fifty feet over our heads is tantalizingly close, but it still doesn't get us what we need."

"Why don't you just shoot it down?" Edwards suggested.

"No way," Jane scoffed, "for two very obvious reasons. Number one, we might damage the unit, rendering it useless, and number two, we don't have a gun."

"He's got a point, though," Birch mused thoughtfully. "I don't think we have time for subtlety. We need to go for the direct approach."

"You want to shoot it down?" Jane's voice, even crackling through his headset, betrayed her disbelief.

"Not exactly, well, at least not in the way Edwards intended. I think we could use the same principle though to get that probe down without damaging it."

"And how exactly are you going to do that without a gun? And even if you could do it using rocks or some other primitive projectile you've got in mind, how could you bring it down without damaging it? There's just no way to make that work."

"There is a way," Birch answered quickly. "Listen, a base like this has to have data-flares, right? It's regulations. I'm sure you know that, Jane."

"Yes," Jane answered frostily. The word 'regulations' was usually shorthand between Birch and Jane for 'let's fight'. It was a constant source of contention between them that Birch was willing to do things his own way and Jane wasn't.

"Well," Birch continued, "what if you call down that probe and I shoot it with the data-flare. You might be able to get control that way and bring the thing down."

"That might actually work." Jane's voice was thoughtful as she considered the possibilities of what Birch was suggesting.

Data-flares, as their name suggested, were a more effective

modern alternative to the old signal flares. As a distress or warning beacon, they were far superior to the old fleeting trail of phosphorescent light that ancient flares provided. Once launched data-flares could stay aloft for hours, transmitting information and relaying instructions. With a little modification they could even send signals that would instruct and commandeer automated mechanical devices and transports, bringing rescue where no human assistance was available. It was a feature jokingly referred to as the 'Lassie Mode' for its ability to bring help.

Jane nodded, that might actually work.

"Okay, how are we going to do this?" she asked.

Birch's mind had been whirling with that very question, but the answer had only just come to him moments before Jane had asked it.

"Time's short," Birch answered quickly, "so we've got to be smart." His words came fast, clipped to a minimum to save every second. He had difficulty speaking slowly enough to be understood. He was trying to explain complex plans quickly, and it wasn't easy.

"It'll be your responsibility, Jane, to get the probe launched and guided over *Colony I.* Edwards and I will shoot it down. There's a communication tower that has an access hatch about four sealed doors away from where we are right now. Make sure and guide the probe over that. We'll shoot it down from there.

"We'll rappel down the tower, get the energy cells from the downed probe and bring them to you.

"There will be seven sealed doors between the nearest airlock and your computer station. You need to get those open before we get there, so we can just run through with the energy cells. I'm sending a layout map of our path. Any questions?"

Jane paused for a moment, trying to take in everything he had just said, to work out the part they each had to play. "No," she finally answered, "that all seems to make sense.

You'll have to reset all the gauges at main control to the startup position before you leave, though, as you won't be there to do it later. That should work; it's going to be very tight, though. It won't give me much time to actually overcome the problems with the autodestruct, get the power back on, and the atmospheric control working before your six hours is up."

Birch shrugged. "I guess we'll see. Let's get started!"

NINETEEN

After a last check of the gauges, Birch grabbed a long coil of electrical wire from a supply cupboard, flung it over his shoulder, and ran for the door. Edwards followed behind.

Sometimes, when everything goes right, you might feel like it was your lucky day. Birch could never remember feeling that way. There were good days and bad days, but never lucky days. When things went right for him it was hard work that made it happen, and with this plan, it was no exception.

The first part was supposed to be simple- open four sealed doors and climb up the communication tower. The internal doors were easy enough; they opened with the usual amount of sweat and effort. Even the uncertain part of the plan seemed to fall into place when he found the hoped for data-flare with five flares stored in its assigned place in the emergency panel of the airlock. But then things got harder. Twenty minutes of shoving and grunting by both Birch and Edwards hadn't budged the final external door.

"Must be another of your 'rusted out bolts' or 'missing springs', Major," Edwards observed gloomily as they rested from their exertions. "I'm not sure it'll ever move."

"Maybe," Birch answered, "but let's see if we can convince it otherwise." He stood up, flexing his fingers for another attempt.

"I think that's why I'd rather take my chances with the slime worms or the space zombies," Edwards muttered, "they're a lot easier to convince than inanimate objects."

"Get up," Birch ordered. "We're going to try this together, rocking the crank back and forth- then giving it a big shove to the left. Then we try the same to the right, then back to the left. We'll keep going until something gives."

Edwards got up, but there wasn't much enthusiasm in his step as he approached the door. It didn't take long for his mood to improve, though. Birch's idea worked. Slowly, slowly the crank loosened. Finally, it turned. They kept it turning. They could hear the faint hiss of air seeping into the compartment long before they could see any opening, but soon a crack appeared, gradually growing until it was large enough to allow them to get out.

Sand and wind filled the airlock. "Let's go!" Birch shouted over the howling gale.

They squeezed through, leaving the door to ease shut behind them.

The weather hadn't improved during their time inside. Visibility was still limited to a few feet as the blowing sand choked the air and colored the sky in its gray, dusty hue. Birch had to use his wrist computer to find the tower, even though its base was located near the airlock.

"Follow me!" Birch shouted back to Edwards and shuffled through the tall drifts as best he could.

A few minutes later they reached the bottom of the tower. Birch adjusted the coil of wire around his neck and quickly started his assent. Edwards took a few minutes longer, fiddling with his suit, trying to get more comfortable before starting another long round of physical exertion in the constriction of his cumbersome spacesuit.

Their progress was pretty good under the circumstances. The wind and the sand dominated everything. The only solidity in this world was the feel of the metal rungs beneath their hands and feet. The tower swayed in the wind, and Birch found himself wondering how any structure subjected to this type of punishment for so many years could possibly be strong enough to support them.

Rung after rung, they climbed. Birch tried to take them two at a time at first but found it hard keeping his footing with a thick layer of dust coating everything. He didn't pause. It was a grueling ordeal in their suits, but Birch was used to climbing both in and out of them. Edwards was not, and as usual he was left lagging far behind. Birch didn't notice. He was too busy getting to the top.

Birch didn't notice much. If the conditions had been better he might have looked below and seen the whole of *Colony I* spread out beneath him. He might also have looked to the east, to *Primary Base*, and wondered about that green ray that brought their pod down. It was even possible that he might have glanced to the south, to the mountains, and shivered at the memory of distant times and events, but none of these things were visible, and none of them were on his mind. Time was running out and he was going to get to the top.

Finally, he made it. There wasn't a platform or any convenient location to set up. Immediately above him was a series of dishes and antenna arrays that he thought it wise to avoid. All he could do was to hang on to the rungs and get ready for the next part of the plan.

"Jane!" he shouted into his mouthpiece, struggling to be heard over the elements. "We're all set out here. How are things at your end?"

"Good, Major," Jane's voice crackled back almost immediately. "We've got the probe launched. I've got your current location locked in, so it should be making a pass near you in about five minutes."

"Great, just make sure you've got all those doors open when we need them!"

"I've got Lauren working on that right now. For now, my hands are full getting the probe to you, but once you bring it down we'll both be giving that our full attention. Hopefully, we'll have them all ready when you need them. That's the best I can do right now."

"I know," Birch answered. "Thanks."

The radio went silent.

Birch waited. Still, the wind swirled and the dust blew around him. Would this storm ever give up? He unstrapped the data-flare device and pulled two cartridges out of a Velcro lined pocket in his suit. The device looked very much like an ordinary flare gun, though somewhat larger and more powerful to accommodate the bulkier data-flares. It was also bright orange, which gave it the look of an oversized toy gun. It was no toy. In fact, the specifications needed to get it to launch a data-flare were such that it had a harder kickback than a rifle. The uninitiated were often taken by surprise and had to pick themselves up out of the dirt after their first attempt at firing one.

Birch was sweating as he opened the gun and slid the first cartridge into the chamber. He wasn't going to get much of a shot here. With only a few feet of visibility and the speed of the probe, this was going to be hard. It would take a direct hit to attach the flare, anything less could be easily shaken off by the probe's superior power and speed. This was a one shot deal. If he missed then they probably wouldn't get another chance.

He took a deep breath, collected his thoughts, and leveled the gun in the direction of its approach.

Birch could feel the ladder shaking beneath him. He looked down. Edwards was finally approaching. He wasn't even sure why Edwards had come along at all. He had tried to talk him into waiting at the bottom of the tower, to meet up with him after all the hard work was done, but Edwards wouldn't listen. For once he seemed more engaged and interested in what they were doing than in complaining about being here. Perhaps the realization that this was it- life or death- had finally focused his mind.

"Probe approaching," Jane's voice crackled through his headset. "Get ready to fire."

"Ready," Birch snapped, bracing himself against the kickback. He hugged the ladder with one arm, extending the other out with the data-flare pistol, ready to fire.

Almost before he could register it the cylindrical gray probe was half way across his field of vision and moving fast.

Birch squeezed off the first shot more in reaction to the noise than what he saw, and as a result, he had shot behind the probe, which was traveling much faster than he had calculated. By the time he had reloaded the probe was well past him and he missed again. Two shots wasted.

Desperate now, believing the probe would not return, Birch fumbled in his pocket, grabbing for another flare that slipped through his fingers and fell, clattering against Edwards' helmet before disappearing into the darkness below. Three flares wasted.

"Wow," Edwards commented as the probe streaked off into the darkness, toward an unseen horizon. "You stink."

Birch said nothing.

"You missed," Jane's voice was flat, emotionless.

"I know. Any chance of bringing it back for a second pass?"

Jane sighed. "The probe's on condition yellow, registering potential threats from your area, but nothing permanent yet. It's a good thing your shots were so bad. Nothing got close enough to take it up to red status and send it scuttling back up to the ship. Another miss like that though and you can forget it."

"I've only got two more flares anyway. It's hit or miss this time."

"Okay. I'm taking it easy on the probe right now. I'm sending in on a loop, off to scan the mountains in the south before bringing it back to you. That should give it a chance to settle its little electronic nerves before we take another crack at it."

"Roger that." Birch had another flare out and slid it into the chamber, clicking the gun shut. He braced himself. It would be a few minutes before the probe got back but he wasn't going to be caught off guard this time. He was going to stare at the horizon until the thing appeared. He would get it this time.

"Give me the gun."

At first, Birch hardly registered the words. They were so unexpected, so sudden, that he almost wondered where they came from before he looked down to see Edwards' extended hand beneath him.

"What?" Birch asked. "What did you say?"

"I said, 'give me the gun'." His hand reached further up, demanding the pistol.

"Are you crazy? This is a matter of life and death. We've got two shots, one more chance, and if we miss we're dead."

"Exactly, give me the gun, Major."

Birch hesitated, Edwards was so inept at everything. Back on Earth, he had seemed competent enough, but in space he was hopeless. It was hard to take anything he said or did seriously.

"I don't think..."

"Look, Birch, "Edwards snapped. "We're about two minutes away from that probe getting back. Let me make this easy for you. You're an astronaut, you fly things. I'm a Special Operative, I shoot things. It's part of the job. You may be okay at blasting the Ares horde when they come at you thick and fast, but this is precision shooting. This is what I do. Give me the gun."

Birch gave him the gun.

"Here," Birch reached in his pocket for the final spare flare.

"Keep it," Edwards muttered, "if I miss it in the first shot there won't be a second chance. That thing's going too fast."

Edwards braced himself against the ladder, pulled the gun up ready to fire, and waited.

To Birch, it all seemed to happen in an instant. The roar of the pod's engines, its long metallic frame shooting into view through the swirling dust, the cracking boom as the flare was fired, the tower shaking under the reverberations of the shot, all were merged, compressed into this one single moment.

It hit! There was no immediate effect on the pod, but the spurting stream of the flare's flaming tail clearly smacked into its metal hull. Then the whole craft disappeared into the gloom.

It was an anxious moment, waiting to see what would happen next, waiting to see if they would live or die. On these next few moments, their existence depended. They had done all they could, now it was up to Jane and the 'Lassie Mode' to save them.

"Okay, we've got it!" Jane's voice confirmed. "Just trying to establish control now."

"Good," Birch was already pulling the coil of wire from his back, tying one end to the ladder, and dropping the remainder down into the darkness.

"Let's go, Edwards." Birch had snapped the wire into a clip on his suit and was about to descend when Jane's voice came crackling through."

"Trouble!" she rasped. "The pod's not responding as it should. It's heading back your way, the way I sent it, but I've lost control!"

As if to punctuate the remark a thundering whoosh of the pod's engines roared as it flashed by, nearly clipping the tower and rocking the structure to its foundations, sending both Birch and Edwards sprawling. Birch quickly caught himself, aided by the wire he had just attached, but he was horrified to see Edwards disappear, falling into the darkness.

"Edwards!" he shouted. "Edwards, I'm coming! Hang on!"

Another impact shook the tower, less violently this time, but enough to force Birch to grab the ladder again to avoid dropping off. The probe had come down somewhere nearby, but that wasn't his chief concern right now. He was rushing to get Edwards, to see if he was alive.

Birch rappelled swiftly down the tower. The wire was not

an ideal replacement for a rope; it was stiff, brittle, and rubbed awkwardly against the clip as he descended. It squealed and warmed with friction as he plunged down to rescue his comrade.

Birch heard him before he saw him. An agonized moan from Edwards somewhere below sounded in his headset.

"Edwards, are you alright?" Birch scanned the darkness but could see nothing. A wheezing groan was his only answer. "Come on, Edwards!" he shouted. "You can do better than that! Are you alright?"

"Y-yeah," the answer finally came. "I... uh, I think I damaged my suit... hit pretty hard, on the chest. Caught something on the way down, before I hit the ground, but hit hard... um, if you could get here real soon that would be wonderful."

"I'm on it. I see you now!" Birch could just make out the dull flicker of Edwards' helmet light going on and off, like an old worn out neon bulb.

It didn't look good. Edwards was lucky, he had fallen onto an outcrop, one of the branches off the main tower where weather and other monitoring equipment was attached, but had he been lucky enough? The suit had taken quite a hit and now its electrics seemed to be struggling to function. His light went out and the emergency restart didn't work. Birch resorted to a punch start, smacking his helmet hard with the palm of his hand. The light came back on and Edwards started, as though woken from a dozing slumber.

"Don't try that again," Birch shouted. He hadn't expected the chance to repay Edwards so quickly, and he wasn't going to let the score go unevened. "You're not dying today, not while I'm here, got that?"

Edwards groaned a response.

"You better watch me," Birch barked. "Watch everything I do. I'm crazy you know. If you don't watch me I'm liable to do something crazy, like drop you. I'm in my hurry to get you down, so you watch every move I make, tell me if things start getting fuzzy again. Got that?"

"Yeah, I got it," Edwards mumbled.

"Good, because if you don't I'll slap you again!"

Birch hauled Edwards onto his shoulder, took a moment to check he was secure, then leaped back into the darkness.

TWENTY

Their descent didn't go exactly to plan. Birch had meant to ease up, to take it slowly at the bottom and make a soft, controlled landing, but Edwards' helmet light had gone out again, and he panicked. He didn't have time for finesse. They tumbled down the last eight feet quickly, making a barely controlled, bumped landing into the dirt at the tower's base.

The sand cushioned their impact, but it still hurt. Birch didn't waste any time over his bumps and bruises, though. He was immediately on his feet, quickly working at getting Edwards' suit going again. It took a moment longer this time, but the light came back on and Birch dragged the disoriented man to his feet.

"Okay," he panted, "I'm going to have to carry you, Edwards. Your suit's pretty messed up. Your power's low and not functioning properly, and the less exertion you have to make the better. It'll save energy. Just relax, we'll make it."

"Won't that put too much strain on your suit?" Edwards' voice was slurred, but his words made sense. "You don't have enough power left to start with. You can't afford to lose any more time or power…"

"Shut up, Edwards," Birch snapped. He knew where this conversation was going, and he didn't want to hear it. He had already had enough of leaving people behind. His wife, Sarah, and the whole world with her, and Ratliff, and then Karla out on the empty prairie, no, if anyone else was going to be left behind it was going to be him. He wasn't leaving anyone again. The chain of guilt dragging behind him now was too well forged for him to ever escape again. If Edwards couldn't make it with him, they wouldn't make it at all.

Birch heaved him over his shoulder and staggered into the storm. Their progress was slow. Everything was dust and sand. Birch was sick of dust and sand. The wind still howled, but he kept walking, following his sensor readings. The only good thing about the probe's near miss was that it hadn't crashed too far away, but still, it took time. With Edwards slung over his shoulder Birch's boots sank deeper into the clinging sand. Every step was a fight against this planet and its gravity, and Birch wasn't sure he was winning.

Finally, he saw something else, something that wasn't dust and dirt, the welcome glint of an electrical pulse. The probe! He stumbled on toward its light.

He should have left Edwards behind, placed him a safe distance from the probe in case the whole thing went up in a massive explosion, like the pod had done, but what was the point? If the probe blew up they were all dead anyway, may as well make it quick. Besides, he needed to keep a watch on the reluctant astronaut, in case his suit gave out again.

"Here you go," Birch set Edwards down, positioning him so that he could watch as he took the machinery apart.

Birch quickly opened the panel. Using his suit's built-in tools he swiftly cut through layers of electronics, working his way down to the vital life-giving energy cells. There were other important systems here too, other equipment that might be useful for their survival on this barren world, but for now, he wasn't interested in any of that. All he wanted were those energy cells and the life they provided.

He was soon up to his elbows in wires, pulling, cutting, breaking, doing whatever was needed to get at the power. In an odd way, it reminded Birch of fishing, when the fisherman gutted his catch. They had reeled the probe in, pulled it unwillingly to shore, and now here he was ripping out the unwanted for what they could consume. The image brought his mind unwillingly back to Karla. She was fishing on the banks of that Rocky Mountain stream, bringing him her catch, touching his hands, making them better, making him better He shuddered, the cloying memories smelt like sweet death and he shook his head, trying to clear his brain.

He worked on with gentle impatience, trying to do as little damage as possible in the short time he had. It was hard to resist the urge to just pull everything to pieces to get what he needed, time was so short, but he would regret it later, if there was a later. He might even regret it now. Being too hasty could easily damage the precious circuits.

Finally, he had them. The energy cells were in his hands. Gently, he eased them out, careful not to damage them. Long boards, golden circuits, like honeycomb, glistened, even in the dim light of R67.3. It was a rare thing to hold your own life literally in your hands, but that was what Birch did now. These energy circuits were their life. Now he had to get them back to Jane as quickly as possible and save them all.

Birch turned to show his prize to Edwards, but he couldn't see him. His light had gone out again. Birch had been so preoccupied with working on this last delicate part of the procedure that he hadn't seen anything, and now Edwards was dying.

"Edwards!" Birch rushed to his side, smacking his helmet again and again, trying to get it restarted. It took a few hits this time, hard ones, full on punches that probably did more harm than good, but it was the only thing that had a chance of restarting his systems at all.

It worked. The light flickered weakly and came back on. Edwards wheezed, sucking down air in rasping gasps that choked him. He coughed, struggling to relearn what it was to breathe. Birch pulled him up, straightening his diaphragm, making it easier for the air to flow.

"I guess I wasn't made to live in space," Edwards

mumbled. He was giving up. The light in his suit was dimmer now, flickering faintly on and off. His sweating face faded in and out in profile. His suit was going to die any minute now, and Edwards was going to die with it.

"You weren't made to die in space either," Birch shouted shaking him back to consciousness. He tried to remember why he had even brought Edwards along. What had made him force this man to board the ship with them when he had pleaded to be left behind, to be left to the life he knew and understood back on Earth. He couldn't remember. Maybe he hadn't even really known the reason himself, except that Edwards hadn't wanted to go, and that had made him determined that he *should* go. After all, Edwards had dragged them across the country into his trap, a life under glass- as specimens in a zoo, and the last thing Birch had wanted to do was give him anything that he wanted. It was revenge- that was it, and now Edwards was going to die, and it was revenge indeed, but he didn't want it anymore. Watching this man choking, his life slipping away, gave him no satisfaction. He had never wanted this, even when he thought he had.

Flinging Edwards over his shoulder, Birch ran blindly for the designated airlock. It was at least half a mile to the door. With the perpetual wind and sand in his face, with Edwards slumped over his shoulder, and with the precious golden circuits clutched in his hands, he ran as best he could.

He was weakening. The sand beneath his feet seemed heavier now, more persistent, holding him back with every step. His leaden legs pumped, stumbling mechanically on.

He couldn't keep on like this. A sick knot was eating away at his gut, starting there as a dull center of nauseated confusion that quickly spread over his whole body, robbing him of all sense and understanding, save for the one single instinct to run and even that was beginning to fade as exhaustion strove to overcome him.

Edwards' light went out again. It wasn't sudden or dramatic like before. It was more like the dimming of a bulb until the power had finally dripped away. Birch dropped Edwards; he could see that now was the time for something beyond desperate. Hitting the suit to restart the electrics wasn't going to work this time, it was going to take something spectacularly stupid to keep him alive.

Birch shook him, trying to get a little more juice to his suit, just enough to keep him breathing while he worked on his ridiculous plan.

"What are you doing?" Edwards mumbled. His breathing was too shallow, too uneven to even manage the gasping, retching coughs that had previously marked his return to consciousness.

"Something stupid," Birch smiled thinly.

Edwards groaned, more in pain than in response to Birch's words. Bur his head was gently shaking.

"You know how much I hate your stupid plans..." his voice trailed off and his helmet light dimmed to little more than a memory of a flicker.

"Yeah, me too," Birch muttered, pulling wires from Edwards' EVA suit, "but when stupid's all you've got left then you've gotta go with it!"

He had the end of Edwards' connector port wire between his finger and thumb. His hand hovered over the power cells. He hesitated briefly.

This plan wasn't stupid, it was suicidal, and no sane commander would have tried it. The power cells were their last chance, their only hope of getting *Colony I* running again. If he messed this up then there was no plan B. They would all die. No one knew that better than him. With little more than an hour's worth of power left in his own suit he knew the meaning of this decision, but what could he do? Watch Edwards die as he had watched Karla die? No! He could never do that again. Edwards was dying now. He could stop it, and if he got this right the power cells wouldn't totally discharge, wouldn't explode, and wouldn't melt or corrode to useless junk in his hands. While it was a risk- a big one in fact-there was still a chance that he could save everyone. That was something he just couldn't refuse. Even if he should die for it- he would always choose life.

He put the wire to the circuits, tentatively, expecting the worst. But they didn't explode. Instead, they warmed and glowed in his hands as their energy flowed into Edwards' suit. His darkened light clicked on, powerful and radiant in the darkness, brighter than Birch's own. His breathing steadied, becoming more pronounced as the suit's medical systems kicked in, aiding his labored respiration. He was going to live!

Birch was elated, but the illusion of success didn't last long. Edwards' suit was more damaged than he had imagined, and as soon as he removed his port wire from the power cells the suit's lights dimmed. Edwards slumped over again, finding it difficult to breathe without the suit's assistance.

"Okay, let's just make this harder then," Birch growled, pulling Edwards to his feet. For a moment he struggled to lift him up, to put him on his shoulder and carry on walking to the airlock, but his body wouldn't cooperate. His arms were like water, there was no strength, no substance to them, and it was all he could do to stop himself from dropping Edwards back into the dirt.

"Can you move at all?" Birch panted.

Edwards' head fell forward, wobbling slightly side to side. Birch couldn't tell if that was supposed to be an answer or was just another indication of his complete inability to control his movements. Either way, he knew he couldn't expect much help from him.

"Okay," Birch spat, holding Edwards' helmet with his hand so he could see his face. "This is it. I'm not going to leave you here to die. I'll drag you in if I have to, but any help you can give would be appreciated. Come on now, lift a leg. Step, step, step, one at a time. Move!"

Edwards' eyes rolled, Birch wasn't sure that he had under- stood, but he moved, a faltering, half falling, half walking step.

"That's it!" Birch shouted. "More! Move, move, come on!"

They stumbled on, a single step at a time toward the air-lock. Edwards' light kept fading in and out. Birch was trying to be judicious with the power cells, to save something for their attempt to override the self-destruct mechanism at the base, but every time Edwards' light dimmed, and his head slumping forward, he was left with that same simple choice to either let the man die, or risk all of their lives by giving him 'just one more' shot of power.

He could hardly go on. Another few hundred meters was all it would take to get them into the airlock according to the readout on his screen, but that felt like a hundred miles. Edwards was heavier than ever, slipping from his grasp, and it was all Birch could do to keep himself upright, to keep his own legs moving. The burden of Edwards was just too much for him.

Edwards tripped, fell to his knees, and pulled Birch over with him. Birch rolled over onto his back and lay there, panting. His eyes blurred as he squinted at his wrist display, the green dot of their location seemed to smudge, to jump and merge, separate and swirl in a hazy double vision. They were coming from the airlock, walking out into the planet's barren waste. Or were they walking toward the airlock? He couldn't work it out, and in his muddled mind, it somehow didn't seem to matter anymore.

He was an explorer in the ancient Sahara, chasing mirages across the desert, dying of thirst. Bones bleaching in the sun. They would never make it. Bones bleaching in the sun...

The sun? It was the sun that brought Birch back. This wasn't his sun. There was no heat, no warmth, no light, no life. This was an alien world, a place where he would die, where they all would die if he didn't get up- if he didn't get the energy cells to Jane soon.

He struggled to stand, to regain his footing, but he fell over onto his back again. He couldn't move. He could only watch.

The wind, the sand, the gray alien sky above, these would be the last things he saw.

Faces passed his vision. Sarah, Ratliff, Karla, Edwards, he had failed them all, and now he had failed his crew this one last time. He would never get back. The energy cells would be lost out here with him. Lauren, Jane- he had let them down too. He let everyone down.

He saw Jane's face, reproachful, staring down at him. Lights were glaring, he winced against their beam. It was almost too real.

"What are you doing laying around out here?" Jane barked. "We've got lives to save! Get up, let's go!"

TWENTY-ONE

The face was real, but it took him a while to realize that. Once he did he quickly struggled to his feet.

"Jane," he stammered, "what... what are you doing here? How did you get here?" He swayed dizzily, almost falling back down again. She caught him in her arms, holding him for a moment, gently steadying him with her hand.

"We've had the doors open for twenty minutes now," she answered. "Once you were outside we could watch your progress on the monitor, but then you slowed down and eventually stopped. We came out to see what was happening. Have you got the energy cells?"

Birch nodded, holding them out to her with unsteady hands. "Just watch out for him," Birch gestured toward Edwards, who was being helped up by Lauren. "His suit's been badly damaged. He's losing charge. I've had to top him up with the cells. If he seems like he's going down again you'll need to give him another quick jolt to keep him going.

Jane's eyes narrowed. "You've been draining the cells into his suit?"

"It was either that or let him die."

"That's never been a problem for you before."

Birch's head shot up at that. He pulled himself up, despite his exhaustion, towering over her, fury in his eyes, but Jane swatted him away with the back of her hand.

"Unless I'm mistaken, Major, you have about an hour's worth of power left in that suit of yours. So, unless you really want to spend your last breath arguing with me, then you'd better let me get on and do something about it."

She didn't wait for an answer. She sidestepped Birch and was gone, running back in the direction of the airlock, leaving Lauren to help the two of them as best she could.

It made sense really, she had to get started, to try and get the environmental controls back online before their time ran out, but still he felt betrayed. Watching those cells disappear into the darkness he knew that Edwards was now one shutdown away from death. There were no second chances. They had to ease him back to the base and hope his suit held up long enough for them to get the air back on.

"We're going to have to carry him. Can you help me?" Birch asked Lauren.

"Are you up to that?" She replied, glancing doubtfully at Birch. Swaying unsteadily on his feet, he hardly looked strong enough to get himself inside, much less carry anyone else.

"I'll manage."

They stood on either side, lifting Edwards up. Forming a support with their hands, they placed him between them and walked as quickly as their burden and Birch's exhaustion would allow.

They were closer than he had imagined and, working together, it didn't take long to arrive at the airlock. The great gray mass of the building seemed to rise up suddenly out of the dust. Strangely, the door was open. Jane and Lauren had wedged them all open to save time on their return. Now Birch slammed it shut, finally blocking out the choking reality of the planet they now inhabited. He would have gladly locked it out forever, but he knew that the respite was only temporary. If they survived beyond the next hour there would be answers to find and problems to solve that would take them out there again.

They stumbled through the corridors, slamming doors shut behind them as they went. Without the constant blast of the storm sounding in their ears, the rasping wheeze of Edwards' irregular breathing was more alarming. The slightest bump seemed to make a noticeable difference in his condition. They tried to be careful, to be swift but gentle, but nothing helped. They were running out of time.

It was a race now, a race with four contestants: Edwards, Birch, and Lauren against death- and it was starting to look like death would win.

Edwards looked bad. His skin had turned to a perspiration-soaked alabaster, his head lolled as he drifted in and out of consciousness. He had been unresponsive for a while.

Birch was having his own problems. His suit was about to give out too. His power levels were below five percent and important features were already beginning to shut down. Temperature control hadn't functioned for a while and he was shivering away the sweat that his exertions had produced. His visor was fogging. He tried to wipe it clean, but the mist was inside and had started to crystallize, freezing in jagged patterns that coated the glass, reducing everything around him to a wintry blur. His internal light was flickering weakly now, like Edwards', and he knew it wouldn't be long before he was in the same condition as him.

"Wait," Birch panted, coming to a stop, trying to catch his breath. Their pace was slow and the burden wasn't getting any lighter. He was tempted to leave them behind, to rush on and help Jane. Maybe that was the only way he could save them, to help her get the systems back on quicker, but he knew he couldn't do it. Lauren couldn't manage on her own, and if he left Edwards now it was almost a certain death sentence. Even if they did manage to get the air back on, it wasn't going to magically flood the whole base. It would take time. Jane would have to concentrate everything on one place, flood one location with oxygenated atmosphere and then let it permeate through the rest of the base later. In other words, they all needed to reach the same location to survive.

"Okay," Birch muttered through gritted teeth, "let's go!"

They lifted Edwards again and clattered down the remaining corridors, finally reaching Jane's location ten minutes later. With a heaving sigh, Birch set Edwards down and slammed the final door shut.

Jane was busily typing at the only illuminated console in the room. The golden energy cells glowed and hummed quietly on the desk beside her, wires from it feeding into the computer.

She raised a finger in a gesture for silence as they approached. "Just wait," she snapped. "I'm about five minutes away from getting it. I've cracked it, but these systems take a lot of navigating."

"I'm not sure he's got five minutes." Birch gestured to Edwards.

Jane looked up. Her eyes lingered on Edwards a moment and then turned quickly back to her screen. "I'm trying," she mumbled, clearing her throat. "I really am. Now shut up and let me concentrate."

Her hands flew furiously over the keys. Her fingers were a blur of movement. Birch could see the images on her screen flipping and changing as quickly as the speed of thought. She was doing her best, maybe even a little better.

"I need you to check all the vents," she called over her shoulder. "I can't waste the time or the energy it would take to do it through the computer, so I need you to make sure this room is sealed off from the rest of the system. Only the main vent should be open. When I've bypassed the autodestruct I'll localize the airflow to this room. That should speed up the process a bit."

Birch nodded and got going with the task. He was shivering visibly now. The cold was getting to him. His fingers tingled painfully and he had lost all sensation in his feet. He struggled to keep his hands steady as he checked the vents. Lauren tried to get him to sit down, to rest and conserve his energy as Edwards was doing, but that wasn't something Birch could do. The one thing he never could do was nothing.

"Right," Jane shouted a moment later, "this is it! Hold your breath. This better be right, if the number countdown comes back up we're done, because with three seconds left to go there'll be no way to stop it this time.

"Here we go!"

She hit the button. Instantly the lights came on and the air coughed, sputtered, and then whooshed through the vents. All of this was wonderful, but it went unnoticed, for they were all transfixed by Jane's screen and the feared digit- the number 'three', that had now appeared on it. The countdown was back!

It seemed a long second before that number finally faded, but not to be replaced by a 'two', then a 'one', and finally the death that they all now expected. Instead, the number faded into nothing. The countdown hadn't restarted! They were going to live!

They cheered. Birch pumped the air with his fist, but his celebration was truncated as he caught sight of Edwards slumped over on the floor. He shot a glance at Jane.

"How long until the air's breathable?" he asked.

She shook her head. "A few minutes yet, and it'll be quite a while after that before it's even close to optimal."

"Who cares about optimal?" Birch snapped. "Tell me the second it's barely adequate. He's going to suffocate in his own helmet if we don't get it off soon!"

"Well, depending on how bad his condition is, I guess you could risk it any time now. It *will* be a risk; the air's still pretty thin. I'd still wait a minute or two, just to be sure."

Birch was already moving before she had even finished her sentence. There was no time for caution. He leaped to Edwards, pulling at his helmet, fumbling with the clasps, trying to wrench it off. As bad as the air was out there, Birch knew it was no worse than what Edwards was struggling to breathe in his suit right now, and it was only getting worse.

The helmet finally came off with a hiss. The air around them had quickly improved and was already comparable to what could be found on the higher mountain peaks. It wasn't exactly comfortable, but it wasn't fatal either, and it certainly seemed to be helping Edwards. In the short time out of his helmet, he was breathing more regularly and the color was returning to his cheeks.

Birch collapsed, exhausted. His whole energy had been given to keeping Edwards alive, and now that this had been achieved he had nothing more to give. He slid down the wall, hunched over, barely able to move. He pulled awkwardly at his own helmet, but he no longer had the strength to move it. His arms fell limply to his side and his breathing grew labored as he gasped against the foul air his dying suit pumped into him. His respirator was shutting down, but there wasn't much he could do about it. He was too cold, too drowsy, too tired to think about such things.

Jane put a hand on Birch's shoulder. With her best attempt at an air-stewardess smile, she leaned over him, asking lightly, "Don't you think you should get your helmet off too? The air quality's pretty good in here now." Her own helmet was off. A few stray strands of dark hair had escaped her hair band and brushed against his visor.

Birch gagged, trying to make a sound, but he didn't have the air to do it. He couldn't breathe. His arm twitched reflexively, but he had lost control of his body.

Jane quickly noticed. Her smile faded and she grabbed his helmet, unclasping it swiftly and pulling it off.

Birch lay for a moment gasping but waved Jane away when she leaned in closer to help him. He would be okay if he could just have a minute to get some air into his lungs.

"That was a pretty dumb thing to do," Jane scolded. "You should always attend to your own needs first, and then help others. When you're in that kind of condition it's too risky to do anything else. You could have died."

Birch didn't say anything. He was already slipping into a semiconscious stupor. He was vaguely aware of Jane's words, and of the need to do something. Their fight for survival had only just begun. There was the base to search, provisions to find, and questions to be answered. All of these were important, but none of them seemed to matter. All he could do now, after the long fight for life, was fall into the darkness that opened up before him.

TWENTY-TWO

It was something like sleep, only deeper, more penetrating. Brought on by exhaustion, it left no room for anything but itself. Birch had no way of knowing how long it lasted. It might have been hours, days, or even weeks. It was a dreamless, timeless void, and he had embraced it like home. It was an escape. Even in stasis the echo of guilt and memory seemed to linger in the synaptic connections of his mind. He always awoke with the bitter taste of it on his tongue, but here he had fallen into the nothingness, and when he had finally opened his eyes his only regret was to have left it behind.

He was alone. He didn't know where he was. Sitting up in a narrow, hard bed, he glanced around, taking in his surroundings. It was a small room, probably once the cabin of a menial worker at the base, he imagined- nothing special, small, cramped, and functional, but interesting all the same. It wasn't the room itself that held his attention, though, rather it was what was in it.

This place looked lived in. Everywhere else they had seen in *Colony I* had been the common areas, the corridors, central control, and the computer center. There was nothing personal in any of that, and so it hadn't somehow registered that this was a home, the residence of hundreds of people who had all somehow disappeared. This room made that real.

It was a squalid little abode. If there had been any life here at all he would have expected to find vermin of some kind sharing it with him. Even though he knew it was impossible on this dead station, he still felt the itch of imagined flea bites as he climbed out from beneath the soiled covers.

He stretched, blinking away the blur as his eyes adjusted to his surroundings. Posters covered the walls, all depicting the same sterile, idealized female form. No other decoration was present. A shaving brush and razor on the sink, some clothes on the floor, and a computer pad lying dead on a bedside table all added to the impression of life. The tiny closet and drawers were all filled with a few shabby clothes and other personal possessions. This place was just as it had been left so many years ago, and it made Birch shiver to think of it.

Where exactly was he? How had he gotten into this room? He was stripped down to his boxers; his uniform was hanging on a peg beside the door. Probably Jane had just shoved him in here, into the nearest residential compartment she could find for him to sleep it off. She certainly hadn't wasted any time looking for the best place for him. He would have to remember never to ask her to pick out the motel on a road trip. He wasn't sure if it was the moldering decay of this newly oxygenated room or just his own unwashed body, but something didn't smell too good either. Birch pulled himself off the bed and tried the faucet, but no water came. He had expected that, but he felt he needed to wash off the grime and memories of his fight for life.

He rubbed his face in his hands. Catching sight of himself in the mirror he frowned. The signs of his struggles were clear. The graying of his hair seemed to have spread. His eyes were sunken, the lines around them more pronounced. He looked tired, more tired than any sleep could ever remedy.

Birch pulled on his flight suit and boots. He took a last look around the tiny room. He wouldn't be coming back here again and this place would fade again into its forgotten obscurity, just as its occupant had. Whoever had lived here was less than a footnote in history. They hadn't made an impact. Even their own home said very little about them. Whatever insignificant life they had played out between these narrow walls had disappeared long ago, and no one remembered. Did anyone care? That was the question. Karla had once said that lives were like stones thrown into the water, making waves beyond their actual impact, but was that really true? What waves had the life of this room's occupant really made? None, nothing lasting anyway. He had been little more than a pebble thrown into the ocean of existence, and the ripples were already lost. Karla had been wrong. Nothing lasted, but at the same time, he yearned for something more. If this was all there was it wasn't enough.

Birch sighed. He thought about that sort of thing too much. Back on Earth, he had fought the same depression that was sweeping over him now. Denver and the rest of the destroyed towns on the plains had haunted him, and then he had lost Karla, and it had almost been too much.

He hated decay, it was a demonstration of the inevitable collapse of human dreams, but *Colony One* was a towering monument to that very thing. Somehow he would have to find a way to cope with it here on R67.3 or be swept away with the feelings he had been trying to outrun. They would all have to be strong to survive on this failed world.

Birch strode out into the hallway, letting the door slam shut behind him. There wasn't anyone there. The corridor looked similar to the ones he had been through earlier, though this one was in a state of disorder. Debris lay everywhere. Parts of ceiling tiles, pipes, and bits of metal fragment crunched underfoot as he stepped across the floor. Birch wasn't sure if this was the result of some conflict or just the natural erosion of an abandoned base. He was inclined to believe the former. A few telltale scorch marks along the walls seemed more indicative of some sort of weapons discharge, but there wasn't any conclusive proof. All he could really be sure of was that the place was empty now and had been for a long time. How it had gotten that way was the question they still had to answer. Knowing that was vital; it could mean the difference between death and survival. Whatever had happened to the colony could happen to them, and they had to be prepared.

The smell of food interrupted his thoughts. It was only now that he remembered that he hadn't eaten since yesterday, or maybe longer, depending on when yesterday actually was. He had been asleep so long he couldn't really be sure. The smell wasn't exactly good, more the sickly aroma of stale confectionery wrestling against the acrid bite of strong coffee, but he didn't really care. It smelled like something he could eat, and that was the only thing that mattered.

Birch followed his nose, sniffing out the source of the smell through the corridors. Eventually, it led him to a communal kitchen. It seemed empty from the outside, but it was difficult to tell- the lights were back on, but everywhere was still only dimly illuminated.

"Oh, you're up," a voice observed in the semidarkness. Startled, Birch turned in the direction of the voice. It was Lauren, leaning against the counter, cradling a cup of steaming coffee in her hands. The base was a little chilly, and its warmth looked good.

"Got a spare one of those?" Birch asked.

"Sure," Lauren reached over and pushed a button on the coffee machine. A cup slipped into place and a strong smelling stream of black liquid oozed slowly into it.

"Is that drinkable?" Birch asked, dubiously eyeing the pungent brew as the last drops dribbled from the machine. It smelled something like coffee, but probably one brewed with fifty year old stagnant swamp water. He held the steaming cup up to his nose and immediately regretted it. His eyes watered as the bitter vapor assaulted his senses.

"I'd recommend plenty of sugar," Lauren smiled thinly. She almost seemed to enjoy his response, "but not the creamer. And just wait until you try the food."

"What is there to eat around here?" Birch asked, taking a

first cautious sip of the coffee. He coughed, took a deep breath, and reached for the sweetener.

"This," Lauren answered, handing him an oblong package wrapped in cellophane.

Birch winced. "Survival rations? That's it?"

"Pretty much. Don't forget these, though." She handed him a supplement pack containing vitamins and other nutritional necessities. "You need to keep up your strength."

"Yum," Birch muttered, peeling the cellophane away from his 'breakfast'. The solid portion of his meal was a standard issue survival ration. Developed by the Space Agency in the early years of the program- with a few additional dietary supplements they could keep you in the peak of health for years, and better still, their shelf life was almost indefinite. You could eat the stuff five hundred years after it was sealed and it would be virtually the same as when it was fresh. The taste certainly didn't improve with age.

In a pinch, you could eat a survival ration as it was. It would have to be desperate times indeed though for that to happen. It was a lump of gelatinous vegetable matter that, when prepared properly, had a nasty undertaste. When you didn't prepare it properly it was the awful overtaste you had to wrestle with.

Birch slammed the ration into a reconstitutor. Here the vegetable matter would be shifted, shaped to something approximating food. He set it to bacon and eggs, good breakfast food, and took another hesitant sip of coffee.

"Where's Jane and Edwards?" he asked as he watched his food transform in the machine.

"Major Grey is still at the computer station. She's hardly slept at all. She's been working on things, trying to get all the systems up. It's been slow. Edwards is still in bed. I haven't seen him since we put him in his room over a day ago."

The machine dinged and Birch pulled his steaming plate out and placed it on the counter. His meal had now been transformed and looked a little like bacon and eggs, and even smelled something like them too, but he wasn't fooled. He put a tentative fork into it and took a bite. It tasted like survival rations with a hint of bacon and eggs added for effect. He didn't care. It was food, and he shoveled it in.

"Okay," Birch said between bites, "we need to get going. I'll get Edwards. You go tell Jane I want her to be ready to report in half-an-hour. I need to know exactly what the situation is. We'll meet up in the computer room and make a decision on how we proceed from there."

Lauren nodded and left to find Jane. Birch took a last sip of coffee and went in search of Edwards. He wasn't hard to find; he was exactly where Lauren had told him they had put him. Without waiting to knock Birch pushed the button, opened the door, and strode in.

Edwards lay sprawled awkwardly across the bed. The covers and pillows had been thrown off in his fitful sleep. He was totally out and didn't look ready to get up, but that was too bad. Birch shook him. Edwards awoke with a start. Scooting back, he fell off the bed onto the floor.

"Time to get up," Birch barked, ignoring Edwards' discomfort. "We have twenty minutes before we're having a strategy meeting in the computer room. You need to be there." He took Edwards' clothes off the peg and threw them onto the bed. "Get these on and come straight out. I'll be waiting in the hall." With that, he strode out.

Edwards, having only recovered sufficiently enough to poke his head up from behind the mattress could only blink dumbly as Birch left.

A few minutes later Edwards emerged from his room, rubbing his eyes wearily. He barely looked awake. Birch guided him to the kitchen and tried to get some food and liquid into him before the meeting. It wasn't easy.

Edwards didn't want coffee. He wanted hot tea, and it took Birch a lot of cupboard searching to find any. It didn't taste any better than the coffee judging from his expression as he tried to drink it. It took some persuading to get him to try anything else after that. He pecked at a few things until finally, he had consumed enough for Birch to be confident that he wouldn't collapse.

"Alright," Birch announced impatiently. "It's time to go." He strode into the corridor, leaving Edwards to catch up. Birch couldn't wait any longer. He had played nursemaid to this reluctant astronaut long enough.

As he walked ahead Birch's mind raced on to that most dangerous, yet most necessary topic- the future. He wanted to hear Jane's report, to finally know exactly what they were dealing with and what their chances were. He was tired of bumping along, reacting to circumstances rather than making them. Maybe, finally, this was their chance to change that. Maybe for once they could shape the future rather than let it shape them.

TWENTY-THREE

Jane and Lauren were already there when Birch arrived. Edwards burst in a moment later, puffing from running to catch him. Quickly they found a place at the table and the meeting began.

"Well," Jane began before Birch could get a word out, "here we are, survivors of your spectacular landing. With no way to get back up to the ship and short supplies, the only thing marring this perfect little scenario is worrying about how we're going to deal with whoever shot us down!"

"Nobody shot us down," Birch muttered. "There were no life readings down here. It must've been an automated system that got us. I've never heard of anything like it; it doesn't make sense a colony having that sort of weapon. It's familiar, but not from any NASA technology of our time."

"So what are we going to do?" Edwards asked, anxious to know their chances of survival.

"The way I see it," Birch replied, "we've got two options. We either stay here on R67.3 and try to make a go of it, or we get off this rock and find a better location to settle."

Jane was rubbing her forehead with her fingers, as though trying to soothe away a particularly persistent headache.

"That seems a rather academic choice, Major," she replied wearily, "given that we have no way to get back up to the Hypnos. The computers list no spacecraft remaining here at all. That's zero, so why don't we just concentrate on reality and try to figure out the best way to get this station running? Anything else would just be a waste of time and energy."

"I don't agree," Birch answered evenly. He was keeping his temper with Jane for now. "Computers can be wrong, and what happens if we put all our resources into one plan? Let's say we decide that the only plan we'll pursue is to get off this planet. What if we hit a dead end, there is no way off, and we're stuck here? Our resources would run out and we would die. That would be stupid. But it would be just as foolish, Major, to follow your plan and only concentrate on staying here?"

"It's not *my* plan, Birch," she snapped. "It's the only logical path forward. There's no way out of here."

"Okay," Birch continued. "What if we follow *the only logical path forward*, only to find out that it's a dead end? We'd be stuck without another option. Don't forget, Jane that we're in a base that once had a lot more colonists than our small group here, but it died out. What happened to them? Have you figured that out yet?"

Jane shook her head. "Those records are still sealed."

"So, we're not even sure if staying here will be an option in the end. Whatever happened to them could happen to us if we stay. We have to try to keep both options open. I don't want to be stuck without a second choice."

Lauren and Edwards both nodded, it made sense to them, but Jane just glared down at her computer screen. The room fell into silence as Birch waited for her response, but she wouldn't speak, wouldn't even lift her head to meet his gaze. Jane could be so petulant sometimes. Birch finally shook his head and moved on.

"Okaaayy then," he drawled, "let's look at what we've got to get done.

"First there's the easy plan: getting off this planet. It's not the 'easy' plan because it's easy to do, or because it'll succeed, there's just not as much to it. If we're lucky it'll be easy, and if we're not it'll be impossible. We're obviously not going to build a spacecraft from scraps down here. Let's be realistic; that'll never happen. The only chance we've got is that hidden somewhere on this rock there's a ship we can use. We have to find it. I'm not sure how many places we can expect to find something like that, not many. Maybe the computer's wrong and there's something here or over at *Primary Base*, but remember, there are also secondary bases, smaller outposts, and science stations where some sort of ship might be found. It's a long shot I know, but we're going to have to be thorough and consider every possibility. And then, even if we do find one, there's still likely to be mechanical issues to overcome. It's not likely we're going to find a ship that'll just start up at the push of a button. Jane and I will have to deal with that issue when we come to it, and who knows if there will even be any parts to fix them. It's all a long shot really."

"What about the pod," Edwards asked anxiously. It was obvious that he was in favor of leaving the planet and wanted some glimmer of hope. "Couldn't you salvage something from that?"

Jane looked up from her computer. "The only thing you'll get from that is ashes," she remarked sourly.

"She's right," Birch sighed. "Anything we need will have to come from right here. I'm guessing, after what happened with the last probe, the ship won't be sending down any more help either."

Jane nodded. "I've already tried communicating with the Hypnos computer. I'm locked out. It seems like it's calculated my channel as rogue input. It's not listening to me."

"So," Birch continued, "to get off this planet we'll need to search every possible location, smaller outposts, even some of the local terrain, to see if there's anything left we can use. It'll be a lot of hard searching and then most likely a tough mechanical job after that. That'll probably take weeks, if we're lucky. Maybe months."

"If that was the easy plan, I'd hate to think what the hard one's going to be like," Edwards grumbled.

"Harder," Birch admitted, "but probably more doable. Getting this station going and keeping it running will take a lot of work. We're talking about four people doing the job of a whole colony. It's hard to imagine that going well."

"I've been thinking about that," Jane said. "It's all a question of scale really. Of course, we can't do the job of a whole colony, but maybe we don't have to. Everything can be scaled back. Food production only needs to be a fraction of what it would have been. We could limit our living space to a few areas, and so reduce energy consumption and maintenance. Under those circumstances, I think it's very doable."

"That makes sense." Birch rubbed his chin thoughtfully." I was hoping to get more of the base back online, though. I think there's some vital systems here we'll need to utilize, lots of work we need to do, and going small scale will limit that. If we stay we need to get this base working, doing what it was meant to do. I don't plan to spend the rest of my life huddled in these few rooms surviving. I want to live."

Jane shrugged. "That's possible in the long run maybe. That's what I'll be working toward, but for now, it's all about survival, and we haven't got much to work with."

"She's right," Lauren agreed. "Looking at the records here I'd say we've probably got eight months to a year's worth of food supply left. Processed, preserved stuff mostly, nothing good. As you'd expect, it seems that they had established an efficient food production network, hydroponics, bio-domes, all that sort of thing, but all of that collapsed of course once the base was abandoned."

For once Lauren seemed at ease, speaking without her usual reserve. It was always that way when she talked about her work. Her area of expertise, surviving on distant planets, was certainly going to come in useful now. Her final goal had always been to prepare the planet for terra-forming, but that was the work of years. That wasn't even a consideration for R67.3 right now. It was all about initial survival.

"What are our chances?" Birch asked. "Is there enough left to work with?"

Lauren shrugged. "Possibly, the computer records are a little sketchy on that. It doesn't look like things were exactly getting done by the book at the end. Some automated computer inventory was completed, but everything else is a mess. Things got stolen. It looks like everything broke down, the chain of command, everything. Things were taken without authorization. Emergency seed stores were raided. They were taken for food I guess. It doesn't look like they had any long term plan for the survival of the base. They just took what they wanted."

"You're saying there's no seed store left?"

"Not on record," Lauren's voice was remarkably calm.

"You don't seem too worried about that!" This was why Birch had no patience with Lauren. She never really seemed to exist in the same world as everyone else. If there was no seed store then there was no future on this planet. They would have to get off or die.

"Something will turn up," she answered blandly. "There's a chance. This is a big base and it had a well developed agricultural system in place. I'm pretty sure there have to be some residual remnants left. We'll find them and start from there."

"It sounds like the hard option just got a lot harder," Birch muttered. "You're talking about crawling around in the dirt looking for seeds, aren't you?"

"Yes."

"Has it come to that, sifting through the dirt to survive?"

"Yes, it has."

"Well, "Birch laughed bitterly, "I guess that's how it all started, so why not? Even astronauts must eat their bread by the sweat of their brow." Everyone was silent. There was no answer to that, but no one looked happy about it.

"Okay, Birch finally spoke again. We've got to follow the two-pronged survival plan. Lauren's obviously the lead player on the seed reclaiming and agricultural side of things. As you're so anxious to stay here, Jane, you can work with her on that. Edwards and I will start the search for a ship to get us back up to the Hypnos."

Jane glared at Birch, but he ignored her.

"It'll take a couple of days for Edwards and me to get our suits fixed. Maybe longer, we'll see. How much of the station have you been able to reintroduce atmosphere to, Jane?"

"Not much," she admitted. "Just this little section here so far. There's not much power getting through, so I don't dare expand the range yet. I could power the whole base, but it would probably blow the feed within the first half hour and leave us with nothing. I've had to rein it in and keep it to a minimum for now. It'll hold indefinitely in this small part. The power feed can sustain that, but that's it. If I had the time to work on it," she added pointedly, "I could get a lot more done."

"That's true," Birch agreed. "And I want this base running as much as you do, but like you said, the oxygen and power will hold here, so that's not the priority. We can use our suits in the rest of *Colony I* for now and come back to recharge when we need it. It's more important that we get food production going. It'll take a while to establish that, you can't grow things overnight, so we need both of you to start on that right away. I'd rather have you both working together. Even if you don't know as much as Lauren, you can figure it out. Two's gotta be quicker than one, right? And that's what we need right now: speed."

"That's not the best use of my time," Jane snapped back.

"That's an order, Jane," Birch replied coolly. "Besides," he added, "I'm not letting anyone go off unaccompanied into the base right now. There are too many unanswered questions. We just don't know what happened here."

"You said yourself, no one's down here. What danger could there be in an empty base?" Jane asked impatiently.

"I don't know," Birch shook his head. "I don't like that green ray, and if they had one automatic defense mechanism in place there may be more, other ones we don't know anything about, stuff inside. I'm not going to risk it."

"What was that ray anyway?" Lauren asked. "I've never seen anything like it before."

"I have," Birch observed darkly, "but I'm not sure how it works. Obviously, it's powerful. What do you suppose it is, Edwards?" he asked, his eyes narrowing to take in the man.

Edwards seemed flustered for a moment. The unexpected attention was not welcome and it took him a moment to recover.

"I don't know," he finally stammered. "I, um... hate to admit it, but I had my eyes closed during the whole thing. I don't like flying much."

"That figures!" Birch snorted, rising from the table. "Well, that's all we've got then. You two can start your *farming* as soon as you're ready. When I'm done repairing our suits Edwards and I will explore the base, looking for transport."

Birch paused, standing behind his chair.

"Just one more thing, as well as your primary job, I want all of you to keep your eyes open for any indication of what happened here. Obviously, something happened to the people on this base. We haven't seen any sign of bodies or anything like that. They're just gone, but where? We haven't been able to get into the records and logs for the station yet, so we're in the dark right now, literally. Anything you find that seems unusual or noteworthy, report it to me immediately. I need to know. I've got a feeling that whatever happened here in the past has a lot to do with our future.

"Above all, be careful out there. Okay, that's it. Let's get started."

TWENTY-FOUR

It took a few days to get their suits working again. Birch's unit wouldn't take a charge and had to be rewired to get it going. Edwards' suit was even more of a challenge. His fall had damaged the Primary Life Support System. Looking at it now it was a miracle he had made it at all. It took a lot of scavenging and improvisation to get everything back into functional order, but finally, Birch was confident that it was safe enough. After the last few preparations, they were ready to go.

He might almost have felt guilty, working comfortably in his makeshift lab while Jane was out every day in the bio-dome, on her hands and knees scraping around in the dirt for the tiniest seeds, but he wasn't. Jane came back every day dirty and grumpy. Banging her dusty helmet into a storage bin, stripping off her dirt smeared suit, she would slump down into a cushioned seat and brood. It seemed an amicable enough arrangement to Birch, after all, she was the one who wanted to stay, or at least she was the one unwilling to consider any other option. He was the one who still had faith that there was a way off this planet. So, it seemed only fair that she should work toward her goal by sifting through the dirt, and he should work toward his by searching for a ship.

Despite Jane's gloom, the news of their progress from the bio-dome had been encouraging. It was meticulous, dirty work, and it took longer than any of them had hoped, but it was producing results. Their seed haul hadn't been too bad, and by the end of the third day, they had collected some twenty specimens that Lauren was hopeful might germinate under the right conditions.

Birch stared at those twenty seeds, holding their sealed glass container gingerly in his hands. Perhaps this was their future. Twenty seeds to plant their garden, to create their world. It wasn't much to build hope upon, but maybe it would be enough. These seeds were hardy. Like Birch himself, they were resilient enough to survive. The result of special cross breeding programs and genetic modification, they were supposed to last forever, to conform to the rigors of an alien world, but as he held them up to the light Birch couldn't help but wonder. He wondered what President Michaels had told him of the results of scientific meddling back on Earth, of how their attempts there to improve crop yields had doomed their race to biological oblivion. Were these modified seeds here any different?

On Earth, humanity was only a few generations away from extinction because of what they had done. Had the same happened here? Only, on this smaller scale, its destruction had been more immediate, more potent? There was no way to tell until he got into the colony's records, but neither he nor Jane had had any success with that yet. So, for now, all he could do was look at these seeds and wonder if he was looking at the means of their deliverance or their destruction.

Finally, Birch finished the last of the repairs to the suits. Jane had made a final attempt to convince him to concentrate all their efforts on the seed gathering. "We could double our chances with you two out in the dome with us," she had coaxed, but Birch had shrugged the suggestion off without comment. He had already said everything he intended to say on that subject.

Birch and Edwards slowly clambered into their suits. Stretching fingers into gloves, snapping clasps shut, tightening, buckling, adjusting equipment- they methodically prepared for the hostile environment outside their tiny enclave.

They didn't look like much. Birch's suit still had the heavy black scorch marks from his encounter with the door at Main Control. Edwards' suit didn't look any better. It had two prominent dents on the chest plate, a scrape down the side of his helmet, and a slightly odd, disheveled look to it, as though it had been put together with odd parts that didn't really match. Despite all that both suits seemed to be working well enough, so they were ready to go.

They trudged down the walkway and opened a sealed door to another corridor that served as a makeshift airlock. The door clanged shut behind them.

Already Edwards was showing signs of distress. His breathing was irregular and he kept looking behind him, as though seeking escape. Birch understood, he hadn't exactly been excited about trusting his life to a suit that had almost killed him a few short days ago, but this was about survival. If they were going to survive they would have to take risks.

"Keep it cool, Edwards," Birch rasped as he punched the keys working the final door's mechanism. "You can't stay in those few rooms the rest of your life, you know."

Edwards didn't respond, but straightened up, lifting his head in an apparent gesture of renewed resolve.

The door creaked stiffly to one side. This was the same exit Jane and Lauren had been using to get to the bio-dome over the last few days, but repeated use hadn't made any improvement to the decrepit portal.

They stepped out into another passageway. It was dark; the power was still out across the base except in the little living space they had established.

"Jane?" Birch spoke into his headset. Jane and Lauren had

already gone on ahead for their day's work at the bio-dome.

There was a moment's pause.

"Yes, Major?"

"We're leaving the habitat zone now. We'll be headed to the hangar directly. With all of us out here, we better increase the number of check-ins. Contact every ten minutes, got that?"

"Yeah" she answered simply.

"Okay. Keep me posted."

They had reached another door. Without power, they were back to manual opening, but he and Edwards had mastered the technique pretty well by now, and they were able to get them open in a few minutes.

They progressed quite well, but they soon began to notice a difference. The further they went into the base, the more pronounced the destruction became. Something bad had happened here. There were holes in the walls and strange scratches on the doors. It was difficult to get through some of them. So much debris and junk was piled up in the way that it took both of them pushing hard to get them clear.

There was a pattern to the devastation. There were weld marks on the doors, but the seals had apparently been broken by some massive force. It looked like the colonists had tried to shut something out, to seal themselves off from whatever was coming after them. It didn't look like they'd had much success.

"What do you think happened here?" Edwards asked, shining a light through a broken door, down another crumbling corridor.

"Who knows," Birch answered cagily and quickened his pace. The more he saw of this place the more he wanted to find a ship and get away.

Finally, they arrived. A crooked sign hung from a single screw, informing them that this was the hangar deck. It wasn't a cheering sight. On the good side, it wasn't as hard to gain access as Birch had feared. There weren't any codes or other elaborate security procedures to get through. In fact, there wasn't any door. It had been blown off. A great metal chunk of it lay thirty feet up the corridor. The rest was strewn about in little pebbles and pieces of debris that crunched underfoot.

"This looks bad," Edwards muttered. His voice was thin, almost inaudible, even in the stillness. Birch ignored him and strode into the hangar.

The computer had been right. It was empty. At least it didn't have anything resembling a working ship in it. There was a pile of junked out wreckage near the bay's outer doors that might have once have been a transport of some kind, but it wasn't in any better condition than the pod they had crashed a few days ago. There wasn't much chance of salvaging anything from that.

Birch sighed. Without hope, he searched the hangar's cavernous space more thoroughly. There was nothing to help them- no hidden ships, no secret compartments, only a dark emptiness and everywhere evidence of a desperate battle that must have been lost by the inhabitants of this base. Shattered terminals, gaping holes, and burned out equipment made that clear, but there were no bodies or remains of any kind, not even any sign of blood. Whoever won the battle here had left the base itself a ramshackle mess, but had been very meticulous in cleaning up every sign of the human carnage. There wasn't a microbe or a cell to indicate what had happened to the people here. If this was a crime scene then forensics wasn't going to clear it up for them.

"Check in, Major." Birch flinched involuntarily, startled by the crackle of Jane's voice in his ear.

"Birch here," he answered. He hesitated. Maybe he would wait another ten minutes to tell her about the hangar. Even a short delay of her triumphalism and the inevitable, 'I told you so' speech would be welcome.

"So," Jane persisted after a silent pause, "what's the news on the hanger?"

"It's empty," he finally answered flatly. "We're about to

start back. I'll tell you more when we get there." He clicked off without waiting for a reply. He was sure to hear plenty when they got back. There was no need for a preview.

Birch took a last lingering look around the hangar. It remained depressingly empty. There was room for a lot more. This place would have once been full of ships. They must have all gone somewhere. Maybe they were over at *Primary Base*, or perhaps scattered among the smaller outposts, but Birch's pessimism wouldn't allow him to believe it. The kind of devastation he saw here had the look of a mortal struggle, a final fight for survival, and if anyone had escaped in these missing ships, it didn't seem likely they would have just made a short hop to another base and hoped for safety. No, that would have been stupid. They would have been looking to get right out of here, to some safe place, somewhere off-world. But where? That was the question he couldn't answer.

Birch ran his fingers along the dead console. If he could get these running he might find the answer. Not that it would do much good right now, not while they were stranded on the surface. For now, they were stuck here, and he didn't have much faith in Jane's *stay here and grow things* idea. He had to find a way off this planet. Whatever had happened to the colony could happen to them. Evil was here. He didn't know what it was, but he could feel it around them, embracing them. It would never let them go. He shivered.

Birch shook his head, ashamed of his rising fears.

"What now?" Edwards asked. He was at his shoulder, his body language making it clear he was ready to go. "Anywhere else you can think of looking for ships?"

Birch shrugged. "Not here. Probably *Primary Base* or somewhere else, but that's a job for another time. We may as well get back. There's nothing for us here."

They left the hangar. Trudging silently through the gray corridors, they made their way back toward the habitable zone. Birch was following their progress on his map display when the blue maze of walls and rooms gave way to a gaping, dark space to the east. It was a large open area at the center of *Colony I*. It was *Town Square*, the hub of this tiny society. The governor's offices were in *Town Square*. Birch instantly knew the significance of that. If anywhere could tell them what had happened to this base it would be there.

"Jane," Birch spoke into his mouthpiece.

"Yes, Major?" Jane's distorted voice came back faintly.

"We're pretty close to *Town Square* here. Edwards and I are going to make our way over there now. We're going to check out the governor's offices and see what we can find out. We'll return after that."

"Okay," Jane answered simply. "We were heading back ourselves soon. Do you need any assistance?"

"Negative. We can handle it." He clicked off and gestured Edwards in the direction of a side passage leading toward the empty space on his map.

TWENTY-FIVE

At first, this passage looked much like all the others. Soon, however, it opened out into a wide foyer where plush carpeting, floral wallpaper, and sculpted glass lighting replaced the stark functionality of the rest of the base. There was an elevator at one side, but it didn't work, and next to it was a large pair of frosted glass doors with long, dulled brass handles. This was one of the many entrances to *Town Square*.

Birch pushed through the doors, stepping out onto a landing at the top of a wide stone staircase. Edwards followed a moment later, gasping at the size and grandeur of the place. From here they could see everything. The weather outside had cleared enough to allow the thin gray light from R67.3's ever-gloomy sky to dimly illuminate the area.

Town Square lived up to its name. Under a high dome of glass, there was an idyllic little village, a tiny town, like something from a picture-perfect calendar. There were maybe a dozen or so small, gray, stone buildings. Some of them were independent structures around the middle of the enclosure; others jutted out from the sides and were illusions of buildings- fronts attached to interior walls of the base to make the impression of a larger town.

"How on earth…" Edwards' voice trailed off as he turned every way, taking in the uncanny reality of the scene. "How did they do this?" He glanced over at Birch, remembering his role with the Hypnos missions. "How did *you* do this?"

"Birch shook his head. "We didn't."

"Then who…"

"Well, obviously somebody did," he snapped back impatiently. It just wasn't us." He was trying to figure it out himself.

"So how could they make this place so earthlike," Edwards persisted, "and where did they get the time or the materials to build it out here?"

Birch had started down the steps, but he knew he couldn't escape Edwards' questions so easily. "There's nothing spectacular here," he answered, pausing at the bottom for him to catch up. The rookie astronaut was still slow and cumbersome in his EVA suit. "Everything is just like we planned, except that it shouldn't be here."

"So, how do you think it got here then?" Edwards panted, finally reaching the bottom.

"I don't know. Like I said, we didn't build it." Birch knew he wasn't going to get any peace from Edwards if he didn't give him at least some explanation, so he decided to tell him just enough to shut him up.

"Look," he continued, "the way the Hypnos missions worked we were supposed to have *Primary Base* ready before the first colonists got here. We had to build it, but we didn't do the construction ourselves; we supervised it. The machines we brought were supposed to do most of the work. We would spend a lot of time in stasis, just being woken up when there were things to do that couldn't be handled by the machines, stuff that needed human insight and human supervision."

"That doesn't sound like much of a life," Edwards remarked.

"Well, you didn't read the brochure then, did you? We were the heroes, the visionaries who could guide all humanity to the new land of milk-and-honey. We were legend." Birch's voice dripped sarcasm. "Only problem was, we didn't do any of it.

"Most of what we brought with us," he continued, "was construction and maintenance equipment. All the other materials had to be available on the planet we chose. At first, this place seemed like a good location, and everything worked out okay for a while, but then about a year into the project one of those storms hit, only it was worse. We'd never seen anything like it. We thought we'd prepared for everything, but that was something else. For five days it blasted us. The wind almost ripped us to pieces. We survived, but by the time it was done all our work had been wrecked, and the equipment was junked. There wasn't much more we could do, so we abandoned the project."

"But you came back without your commanding officer, how did that happen?" Edwards asked.

Birch flinched at the question. They had been walking along an artificial, molded dirt road toward the cluster of gray buildings at the center of *Town Square*. He stopped suddenly, turning on Edwards. For a moment he didn't speak, and when he did the words came clipped and hard.

"He went out to secure the equipment at the quarry before the storm. He never came back."

They walked on in silence. Edwards seemed to sense that the conversation was over and didn't pursue the subject any further.

They passed through the crumbling remains of a miniature forest. The false dirt of the fanciful country road gave way to a cobbled street leading to the center of town. As they walked the road twisted, taking them between the first two buildings. Edwards stopped to look at one. It had a large window, intact, but impossible to see through because of the dirt smeared across the pane. Wiping it clean, he looked in.

"Junk," he muttered, shaking his head.

Birch looked in. It was junk. It was a display window filled

with dusty, moldering stuff- knick-knacks and an odd assort-
ment of useless items, all arranged in a symmetrical display.

"I don't believe it," Edwards said, bending down for a
second look. "It's a store! They go to all the crazy lengths of
building a base out on a piece of rock like this and what do
they do with it? Turn it into the galaxy's most remote
shopping mall! What was NASA planning to work on next-
the first interplanetary burger chain?"

"Sure," Birch answered grumpily. Edwards' attitude
annoyed him, even if it agreed with his own. It was okay for
him to think NASA's deals with Industry had turned it into an
enormous joke, but he didn't like anyone else pointing it out.
Besides, the final decision to include these things had been
based on sound research and considered opinions on the
psychological needs of the colonists. *Man shall not live by work
alone*. They needed to shop. They needed somewhere to let off
steam, somewhere to live a normal life, and *Town Square* was
designed for that very purpose.

"Do you suppose one of these places here does mani-
cures?" Edwards smirked, glancing around the town. "I could
really do with a good manicure! Too bad I forgot my wallet."

"Don't get cute," Birch snapped. "You weren't exactly
above making a buck yourself, were you? You all had a pretty
good angle going back on Earth with your Ares zoo act. *'Roll
up, roll up! Take a peek at the freak- for a price!'* You've got no
room to talk."

Edwards' expression darkened. "It wasn't like that," he
replied hotly. "We were researching, trying to find ways to
help the Ares. A lot of people just wanted to kill them out-
right, wipe them out for what they'd done. They've destroyed
whole cities, hundreds-of-thousands have died. They're
bloody savages, but I wanted to help them. If we could find a
way, maybe through selective breeding, or therapy, or drugs,
then maybe we could tone them down, rehabilitate them, and
bring them back into society. It was for their own good, and
they wouldn't even know what was happening. In the enviro-

dome they could live out their lives without ever seeing how we were helping them. In that way, we could save them."

"Now *that* doesn't sound like much of a life." Birch shook his head in disgust. "You talk about them like they're animals, some kind of species to be bred."

"What do you expect? They act like animals! I didn't see you doing anything different with that Ares kid when he killed your friend. You almost beat him to death, and that was over a single life. Imagine how you'd feel seeing whole cities burned, and they're still doing it! They'd do more if they could. Maybe, in the end, the only way to stop them is to kill them, but I'm willing to try something different."

For a moment both men were silent. Edwards' words had struck a little too close to home for Birch's comfort. There were many times since then when he had come close to killing the Ares kid. He still might do it, he knew that.

"I suppose," Birch finally answered bitterly, "that it was all for our own good too when you led us by the nose to be the next big exhibit in your president's personal petting zoo?"

Edwards sighed. "I didn't know anything about that. I'm just a very small cog in a very big machine. All I was told was that because of my knowledge of the Ares I was assigned to help take you across the country. That's it. I knew as much about their plans as you did."

"Well, I didn't exactly see you jumping to our rescue when you did find out!"

"If I had tried, you wouldn't have seen me at all. Going against them openly, right under their noses, would have been stupid. I didn't agree with what they did, but there wasn't anything I could do about it."

"Maybe," Birch admitted reluctantly, "but why didn't you try to help us later, when we got free? Instead, you just spent the whole time trying to talk us into going back to the zoo or begging us to leave you behind. Why would you want to go running back to Michaels instead of going on with us if you were really on our side?"

Edwards laughed scornfully. "What, stay behind and miss out on all of *this*?" He gestured with open arms, taking in the wide scene of desolation around them. "Oh yes, I can see your point! What could ever possess me to want to stay home instead of experiencing this trip of a lifetime to a dilapidated, abandoned, interplanetary shopping mall? You missed your calling, Birch- you should have been a travel agent. All aboard for the *Major's Magical Mystery Tour*! Destination: death most likely." Edwards turned away from the window. His voice had risen almost a shout, but now it dropped again to little more than a whisper.

"We should never have left. You would have been safe, and I would have been home," he mumbled. "You know, I never expected much, and I got what I expected, probably less, but at least it was something. My whole life I've done what I was supposed to do. Forced to eat, drink, and think the way I was told. I couldn't breathe, except maybe for a few minutes early every morning when I was alone at the zoo. Then I could be free. I could breathe it in, great gulps of the stuff, packing it into my lungs, stuffing myself with it so that I could hold my breath, keeping the freedom inside until the next day when I could fill up on it again. But now that's gone. Because of you, I was forced onto that fool's mission across the country that almost killed us all. Because of you, I've been blasted into space, and now because of you, I'm standing here on this dust-ball of a planet looking at rotten old knick-knacks through the dirty shop window of a dead colony's shopping mall. Everything I do is because of you. I'll never be free of you. Here I am in the vastness of space and I'm still as trapped as I ever was."

Birch shrugged. "Nobody's free," he answered coolly, "not even for a few minutes. Some of us are just unlucky enough to know it. Maybe you'd rather be one of your Ares."

Edwards said nothing, but his eyes blazed with fury. His lips moved slightly, as though he was struggling to say something, but no sound came. He walked away.

For a time Birch simply watched him go, expecting him to turn back at any moment, but he didn't. He just kept walking, never looking back, until finally, he disappeared through one of the exits. Birch let him go. He wouldn't stray too far in a place like this. Where could he go?

Birch walked toward the center of the enclosure. On either side, he saw the outer walls of *Town Square*, made to look like the exterior walls of a row of classical European apartments. Their darkened windows stared down at him, like the hollowed out sockets of empty skulls. Each had a balcony. Some still had chairs sitting out, ready for the occupants to come out and sit on them. Nothing moved, but he could still feel the windows watching him.

Birch knew how it worked. Those apartments had been reserved for the important people. Even in space, there was a hierarchy. You could never escape that- no matter how far you traveled. The accommodation surrounding *Town Square* was as close to an earthlike existence as anyone could expect out here, and so naturally they would have been set aside for only the most influential members of the community. The governor, top administrators, military brass, wealthy and influential citizens- those were the type of people who would have lived here. Birch made a mental note to check these homes later if nothing turned up at the administrative offices. There was always the chance that their personal records might hold some clue about the fate of the colony.

Birch approached a small stone bridge spanning a dried up riverbed. This marked the entrance to the very center of *Town Square*. The governor's office was on the other side.

Everywhere signs of a forgotten normality persisted. A half filled trash can, empty park benches, a vacant food stand all spoke of the lives that had once existed here. On the riverbed, there rested an old miniature riverboat lying crookedly on one side. Its jolly, red paint faded to a murky brown, and the tattered ribbons of cloth that might once have been festive bunting hung limply over its side.

The river and the boat had been part of the original plan, Birch remembered that. It was all about 'putting the *fun* back into functionality', as NASA had termed it. The river had been both. It served as an irrigation system, fed by the underground ice lake discovered by Birch's crew during their survey mission. Equally important however was the river's decorative aspect. It had long been recognized that over an extended period the human mind craved its natural surroundings. Short missions were not a problem, even a mission of a few years was manageable for a hardened astronaut, but it was a problem for permanent colonies. Too long without the green and blue of earth and sky caused mental disorientation. It led to dangerous psychological problems, and eventually even psychotic episodes. Somehow we were just hardwired that way. Take us too long from our intended Eden and we would surely die. Training didn't help, even upbringing made little difference. Too much time in space would kill you or lead you to kill someone else. For that reason, the river and *Town Square* were vital for the colony's long-term survival. The flowing water, the green vegetation, even the simulated blue of the sky projected on the glass overhead were all important elements of this survival.

As he crossed the bridge he heard something. He had become so used to the silence that it startled him. At first, he thought it was a voice calling his name, but the impression melted into a high pitched electrical hum, like the sound of a powerful amplifier waiting to be used. That was strange. There wasn't any power getting through to *Town Square*. The little energy they had managed to produce was all concentrated on their living quarters.

Birch looked down at his suit's computer screen. Edwards' reading was still there. He was some distance away. It looked like he had been heading back to the habitable zone, but he was coming back now. His dot was moving fast. It looked like he was running.

"Edwards," Birch radioed, but there wasn't any answer.

"Edwards!" Birch tried again, but still, he didn't get a reply.

"Jane, have you gotten any word from Edwards over the last ten minutes?" No answer there either.

"Jane, are you there? Respond please," but still there was no answer. Birch tapped his helmet, trying to adjust his settings, but could still only pick up static.

"Great," Birch muttered looking down at his display again. Edwards was still moving fast. He would probably be in sight in a couple of minutes, but Birch had no idea why he was running. Was he being chased and if so by what? Was there anything he could do to help? He decided to try.

He glanced around, looking for something he could use as a weapon. There wasn't much. Finally, he noticed an iron bar that had been the crossbeam to an ornate iron lamppost. It wasn't much, but it would have to do.

He ran for a nearby set of stairs. He was a quarter of the way up when the buzzing intensified into a painful screeching howl. Birch instinctively put his hands to his helmet, and in the movement saw the sky flickering from its natural gray into an unmistakable Earthy blue, but the impression didn't last. The glass panels quickly crackled and fizzed, before settling into an angry, rolling bank of red cloud.

Suddenly Edwards appeared through the door at the top of the stairs. He ran awkwardly down, two steps at a time, waving his arms wildly. He seemed to be trying to shout something to him, but Birch's headset still wasn't functioning properly, and even if it was the only thing he could hear was the deafening electrical screech.

Tightening his grip on the metal bar Birch ran up, ready to take on whatever came, but nothing appeared. A few seconds later Edwards had nearly reached him, and launched himself at Birch, sending them both toppling over, crashing down the steps to the street below.

What happened next was a jumble of events that Birch could make little sense of at the time. The metal rod flew from his hand, landing further up the steps, before clanging down after them. Edwards was on top of him, his weight pushing them down the stairs, his face contorted in a fruitless attempt to communicate without sound. Above the screeching, Birch heard the striking of the bell from *Town Hall* clock, this despite the lack of power and the fact that the time only read *ten minutes-to-seven*. The clock tower was directly opposite now and, even as they fell, Birch saw scrawled across the clock face in giant red letters that same word, 'EVIL', just as they had found in *Main Control*.

More troubling still was the sky. On his back now, looking up he saw massive swirling red clouds twisting and turning across the glass ceiling. It looked like the satellite picture of a hurricane descending upon them. Birch was just attempting to warn Edwards of their impending doom when the 'eye' of the storm began to glow, radiating a harsh pulsating light. The hum of electrical current intensified, surrounded them, and they both looked up in time to see a bolt of power crashing down to obliterate them.

TWENTY-SIX

Birch didn't see what happened, but he felt it. A flashing bolt of electricity crashed down nearby, striking above them, further up the stairs. He didn't realize it at the time, but the motion of the metal bar flying from his hand had provided enough distraction for the electrical charge to target it instead of them. The impact shook the ground and Birch's helmet hit the pavement.

Turning over, Birch saw the sky. The lightning seemed to have relieved the pressure, it had mellowed, but it wouldn't last. Already the clouds were beginning to swirl back into the same storm pattern he had seen a moment ago.

Birch struggled to his feet. Edwards was up already and grabbing his arm, trying to pull him up the stairs, but Birch shook him off and ran to the center of *Town Square*. Edwards hesitated, apparently torn between the safety of the exit and the danger of following Birch. He followed him.

Birch ran for cover. His best chance was a portico with pretentious Greek columns a few feet ahead. Glancing up he could already see the same white effect glowing at the center of the cloud formation. It was going to strike. Looking back, he saw Edwards lagging behind, puffing his way toward him. He wasn't going to make it. In three swift steps, Birch was at his side again, pulling him toward the shelter. The white glow intensified, the strike was seconds away. Without thinking Birch shoved Edwards hard, sending him toppling the last few steps toward cover, before launching himself after him.

With a thundering crash, the lightning fell. Birch barely made it. He landed under cover just as the bolt hit, sending sparks flying up from the cobbled pavement where he had stood just a moment before.

"That was too close," Birch muttered, but no one could hear him of course; he was still getting interference on his headset. He pulled Edwards toward him and gestured to *Town Hall* across the street. They had to make a run for it. Edwards nodded to show that he understood, but he didn't look very happy about it.

Birch looked up again. Already the clouds were gathering and swirling in preparation for the next strike. He sighed. They didn't have long. Maybe it would have been smarter to stay under cover and catch their breath for a minute, but he didn't trust that lightning. He wasn't sure how safe they were, even under here. Clearly, it was following them and he felt it was better to be a moving target than a sitting duck.

Tapping Edwards' shoulder he gestured out into the street before running for the main entrance of *Town Hall*. Edwards sighed and followed after him.

In the open again, he could hear the sound of the rain beating heavily on the cobblestones around him, but there was no rain. The street was perfectly dry. It must have been a trick of the environmental system. *Town Square* was designed to simulate weather patterns as a way to maintain an earthlike existence for the colonists. Without a ready supply of water from the ice reservoir, it must have been reduced to this dry storm. Obviously, the lightning was still working, but even that wasn't working as it should. It was supposed to provide a harmless visual display to accompany simulated storms- not become a deathly menace targeting people in the street.

They made it before the next strike landed. The lightning

came down with a crash in the street, sending more sparks showering around them.

The wind was picking up now. Somewhere high above their heads the giant fans, that were supposed to produce a gentle breeze, were whirring above their recommended capacity, blowing a gale that threatened to send Birch and Edwards flying back into the street, out into the electrical storm.

"Something doesn't want us to get in!" Birch shouted above the howling wind, but of course, Edwards couldn't hear him. Communication was still dead.

Birch lunged for the door. Holding the ornate brass handle tightly with both hands he pulled himself up and tried to get in, but it was locked. He was confronted with a keypad, but it was dead. Birch didn't know any codes anyway unless it would accept his personal NASA code, but that seemed like a long shot.

He tried to break in- shoving his shoulder hard against the metal door, but it wouldn't budge. There wasn't much more he could do. He tried a few buttons on the keypad again but got no response. He tried pushing the door again, harder this time, but it was futile. He was just resting, gathering strength for another desperate attempt when the keypad sparked, fizzled, and shot a beam of red light into his face.

Birch wailed in pain. Edwards shouted and tried to pull him away, but already the crimson glow had seized him, narrowing its focus to a razor shaft of light that plunged deep into his eye. His body stiffened, transfixed in the flickering beam. An instant later the light turned green and let him go. He fell limply to the ground, unable to move.

There was a slight, almost imperceptible click as the door swung out a few millimeters revealing a tiny slither of an opening. Edwards pulled it open and dragged Birch in, slamming it shut behind them.

The darkness embraced them. It was quite. The storm outside rattled at the door but couldn't get in. For a time all Birch could do was breath. Something had been wrong with that eye scan. He was used to invasive security measures, they were pretty standard for astronauts, but that one had felt more like something alive, something gnawing into his brain, than anything he had experienced before.

Pain throbbed through Birch's skull. It took a while before he could move and even longer for him to struggle back to his feet. When he finally did Edwards had to steady him to keep him from falling again.

In the glow of their helmet lights, they looked around the hall they had entered. It was striking in its normality. It had the look of a standard civic building, like a county courthouse or the town hall in a small municipality somewhere in the Midwest. Marbled floors and a wide staircase with ornate iron railings, doors leading off the hall (no doubt leading to the smaller offices of smaller officials) all were comforting reminders of the bland reality these explorers had left behind.

At the far end of the hall, a large ornate set of double doors invited further investigation. Feeling his strength return Birch limped slowly toward them. Edwards followed.

Beyond the doors, they discovered a small but impressive chamber. A semicircle of twenty chairs and metal tables was facing a stage with a carved railing and an imposing wooden desk rising above them all. Behind it was the seal of the colony- two gloved hands shaking, two worlds on opposite sides of the seal, and a field of stars between. This was the elective body of the colony's government, but the position and construction of the desks made it clear where the power really was. This wasn't a surprise to Birch. It had been agreed early on that survival in space was tough and required strong, decisive leadership. The elective body could advise their governor, but they could not control him. Only in the most extreme circumstances could he ever be challenged.

Birch climbed the stairs to the stage. He ran his gloved hand along the banister, feeling it slide beneath his touch. He sat in the chair behind the desk, but there was nothing useful here, only dust. He wiped it with his hand, looking at the grain of the wood beneath.

Birch looked down at the empty chairs on the floor below. Even now in this empty room, he could almost feel a palpable sense of the power of this place, like the hum of an electrical substation. Everything about it said power. A desk like this could certainly give you a superiority complex, so high above the others and made of wood. Wood was rarer and more valuable than gold out here. You could dig for gold, there was plenty enough of it on R67.3, but you had to grow a tree. That took time. This desk was real wood and represented the undiluted power of the governorship.

Birch shook his head and got up to go. This place wasn't providing any more answers than anywhere else they had explored yet. It was all still a mystery, yet he hoped he might find something more concrete in the governor's offices on the floors above.

They came back into the main hall and climbed the iron staircase up to the third floor where another impressive set of doors announced the entryway to the governor's offices. They were left open, one hung crookedly from its hinges. It was the first sign that anything unusual had happened here. Up to now everything in Town Hall had looked so ordered that it was impossible to imagine that anything could ever have gone wrong. You almost felt that probably everyone was on lunch break and would return at any moment.

They walked through a reception and two smaller workstations before finally reaching the governor's personal office. It was spacious and ornate, as Birch had expected. Art from both Earth and this world lined the walls. All were bright and colorful. Even in the pictures of scenes on R67.3 the artist seemed to have found some light and vibrancy on this dead planet.

At first glance, the only thing that seemed out of place here was that a drawer of the governor's desk was open, but as he approached Birch saw that gouged across its wooden surface was that word again, 'EVIL'.

Birch sat at the desk. From here he could see a large picture window, and through it, *Town Square* spread out in its grandeur beneath it. The artificial storm had died down out there. Perhaps without them, there was no need for such a display.

A sudden movement in the room startled Birch and looking down he saw a screen rising up out of the desk. There was the electrical crackle and groan of an old computer sputtering to life, but the screen remained blank. However, as he watched, the hue of its black began to alter just enough to tell him something was happening.

He waited a few minutes, but nothing changed. He tried a few codes on the keyboard but nothing came up. Finally, he turned his attention back to the desk and the contents of its drawers.

There wasn't anything there, nothing significant anyway. There were a few personal items, but no data documents, no personal recording devices, nothing to tell him what had happened here or what possible danger they might be facing now. Birch leaned back in the chair and sighed before turning his attention back to the computer screen. It flickered white, then flashed the colony seal before settling into the main data page.

Birch let out a low whoop and settled down to the keyboard. He had no idea how the console was getting power, nor how he had gotten into the secure part of the network so easily, but this was his first chance to get at the core data, and he was going to take it.

Within a few minutes, he was scanning the colony's plans, seeking any alternate sites for ships that could get them off the planet. As he had expected Primary Base had a number of ships registered there, and a few of the smaller outposts had lightweight pods that might work too, if any of them were left. Most likely their hangars were empty like *Colony I*'s, the records seemed to indicate that, but maybe one of the smaller bases had something left. He would have to check himself.

Birch was just turning his attention to the governor's records when the display went blurry and disappeared into a single line of gray static. It quickly refocused, the picture changing into a head and shoulders shot of a strange, digitized figure. It was a man with slicked-back blonde hair, a suit, sunglasses, and an impossible leering smile.

"That's it," the man giggled distortedly as a corrugated metal background swayed sickeningly behind him. "Here we go… catch the wave!"

Birch blinked at the screen for a moment, unsure of what he was seeing.

"What is that?" Edwards asked, looking over his shoulder.

"I've got no idea," Birch answered, too surprised to even notice the significance of hearing Edwards' voice again. "It must be some kind of sick joke."

The figure on the screen leaned in toward the camera extending a finger at them "Ohhhhhhhh," he moaned, "your love… it's fading."

"It sure is," Birch muttered, clicking out of the display. He had seen enough. This had all the appearance of a juvenile prank and he didn't have time to waste on it..

"D-d-d-d-on't touch that dial!" the strange figure stuttered as his image reappeared on the screen without Birch restoring it. "Or I shall get very an-an-angry! You wouldn't like me when I get angry!"

"Y-y-y-youuu need to listen. I hate to get all Robinett on you, but if you hope to find me you really have to get the point. H-h-h-h-haaaaaahaha".

"Who are you?" Birch growled. "What do you want?" But the figure seemed stuck, frozen mid-laugh before glitching into a completely unrelated pose. Birch tried again. "Who are you? What are you?" But there was still no answer. The figure only tilted his head awkwardly, as though trying to figure out what was being said. Birch gave up. It must have been some sort of automated program. There was no meaningful communication going on here.

The man froze again, a look of mock terror crossing his elastic face. "Oh no," he cried dramatically, "they're coming to get me!" He screamed.

The screen faded to black. Lines of distortion rolled across the display, and then the original image returned.

Birch and Edwards looked at each other, at a loss for what to say about what they had just seen.

For a moment there was silence. Then a rusty metallic ring sounded from an old push button telephone sitting on the desk. Birch hadn't noticed it before, and he wondered what an ancient relic like that would be doing in the governor's office.

He picked up the receiver.

"Hello?" he answered tentatively, holding the earpiece awkwardly to his helmet.

"I-I-I see you got my message," the same distorted voice answered. "The fact you got this f-f-far proves you're not one of them, but it doesn't prove you're one of us." The voice seemed somber, less crazed than before.

"I-i-it's been a long time, but I know w-w-where you are. Now you have to f-f-find me if you can. You better hurry, though. You don't have l-l-long."

There was a click and Birch was left with the dial tone buzzing angrily in his ear.

TWENTY-SEVEN

"Major Birch! Major Birch! What are you doing out there?" Jane's quivering voice came as a welcome interruption to his thoughts.

"Birch here," he soothed. "Don't worry. We're fine. I think there was some kind of security mechanism in *Town Square* breaking up our signal, but it looks like we got around that once we got into the main computer here in Town Hall."

"Yeah, yeah, that's great," Jane sputtered, "but what are you doing?"

"Well, right now we're sitting in the governor's office," Birch answered with more than a hint of irritation creeping into his voice. "What are you doing?"

"I'm sitting here watching all the power reserves we have being sucked dry at a rate twenty times faster than they were five minutes ago!"

"What?" Birch put his hand to the side of his helmet, as though her words must have been the result of a malfunction in his earpiece. "What's happening?"

"Like I said," Jane snapped, "I've been watching our power drain away for the last five minutes, so let me ask you again, what are you doing?"

Birch and Edwards both looked at the computer. "Wait a minute. I've got some equipment running here, but there's no way it should be draining that much power. Let me check it out, though."

"I suggest you hurry. We're losing months of power by the second right now and if this keeps up we're not going to have any plan A, B, or C to fall back on, only a plan D-E-A-D!"

"Yeah, I'm on it!" Birch pulled the keyboard toward him. His gloved hands tapped furiously at the keys.

"I don't get it," he was mumbling to himself. "One simple computer shouldn't make that much difference."

"Okay," he called to Jane, "I've got everything shutting down. Down in five- four- three- two- one. Okay, shutdown complete. We're offline now."

"It isn't making any difference," Jane shouted a moment later. "If anything the flow has increased slightly. That's not it! There must be some other cause."

"Okay," Birch sighed. "I'm going to reboot the computer here and try and follow up on it from this end. You work on your side and let me know if you come up with anything. How long do you think we've got if the power flow keeps up at its current rate?"

"I don't know," Jane's voice was very small, "three, maybe four weeks. That's if it doesn't get any worse."

"Well, that's something anyway," Birch reasoned.

"Not much," Jane answered flatly.

The computer hummed back to life. Birch was soon facing the same menu he had been exploring moments ago when the bizarre interruption had broken in on him, but there wasn't any sign of a repetition. He tried selecting things in the same order as before, but whatever had triggered the event last time wasn't working now.

Finally, he gave up trying to get back into the program and concentrated on simply finding it. He started scanning files. He wasn't exactly sure what he was looking for, but he was certain that when he found it he would know the cause of the power drain.

Files streamed by, flowing like water across the screen until Birch's eyes glazed over at the sheer volume of the data. For nearly an hour he watched. As a result, he almost missed it when it flew by, but somehow his mind registered it a moment after he had seen it- a file with a familiar word: *Robinett*. He backtracked. Yes, it had almost slipped by, but there it was, the same thing the man in the message had mentioned. That was too big to be a coincidence.

He flagged the file. It was a program buried deep in the base's mainframe. Triple encrypted, it was big and it was running live now, but after a few attempts it was clear that there was no way for him to shut it down or break into it, at least none that he could figure out just yet. There was little doubt about it being the source of the power drain. It was running at a huge capacity, bigger even than most of the base's primary systems.

"What are you?" Birch muttered as the *'Access Rejected: Unauthorized Route'* message flashed up for the fourth time.

"Jane," Birch spoke into his radio mouthpiece as he tapped at the keyboard, "I think I've isolated the rogue program, but I haven't been able to make any progress with it yet. It's running independently of everything else and there doesn't seem to be any easy way to get at it. I'm patching the information over to your computer. You'll have work on it there. We're heading back. Keep me updated if you make any progress."

"Right," she replied simply and clicked off without further comment.

'Access Rejected' flashed up on the screen again. Birch sighed and leaned back in his chair. None of this made any sense. The garbled, crazy message from the computer had led him clearly to this file and, even though it was encrypted and impossible to access, it wasn't exactly hidden. It stuck out a mile if you knew what you were looking for. It was almost as though the computer wanted him to find it, but now for some

reason it wouldn't let him in.

Birch leaned over to pick up the phone again, resorting to a last desperate notion that maybe he could reach the computer through that, but he was startled to discover that it had gone. While he had been engrossed in the files the phone had disappeared. He examined the desk more closely, trying to figure out what had happened to it, but there were no cracks or any other signs in the smooth wooden surface to give any clue. The phone had simply vanished.

Birch shook his head. They had hit a dead end. There wasn't anything more they could do here. He got up and walked to the window. It looked peaceful enough outside, but he didn't trust it. Another storm could start up in an instant. Still, they had to get out of here and there wasn't any other way. They would just have to take their chances, head for the nearest exit and hope that the lightning couldn't keep up.

"Well," Birch said taking a last look around, "I guess we're done here." Edwards nodded and soon they were descending the stairs and exiting the building. The door closed, locking with a click behind them. They paused for a moment under the cover of the arched porch, watching the sky for any change, but it remained an unaltered cloudless blue.

"Okay, let's go!" Birch barked and ran into the street.

He headed for the nearest exit. Ducking and weaving, they sped along as best they could in their cumbersome EVA suits, trying to avoid a renewed onslaught of electricity, but nothing happened. The sky didn't darken, no clouds formed, and no lightning came. If anything it seemed to be brightening, clearing into the golden glow of a perfect day's sunlight, but in Birch's mind, this wasn't an improvement. There was something unsettling about seeing this dead place bathed in such lively light. It was out of place, like a sunny day in a country graveyard. Everything seemed so beautiful and perfect until you considered what lay beneath the surface.

Reaching the stairs, Birch paused, waiting for Edwards to catch up. It seemed pointless to run. It was clear by now that they were no longer a target. Whatever had been directing the storm against them earlier had somehow been mollified by what had happened in *Town Hall*. Birch didn't know why-they hadn't disabled the defense system or entered any codes, but somehow it seemed to have accepted them.

Edwards reached him a moment later. Puffing from the exertion, he barreled past Birch without even looking and hurled himself at the stairs.

"Calm down," Birch snapped impatiently as Edwards jumped the first ten steps in three leaping bounds. "The boogie man's not going to get you. Look." He pointed to the blue skies above. "See? *Clear sky at day- astronauts not run away!*"

"Sorry," Edwards replied, stopping on the stairs. "I just put my head down and ran for the exit." He looked up at the sky. "Why do you think it's stopped trying to kill us?"

Birch shrugged. "Maybe it hasn't. With just three weeks of power left, we'll end up just as dead if we don't figure out how to shut that program down. We should get going."

Birch hesitated, though, lingering for a last look at the elaborate normality of Town Square. It was all a beautiful lie of course. The idea that things could be like Earth out here was a dangerous illusion. Things were so easy on Earth. It was like breathing. Everything was natural. You didn't have to think about it; it just happened, but out here nothing was easy. You had to struggle for every breath, and with just three weeks to save themselves Birch knew it was going to be another tough fight.

"Okay," he finally said, turning his back on *Town Square*, "let's get out of here." They marched up the stairs, through the double doors, and into one of the base's many uniform gray corridors.

The walk back was mostly uneventful. At times they caught the impression of a flashing light or heard a bleeping ping where formerly everything had been silent and still. He had the uneasy suspicion that they were being watched. Their little detour into *Town Square* had been a disaster. They hadn't learned anything useful. What they had discovered had only added to their confusion, and in the end, their bungled attempt had awakened something that had a good chance of killing them in three weeks. He didn't look forward to hearing what Jane had to say about all that.

As it turned out Jane had nothing to say about it at all. She showed no interest in the whys and wherefores of how it had all happened. Instead, she was already diving enthusiastically into a plan to get them out of it. When he arrived Birch hardly had time to get his helmet off before she was at him, bombarding him with all the details of how it could be done.

Birch didn't like her plan much. It was risky, dangerous, and probably their only chance of survival. They had to split up. Jane and Edwards would go to *Primary Base* and see if there was a chance of repairing the power systems there. If they managed it *Colony I* would be abandoned and they could start over again, setting up habitation in the older base.

Birch and Lauren meanwhile would stay behind at *Colony I*, working on shutting down the rogue program and stopping the power drain. If they succeeded Jane and Edwards could return and they would all resume their work there.

The plan made sense. It gave them two chances, a 'plan A' and a 'plan B', but he still couldn't make himself like it. Sending Jane and Edwards over there alone seemed like a bad idea. They still didn't know why *Primary Base* had shot the pod down. They had all dismissed it as some sort of automated defense system, but that was just a guess. Was there something over there, something that had targeted them, something that would be waiting for them when they arrived?

And then there was that voice on the phone in the governor's office. It had said something about knowing where they were. Was there really someone else here after all these years, alive and watching them? The voice hadn't directly threatened them, but the tone of it made Birch uncomfortable. It had sounded crazy, and crazy people could do anything. For both these reasons, Birch didn't like Jane's plan. He argued that he should be the one to go, but Jane wouldn't accept that. She had been quick to point out that he wasn't qualified for the job. She knew much more about the power systems and would have a better chance of getting things running over there. Birch couldn't argue with that, and when she reminded him of the limited time they had to get it done he had to admit that she was right. Besides, he reasoned darkly, who knew if anywhere on this world was safe. There was just as much potential danger staying here as going over there.

That was it then. Against his better judgment, Jane and Edwards were going over alone, and Birch was left to hope that for once the gnawing feeling in his gut that warned him of impending doom was wrong.

TWENTY-EIGHT

They were ready to go the next morning. Surprisingly little had remained to be done. By the time Birch and Edwards returned from *Town Square* Jane had it all in hand. She hadn't waited for Birch's approval; she had started getting things ready immediately. She had set aside oxygen supply, food, power cartridges, and tools. She had downloaded maps and schematics into her suit's computer. She had put together a timeframe that planned their movements to the minute to maximize their efficiency and increase their chances of success. After a fitful night's sleep, she was ready.

Birch could only marvel at Jane's quiet efficiency and fore-sight. She even had her transportation ready. In the bio-dome, she had found a couple of small two-man-buggies that she had been drip charging over the last few days before the power supply had gone critical. The fact that Jane hadn't seen fit to inform him of this little discovery before now irked him, but that was typical of her. For all her professed love of protocol she was still more than happy to leave Birch in the dark and forget that, as her commander, she had to tell him everything. But then she didn't see him as her legitimate commander. She had made that clear from the day he had taken over, and Birch was smart enough to realize that her recent silence on the subject didn't represent a change of heart, just a change of approach.

"Everything's stored, checked, and ready to go," Jane said, waving curtly to the camera above her head. She and Edwards were alone in the airlock. Birch and Lauren were at Main Control, watching their progress on a monitor as they worked on a solution to the power drain.

"Okay," Birch replied. "Stay safe and keep in regular contact. I want to hear from you every thirty minutes."

"Yeah," Jane answered flatly as she hit the button releasing the door mechanism. Birch looked up, trying to see her face, but she had turned away. The only thing he could see was the grainy outline of their suits passing through the doorway into the gray light of the surface.

Birch switched to an external camera and saw Jane and Edwards approaching the buggy. It was a squat little vehicle with two seats, big wheels, and a storage bin at the back piled high with necessary supplies to keep them alive over the next few weeks. They didn't need much more than that. If things hadn't been fixed by then they were all dead anyway.

The buggy's wheels spun in the dirt, kicking dust into the air as it pulled away. One of the suited figures looked briefly back. It was Edwards. He hadn't exactly been thrilled at the idea of heading over to *Primary Base*, but he had no choice. He never did, so as usual there hadn't been any more he could do than just shake his head and resign himself to whatever life threw at him.

"Report, Major Gray," Birch spoke into his desk microphone a few minutes later. "How's the equipment performing? Does it look like the buggy will hold up?"

"It's fine," she responded tersely. "I'll see you on the other side," and she clicked off.

Birch blinked at the screen, watching the buggy speed away toward the distant, dark blotch on the horizon that was the only sign of *Primary Base's* existence from here. He zoomed the camera in on the base, taking in its darkened dome, filling his screen with it. It was dead. No light or energy emanated from it. Like a massive black beetle caught scurrying across the planet's surface, it lay squashed and lifeless in eternal repose.

Birch shook his head, pulling the focus back from *Primary Base* to Jane and the buggy before turning his attention to his work.

For the first time, Birch had the tools to achieve something. As it turned out, their journey to *Town Square* hadn't been a total disaster. Obviously, it had compounded their problems in a lot of ways, but at the same time it had freed up a number of the base's computer operations. Without knowing exactly why it had happened, he gratefully noted that a large number of the records and files that had been blocked to them before had opened up since their return.

Birch and Lauren had relocated to Main Control. The slight increase in power consumption there was greatly offset by the greater efficiency of its superior equipment. Even so, they only used what was absolutely necessary. The lights were dimmed to a dusky gloom. Most of the control panels were dark, and the few that were lit were only kept running long enough to do what was needed before being shut down again.

In the dim glow of their workstations, the shadowy figures of Birch and Lauren could just be made out. Lauren was working on the direct approach. She was trying to break through the coding to get into the Robinett program. Her chances of success were slim. She wasn't exactly an expert in the field, but she was smart and probably had about as good a chance of breaking through as anyone did.

Birch had the harder job because it was possible. If Lauren succeeded it would be a miracle. If Birch failed it would be a disaster. It wasn't going to be easy. He was trying the indirect approach. Rather than attempting to break into the program he was searching the entire base's database, searching for any clue to who wrote it and why. If he could solve that little mystery he was sure he would have a better idea of how to access it and shut it down.

He started with the obvious, looking for any mention of the filename, *Robinett*, but he got nothing. He tried a few other snippets of speech he could remember from the crazed ravings of the man on the computer. He tried *'Catch the Wave'*, but got nothing again. He typed *'Fading Love'* and a single match flashed up on the screen. It was a music file with the title *'(I Know) I'm Losing You'*. Birch clicked on it and a muffled strain of guitar and cymbals sounded from a dusty speaker in the desk. "*Ooooooo*," a voice crooned in classic Motown style.

The music echoed through the room, reverberating in the rafters above them. Lauren looked up, puzzled by the sudden intrusion into their silence. The song itself was a simple one, a plea for the love of a wayward lover, the kind of thing probably sung, spoken, and sighed millions of times by millions of men and women, and yet in these gloomy surroundings the words somehow took on a deeper, darker meaning.

What was it the song had said? Something about seeing someone else in their eyes… about becoming cold and losing their soul… about being empty… and about how those effects were carried around in the air. No doubt these were originally intended as meaningful metaphors, beautiful words to convey the sorrow of a lost love, but Birch couldn't escape the feeling that the man in the computer had mentioned this song for another reason. He was trying to tell him something.

'Losing your soul', that was the gist of the words as they echoed in his brain. He glanced up at Main Control's large viewing screen where the word *'EVIL'* had been scrawled in massive red letters. This place was starting to get to him.

Birch leaned forward, staring down at his screen again. There was no way of telling who had posted the song. The date of the upload put it about a week before the last log entry from *Colony I*, but that was all he could find out. Birch was pretty sure it must have been the same person responsible for the crazy computer message, but that didn't get him very far. He still had no idea who it was. Everything he discovered only seemed to add to the mystery of the colony rather than help him solve it.

Birch tried a few more keywords, but every time he only hit another dead end. It was always the same. Every entry produced either no result at all or far too many to sift through in the time they had left, and so he had decided on a different approach. He would try to piece together the events that had led to the demise of the colony.

The messages were the key, he was sure of that. Someone in the middle of all the turmoil had left this trail of bread-crumbs to follow. Why? Were they intended to help or harm them? That was something he really couldn't answer yet.

He decided his best chance was to scan the base's voice logs and sort them according to emotional content. The computer could detect the slightest inflection in the voice and rate each entry according to the mood and the frame of mind of the speaker. Birch had them divided into three categories: calm, anxious, and panicked. The typical log would show up as mostly calm with a few anxious incidents and a very small number of panicked moments. *Colony One*, however, didn't match the usual model at all.

The computer started chronologically, sorting all the voice files in its memory. The pattern was striking. The three cate-gories were color coded- green, yellow, and red according to the level of emotion registered. The early entries tended toward green with a number of yellow and a few reds relating to technical issues and teething trouble at the base during its early days. Things settled down shortly after that into a pretty steady green with a few intermittent yellows and some very rare occurrences of red. Things had gone well.

The random sampling of the reports told Birch that every-thing had started smoothly. That was puzzling enough given that Birch's team hadn't laid the groundwork for that, but he had enough to worry about trying to figure out how things ended here at the colony without troubling himself too much with how they began.

He caught a few of the highlights. The first marriage (one of the advantages of being a colonist rather than NASA personnel was the allowance made for romance), the first birth (a girl with the most ominous historical appellation- Virginia Dare Chalmer), and the first death (an accident- Second Grade technician Bruce Marlowe fell into a ravine on the lower levels of *Primary Base*. His body was never found.)

Birch took in just enough to get a flavor of life in the colony, but these early green and yellow reports held little useful information. By the time a few years had progressed however the nature of the logs began to change. He could see that very visibly as the predominately green lines of data began to show gradual increases of yellow and red. Like the changing of the autumn leaves the transformation was gradual, with a few yellows and reds here and there, but once it took hold the change was swift and complete. The lines switched to mostly yellow with only a smattering of greens, then quickly transformed again into a wall of red. Entry after entry flipped by on the screen- red, red, red, red, yellow, red, red, red, red, red... by the last few months, the entries were uniformly red. Something had gone terribly wrong and panic had set in. Then the lines went blank. For some time after it seemed the power remained on and the computers made automated date checks, but there were no new entries, just dates. These numbers weren't green, yellow, or red, just a lifeless dark gray. They filled the screen, crawling past like the flat-lined heart rate of the dead.

Birch stopped the data and scrolled back up to the point where the log entries began turning consistently yellow. He resisted the temptation to simply play the colony's last log. Experience had taught him that the last gasping cries of a dying society weren't likely to give much enlightenment, just a sense of the panic and despair that was so natural when you reached the end. He had no desire to see that again. No, he was sure the answer wouldn't come at the end. It would come somewhere in the humdrum details of everyday life. Despite our human fears disaster rarely strikes suddenly. It creeps up on us. It slinks into our lives, unnoticed at first before it grows into what finally destroys us. This was what Birch looked for now- the subtle beginning of the end. He was sure this would tell him much more about the causes of this catastrophe than their final death cries.

It didn't take long to prove his theory right. His search started back where the green entries transitioned into yellow and red. Even after only the first couple of logs, it was clear that this was no ordinary concern. For a time it wasn't really clear what it was about. Some ominous cloud hung over the settlement, but no one seemed willing to name it, as though naming it would make it real, and so only vague fears were expressed.

It was a young Level Three technician that first named it. Perhaps he was too young to know the danger of being the first to be right, or perhaps he was just too scared to care, either way, his log was the first to openly acknowledge it. His face was blanched and his eyes wide as he reported,

'I think I saw Bruce today.'

Birch's eyes narrowed at that. Bruce? Bruce who? *Marlowe?* Birch pulled his chair closer and raised the volume on the speaker, trying to catch every word.

*'The guys have been slacking hard on me the
last few weeks, especially when they knew I had
duty shift down on The Lowers. I wasn't going to
let it get to me, but maybe I did. I don't know. All
I really know is that one minute I was working on
a power coupling off the main shaft, the next
something rushed by, knocked my light down and*

*broke it. I couldn't see what it was.
At first, I thought it was the guys trying to have
some fun with me, but after a minute or so
it came back. I'd been trying to feel my way back
up to the main shaft when it came back. I couldn't
see it but I could hear it, growling and snuffling
like an animal looking for food. I didn't care where I
was going, I ran for it and ended up back in the main
shaft. I was done for the day. I think I'm done for good!*

*I've never been one for all of those old Primary Base
scare stories, but I've had enough! If I can get a
transfer to Colony I I'll take it! It'll mean less pay but
there are some things that money can't buy.'*

"Lauren," Birch called across to her from his workstation. She looked up. "Get Jane on the radio. Warn her to watch herself over there. It seems like *Primary Base* had some unexplained problems." He felt stupid, even as he said the words. Warning Jane of a long dead threat made no sense, but then he wasn't sure of anything in this place. "Just tell her to keep a look out for trouble," he concluded weakly.

Birch turned his attention back to his own screen. He noted the young technician's name, Bill Parsons, and looked for further entries to follow up on his suspicions, but there were none. He had disappeared.

Birch finally found him. A few weeks later he had been listed as dead. He never got that transfer. The details beyond that were very sketchy. It looked like a cover-up, but you never could tell with these things if it was willful or natural ignorance at play.

"Um, Major," Lauren faltered, "I can't reach Major Grey. We seem to have lost her!"

"Lost her? What do you mean 'lost her'?"

"Well, she just isn't there. I've tried to reach her, but there's been no response. I've tried her tracking signal, but I got nothing. I've tried to get a visual on her but none of the cameras are picking her up. She's just disappeared.

Birch pulled his monitor toward him and switched to camera mode. He scanned up and down the route to *Primary Base*. There was no doubt about it, Lauren was right. Jane was gone.

TWENTY-NINE

Birch could have kicked himself. Letting Jane and Edwards disappear like that right under his nose was about the stupidest thing he could have done. He just hadn't believed they could be in any real danger out in the open, and so he hadn't been watching.

Again he scanned along the route to *Primary Base*, but there wasn't any trace of them. He was stumped. He couldn't imagine how they could have vanished so completely. Then he had a thought. He knew where they were.

It was a wide horizon of gray dirt, and if he hadn't had a premonition he probably would never have found them, but there they were. He saw them first as a small plume of gray dust heading away from *Primary Base* toward the foot of the mountains. He zoomed in to get a better look. Yes, Jane and Edwards were there. With their backs to him, it was difficult to make much out, but the buggy was traveling quickly, bumping and rolling across the rutted landscape.

"I've got them," Birch informed Lauren.

"Where?"

"Heading for the mountains."

Lauren shot a meaningful glance in Birch's direction, but as usual she kept her thoughts to herself. She pulled the location up on her own screen and for a moment they both blinked dumbly, watching the events unfold in the gloomy stillness of main control.

***

Edwards had no idea where they were going. It was a sensation he had grown accustomed to, only this time it had come as a surprise because for once he had thought he did know where they were going. They were supposed to be on their way to *Primary Base*, a place he had little appetite for visiting, but which now looked oddly desirable after Jane had veered away toward the distant mountain range.

"Where are you going?" he asked, but Jane barely acknowledged his question with a slight instinctive turn of the head. "Where are we going?" Edwards persisted, but he still got no response.

Edwards turned in his seat. The dust was flying up from the thick, black tires, choking the air about them. Through the haze, he could just make out the dark outline of *Primary Base* disappearing into the distance. Ahead there lay an expanse of dust, a barren plane leading to the foot of great gray mountain range. She was leading them into death.

"Have you gone off your nut?" Edwards snapped grabbing Jane's arm.

She swatted him away with surprising ferocity, hunching over the steering wheel like a mother bird guarding her nest. When she finally turned to address him her words were calm and reasoned, but there was something in her eyes that Edwards didn't like. She looked more like an Ares than a human in that moment, and he feared what she might do if he pushed her too far.

"You shouldn't worry so much. You'll be fine," she soothed icily. "I've got a little job to do first, then we'll get back to our safe little base. There's time for both."

Edwards watched the empty horizon before them and

sighed. Once again he was along for the ride, wherever it took him.

***

"Buggy One, this is Main Control seeking confirmation. You are off course, do you require assistance? Repeat, do you require assistance?" Static was the only answer. Lauren tried again, "Buggy One, do you require assistance?"

"Jane," Birch broke in, "where are you going?" but there was still no answer. He turned to Lauren. "Are we getting through?" he asked.

Lauren nodded. "We're transmitting okay. I'm not sure about their reception. It should be clear enough. There's no interference."

"Try concentrating on Edwards? Maybe he'd be more likely to answer."

Lauren shrugged. "I've tried that, but I got nothing from him. Either there's something unusual blocking the signal or they're just not answering. Whichever it is I don't see that there's much more we can do unless we go out after them."

The buggy sped across the screen. "Jane," Birch repeated, "where are you going?" Still no answer. "Where are you going, Jane? Report Major Grey- where do you think you're going?" He paused. "Jane… Jane, I *know* where you're going." He was sure she could hear him now. He saw her head came up on the screen, but she kept driving.

"You're wasting your time, Jane. You're wasting all of our time. Get back to *Primary Base* immediately!"

Jane ignored his order. If anything her speed only seemed to increase. Lauren was right. The only way he could stop her now was to go out and get her himself.

***

Edwards grabbed the hand-bar as the buggy took another

rut at top speed. If they didn't shake apart it looked like they would reach the foot of the mountains in the next twenty minutes. They loomed ever larger as they approached, but the closer proximity didn't improve their appearance. A stark, rocky wall of stone shot skyward. The dark gray cliffs almost merged with the powder gray of the dusty sky. This was a terrible place. If Jane planned to ascend those mountains he had no idea how they would manage it.

A short time later they skidded to a stop. There was nothing remarkable about this place. Jane had been looking down at her wrist computer, checking on something before they had pulled up. She was glancing at it again; then scanned the horizon, trying to get her bearings, before climbing out.

"Well, this was definitely worth a visit," Edwards observed bitterly as he stepped out of the buggy. "Show me to the souvenir shop. I bet it's a doozy!"

"Shut up, will you, Edwards; I need to concentrate. You know, I think you've been around Birch too much. You're starting to sound like him."

"I've been around all of you too much," Edwards responded gloomily as he looked around, trying to see the significance of this desolate place. There wasn't much. A few large stones lay scattered haphazardly around. Some of them had smooth edges but all were cracked and crumbling. Apart from that, there wasn't anything different here, except for the sheer cliff face of the mountain some fifty meters away.

Jane was at the back of the buggy, taking out a shovel, some brushes, and other technical equipment he didn't recognize. She was looking down at her wrist computer again, checking something on it against the landscape, and walking slowly toward the mountain. Finally, she stopped, dropped to her knees and began to dig.

"What are you digging for," Edwards quipped, "gold, oil, power cells?"

Jane didn't look up. "Something more valuable than any of those, but shut up Edwards. I'm trying to concentrate."

Edwards shrugged and walked away. From here *Primary Base* was nearly as far as it had been when they had started from *Colony I* earlier in the day. It appeared as little more than a dark smudge on the horizon. He grabbed a set of binoculars from the buggy and held them to his helmet. Through the electronic display, he zoomed in on the base. Up close it was as dark and dead as he had expected. He panned around, looking for *Colony One* and found it. From here it looked just as dead as its sister base. There was no clue to indicate that anyone was alive and working in there.

He lowered the binoculars and looked around. He was overcome with an immense feeling of his vulnerability. He was nothing more than a tiny speck of life in this hostile environment. How could he hope to survive?

He raised the binoculars to his face again. *Colony One* was dark and solid, but behind in saw something that made him catch his breath, the gray sky behind was swirling, darkening to an iron-gray. A storm was coming in.

***

Birch hadn't seen it on the radar. He hadn't even bothered to check before Jane and Edwards had left because she was smart enough to look for herself. She had everything ready for their departure, so how could she have missed such an obvious step. The unpalatable answer was that she hadn't. She must have seen that the storm was coming, but she had gone ahead anyway.

There wasn't much Birch could do. If he went after them he probably wouldn't get there before the storm hit, and even if he did, what good could he do? It would just mean three of them trapped out in the storm instead of two.

"Jane!" he barked into his microphone. "I know you can hear me, you ignorant excuse for an astronaut, so don't give me any of that *'my radio doesn't work' stuff.'* Look, there's a big storm coming your way. Worse than the last! If you both catch the brunt of that it'll rip you to pieces. I don't care how important you think your little egg hunt is, if you don't get moving now you will die!"

Jane didn't answer, but her head lifted slightly as she glanced back over her shoulder. She kept working.

"Maybe I'm being a little too subtle for you, Grey!" he bellowed into his microphone. "Let me spell it out for you, leave or you're going to die! Not that I care much either way about you right now, but your reckless stupidity is going to get everyone else killed too. We all need you to complete your mission!"

Jane didn't even look up this time. She just kept working, and there wasn't a thing he could do to make her stop.

***

"Um, Major Grey," Edwards stuttered, "we've got a problem." He pointed to the advancing clouds, but Jane didn't stop to look.

"I know," she muttered impatiently and kept digging. "I just need a couple of minutes and we'll be ready." She reached for a data pad, tapped it a few times and nodded. Lifting an object from the hole, she put it into her pocket. "Okay, that's it." She leaped up, grabbing the equipment. "Let's go!"

She ran for the buggy with Edwards a few steps behind. Throwing the equipment in the back, they jumped into their seats and had barely landed before the buggy peeled away toward *Primary Base*.

***

Birch caught a last glimpse of Jane and Edwards as they pulled away from the mountains. He had no idea if they had enough time to make it. The sky was still clear where they were, but already *Colony I* was feeling the effects of the storm. The base shook and rattled as the howling winds descended.

Black clouds swarmed across the sky. The dust swirled, and Birch lost the visual feed. His screen went blank. They were gone.

"Good luck," Birch murmured into his microphone. If Jane heard him she didn't answer.

***

The buggy leaped forward, shooting along on an intersecting course with the storm. It was a race to *Primary Base*, and Edwards wasn't sure they were going to win. Already the storm had reached *Colony 1* and a moment later it disappeared in a whirlwind of cloud and dust.

"Hang on!" Jane shouted as she swerved off the smoother path onto rocky ground. There was no time for caution. They either had to get there fast or not at all. She jammed the buggy into high gear and took the harder, more direct route to the base.

The buggy lurched and jumped as it hit the stony ground. The vehicle was designed for all terrain, but the speed it was traveling wasn't exactly to manufacturer's recommendations. They zoomed and weaved through the boulder strewn surroundings. Rocks of all sizes lay about them. The smaller ones jostled and bumped them as they ran over them. The bigger ones had to be avoided. Edwards thought his guts were going to be shaken to bits when they hit another sizable obstacle at full speed and went flying briefly over it. They landed with a grinding crunch.

"I wouldn't mind at all," Edwards shouted over the sound of the approaching storm, "if you missed a few more of those! I really wouldn't!"

Jane ignored his comment and kept driving, her eyes glued to the way ahead. She swerved quickly to the left twice in succession, only barely missing large, jutting stones, and then hit a smaller rock that briefly sent the buggy airborne and directly into the path of another boulder.

There wasn't time to avoid it. Jane wrenched at the wheel and tried to slam on the brakes, but it was too late. They spun, sideswiped the boulder, hitting it full force and sending the buggy teetering on its wheels before and toppling over on its side.

The world was spinning. Edwards shook his head, trying to clear his mind. He unclasped his belt and tried getting up, but he lacked the strength and could only lie there. He needed to rest and catch his breath, but Jane wouldn't let him. She was already up and quickly grabbed his arm, pulling him to his feet.

The buggy's wheels were spinning. Edwards panted, leaning heavily on the disabled vehicle. He looked around, taking in the situation. On the good side *Primary Base* was probably less than half a mile away now. On the bad side, the storm was right on top of them.

"Take cover, fool!" Jane shouted, ducking behind the rock that had felled them. Edwards only just had time to follow her before a curtain of dust and ash descended upon them.

THIRTY

Birch kept checking his screen, even though he knew nothing would change. The video feed had gone down as soon as the storm had hit and now, as it continued to rage outside, the display remained stubbornly blank. Only the indistinct pattern of blowing dust remained, but he kept on checking, watching for even the slightest sign that Jane and Edwards were still alive.

Between checks Birch was back at the records, looking for any clue to help him overcome the power drain. It was only now that he was becoming aware of just how extensive his access was. The computer had almost opened up too much for him. Every file was available. All of them. Important political plans and military records, insignificant personal and private messages, secret memos, and janitorial supply requisitions- literally every piece of electronic data recorded in the history of the settlement on R67.3 was available now for him to read.

Birch's eyes narrowed as he took it all in. No one should have had this kind of access. All that personal, private data- all those government secrets- it could only mean one of two things: either this system access was the work of someone who was very well connected, with top security clearance, or it was the opposite- some lowly hacker with ridiculous skills who had broken into the system and high jacked the data.

Birch was leaning toward the hacker idea simply because it made a lot more sense. The way everything had been set up pointed in that direction. The craziness of that original transmission in the governor's office and the subsequent power-sucking "Robinett" program all suggested a hacker. No legitimate colony official would have done anything so nutty. If they had wanted to leave information for future visitors it would have been put in a direct message, encrypted for security, and left somewhere sensible that didn't require an elaborate egg hunt to find it.

He was sure he was on the right track now, but the question remained: what sort of hacker could pull off something this big? Unlocking every public and private message was remarkable, and gaining access to the governor's personal computer system was equally impressive, but hiding a program the size of the Robinett file on the mainframe, and setting it up to leech off the system without getting caught was outrageous. Birch was sure now that the only reason he had found the file was because it wanted him to find it. The voice on the phone had made that clear.

Clearly whoever had done all of this was very good. Someone with that level of skill would be hard to hide. Birch set the computer the task of finding them by listing the best computer technicians on the base. Of course in a facility like this, the list was long. Forty-three names came up.

He needed something more to go on. He decided to backtrack, go back to his previous line of inquiry and look for some kind of link to the ending events on *Colony I* and those forty-three names. He started with Bruce Marlowe to see if there was any connection between him and any of them. There didn't seem to be. Marlowe was a nobody, a low-level grunge worker, and the forty-three were the All-Star team. They were the best and brightest. Researchers, programmers, and military personnel, none of them moved in the same circles as Marlowe. They were as far above him as the heavens were from the earth.

Birch broadened his search, looking for any more question-able deaths, ones that couldn't be easily explained. He found plenty. Marlowe had been the first, Bill Parsons the second, and the pattern had continued, slowly at first, but over the years it had grown, escalating into a crisis. There didn't seem to be any direct link between any of the early deaths and the forty-three, and by the time there was any connection the cases had become so widespread that it hardly seemed to indicate anything. By that time everyone knew someone who had died mysteriously. Birch sighed. His idea had just led him to another dead end.

His search wasn't entirely fruitless, however. He was begin-ning to see a pattern in these events. All the early incidents had been over at *Primary Base*, and at first, they had been shrugged off as workplace accidents. Rumors swirled in the private messages, but that had hardly mattered. *Primary Base* was the industrial heart of the colony. It produced most of the power in its geothermal plant and provided much of the ore in its mines, but it was a dirty, run-down, ramshackle limb of the colony. It was where most of the indentured colonists worked and lived. They were the grunge workers, the ones who had signed up, not for the adventure, the glory, or any higher ideals, but simply to escape the grinding poverty that Earth had fallen into after the first Hypnos missions. Grunge workers, like the Hypnos crews, had guaranteed the financial support of their families through their inclusion in the colony missions. Unlike the Hypnos crews, however, the payments were at a mere subsistence level. Their families back on Earth would survive, but only just. At least that gave them a chance. The volunteers had mortgaged their lives for that chance, and if nothing else, at least they knew they would be fed.

From the secret messages, it was clear that the governor's office took the situation much more seriously than their pub-lic communications seemed to indicate. They were still telling the colonists that everything was fine as they privately laun-ched a full scale investigation.

Secretly the early inquiries had focused mostly on the possibility of a serial killer. It seemed to fit. Many of the inhabitants of *Primary Base* had questionable backgrounds. None of them were exactly hardened criminals, but neither were they model citizens. A number of them had a history of minor brushes with the law, but that hadn't worried the Selection Committee. They were hard workers and they were cheap. Besides, the thinking behind the policy was that their petty criminal behavior had been the result of their surroundings and social context. It wasn't their fault. It wasn't a reflection on their personal character. They would improve in the cleansing atmosphere of outer space and through the guidance of hard work. That had been the theory. It hadn't quite worked out that way, however, and *Primary Base* had acquired a reputation for being 'the wrong side of the tracks' to the rest of the colony complex.

It hadn't taken much imagination to see any number of the inhabitants of *Primary Base* as potential murderers, and the governor was a man of limited imagination. He had ordered increased surveillance and patrols, but it hadn't made any difference. Things only got worse.

A pattern emerged, but it didn't move the investigation any further. Most of the bodies were never found, the few that were had been horribly mutilated. Gashes, gaping wounds like the incisions of sharp knives or claws covered them, blood was everywhere, but never any traceable evidence. No footprints or fingerprints, no DNA, just a discarded body somewhere on the lower levels.

They were able to contain the panic for a while, but eventually the accident story had worn thin. People were asking too many questions and the governor's office provided too few answers. The gnawing terror that had been nibbling at the edge of their society was only now coming fully into view, but the repercussions didn't really start until two separate and climatic events. The first was a nasty surprise, the disappearance of Security Chief James Miltant and five of his constables while patrolling *The Lowers* in a high profile publicity stunt designed to demonstrate the safety of *Primary Base*. It had all happened live on camera. Miltant was all guts and bravado. Leaning on his holstered pistol he had looked directly into the camera and assured the safety of every colonist. The people of *Colony One*, *Primary Base*, and all the outlying stations had nothing to worry about as long as he was around. His stony face and imposing muscular presence were a comfort. But then before their eyes, he had disappeared.

> *"This part of The Lowers was carved out by the automated constructors left by the original Hypnos crew years ago."*

He patted the smooth stone walls and walked on down the long, dark tunnel, illuminated only by the light bar he held above his head. He turned back occasionally to address the camera as he strode forward, perfectly at ease in his surroundings.

> *"You may have heard some stupid rumors flying around about how dangerous it is down here. Well, I'm here to tell you that those rumors are absolutely true, but not in the way you might have imagined.*

> *"Over the last few months, my men and I have made a thorough search of all the lower levels and investigated every instance of disappearance, injury, or death, and we can tell you beyond doubt that there is no real threat down here, but there is danger."*

He stopped and the camera came up beside him, taking his face in profile before turning its attention to their surroundings. They had entered a large natural cavern. The beam of their lights crossed the ceiling, making the natural crystallization in the rock sparkle and glisten like stars above.

They came out onto a narrow steel balcony overlooking a deep abyss that glowed hotly beneath them. The camera zoomed in- down the long chasm toward the glowing molten liquid that bubbled far below as Miltant's voice continued.

"This is a danger. Primary Base has lots of dangers,
but none of them are any more unusual than the natural
hazards of working in these extreme circumstances.
That's what makes everyone one of us here a hero.
We chose this life.

"Yes, we have lost friends here. Our fellow workers who
gave their lives to make this life possible for us all, but
there is no evidence to show that these were anything
more than terrible accidents. Follow me now as we share
our findings with you."

Miltant smiled reassuringly and swung out onto a metal ladder stretching out beneath them. The cameraman followed, puffing hard. The other constables followed after them and the picture shifted between the officers above and their commander below, leading the way.

The picture grew fuzzy and indistinct, but the transmission continued, all the while punctuated by Miltant's soothing voice making the terrifying seem mundane. It was strange, like watching an infomercial for peace and safety. Birch wasn't sure if anyone bought it, but there was no doubting that Miltant was a persuasive salesman. He was very convincing right up to the point that he disappeared.

They had all disappeared together. One minute the picture grew fuzzy and Miltant's voice distorted, the next moment there was nothing, only a blank screen and then a break in transmission. They were gone.

That had been impossible to smooth over, panic had set in, but even that was as nothing compared to the reaction when less than a week later the first disappearance from *Colony One* took place. Losing a few indentured colonists over at *Primary Base* was one thing, but with death roaming their own corridors blind terror had seized the entire settlement, and it didn't really come back from that. It was another six months before the final silence, but a chattering fear had gripped the station and wouldn't let go until it was finally dead.

Birch slumped deeper into his chair, staring at the screen. It was a few minutes before he moved again. He knew what he had to do. He had scanned a wide sample of the entries from over the years. He had learned a lot, but there was still more to discover, and he couldn't put it off any longer. To truly understand what had happened here, and to figure out how to overcome it, he had to look at the entries for the last week of the colony. He had to watch them all die.

Rising from his chair he crossed the room to a large shiny silver urn and poured himself a steaming cup of sludge that passed for coffee in this place. He gulped it down, but it didn't disguise the leaden taste of defeat, and its heat couldn't warm him. He glanced up at Main Control's oversized screen. On its darkened display the word 'EVIL' was still clearly visible, scrawled in giant red letters that seemed to glow in the semi-darkness. Had they found it here, or had they just brought it with them? You could never tell. It was time to find out. He walked back to the computer.

"Major," Lauren's voice broke in as he settled into his seat, "change in weather coming. I've tried to message Major Gray again but there's still no response."

Birch sat up in his seat, flipping his display from the records back to the camera. He gasped, then switched over to the computer's weather modeling program. His eyes narrowed.

"Are you sure she's not getting your signal?"

Lauren shook her head. "I'm not sure of anything except that she's not answering."

"Yeah, that figures," Birch muttered. "Okay, try sending

the update through text only directly into her computer. I'll do the same with the data that I've collected from the records. If she doesn't want to answer the phone then maybe she'll take a message."

Birch was already working on his message. It would take a while. Firstly he had to warn her about all the events in *The Lowers* and the dangers there, but he also was trying to give her enough information to get her to help him solve *Colony I's* mystery. There were things he needed to know, questions about what had been going on over in *Primary Base*, people he wanted investigated. He tried to condense it all down into something she could follow, a trail of clues that could lead him to the author of the Robinett program.

Lauren's message was simpler and only took an instant to send.

Weather coming!
If outside MOVE NOW!

THIRTY-ONE

Edwards clung to the rock. He had fallen into the fetal position behind Jane. Her boots were inches from his face, but the only thing he could really see was the faint ember of her helmet light glowing in the darkness.

She kicked him in the shoulder. Not hard, but firmly enough to get his attention. His suit's wrist computer lit up. Squinting down at the screen he could just make out her message.

Storm's getting worse,
WE HAVE TO GO!

The words faded into the digital display. Staring out into the darkness Edwards couldn't see what had alerted her to the change. It didn't look any different to him, and he couldn't imagine it getting any worse. A muddy darkness had swallowed the world and spat the chewed up clumps of dirt and sand back in their faces on the howling wind. Edwards wasn't sure he could even stand in these conditions

"Get up!" Jane shouted clambering to her feet. He struggled to follow but stumbled, leaning against the rock, trying to focus on something that would stop the world from whirling around his head.

"Move it!" Jane barked, her voice barely audible over the

storm. She was already on the other side of the rock, grabbing the shovel and digging furiously to free the half buried buggy from the dirt. A moment later he was at her side, using his gloved hands to scoop as much of the gray soil as he could manage without any tools.

"Okay, let's try it," Jane ordered a few minutes later, and they put their shoulders to the buggy. It rocked a little on its side but didn't move.

She grabbed the shovel again. "More, more! Let's go, let's go!" Her words matched the rhythm of her digging as she flailed away at the dirt. Edwards wasn't far behind in his efforts. His hands flew, pulling and scooping as much away as he could.

"Try again," Jane shouted moments later. She was already up again pushing against the body of the buggy. Edwards joined her. It moved more this time but still stayed stubbornly in place. With the wind flinging dirt at them almost as quickly as they could remove it their progress was slow.

Edwards hadn't thought it possible but the sky was looking worse. Maybe it was a trick of the light caused by the great red sun shining far above the planet's opaque atmosphere, or perhaps it was something to do with the changing cycle of the storm, but for whatever reason, the sky had taken on a strange crimson-black glow. Something was building up, he could tell that much. He could feel it crackling like energy in the air around him.

"Push harder!" Jane urged, straining against the obstinate vehicle. Edwards glanced over again at the ruddy clouds and made a last desperate effort, launching a lunging shoulder tackle against the buggy. It teetered, wobbled, and fell, bouncing back onto its wheels. Edwards went over with it, his feet kicking wildly as he sailed over the vehicle and landed in the dirt on the other side.

"Are you okay?" Jane gasped, rushing to where he lay.

"I think so," Edwards groaned, dusting himself off. "But I'll worry about that later, let's go!"

Jane nodded and jumped into the driver's seat. Edwards limped in beside her and a moment later they were racing toward *Primary Base* again.

The buggy started up quickly enough, but soon it became clear that all the dust and dirt were affecting the engine. It sputtered, shook, and slowed.

The ribbons of fiery cloud were closing in.

"Can't you make this thing go any faster?" Edwards shouted, glancing back to the advancing curtain of cloud. Jane gave him a brief look and shrugged.

"Maybe, if you push."

By now they were barely traveling at half speed. The slowdown was exasperating, but probably a good thing for their safety. They were driving blind. More than once Jane needed to swerve at the last minute to avoid impact with another boulder. At a faster pace, they probably would have crashed again, maybe fatally this time.

The wind was changing. Up to now, it had been at their backs, pushing them on toward their goal. Now it suddenly shifted in the opposite direction, blowing into their faces, making their progress harder.

"Oh great, here we go again!" Jane shouted glancing over her shoulder.

"What?"

"I've seen this before. It's building up to a pneumatic blast, a little like the way a tsunami sucks water up from the shore before it crashes in to destroy everything in its way!" She leaned over the steering wheel, willing the buggy to greater speed. "It's pulling in air now, so we're probably about two minutes away from getting hit by an explosion of gasses that'll make a tornado feel like a two year old blowing out the candles on their birthday cake!"

Edwards wondered if she was exaggerating, but the panic in her voice seemed pretty clear.

"Um, so, are we nearly there yet?"

Jane grimaced then glanced down at her wrist computer

again. "Yeah, about three minutes away, if we don't slow down any more."

"I don't like your math much!" Edwards muttered. "If it's going to hit us in two minutes and we're going to get there in three, that doesn't exactly sound like a happy ending."

"It is what it is," Jane snapped. "Maybe we'll get lucky." Her foot was already to the floor, but she gave the accelerator an extra shove, trying to squeeze the last particle of speed from the sputtering engine. "Just be ready to jump out as soon as we stop! I'm heading for the nearest airlock. Run for the door and don't look back. It'll be close!"

Jane coaxed the buggy along. It didn't lose any more speed. If anything it seemed to quicken slightly, and a few moments later they were skidding to a halt at their destination.

It was only at this proximity that Edwards could finally see anything of the smooth, black walls of *Primary Base* sloping up beside them. Jane rammed the buggy into reverse and gunned the engine, pulling back to the wall as fast as the ailing vehicle could manage. The airlock door was just behind them. Jane had done it. She had led them right to the entrance. They were going to make it!

The wind suddenly died away and everything went silent. Edwards paused, surprised at the unexpected change in the weather. Dust floated gently in the air and the faint reddish hue of the sun somewhere above the clouds warmed the cold, gray world. Edwards shook his head. Jane had certainly overstated the power of the storm. It wasn't much more than a damp squib.

"Out, out, out!" Jane was shouting as she leaped down and rushed to the back of the buggy. She had grabbed as much equipment as she could and was running for the airlock. Edwards followed, but his earlier hesitation cost him dearly as he hadn't progressed more than a few steps when it hit.

It started as a sound, a thin tinkling as a faint gusty breeze caught a stray piece of metal off the structure of *Primary Base*. An instant later it boomed with a thundering crash as the air exploded around them. The sound was so intense, so beyond anything Edwards had ever experienced, that it registered more as pure pain than any audible noise that Edwards' ears could detect.

He had the brief sensation of being airborne. There was a sudden crash and reality struck in the form of a hard, unyielding object. His helmet light went off and he rolled, coming to rest in the gray dirt.

THIRTY-TWO

For the second time that week Edwards' suit went critical. Last time Birch had been there, holding it together long enough to keep him alive. There wasn't much hope of anything like that this time. Jane was somewhere nearby, but his suit was completely dead. All operations had ceased. Air, temperature control, computer functions, everything was gone, and in a few minutes, he would be gone too.

Edwards couldn't see much. His visor was already icing up. He had fallen face down in the dirt, and he hurt too much to do anything more than roll over on his side and breathe. The breathing was coming harder, and the only thing he could see was the gray smudge of the planet's surface.

There was a quiet stillness in the certainty of death. All the doubts and struggles melted away. He had always heard that your life flashed before your eyes just before death, but Edwards wasn't susceptible to that. Memories tried to come, but he brushed them aside. He hadn't done anything worth remembering. He just waited for the darkness. There wasn't anything more he could do.

He was floating, drifting into the comfort of oblivion when he felt himself being lifted. His first instinct was to fight it, to pull away and go back to sleep, like a kid fighting a wake-up call on a school morning, but he didn't have the strength. It didn't matter anyway. Everything was futile. His suit couldn't be fixed in time, and he didn't know why they didn't just leave him here to die in peace.

The hands carrying him weren't strong enough for the job. They dropped him, and rather than try to pick him up again he was dragged along in the dirt. There wasn't anything Edwards could do to help. He was dead weight. He felt his eyes rolling into his head and his face burning. The darkness was approaching.

***

Fortified with coffee, Birch got back to the job at hand. He paused briefly to check the video feed, but it was worse than ever. There was no way he could do anything for Jane and Edwards until the storm let up, and the frustration of that reality did little to improve his mood.

He gritted his teeth and got back to the records. There was no more delaying it. It was time to see the end. He decided to approach it from the same angle he had been following before. He started by looking for any links between the disappearances in the last few months of the colony. What he found was unsettling. Bruce Marlowe and Bill Parsons had become the boogiemen of *Primary Base*. If anything went wrong over there it wasn't considered an accident any longer, it was a "B.B. Parlowe", an amalgamation of their names to describe any unexplained or unfortunate occurrence.

Mass hysteria took hold. Reports started filtering back to the governor's office claiming sightings of Marlowe and Parsons wandering *The Lowers*. The stories caught on and people started seeing everything, Marlowe and Parsons at first, then Chief Miltant and his five ghostly constables. Later, when the panic was complete, people were reporting all types of sightings in all sorts of places. Nowhere was immune to the madness.

The governor's office was not equipped for such a general

breakdown of order. There were a number of attempts to regain control, but once Miltant was gone things really fell apart. The governor took on a bunker mentality, raging at the unfairness of it all as the world broke to pieces around him.

Birch skimmed through the governor's private messages. He had read a number of his entries already and hadn't been impressed. Governor Braxley P. Pickett was an obvious political appointee, the sort that has bedeviled every endeavor since the dawn of human effort. He knew the right people, belonged to the right organizations, believed the right things, and kissed the right rings. He deserved the job because it was his turn. Unfortunately for him, his turn came up at a time when all of his political skill, all of his powerful friends, and all of his mental orthodoxy counted for nothing. This was far beyond anything he could handle.

One thing caught Birch's attention. In the final stages of the colony's life, as the deaths and disappearances mounted up, and the inevitable grimness of their situation became clear, the talk had turned to a more drastic solution- escape. Nothing else had worked. They were vulnerable here on this tiny speck of livable space in the vast inhospitable universe. Something was stalking them, hunting them to extinction, and if the danger had been tangible, something they could understand and resist, they might have stayed to fight it. But an indistinct terror took hold of them all. It felt as though they were opposing something elemental, a primary evil that was always there and would destroy them all if they stayed. And so it had become an inevitable decision to leave.

This final conclusion had not united the colony at all. What Birch noticed was a real sense of paranoia on the issue. It seemed that there were rival camps trying to find somewhere to go, and neither side trusted the other. The divide wasn't helped by Pickett's decision to seal off *Primary Base*. He had done it immediately after the disappearance of Miltant's patrol, but before the first occurrence at *Colony I*. It was a panicked reaction, but Pickett had seen it as a necessary evil.

In public messages, he had presented it as a temporary precaution. In private communications, his explanation had been blunter.

> *"Primary Base is a cancer. We did what we could*
> *to treat it, but the patient has not responded.*
> *That leaves only one course of action. The affected*
> *area must be cut off."*

> *"Starting immediately, all contact and personnel exchange*
> *between the two sites will cease. Full compliance*
> *is required. No exceptions. They can stay on their*
> *side and we'll stay on ours. That way the cancer*
> *won't spread."*

It was a desperate move, and ultimately an unsuccessful one. The cancer spread anyway. People disappeared from *Colony* I. Even so, Pickett kept the barriers up to the end. He didn't know what else to do.

The people of *Primary Base* weren't fooled by the governor's talk of 'temporary' or 'precautionary' quarantine. They knew what was happening. They were being left to face the terror alone. *Colony I* still wanted their energy to power their station, and in return, they continued to send food supplies through automated drop-offs, but they didn't want *them*. They didn't care if they lived or died. They were the plague house, marked for death so that the contagion wouldn't spread.

Primary Base's leaders had briefly considered retaliating by cutting off the newer base's power supply, but that was futile. They were too dependent on their neighbor for that. *Colony I* probably had enough power production capacity to limp along at a reduced level for months, while *Primary Base* would quickly run out of food. *Colony I* had all the advantages. That was the way the system worked, and if they planned to survive then the people of *Primary Base* would have to do it without any help from their sister base. That left two simple options - solve their own problems or die. The latter seemed the most likely outcome. After all, they were an industrial complex manned by grunge workers. What chance did they have? They were trapped, left to die, and for that reason, the people of *Primary Base* were the first to look for an escape. They were the first to give up on R67.3 and so, for once, they started ahead of *Colony I*.

As the situation worsened both sides planned their flight, but both camps were hindered by the lack of cooperation. Working together they might have come up with a destination and a feasible plan to get there, working apart, it was chaos. They couldn't leave. A large number of colonists fleeing blindly into open space without a working plan and adequate resources wasn't likely to end well. Survival on other worlds took a lot of work and preparation- that was what the Hypnos missions had been all about. Without that planning their chances were slim, and the colonists weren't ready yet to abandon their tenuous toehold on existence here for the uncertainty of a poorly resourced journey to nowhere. That would only be the last resort.

Significantly there was no mention of a possible return to Earth. That idea never even came up. Perhaps it was just another indication of Pickett's paranoia, or maybe they had gotten wind of how things were going back on the home-world, but for whatever reason, all communication Earthward had been cut early on in the crisis, and any attempt to get a message out had been blocked on the governor's orders. That evidently was what had almost ruptured Edwards' ears when they first approached the planet. He had tapped into the stored messages, getting them all at once in a burst of deafening noise.

With a return to Earth out, and life on R67.3 becoming impossible, only one option had remained. They needed to find where the other Hypnos missions had gone, particularly the later ones. On the surface that appeared hopeless. There was no direct reference to them in any communication. They seemed to simply disappear, but in the last few months before they lost contact the messages from NASA took on a cryptic, almost garbled tone.

It became a common belief in the colonies that these final messages were not the staticky nonsense-filled mess that they appeared to be. Perhaps these messages weren't garbled at all. Maybe they were just what they were intended to be, a sly attempt to get some information out in such a way that it couldn't be detected. The problem was that no one here could detect it either. They were sure there was something more to these messages, but whatever it was, they couldn't find it.

This was where Pickett's paranoia kicked in. He was sure that, despite all their disadvantages, somehow a group over at *Primary Base* had gotten the jump on them. From the messages he had intercepted from them, his suspicion was that they were on the verge of piecing together the location of another colony. The irony was that in sealing *Primary Base* off to protect themselves, he had cut off any chance of cooperating with them. They knew something, he was sure of that, but they weren't sharing it.

And then came the silence. It didn't cause much alarm at first. It happened all the time. During storms communication usually went down, so when *Primary Base* went quiet during one of those five-day sand blizzards it wasn't exactly a surprise, but when it failed to reestablish contact afterward news quickly spread around *Colony One* that the crisis had finally come to a head. The end was now. They were certain of that.

All attempts to raise *Primary Base* had been fruitless. In the end, Pickett had had no choice. He needed to know what was going on over there. He had to send over an investigative force, the first since Miltant and his team had disappeared. There weren't many volunteers.

THIRTY-THREE

Everything was white. Edwards blinked hard against the contrast as he tried to adjust to his surroundings. It was so bright and so piercing that his first thought was of heaven or some other spiritual experience, but the light was too cold and clinical for that, and it flickered dimly every few seconds.

He sat up quickly and bumped his head on the equipment stretched out above him.

"Lie back down," Jane's voice came from somewhere behind him, as crisp and cool as the room they now occupied. "I'm not done with you."

Edwards fell back onto the cushioned table, breathing awkwardly. From where he lay, he could see the stark white tiled room he had been brought to, but he couldn't see anyone. Electronic panels bleeped and pulsed on one wall, but their light didn't add any cheer or color to the room.

Finally, Jane was at his side pulling him slowly into a sitting position. "You're going to be fine," she assured him flatly as he leaned heavily against her. "Just take it easy for a bit." She handed him a steaming cup of something and smiled thinly. "Just hurry up about it, though, will you?" She gestured to her wrist computer. "We've got places to go, people to see, you know."

Edwards coughed heavily, his breath coming in rasping

gasps. It was a few minutes before he could say anything, and when he finally did it was a single word that encapsulated the great question in his mind, "How?" He started coughing again without getting another word out, but Jane knew what he meant.

"Well, I guess we weren't right about the condition of this base. It's not the broken down wreck we all imagined. When I dragged you in here everything was on, lucky for you, too. I was able to get you to this med center and here you are, alive. If the oxygen had been off or everything else hadn't been working you wouldn't have made it. Your suit was too far gone; your condition was too critical. You would have been dead."

"Where..." Edwards wheezed groggily. "Are there... are there any people left here?"

Jane shook her head. "No, it looks like things have been left to run automatically. This base is on an energy source that'll run it forever. I guess they weren't too worried about paying the bill. They left the lights on. From what I've seen there's no life. It's pretty clear that this place has been empty for a long time. It's kind of unsettling in a way, but it could be our chance. We could live here."

"What does Major Birch think of that?" Edwards asked.

Jane frowned at the mention of his name. "Who knows?" she snapped, but immediately she regained her composure. "I don't know. I lost the signal some time after the storm hit. I haven't been able to reestablish contact yet. I'm sure we'll hear what he thinks soon enough."

Edwards slid off the table, testing his weight on unsteady legs. He was wearing only his boxers, t-shirt, and socks. Jane must have stripped him down to hook him up to the equipment. He grimaced, rubbed his legs, and glanced around for his clothes. Jane seemed to sense his discomfort and took a step back, gesturing to his flight suit draped across a nearby chair before exiting the room through a dinged up white metal door.

"Hurry up," she added, letting the door swing shut behind her as she left.

Edwards pulled himself into his clothes. He paused as he stooped to zip it up. For the first time, he noticed the examination table he had been lying on. It was made of some gray metal. The cushions were supposed to match it, but they didn't. They were red, stained all over with dried pools of a red liquid that he knew must be blood.

His head swam and he staggered back, bumping into the smooth, cold tiles behind him. The walls weren't perfectly white either. Closer now, he could see splatter marks, like a thousand tiny stars in a bloody constellation. Blood had seeped into the cracks. It had dripped down and settled into congealed pools that had hardened and coated the floor in a carpeting of gore.

Edwards took a deep breath, zipped up his suit, and bolted for the exit. On the other side, he slammed the metal door shut and leaned against it, panting heavily.

"I guess you noticed the blood then?" Jane observed coolly.

"Well, yeah," Edwards admitted through puffing breaths. "You might have told me I was lying in a pool of dried blood!"

"It didn't seem important while I was saving your life."

"I suppose not." Edwards glanced up and down the long corridor. There was more dried blood here. Smears and blotches all around, on the walls and along the floor, whatever had happened here nobody had bothered to clean it up. Maybe after what happened here there wasn't anybody left *to* clean it up. But there weren't any bodies and no evidence of any remains that might have been the source of all this gore.

"Something really bad happened here," Edwards murmered.

"Yeah, I think you could pretty safely say that," Jane responded dryly. "Come on, let's go."

"Is the rest of the base like this?" Edwards asked, hurrying to keep up with Jane who had started up the passageway.

"I haven't seen the rest of the base. The little I saw while dragging you in here didn't look a whole lot better. Not as much blood, but plenty of destruction and mayhem. I don't know. We'll find out soon enough."

They entered what looked like a locker room with gray storage compartments lining the walls. Jane's EVA suit lay on a metal bench that divided the room down the middle. Edwards' suit was nowhere to be seen.

"Your suit's completely shot," Jane explained as she opened one of the compartments. "Fortunately I found a working one you can use." She handed him a suit and started to put her own on.

"Suit up, Edwards," Jane said. "It's time for you and me to do some exploring."

***

Birch found the file of the last expeditionary mission to *Primary Base* pretty easily. It was flagged prominently and was referenced in a lot of the other communications that flew around in the last few hours of the colony.

Birch found the unedited copy that hadn't been sanitized for public consumption. He clicked on the file. A small window popped up on the screen. A grainy video feed from the task force helmet cameras came on. The display kept switching from one camera to another, giving a different view of the action every few minutes. A box next to the video window showed the vital statistics of the six-member team. Their heart rate bleeped next to their picture. Their name lit up whenever they spoke and beneath that was their present location. It put you at the heart of the action, but the overall impression was so much like a video game that Birch had a hard time reminding himself that these were real people with real lives that couldn't be replenished if they were lost.

"It's locked!"

Team leader Flack grunted as they tried to work the door mechanism. After a few minutes effort, they managed to push it aside.

"Okay, we're going in."

Flack gave the thumbs up and slid through the gap.

The next few minutes were a jumble of mixed images. Flack and his men were coming out of the airlock and entering the base. They proceeded a short distance down a passageway and then out into the open space of *Main Dome*. The camera switched quickly between views. The surroundings were dark and it wasn't easy to see much more than the faces of the men in the light of their helmets. Flack spoke and his face was profiled from different angles by the cameras of his men.

> *"It's empty so far. Everything's quiet here. The power's down too. No lights, nothing. It looks like you were right about the base. I think they all left. As per orders: I'm sending half the contingent along to the hangar see to see how many ships are missing. The others are coming with me to Command Post to get the power up and retrieve the records."*

Flack signaled his men and they divided up, two groups walking in separate directions. Governor Pickett's voice came over the speaker.

> *"Carefully does it, men. Remember, your main objective is to find out where they went. The future of the colony depends on you. Every life, your families', your friends', your colleagues', we are all depending on you."*

No one answered that. They knew what was at stake.

They walked on. Each member of the team was armed with

a heavy assault rifle and weighed down with extra ammo. They were prepared for the worst.

For a time only the sound of their breathing and an occasional muttered comment could be heard. A little later the weight of their responsibility became clear. The voice of one of the men heading for the hangar broke in on the silence.

"What is that?"

Two streams of light crisscrossed, wobbling as they focused in on a patch of floor. One of the men reached down, rubbing a gloved hand against the dark patch.

"It's blood, still damp too."

He held his sticky fingers up to the helmet camera of one of the other men. His voice remained steady, but the pulse monitor beside his picture spiked. All their pulse monitors spiked. The man turned and examined the floor more closely, following a dark trail with his finger.

"Drag marks... I'm not sure the people here
went anywhere."

The view switched between cameras, wild, random cuts trying to make sense of the darkened world around them. A few steps further on and there were more marks. The floor and walls were splattered with more crimson stains that in the gloomy distance showed up as indistinct black patches.

The party hesitated, apparently unsure if they should proceed. Governor Pickett's voice crackled over the radio again. It seemed he had assumed direct control of the mission from the safety of his office in *Colony One*.

"Continue to the hangar bay, Party Two. Once
there you must calculate the number of ships gone

*and access the flight log data. We must know where
they went. It's our only chance."*

They still hesitated. Finally, the leader took a few faltering steps and they started moving again in the direction of the hangar bay. A moment later they stopped. The men were looking around. They seemed to almost be sniffing the air, trying to detect something they couldn't quite identify. The leader had his hand up, calling for silence.

"Did you hear something?"

No one answered. One of the men cleared their throat nervously and turned to look to the rear. In his camera a sudden flash of gray motion burst upon him, sending him crashing to the floor. The picture fuzzed and died.

The others reacted instantly, turning to their comrade, guns raised, but in that instant, the leader was shoved from behind, smashed into the wall then collapsed to the ground. The last man screamed and fired indiscriminately into the darkness. The light from his helmet spun wildly as he swerved and turned, searching for their attackers.

CRACK! CRACK! CRACK! The shots went off. His helmet and face were illuminated in the flash of each shot. There was nothing there. He stopped firing and stood, breathing heavily, looking for the danger. His light went up and down the corridor, but he couldn't see anything. It was almost as if it had all been his imagination, the effect of these surroundings, except that two men lay at his feet.

The heart monitors of the two men flatlined. One of their cameras was still transmitting, and occasionally the main display switched from the last living man to a view of the floor from the dead man's helmet.

The survivor started running. It wasn't an ordered retreat. He plunged back up the corridor. His feet echoing on the steel floor as he fled into the darkness.

Fallback

*"Party Two, Party Two… what happened? What
did you see? What did you see?"*

Pickett's words showed the strain. Panic was creeping into
his voice. No answer came, only heavy breathing and the
blurred image of the man's surroundings, illuminated in his
suit's light as he ran. Then there was a loud crack. The man's
suit crunched as he slammed into the wall. The video feed
showed the world turning briefly upside down and then
distorted into waved lines that finally dissolved into nothing.
The main display went briefly blank and then reverted back to
the only view left to it, the floor from a dead man's camera.

THIRTY-FOUR

Everything went silent. Party Two's video feed was reduced to two channels of static and one view of the floor. Two of the heart rates had flatlined, but the third continued and, after a wild fluctuation, settled into a steady, easy rhythm. Perhaps the survivor had passed out.

Flack and his men had heard all of this but couldn't see any of it. Flack finally broke the silence.

"What just happened?"

There was no answer until Pickett eventually spoke.

> *"We just lost Party Two. It's up to you, Party
> One. I know it's hard, but we need you to find out
> where the people of Primary Base went. You're our
> last chance."*

Flack shook his head, but despite his obvious <u>reservations,</u> he continued on to Command Post. Birch never found out if they made it because a few minutes later the feed cut suddenly from their camera display to something more pressing. Something was coming. There was no audio at first, but the short film zoomed in fuzzily to what looked like a throng of space-suited figures streaming out of *Primary Base*, coming toward *Colony One*.

"Who are they?"

Pickett spluttered. The quick conclusion was that the rabble of *Primary Base* hadn't gone anywhere. Their silence had been a trick to break quarantine. They had set a trap, lain in wait for the investigative force, and now they were invading *Colony One*. They could try, but this was exactly what Pickett had prepared for. An invasion was something he could deal with, and now that they had come out into the open he could finish them off. He gave the order to fire mortars at the advancing throng.

***

Jane and Edwards entered *Main Dome*. *Primary Base* was built on a very different design to *Colony I*. *Colony I* was an attempt to replicate an Earth-like existence as closely as possible. It was an extravagant statement of intent about the future of humanity in space. *Primary Base*, as the earlier station, was built solely for function. It was all about survival. Nothing was done that didn't have to be done. *Main Dome* was a striking example of this reality.

Beneath the dome, there was a miniature city of sorts. A number of squat, gray buildings all squeezed together in the space between the dome's tinted glass ceiling and the gray concrete floor below. The glass of the dome itself protected the settlement from the harsh elements outside, but there was no breathable atmosphere here. That was reserved for smaller internal spaces. For that reason, a number of the buildings had skyways, enclosed glass walkways connecting them high above the ground.

The dome creaked; its glass rattled as the pounding wind beat against its panes. It reminded Edwards of the stormy nights back on Earth when he had lived by the ocean. At the end of the longest days he could leave the world and shut himself away, comfortable in the knowledge that, rattle as it might, it couldn't get in. He was safe until the next morning. Of course, if the wind whipped hard enough that comfort was replaced by a more immediate fear that the outside world might break in prematurely. That was his fear now as the old dome groaned under the punishing wind.

Jane seemed unconcerned by any of this and was already making her way toward a building at the center of the dome. He hurried to catch her.

"Where are we going?" Edwards puffed.

"Command Post", Jane answered over her shoulder as she walked. "Major Birch gave us a to-do list before we lost his signal. I'm not usually one to jump when the *Beloved Leader* barks, but he actually had a good idea for once. I'm following up a couple of leads before we move on."

Command Post was a solitary building at the center of the dome. Unconnected to the other structures, it stood as a single prominent example of colony authority on the base. Being at the center of the dome, it was taller than any other building, but it was also more substantial and decorated in an ornamental style. All the other buildings were a testament to drab functionality. Command Post was built of the same gray rock as all the other structures of the base, but there was evidence that it had once been painted. Most of the paint had faded and peeled away by now, but enough of the original color remained to remind them of the grand impression it was supposed to make.

They entered the building through its main double doors. Inside they passed through an airlock and further in discovered a changing room similar to the one they had recently left in the Medical Center- only this one was more plush. The benches were thickly upholstered, the light fixtures ornate, and the walls decorated in classical style. They removed their helmets before moving beyond into the main foyer with a stone floor and a narrow metal staircase. This was as close to the grandeur of *Colony One*'s Town Hall as *Primary Base* could manage. It wasn't much, but it was more than most of the base's inhabitants would ever see anywhere else.

Jane and Edwards didn't climb the stairs; instead, they turned the corner and took another set of steps down into the basement. On the way down Edwards noticed another of those ominous red stains, but he didn't stop to examine it. At the bottom, there was a barred gate that swung crookedly on its hinges admitting them into the lower level. This must have been a secure part of the facility once, but the lock was broken and the gate hung freely now.

They stepped into a wide room as gray and drab as all the others. A rat's maze of cubicles stretched out to the far wall. By the near wall was an imposing upper desk. Behind it was a large viewing screen and a detailed map of *Primary Base* with red pins stuck in it.

"What do you suppose those pins represent?" Edwards asked, looking at the map.

Jane glanced up and shook her head. "I wouldn't like to guess," she answered darkly and headed for the nearest cubicle. She sat at the workstation and reached down to put her helmet on the floor, but instead of leaving it there she pulled another one out. The ownerless helmet was dusty; it must have been there a long time. Edwards picked it up and examined it. It was different to the NASA helmets the Hypnos crew wore, and it was different from the helmet of the replacement suit Edwards had picked up here. It was a slightly different shape, outlined in gold, and with the letters C.I marked in gold along the side. It was a lot nicer than Edwards' dirty, dinged up *Primary Base* helmet. He wondered why anyone would leave their helmet down here. Perhaps that was another thing that it was better not to try and guess.

Jane was already working at the computer, scanning through files at speed.

"What are you looking for?" Edwards asked.

Jane didn't look up. "I've got to unlock some of the quarters on the lower levels." Her screen flashed and changed quickly as she sped through codes. "Command Post is the place for that. This is where they controlled and watched everything that happened on the base, at least they tried to. It doesn't look like it did them much good in the end." She bit her lip in concentration. "Let's just see if Birch got it right for once and sent us some useful information."

"You don't like Major Birch much, do you? Edwards observed. Jane didn't bother to answer but shot him a steely look that said more than words. She turned her attention back to the screen. "What is it with you two anyway?" Edwards persisted. "Why do you hate him so much? I mean, I know he's kind of irritating sometimes, but he seems to be genuinely trying to do what's right most of the time."

"That's not my experience," Jane replied without looking up again.

"Well, he saved my life."

"You're the lucky one. He's killed more than he's saved. Remember what happened to Karla and DeSante?"

"That's not really fair," Edwards replied. "He tried to save them."

"Yeah, that's what he always says, but somehow he always comes back alone."

"You've said that before, when Karla died... was that what happened to Colonel Ratliff?"

Jane's head shot up at that. "Yeah," she blinked and stared back down at her screen. "That's exactly what happened with Colonel Ratliff. They were both out at the quarry alone carrying out repairs. A storm hit, and three days later Birch came back alone."

"What do you think happened?"

"I think Birch killed him."

It was Edwards' head that shot up this time. "Killed? Like murder? What... but why would he do that? That makes no sense!"

"I've tried to figure that out myself," Jane answered. "The

best I could come up with was that maybe something changed Birch's mind about the mission and he needed to get home. I don't know why, but he was never that committed to the idea of the Hypnos program. Well, Colonel Ratliff would never agree to abandon our mission, so maybe Birch had to kill him to take command, and then he'd have the authority to order us to return to Earth."

Edwards shook his head "I don't buy that; that sounds pretty weak. Major Birch doesn't seem the type to go psycho like that. Besides, it didn't look like he was all that excited to be back on Earth when I met him. He's not exactly the 'homesick' type. I've never seen him really happy anywhere, so the idea that he'd miss Earth so much that he'd kill to go back seems pretty unlikely."

Jane nodded. "Yeah, I agree," she looked up from her computer. "If you take it like that it does sound pretty dumb, but I wasn't thinking of any personal reason for going back. You're right about him. I couldn't imagine him missing anyone or anything enough to do anything like that. He's always too busy thinking about himself, but what if he wasn't acting for personal reasons but professional ones instead?"

"Professional reasons? Like what?"

"Look, I didn't know much about it at the time, but from what I understand it seems like the Hypnos missions were being undermined right from the very beginning by insiders working to make it fail. What if Birch was one of those?"

Edwards thought for a moment. "I still find that hard to believe. He just doesn't seem the type. I'd need a lot more proof to think that he could do something like that."

"You want proof?" Jane spat. Her eyes flashed at the memories. "I've got plenty! First off nobody could explain how he even got on the mission. The crew had been set a long time before he came along, but in the last ten months before launch, we lost our pilot to some sort of genetic anomaly that hadn't shown up on any previous tests. Birch was the replacement, but he hadn't even been on the reserve list before that. I just don't see how he was chosen. Everything about him was wrong. He was a good pilot; on short runs to Mars and other routine missions he was considered a pretty handy guy to have around, but there's just too much baggage to ever consider him for a high-profile long-haul mission like Hypnos. He's always been an arrogant, irrational ball of stupidity, and I've done my best to avoid him. About the only thing he had going for him was his blood type, and that didn't make him any more qualified than the other thirty percent of the population."

"Blood type?" Edwards asked, puzzled.

"A+, that was the blood type for the Hypnos III mission. It was a health requirement for every long range operation that all crew members had to belong to an assigned blood group. The mission commander was appointed first- then a compatible crew was selected around him. The idea was that if anything went wrong and a transfusion was needed then there wouldn't be any problem getting a match. Birch fit that requirement, but there were so many better candidates ahead of him. Someone must have pulled some strings to get him on. I'm sure of that. I'm just not sure who or why, but I'm guessing it was someone trying to scupper the mission.

"The second proof is what he did to Colonel Ratliff. It was bad enough that he came back after three days saying that the colonel had been lost in the storm while trying to save some of the equipment out at the quarry, but it was what Birch did afterward that really showed what he was up to. He wouldn't let any of us search the area for him. He took DeSante along with him and did some supposed searches himself, but Lieutenant DeSante was a little puppy, and I'm sure he could easily have been guided away from anything he wasn't supposed to see. After that Birch told us we had to leave, our mission was a failure, and that the only way we were going to survive was if we gave up the whole idea of settling this planet and went home.

"He made us leave, and I never got the chance to look for

Colonel Ratliff, to be sure he was really dead, and I'll never forgive him for that. Never."

"So why didn't you stop him? Why did you just go along with what he told you to do?"

Jane shuddered. "I tried. The others were all sheep. DeSante would obey any order a superior officer gave, Karla could never see the bad in anyone, and Lauren was an Industry robot. Still, I thought I was getting through to them, they knew I was right. They knew we had to try harder, that we had come too far to give up on our mission or Colonel Ratliff until we were sure that both were lost, but then Birch ended the controversy in his own unique style. He drugged me and stuck me in cryogenic storage. The next thing I knew we were waking up as we approached Mars."

"Wow," Edwards' voice cracked. "I had no idea. No wonder you hate him!"

"Yeah, no wonder." She smiled thinly. "And the fact that putting me into cryo-storage drugged up like that ran the risk of causing brain damage only added zest to the mixture. So yeah, I hate him."

"What do you think he was going back to Earth for", Edwards asked, "and why do you think he left again after he'd worked so hard to get there?"

"I think he was expecting to find something that wasn't there anymore. You remember how willingly he followed you all across the country? You were taking him where he wanted to go."

"I'm not sure I'd call it 'willingly'," Edwards scoffed, "but I guess he did get there in the end."

"Exactly. I know he didn't make it easy, he never does, but can you imagine trying to get Birch to go anywhere he didn't want to go? He never would have gone along with you if there wasn't something he wanted to get out of it. Remember how he got separated from the rest of us with DeSante and Karla? He could have gone anywhere, but where did we find him? He was still on his way to Washington. He could have gone anywhere in the country, but he was still on his way to Washington. I think that says a lot.

"That's point number three against Birch," Jane concluded. "He was too anxious to report back to his Washington pals. It was only when he found out that the situation had changed and that his people weren't in control anymore that he ran for it."

Edwards looked thoughtful. "I guess that's possible, but if you don't trust him because of his willingness to go to Washington then why do you trust me enough to tell me all of this? I was the one leading you there."

"For three reasons," Jane laughed. "One: you're alone out here, what are you going to do? Overwhelm us with your awesome power? I don't think so. Two: you didn't want to come with us. You're not a spy or a plant like Birch, that's obvious. Three: If you were a spy you'd have to be the world's worst spy. More likely you're just a guy who hasn't got a clue. I mean, have you seen yourself lately? You can't do anything. Really."

Edwards wasn't exactly sure how to take that. He brushed the comment aside lightly.

"Yeah," he quipped, "and I suppose that since you think you can do everything that makes you a highly suspicious NASA superspy. I better keep an eye on you."

"You better believe it," Jane smiled, making her hand the shape of a gun and pulling the trigger.

Her attention went back to the screen. "Okay, I got it," she announced a moment later. "It looks like we've got a bit of walking to do. It seems as though Birch's interest is in the lowlife of the base, literally. Most of the names he's given me are of lower dwellers, people that live in the communal barracks way down near *The Lowers*."

Edwards gave Jane a look. "'*The Lowers*?' Just how far down is that?"

Jane shrugged. "Pretty far. We had to go down there anyway. I think that's where we'll find the source of *Colony One's* power problems too. I've unlocked the security codes all the way along, so it should be a pretty straight run. No problems."

"Yeah right," Edwards muttered gloomily. "What could possibly go wrong?" Unfortunately, he could think of over a hundred things that could possibly go wrong, but Jane wasn't going to listen to him anyway, so he didn't bother to say anything. They would just have to go down and find out.

THIRTY-FIVE

The mortars never hit. In fact, not a single one was fired. As the *Primary Base* mob advanced Pickett had ordered again and again for them to be launched. By the end, he had been screaming the order out, but his words had been futile. Something was stopping the launch. It didn't look like a malfunction, everything was still showing up green on the panels, but they wouldn't fire.

It didn't take long for Pickett to conclude that this was an act of sabotage, and the fact that a few minutes later his order to break out the weapons and prepare for hand-to-hand combat was met with the perplexing news that they were all gone, only confirmed his assumption. With only a little time left until the colony was overrun he didn't waste any effort trying to figure the how or whys of it. He had to act.

It quickly became obvious that nothing was going to stop the attack. Mechanisms and systems that should have secured the inner ring of the base were going down. Nothing was working and the doors were left wide open. Somehow the rabble of *Primary Base* had figured out all the emergency protocols and overridden them. They were going to get in.

Pickett stared at his screen, watching the figures advance, powerless to stop them. They were getting close now. Alarms sounded and the lighting switched from natural daylight to a bloody, pulsating red. *'Warning: Unauthorized personnel approaching,'* a computerized voice warned.

"We need do something, now!"

one of Pickett's men was shouting. The words seemed to pull the governor from his paralysis.

"Yes, yes... do something. Um... yeah, okay, order all security officers to respond to the threat immediately. They are to hold them back using whatever weapons they can find. Their superior training should still give them the advantage. While they do that we'll perform a precautionary evacuation of all vital personnel. Once they have secured the station everyone will return."

The officer saluted and left to carry out his orders.

'Warning: base breach imminent,' the computer warned flatly. The camera display changed to outside. A mass of figures was at the doors, swarming through the openings, clawing their way into the base.

"Should we get your shuttle ready?"

one of the men asked the governor. Pickett paused for a moment, watching the monitor. He nodded.

"Yes, better prepare the shuttle: it looks like we might need it. Its location is remote enough to keep it hidden from the invaders, but have it ready to go. Let's see if they can be stopped first. I wouldn't want to leave too early. That wouldn't look good."

The pictures from the video feed weren't encouraging. Already the invaders were swamping the first line of defense. It didn't look like it would be long before they would break through and have the run of the base. Still, Pickett did nothing. He sat watching, horror etched on his gaunt face. He was not ready for this, that much was clear.

***

In silence Edwards and Jane left the comparative opulence of Command Post for the gray world of *Main Dome*. With his helmet on again, Edwards was feeling the usual claustrophobic panic that always engulfed him in these suits. It wasn't helped by the stale, rank smell that permeated the air he breathed. It came and went, but there was a distinctly unpleasant odor lurking in there somewhere

"Where did you get this suit?" Edwards asked.

"The medical center," Jane answered noncommittally as they strode across the floor of the dome. They had to watch their step. Chunks of concrete had cracked and broken away in places. The same was true of the buildings. There were large rifts in the walls, broken fault lines that eventually would burst open and send the buildings tumbling to the ground. Clearly, the materials used here were inferior. Perhaps, as the earliest building, *Primary Base* had suffered from untested methods that were later improved in building *Colony One*. Native material concrete could be tricky to get right. Whatever the reason, the whole base presented a picture of creeping decay.

"Where exactly in the medical center did you find it?" Edwards persisted as he caught another whiff of foul air.

"It works, so what does it matter?"

"You're not the one wearing it. Where did you get this suit? Was someone still in it?"

"No," Jane kept walking and didn't look back. "It was empty. I did have to clean it up a bit, but it's all I could find. You're lucky to have it."

"What do you mean, '*clean it up*'?"

Jane spun around, frustrated with Edwards' constant questions. "Okay, just give it a rest, Edwards. When I found your suit it was covered in dried blood and some other residue. Now you know. Happy? It looked like someone may have died in it, but the body had been removed. By who? I don't know! Why? I don't know that either. That's the mystery of it! It looks like a massacre happened here, but somebody took all the bodies away. All I do know for sure is that you got the only working suit I could find and you should be thankful I found that. Honestly, you're such an incompetent sometimes I really wonder how you were ever made a Special Operative or ended up on this mission."

"Not by choice," Edwards replied. "And I don't like you hiding things from me. I've had enough of that. If you had to give me a suit that was covered in blood and guts then you should have told me. At least now I know why it smells like a dead cat in here now. I wanted the truth, that's all."

Jane smiled and nodded. "Okay, that's fair. Well, Edwards, you ready to go? We've got to plumb the depths of a little hellhole called *The Lowers,* and I have to tell you, I'm more than a little nervous about it. I don't know what happened to all the people down there, but it obviously wasn't good. We've got to go down there now, and the same thing may well happen to us, but we have to do it because there doesn't seem to be anything else to do. Something's very wrong there and we've got to try and figure it out now. Is that honest enough for you?"

"Yeah," Edwards gulped. "That's honest enough."

They walked on in silence. Edwards shifted uneasily in his suit again. The smell wasn't getting any better. He knew it couldn't possibly be anything to do with whoever had died in it. That was too long ago. Probably it was some mold, or rotting rubber, or something like that, but that didn't give him any comfort. The reality of death and the accompanying stench of decay had him retching, struggling to keep his breakfast where it belonged.

"Are you okay?" Jane asked as he doubled over holding his stomach.

"I'll be fine," Edwards gasped through clenched teeth. "I'm just having a hard time catching my breath."

"Let me have a look." Jane examined his suit. "Yeah, this isn't exactly working right." She adjusted a few settings and gave him a pat on the back. "That should keep you going, just don't try running any marathons."

After another moment's pause, Edwards finally straighten up and started walking again. Soon they were entering an ugly, squat gray building. Inside, at the center of a wide, stark room of bare concrete, there was a large wire cage with doors on all sides. It was the base's main elevator system leading down to *The Lowers*. Jane walked up and pushed a button.

"We're trusting that?" Edwards asked doubtfully. "If it's anything like the rest of this place it'll fall apart before we get halfway down."

"It'll be fine," Jane assured him. "I ran a check on everything from Command Post and it all tested out fine. Besides, I don't think your suit's up to a mile-and-a-half descent to *The Lowers*. It's the only way, unless you want to wait here alone while I go down and sort things out."

There wasn't really a good answer to that, so Edwards kept quiet and waited for the elevator to arrive. When it finally pulled into the chamber it didn't do much to allay his fears. It was a bare-bones piece of machinery- a rickety wire cage held together by different colored rivets and bits of metal that clearly had been added later as an ad hoc repair. Jane moved forward, pulled the cage door aside, and stepped into the elevator. Edwards followed reluctantly behind.

The floor swayed slightly under their feet. Edwards glanced down into the darkness beneath them. The shaft was much wider than the elevator. It apparently had been designed to allow a large number of elevators to travel side-by-side to minimize delay.

Jane pushed the button and the elevator creaked, jolted,

and began its slow descent into the darkness. They couldn't see much. A naked bulb above their heads cast a thin light, but there wasn't much to see. Stark metal walls, girders, and hanging cables passed slowly as they crawled down to the lower habitation decks. A couple of times they passed other empty elevator cars, frozen in place between floors.

The elevator clanked and groaned on for another fifteen minutes. Edwards wasn't sure if that was the expected speed of the equipment or if years of decay had brought it to this. Either way, the time dragged and every bump and jostle of the compartment had him grabbing the wire cage, preparing for a sudden fall to his death.

Finally, they came to a stop. After all the noise of the descent the silence was deafening. Jane pushed the cage door aside and stepped out. Edwards followed. They were in a round, domed room carved out of the rock. The elevator light winked out, leaving them in darkness for a moment before their helmet lights clicked on. Jane was soon taking the cover off a panel on the wall, trying to get power back to the lower levels. After a few minutes, she shook her head and slammed the panel shut. The lights came back on.

"It looks like we better be quick down here or we'll be back in the dark again," she muttered, starting for the doorway. "Whatever fried the system sure made a mess. I don't think my repairs will hold long."

They walked along a corridor that seemed to stretch infinitely before them. It was circular with a slatted metal floor that clanged beneath their feet. The impression was similar to walking along a giant worm trail burrowed into the earth, and in some respects that probably wasn't far from the truth. Edwards remembered the description of how things were supposed to work on the Hypnos missions and part of that involved machines that would have excavated this type of tunnel, but the Hypnos crew hadn't been here long enough to complete that part of the mission. Again it seemed that the Hypnos mission had been more successful than they knew.

Jane was following a map laid out on her suit's computer. A few minutes later she stopped at a metal door. "This is it," she announced and pushed a button. The door slid to one side, and they entered a small chamber that barely held the two of them together. It was a tiny airlock between the sterile air of the corridor and the oxygenated atmosphere of the room within. A moment later the second door opened and they passed through into the wide room beyond.

There was nothing here, no furniture or personal effects of any kind. It was a long, grim room with blank metal walls, a metal floor, and a low stone ceiling.

"Doesn't look like much" Edwards commented. "You must have gotten something wrong. I don't see how anybody could have ever lived here."

"No, I'm right, but this wasn't just for one person. A lot of 'somebodies' lived here. It's a communal barracks." She pushed a button and a rectangular pallet jutted out into the room. It was a mean little cot that didn't look very comfortable, but it could be stored away quickly to maximize space in the room. She pushed the button again and it disappeared.

Jane removed her helmet, took a tentative sniff of the air, and wrinkled her nose. "Yeah, not too sweet, but breathable. Okay, let's get to work."

"On what?" Edwards glanced around at the empty room as he removed his own helmet. "There doesn't seem to be much here to work on."

"Yeah?" Jane pushed another button and the far wall lit up with a blue neon outline illuminating a number of small doors. "I think there's enough to keep us busy."

She walked over to a keypad and started typing numbers. "Everyone needs a little corner of the universe to call their own," she added, concentrating on her typing, "it's just that some people's corner is a bit smaller than others'. They don't get much smaller than this. A three-foot cube locker isn't much to show for a lifetime's work I suppose, but I guess its about as much as a grunge worker on an off-world base can expect."

Edwards was looking over her shoulder. "They're all code protected. How are you going to get in? You have about a one-in-a-billion chance of finding the right codes."

"Yeah, you'd think that wouldn't you, but no. Not in a place like this. Sure, they have their own little code to keep the riff-raff out of their stuff, but you didn't think that anything they had here was really private? Command Post had an override code. With that, they could access anything, and now, so can I." With a flourish, she finished the code and hit the final entry button. One of the doors hissed, clicked, and swung open. Its light remained on while the rest of the wall darkened again.

"Okay, let's see what we've got," Jane said.

They looked inside, but the contents were depressingly mundane. According to the nametag, the locker belonged to someone called Marlowe, but there wasn't really much there to tell them anything about who he was or what he had done. If this little box was the sole depository of his life's dreams and achievements then it was a pitiful testament to its futility. There were a few assorted papers, mostly work related indenture statements, a few changes of clothes, an electronic data reader that didn't work, and a credit strip used for monetary transactions. One thing did catch Edwards' attention, a grainy black and white copy of a photograph printed on plain paper. It was the only real piece of truly personal property in the locker. Everything else could have belonged to anyone. Sure, the stuff had his name all over it, but none of it told you anything about the man who owned it. The photograph at least was something tangible.

It was a group shot, eight or nine young men and women all merged into one hugging, clinging clump. A couple of them had their fists raised. They were all shouting and laughing. It was a scene of unfiltered joy and energy that seemed strangely out of place on this bleak planet. At least someone here had managed to figure out how to have some fun, Edwards concluded. Still, there was no way of telling who these people were or what their significance was. They were happy, though, and that was enough to make it stand out.

Edwards flipped the picture over and what he saw there was a far greater surprise than anything he had seen on the front. Scrawled in almost illegible letters was that familiar word, 'EVIL'.

***

Birch's eyes blinked open. His head was on the desk. He must have fallen asleep. He hadn't slept well in a long time and exhaustion had caught up with him.

In his mind, he had been with Karla. Somehow she had merged with the base. Her death and its death had become two expressions of the same event, of the inevitable demise of all things. Birch hated death; even in inanimate objects, it pained him. Growing up it had surr-ounded him. It was in the broken sidewalks and the flaking paint of his neighborhood, in the leaking roof and the cracked walls of his family home, and in the worn out promises and the creeping rot that had overtaken their society. They had become a culture of decline. They had dressed it up prettily, said some nice words about sharing the planet and passing the torch, but none of that had been true. That was no Golden Age, the time of global equalization. It had been the death of a dream, one that Birch had loved.

It was this as much as his wife Sarah's cancer that had made him run. She had simply been the most physical mani-festation of the illness. He couldn't stand to watch it, to smell it, the cancer eating from within. He had fled to Hypnos, the last big dream of a dying nation, the last chance to build some-thing new rather than watch something old fall apart. But even that hadn't been true. It had brought him to this dusty world and to this dead base. Death, it seemed, was to be his companion wherever he went. They were all Liberty Bells, built imperfectly and destined for destruction.

Birch's eyes flickered open again. Someone was shaking him. It was Lauren and for once there was emotion in her voice.

"Major, Major Birch!" She shook him again. "There's something on the monitor you need to see!"

Birch pulled himself up, rubbed his eyes, and glanced down at his screen. It took him a moment to make any sense of what he saw, but when he did he shot upright in his seat, fully awake. The storm had cleared and *Primary Base* was visible again. Jane's buggy was parked outside, but none of this was what grabbed his attention.

Five space suited figures had circled the buggy. Each held what looked like a heavy metal bar in their hands and they brought them down again and again on the machine.

THIRTY-SIX

In rhythmic unity, the bars came crashing down, again and again, smashing and breaking the vehicle to pieces with the devestating precision of a ceremonial sacrifice.

"Who are they?" Lauren asked.

Birch was already at the video controls, zooming in to answer that question. What he saw made him gasp. "Well, I guess Edwards got what he wanted!" he answered.

"What's that?"

"Space zombies," Birch blinked at the screen. "Edwards said he'd rather face them than deal with all the malfunctioning doors. It looks like he got them."

"Space zombies, really? That hardly seems likely." Lauren glanced down at the screen again. "There's got to be a better explanation than that."

"No doubt," Birch muttered, "I'm just stuck trying to think of what it could be." He pointed to the screen. "That's the kicker right there." He froze the picture and zoomed in on one of the figures. On their chest, they could just make out a smudge of yellow.

"What's that?" Lauren asked.

Birch zoomed in again. "It's a patch, a security forces patch. I think we just found Governor Pickett's five missing constables!"

Lauren didn't answer. She touched the screen, as though trying to verify the reality of what she was seeing, but it didn't change. Birch started the live feed again and it was clear that they were all wearing the same insignia.

Birch snatched up the radio mouthpiece. He was trying to reach Jane, but he was still only getting static. There was no way of knowing if they were dead or alive, but it didn't look good. For now, all he could do was watch as their transport was destroyed. He was powerless to do anything else.

"Okay," Birch muttered, finally, "I've seen enough of that. I need to get over there." He rose from his chair.

"Is that wise?" Lauren asked doubtfully.

"No, but it's all I can do? I've got to do something. I'm going to need your help, though. I want you to stay here and update me on what happens. If the constables go back in tell me. If they look like they're coming over here then I'll come back for you. While you're here I'll also need you to investigate Pickett's emergency shuttle. He mentioned that it was hidden somewhere. I want you to see if you can find it. I suppose he must have escaped in it before the end, but maybe there's a chance he didn't and it's still here. I need you to find that out. Got that?"

Lauren nodded. "But what do you think you can do over there?" she asked. "Five against one isn't very good odds, and there could be a lot more than that inside the base. I still don't think it's a good idea."

"Maybe not, but I've got to try." He grabbed the data-flare from the desk. "Besides, I'm armed with this little pop gun, and all they have are metal rods. What could possibly go wrong?"

Lauren shrugged. "I suppose you know best. I'll do what I can here." She returned to her seat and started working on her computer. That was probably about as warm a sendoff as he could expect from her, even if he was headed off on a mission of almost certain death.

Birch didn't waste any more time on farewells. He was

soon back in his EVA suit making his way through the corr-idors to the bio-dome. Jane had left the other buggy there. It took a while for him to reach it, it was on the other side of the base, but he passed swiftly through the gloomy passages and arrived twenty minutes later.

He paused at the thick glass doors, panting, trying to catch his breath before going on. He entered. Once inside the scale of the work the colonists had untaken here became obvious. Acres of lifeless, gray soil surrounded him. Perhaps this had once been a thriving garden, but now even the memory of life was gone. It had all turned to dust. A narrow concrete walkway took him through the barren fields to where the buggy waited, parked near the dome's glass outer wall.

Birch climbed in. It started up right away. The engine hummed; Jane had done a good job. The battery was full and everything was ready to go. The only question remaining now was how he was going to beat the odds and get Edwards, Jane, and himself back alive. He didn't stop to ponder that too much. There were plenty of other things like 'space zombies' and actually finding Jane and Edwards to worry about first. He would work out the technical problems of getting back later- if they made it that far.

The bio-dome had a large vehicle-access-airlock for trans-porting loads from the planet surface into the base. Birch drove into it. There was still no power to the doors, so he had to work it manually, but eventually, he was through and out into the open.

The storm was gone, but even now there were flecks of monochromatic dust floating thickly in the air. The feeble gray remnant of sunlight struggled to shine through the clogged atmosphere. In the few instances that it succeeded the light caught the dust and reflected like shimmering snow. It was a rare moment of beauty on a desolate planet, but Birch didn't notice. He was too busy trying to save the world or at least his little part of it.

The buggy's tires spun in the dirt as he pulled away. He

was on the opposite side of *Colony One*, so it took him a few minutes to get beyond it and into the open ground between the two settlements. It was impossible to see from here whether the constables were still outside. The base itself was little more than a dark blotch in the distance. He was going to be cautious anyway. He would take a wide path around and come at *Primary Base* from the other direction. Maybe with the element of surprise he might survive long enough to get something done.

***

Edwards was ready to go. They had been through three barracks by now and hadn't found anything more significant than a few pictures, papers, and some assorted knick-knacks-worthless little remnants of the worthless little lives that had once existed here.

"Are we done yet?" Edwards asked finally as they came out of the fourth barracks.

"Yeah," Jane answered hesitantly, glancing up and down the long corridor. She hadn't seemed any more enthusiastic about poking around down here than he had at the start. She had been more concerned with fixing the power than with any of Birch's theories, but now she paused, as though she was afraid of missing something important. "We can double back through the main lounge and get to *The Lowers* from there. I want to check one more thing before we go down."

They walked on in silence. The lounge, when they reached it, was the first sign of any comfort in the lives of the workers here, but even this was little more than a perfunctory gesture. Cracked leatherette sofas lined the room. A threadbare industrial carpet lay ruckled beneath their boots. Faded posters of long-forgotten movies and defunct sports teams hung askew in battered frames along the peeling walls. Someone had daubed the words *"Homo Fuge! EVIL"* in great red letters across the wall.

"Homo Fuge?" Edwards shook his head. "What's that supposed to mean?"

"*Fly, Oh man*, or something like that. It's Latin," Jane answered.

"Good advice, I wish we could take it."

Jane approached a large screened viewer that spanned the far wall. It had a prominent crack down one side. "These things usually have a memory mode in facilities like this," she explained as she tapped buttons on the side of the screen. "It should have a record of everything that happened in this room in last twenty-four hours before things went down. If I set the parameters to detect loud noises and any voices with a high emotional content we should get some idea about what happened here."

The screen flickered, but instead of lighting into a picture it settled into a jagged purple line condensed narrowly across its middle. "The screen's broken," Jane muttered shaking her head. A loud boom thundered through the speakers anyway and the sound of howling alarms quickly followed. There was the thump of hurried footsteps, something was knocked over and crashed to the floor, but the screen remained stubbornly blank except for the purple line.

"That doesn't shed much light on anything," Edwards commented after a few minutes of listening to nothing but the sound of confusion.

"Shhhh!" Jane leaned in closer to the speaker, but it had gone quiet. That was all there was, but Jane was already back at the keys, rewinding to hear the brief, confusing sounds again, only this time she had filtered out the background noise, focusing in on what she thought was there.

For a moment there was nothing but the sound of static. She tried again and after the initial boom and crash there came a hissing like a suppressed chuckle, snuffling, almost animal sounds, and some muttered words that after a few more repetitions seemed to sound something like "*Marlowe's way*", but it wasn't clear enough to be certain.

Edwards shivered. "What do you make of that?"

"I don't know," Jane shrugged, but her manner suggested that she did. "We've wasted too much time here. Let's get down to *The Lowers* and get the power back on at *Colony One*."

They hurried along the passages and tunnels, back toward the elevator. At each junction, there was a curved mirror, like in an old department store, and in it, Edwards could see the long expanse of emptiness stretching out around them. The empty stillness was not comforting.

"What do you suppose that loud noise on the recording was?" Edwards asked, less from an interest in the answer than from a desire to end the gloomy silence.

"It sounded like an explosion," Jane answered without looking back. "Probably further down in the base."

"*The Lowers*? Are we going to be able to get down there then?" Edwards asked. He was deeply conflicted about their mission to delve deeper into the station. On the one hand, he fully understood the need to repair *Colony One's* power supply. On the other hand, he dreaded going down there to do it. It was like going for a painful but necessary procedure.

"Let's just wait and see," Jane answered tersely as they pushed on through the passageway.

A few minutes later they reached the elevator room. Everything was just as they had left it. Jane and Edwards entered the cage and the compartment shuddered as they began their slow descent. The ride only lasted a few minutes though before they stopped again.

Jane looked puzzled and started pressing buttons on the control panel. They still had a way to go, but they weren't going anywhere. Edwards glanced over the side and gasped at what appeared in the narrow beam of his helmet light. Beneath them was not the long expanse of empty elevator shaft he had expected to see, instead, there was a large metal plate, welded and bolted in place, blocking their way down.

"It doesn't look like we're getting down that way," he commented dryly. "In fact, it looks like they were trying hard to make sure that nothing got through here- either up or down."

Jane nodded, reversing the elevator up to a higher floor. "There's always another way," she added brightly as they crawled slowly upward. "There are a lot of service shafts around here. There'll be another way down."

"Great," Edwards remarked gloomily. "But aren't you at least a little worried about why they blocked the shaft like that. I mean, maybe there's a radioactive leak, or dangerous gasses, or something else that we don't need to mess with down there. They wouldn't have blocked up the main shaft for no reason."

"Stop worrying, Edwards," Jane replied soothingly. "Our suits will filter out any dangerous elements. All we have to do is go down and see why the power flow isn't getting through to *Colony One*. We'll fix it, and it won't take long."

In fact, it didn't take long to explode the false security of Jane's words. The elevator stopped at the next level and it was soon apparent that there had been another brutal fight here. The Elevator room itself was largely untouched, but beyond it, there was incredible destruction. One passage was partly collapsed and the damage grew worse as they drew closer to the place that the map indicated as an access point to *The Lowers*.

"This is it," Jane finally announced as they came to a pile of rubble. She began pulling away stones and soon the remains of the entrance was visible.

It was then that Edwards first heard something. As they were clearing away the last few rocks he imagined he caught a faint impression of a sound, the same snuffling animal sound he had heard on the recording in the worker's lounge. Edwards looked at Jane, but she was busy wrestling the battered door open.

"Did you hear that?" Edwards hissed. Jane didn't even pause to look at him.

"No," she wrenched the door, and it opened with a metallic screech. Inside the faint impression of a narrow staircase stretched up and down into darkness.

The lights went out.

Edwards took a step back, stumbled over a chunk of concrete and fell to the floor. In that moment their helmet lights clicked automatically on. On his back now, Edwards saw Jane turning to help him, but behind her, bursting through the doorway was the spectral image of an astronaut clad in a stained gray spacesuit.

The astronaut landed on her, sending them both crashing onto Edwards. For a moment they were all wrestling and rolling until the attacker was finally still. It was only then that Edwards noticed the half smashed visor of the man's helmet and the pallid, bloodless face beneath it. This astronaut was dead and had been that way for a long time.

"Poor guy must've been trapped when the exit was blocked." Jane panted, climbing to her feet. She glanced in at the stairwell. "Yeah, it's blocked at the top." She dusted off her suit. Edwards took a little longer getting up.

"I don't like the look of him," Edwards commented, glancing down at the dead man's face.

"I'd be worried if you did," Jane laughed.

"That's not what I mean. Look at him. His face is all sucked in, but look at his eyes, there's something wrong with his eyes." There was. The dry atmosphere in this part of the lower levels had mummified the body. He was leathery and withered, except for his eyes. They didn't have the usual glassy, hollow appearance you expected from the dead. They didn't move, there was no obvious indication of life in them, but there was a spark, a slight red tinge that gave an appearance, not of life, but of something more than death.

They were suddenly aware that the animal sounds were getting louder. Edwards and Jane looked down the stairwell toward the source of the noise. In the crossed beams of their helmet lights, they saw a swarm of space-suited figures clambering up toward them.

"Oh great!" Edwards shouted, pulling Jane back into the

corridor. He slammed the door shut and started pulling rocks to barricade it. "Come on!" he bellowed. "*Homo fuge*, and fast!" They quickly finished piling stones into a makeshift barrier and fled blindly back up the corridor toward the elevator. The beams of light from their helmets twisted crazily in the darkness as they ran instinctively for safety.

If they had had time to think they would have realized the futility of running for the elevator when the power had just gone out. There was no power, so of course, it would be dead. It didn't matter, though. Somehow the elevator worked anyway, a fact that they only later realized meant that more was happening here than just malfunctioning power grids.

Edwards slammed the cage shut, and Jane pushed the button sending them slowly to the surface. They stood silently, breathing hard. Edwards looked down, watching for any sign of pursuit, but he couldn't see anything

To his surprise, an unexpected chuckle rose in his throat. It wasn't funny. He wasn't amused. He tried to suppress the sound, but it burst out, escaping as inexplicable, bellowing, laughter. It was manic, an involuntary expression of relief as the elevator slowly pulled them to safety.

Jane didn't join in. She just kept staring down into the darkness.

"Wow!" Edwards finally gasped through heaving breaths. "That was close!" He leaned forward trying to gain control of his voice. "Seriously though, we have got to get out of this place." He straightened up and looked Jane in the eye. "There were a lot of those things down there, and I have the feeling they were planning to do the same to us as they did to that poor guy and everyone else who lived here. We're not safe."

"I'm not sure whether I agree with your panic," Jane responded coolly, "but I do think you're right. We need to get back to *Colony One*, regroup, and figure out where we go from here. We still need to get to *The Lowers* to repair the power systems, but that's a job for another day."

"Yeah, and a job for another guy," Edwards added emphatically. "You can drag Major Birch along with you next time. I'm staying in *Colony One* from now on!"

"He'd never come," Jane answered flatly. She gazed down into the darkness. "Not here."

The minutes passed slowly. Jane's eyes never moved from the yawning space below. Edwards glanced up and caught the sudden impression of a faint light far above them.

"Uh-oh," he muttered, pointing up. "What do you suppose that is?"

Jane followed his gaze. "That looks like a problem," she sighed. "I guess our friends down below weren't the only ones who wanted to greet us."

THIRTY-SEVEN

"They've gone inside," Lauren's voice crackled over Birch's headset. The news wasn't exactly comforting. It was like finding a spider in your bedroom, taking your eyes off it for a second to grab something to hit it with, and then discovering that it had disappeared.

"Okay," Birch responded. The buggy sped across the gray plains.

"Worse news with the weather too, I'm afraid," Lauren's voice came faintly. The interference seemed to be increasing as he approached *Primary Base*. "I'm picking up a sighting, looks like a clipper system coming through in a few hours. High winds, the usual, but it shouldn't last more than a day or so this time according to the readings. You'll either have to finish quickly or wait the storm out, something to consider while you're over there.

"Wonderful," Birch spat bitterly, "any other good news for me?"

"No. I'm sure you're aware of the dangers. I've been re-searching Pickett's shuttle. I haven't gotten very far yet. Most of what I've seen is mayhem and confusion at the end. The upshot is that nobody comes back from *Primary Base*."

"Yeah, thanks for the pep talk. Remind me to look you up next time I need a motivational speaker. You certainly have a magical way with words."

Lauren didn't answer for a moment. "Good luck," she finally replied. "Try to get back before the storm. It'll be easier that way."

"Thanks," Birch muttered and clicked off. That was likely to be the last he would hear from her until he came out of *Primary Base*. He was entering the dead zone around the station where no communication was getting through. He was on his own now.

The base loomed up darkly beside him. Its thick glass dome winked opaquely in the dull sunlight. There was no way of knowing what was on the other side, but he knew it wouldn't be good. At the very least it held the five constables who had just destroyed Jane's buggy. That was enough to worry about, but somehow Birch doubted that was all he would find.

He stopped outside an entrance on the far side of the base and climbed out of the buggy. He had been thinking about how to prevent what happened to Jane's vehicle happening to his. The solution wasn't ideal, but it was the best he could come up with just now. He rigged the buggy's battery to the frame and programmed it so that if anyone got too close they would get a nasty shock. The bad part was that too many shocks would drain the battery and leave him stranded anyway. He didn't have any better ideas. All he could do was get on with what he had to do and hope the buggy would still be here and with a full charge when he got back.

Birch entered by a small service entrance. The door was jammed with age and decay and it took him a while to get in. Once inside he found himself in a dark, narrow corridor that snaked through the less traveled portion of the base. There wasn't any light here and he stepped carefully, unsure of the soundness of the floor beneath his feet.

He followed the wrist computer's map direction toward the center of the base. If there were any people nearby they should have shown up on the same display, but whatever had been blocking outside communication was having the same affect on his readouts. According to his computer, he was completely alone in *Primary Base*. He knew that wasn't true.

He tried the radio. "Major Grey, Major Birch here, respond please." Silence was the only reply. He had expected that. It was never going to be that easy.

Without any readings or communication, it was hard to be certain where Jane and Edwards were, but he was pretty sure he knew where he would find them. Their mission had been focused on one place only, the last place he wanted to go- *The Lowers*.

There didn't seem to be any power in the outer corridors, but as Birch moved closer to the center of the base some limited functions returned. A thin light shone dully from the wall panels and the doors opened automatically again.

Finally, Birch came out into *Main Dome*. He blinked against the brightness of the light. Shading his eyes with his hand, he scanned the cavernous space for any sign of life. There was nothing visible. Empty gray buildings, the dark dome, and the flat gray concrete floor that he grimly noted was marked with dried red blotches. That wasn't unexpected. It looked empty now, but he wasn't taking any chances. According to the map, the elevators to the lower levels were on the other side of the dome, and he skirted around the buildings to avoid walking out in the open.

A few moments later he reached an ugly little gray building that was the elevator station. It was dark inside. He entered slowly, cautiously glancing around for any sign of the five constables. He didn't see anyone. He fingered the trigger of the data-flare. It was a pretty useless weapon, but the solid feel of its handle in his grasp gave him some comfort.

In the beam of his helmet's light, he could make out the mostly empty room and the large wire structure at the center that housed the elevators. He walked slowly toward it, his careful steps echoing in the darkness.

He glanced through the wire mesh, down the shaft into the heart of *The Lowers*. He was surprised to discover that it wasn't dark. Somewhere far below, there was a point of light.

He couldn't tell if it was moving or not, and if it was moving he had no way of knowing if it was going up or down. He couldn't even tell if it was who he was looking for or who he was trying to avoid. All he really knew was that this was the only sign of life he had found so far and he had to follow it. He pushed the button and waited for the elevator to arrive.

***

Jane and Edwards leaped at the control panel in the same instant. Pushing buttons furiously they tried to stop the elevator in the hope of getting off and avoiding detection by whoever was coming down, but the mechanism was too slow. The light was drawing closer, and by the time their cage had come to a stop the floor of the elevator above was clearly visible a few feet above them.

Jane hurled the cage door aside and jumped out, but Edwards stumbled and was caught in the doorway as the mysterious descending elevator passed. At first, all he could see were the feet of the occupants. Then their legs. As the compartment drew level he saw a number of space-suited figures. They were perfectly still. Like marbled sculptures they stood, not turning, not looking, just standing as they passed by. None of them were looked directly at Edwards, and none of them showed by even the slightest tilt of the head that they had taken any notice of him, but somehow Edwards knew they had seen him. He felt it.

Jane had been trying to pull him off, but after the elevator passed she gave up and got back in the compartment. "No point trying to hide now," she muttered and pressed the up button again. "Our only hope is that somehow they didn't notice you. They didn't react when they went by."

"They saw me," Edwards said. He looked down. Briefly, it seemed as though the light was still descending. Perhaps he had been mistaken. Maybe they hadn't really seen him after all, but that hope was a brief one. The light was stopping, and a moment later it followed them up.

"And here they come," Edwards concluded grimly.

***

Birch had been waiting a few minutes when the rickety cage finally clanked and wheezed its way into the main elevator station. He wasn't sure he trusted the thing but he didn't have much choice. If he wanted to get out of *Primary Base* and back to *Colony One* before the storm hit he would have to be fast. This was the only way.

He gingerly lifted the cage door and was pulling it aside when the sudden crash of a blunt force impact sent him hurtling across the room. He lay on the floor, dazed for a moment, unable to comprehend what had happened.

White spots fuzzed before his eyes, He tried to get up but collapsed as his arm gave way under him. He blinked hard against the pain. In the narrow beam of his helmet's light, he could see boots crossing the floor. They were coming for him. He tried to lift himself up again, but only managed to feebly raise his head a few inches, just enough to see the hollow black oval face of an astronaut's helmet, the shine of a golden badge, and the glint of a metal bar as it was raised up to come down on him again.

THIRTY-EIGHT

Edwards was at the control panel again pushing the up button for the fifth time. His finger tapped repeatedly, over and over, trying to squeeze even the slightest particle of extra speed out of it.

"Lay off the button," Jane snapped. "It's not helping."

Edwards stopped and glanced over the side to the pursuing light below. It hadn't gotten any closer, but it wasn't any farther away either. He knew that when they finally reached the top they only had a few minutes to get clear of the cage and run for the exit before the second elevator arrived. That wasn't much time. It probably wouldn't be enough, but all they could do was try.

Finally, the cage clanked and sighed as it pulled out onto the surface and came to a shaky stop. Jane and Edwards immediately lifted the door and launched themselves out into the gloomy room, ready to run for the exit, but something surprised them. There, in this empty mausoleum of a building, two space-suited astronauts were wrestling and rolling on the dirty floor.

***

The pain in his arm had stopped Birch from getting up, but

he could move his legs, and when his attacker came at him again with a metal bar he had been ready. He kicked out, landing a hefty blow on his assailant's knee. There was a crack and an audible groan as the figure crumpled and fell to the floor beside him.

Birch struggled to get to his feet, but before he could take a step his attacker was at him again, knocking his legs out from under him and sending him clattering back to the floor. For a moment they struggled, gouging and pulling at each other, trying to gain the advantage. Birch was losing. His attacker was just too strong for him. With his throbbing arm it was hardly an even fight, and soon the man was on top of Birch, sending a flurry of fists into his stomach. Birch writhed, trying to knock him off, but his weight was just too much for him. He was beaten.

In a blur of indistinct action Birch caught the sudden impression of two more astronauts launching themselves at him. Death was certain now, he was sure of that, and yet he was surprised a moment later when the newcomers pulled the constable off and threw him aside, hitting him until he fell unconscious at their feet.

One of the figures bent over Birch, checking him for any injury. It was Jane. He recognized the suit. The other must have been Edwards, but he was wearing something different, some old gray relic from the colony.

Jane helped him to his feet. Birch winced with pain. He ached, but it wasn't anything lasting. His left arm was still throbbing from the initial blow of the constable's metal rod, but it wasn't broken. A good rest would fix it if he ever got back to *Colony One*.

Edwards quickly dragged the unconscious constable, feet first, to the elevator, pushed him into the cage, hit the button, and sent him to the bottom. "One less to worry about," he explained as he ran back to Jane and Birch.

Birch had bent down to pick up the data-flare when the second elevator arrived. Glancing up, he saw that it contained four more constables. They didn't move. For a moment Birch almost imagined that they might just stay that way, but the illusion was quickly broken as they pulled the door aside and stepped out.

There was a diabolical fluidity to their movement. It was something natural, like the oozing flow of molten lava down the side of an erupting volcano. There was no haste in their action, only a terrible certainty that they would reach you, and when they did, you would dead.

"Maybe we should go," Edwards was edging to the door.

"Great idea, Edwards." Birch was cautiously following, careful to keep an eye on the constables. Jane stooped down to pick up the metal bar Birch's attacker had dropped and followed after them.

They had hardly made it to the doorway before a flash of sudden movement brought all four of the constables within striking distance. Jane lashed out at the nearest figure, swinging the metal bar at his helmet. It landed with a smack but didn't faze him. There was a moment's pause, as though he was calculating the level of pain and the appropriate response, then he snatched Jane's weapon and flung it across the room. She turned and ran.

They all ran. This wasn't an ordered retreat. It was a panicked flight, an unthinking, uncontrolled dash for the exit and any hope of safety. They didn't know where they were going, but by good fortune, they had instinctively run for the farthest point across the dome and came out not far from where Birch had entered earlier.

"Come on!" Birch shouted. "This way!" He guided the others through the narrow opening, into the dark passages that would lead them back to the buggy.

"Here," he handed the data-flare and a fistful of flares to Edwards. "You're better at this than me. I need you to hit each one of them in the chest plate, as near the center as you can manage. Got that?"

Edwards nodded.

They ran on into the gathering darkness, but as fast as they went, it seemed that their pursuers were effortlessly keeping pace with them. Edwards got off a shot at the lead constable. The flare whooshed with a sprinkle of yellow sparks and hit him directly in the center of his chest before fizzling out in a puff of black smoke. It didn't stop him. It didn't even slow him down.

Edwards fumbled in his suit, grabbing another flare from the pocket where he had stored them. It was hard to reload while running, but a few moments later he clicked the barrel shut and took aim at the second constable. He hit again, but with similar results to the first.

"This isn't working!" Edwards shouted, reaching for another flare.

Birch was only a few steps ahead and had seen it all. "You're doing fine!" he growled. "Keep firing. Hit each of them two or three times. I don't care; just hit them all at least once!"

Edwards nodded and took a third shot that missed this time. He grabbed another flare. Every shot cost him a few steps. He was last in line and they were closing in. The constables retained the same languid look they had shown in the elevator room. Effortlessly it seemed they were catching him.

"I really hope you've got a better idea to get out of this than shooting this little pop-gun at them," Edwards shouted, "because it's still not working!"

"We're almost there!" Birch responded. The dim side lights of the corridor had gone out. They were in a part of the base that had no power. This was what Birch had been waiting for. As they turned a corner they came to one of the safety doors that he had opened on the way in. He had left them all open. This wasn't exactly safe, a routine atmospheric breach could prove critical with the safety doors left open, but he hadn't worried about that. He had been more concerned about having a quick escape route. His instinct had been proven right. That was exactly what he needed right now.

Birch paused at the heavy metal door, waved Edwards through, and slammed it shut behind him, turning the crank and resetting the mechanism.

"That should keep them busy for a minute," Birch panted as they started running again. 'They'll have to go through the manual override to get through. We'll have a few more like this before we get outside, so that should buy us ten minutes or so, plenty of time to get to the buggy and get out of here!"

Birch's estimate had been too optimistic. Much less than a minute had passed before they heard the clang of the door opening behind them.

"Wonderful," Birch muttered, glancing back at the not-too-distant constables. "Plan B Jane, I need you to program in on reading 53 and shut everything down, and Edwards, don't stop shooting! Use every flare you've got!"

They ran on. Jane was trying to tap out codes on her wrist computer, Edwards was trying to land a couple more shots on the constables, and Birch was slamming and resetting every door they came to. All of this left them with very little breathing space by the time they finally reached the outside entrance.

Never had gray rock and lifeless soil ever looked so good to Birch. He shut and reset the final door and looked up just in time to see Jane running for the buggy. "No, Jane!" he shouted, but too late. She was already too close and an electrical charge leaped out and knocked her to the ground.

Birch switched off the power and ran quickly to her side. She was alive but unresponsive. She had taken quite a jolt, but already her suit was pumping extra oxygen, stabilizing her readings, and trying to help bring her around.

Birch didn't have much time to think about Jane's health. It wasn't long after this that he heard the familiar clank and rattle of the door's handle as the constables worked the mechanism, they were about to get out.

Birch tried to drag Jane to the buggy, but it was only a short moment later that the door burst open and the four constables stepped out.

Birch didn't have any time to consider his next move. The constables were already moving. They never spoke a word. They seemed instinctively to know what they needed to do, and now as a unit, the four of them drew up their metal rods and marched toward Birch and Edwards.

"Split!" Birch shouted, waving Edwards to the left. "Draw them away and keep them off Jane."

Birch ran right and Edwards went left. It seemed to work. Two constables followed Edwards and the other two came after Birch. Jane was safe for now, but it didn't last. Edwards tried dodging the first attacker, but his maneuver was swiftly countered by the second constable who slammed him to the ground and pinned him there. That now left Birch with three enemies to contend with alone.

"The odds keep getting worse," Birch muttered to himself. He stooped down, picked up a rock, and flung it at the nearest enemy. It hit him hard in the visor, but it didn't have any impact. He just kept coming. Without a weapon, Birch knew he was finished. There was only one thing to do.

Birch doubled back. Dodging the swinging weapons of the constables, he jumped into the buggy, started the engine, and hit the accelerator. The tires spun, dirt flew, and the buggy took off. The constables pursued him, but he quickly left them behind as he sped toward *Colony One*.

Birch kept going for a moment, but the instant he knew he couldn't be caught he pulled the wheel hard and spun the buggy around, facing *Primary Base* again. He glanced down at his wrist computer. Briefly, he considered trying to continue what Jane had started, but already he could see the constables turning their attention to their captives. Perhaps Jane and Edwards only had seconds to live. There wasn't time for the smart plan; he had to go with the stupid one.

Birch gunned the engine and headed back at full throttle.

They saw him before he arrived, but it didn't do them much good. They had gathered around Edwards' prostrate form when the buggy flew at them. They scattered. Birch swerved suddenly, missing Edwards and slamming into a constable that flew across the hood, hit the windshield, and bounced to the ground.

"Two down," Birch muttered as he reversed to clip a second fleeing form. The last two, however, were not so easily dealt with. One jumped into the seat beside him and wrestled for the wheel. Birch elbowed him in the ribs, but before he could do any more the second one had leaped on the other side and was at him, pulling at his helmet, lifting him from the seat. Birch wrenched the wheel. The buggy hit a stone, rolled over on its side, and went skidding through the dirt.

They all flew clear, but the constables came up ready to fight; Birch lay dazed on the ground. They quickly over-powered him. His helmet was smashed down into the dirt. He tried to lift his head, attempting to get up, but heavy hands shoved him down again. All he could see now was gray soil, but in the brief moment his head had been up he had caught sight of something that gave him hope. Jane was conscious again and, unnoticed by the constables, was tapping subtly away on her wrist computer.

Birch was pulled roughly to his feet, but before the con-stables could harm him their suits started whining loudly. There was a brief pause. Their grips loosened. Red lights flashed on their chest panels and both men stumbled. The whine became a screeching alarm. Their hands went to their heads; they writhed and fell to the ground, convulsing, and then they were still.

Birch stared for a moment, unable to believe what had just happened. He looked over at Jane who was struggling to her feet and went to check on Edwards. He was alright, pretty sore no doubt, but he would live. They had all made it.

"Nice work, Jane," Birch smiled. She had been their last hope and she had come though. The data flares had worked. Just like with the probe, attaching them to the constables' suits had allowed her to override the original programming. In this case, she had shut their suits down.

"Thanks," Jane answered coolly, "but we need to get back. I have some things to figure out before we can make any progress here."

"Yeah," Birch replied, eyeing her thoughtfully. "I've got things to do too. Let's go."

The buggy still rested on its side, but it didn't take long to have it upright again, and soon they were speeding back across the gray plains toward *Colony One*. Through the cracked windshield, Birch could see the gathering clouds of another upcoming storm, the one Lauren had been warning him about. It was a race to get back in time, but Birch was determined to win this one.

THIRTY-NINE

He did win. It was a good ten minutes before the storm hit when Birch finally pulled into the entry port of the bio-dome at *Colony One*. The swirling black clouds could be seen hovering ominously through the glass ceiling of the empty dome as they hurried through.

"We're back," Edwards panted as they ran through the corridors. "Anything new to report?"

"Yes, quite a lot," Lauren responded in her usual even tone. "I'll tell you when you get up here."

"Thanks," Birch answered and clicked off. There was no point trying to get any more out of her until they reached Main Control. All he could do right now was hurry and hope the news was good.

It took another twenty minutes to get across the base and into Main Control. Once inside they quickly removed their helmets and gloves. Edwards threw himself into a chair and slumped over, his head in his hands.

"I don't care what anyone says," he muttered between gasping breaths, "I am never leaving this room again!"

"Sure," Birch answered. "At least not until one of those 'space zombies' of yours comes knocking on that door anyway."

Edwards' head shot up. "You don't mean that those things could come over here, do you?"

"Yes, that's exactly what I mean. They've been over here before, near the end of the original settlement, and there's no reason to believe they won't do it again now they're active."

"Great," Edwards groaned, "and what exactly are we going to do about that?"

"Well, that's what we've got to figure out." Birch pointed to the screen displaying the video feed outside. It was now little more than a swirling mass of gray and black dust as the storm rose up to full force. "At least we've got that on our side. I don't think they'll come over until that's blown over, so we have maybe twenty hours to a day to figure it out. That's more than Pickett and his men got once they finally realized the danger they were in."

Birch walked over to the coffee dispenser, poured himself a cup of the noxious brew, and took a sip.

"Okay," he sighed, dropping into a chair and resting his feet on the low table. "Tell me what you've got, Lauren. Any news on Pickett's shuttle?"

Lauren nodded. "Yes, some. I haven't been able to pin down exactly how it's accessed, but the entry port to the secret hangar is somewhere in the governor's personal suite. Everything I've read points clearly to that. There's nothing to say how to get in, though. We'll just have to work that one out ourselves."

"Fine," Birch nodded, "that's more than we knew before. Anything else?"

"Not really." Lauren paused, as though weighing whether she should speak her mind. "Well, there is one other thing. It's that word." She gestured to the large screen with the red, dripping 'EVIL' written across it. "It keeps coming up. You mentioned seeing it. I've been reading it everywhere. It seems it was more than just a simple statement of what was going on here. I think it's trying to tell us something. I don't see how it fits with anything else, but I don't think we should ignore it."

Birch nodded.

"Here's another one for you." Jane threw the photograph

she had found in the worker's quarters at *Primary Base* on the table. "I noticed the same 'EVIL' marking on the back of this and thought it might be important."

Birch picked up the picture and turned it over, examining the writing. The same word was there, though the style of the letters was quite different from the way they were painted on the big screen. These were not written by the same person- that much was clear. That escalated things. It meant that this was a conspiracy of some kind. It wasn't just the ranting of one crazed individual. More than one person knew the significance of 'EVIL' and Birch couldn't shake the feeling that this was the key to something important.

He turned the paper over again, looking at the picture. It was an unusual artifact. The mere fact that it was printed instead of electronically stored seemed to indicate an importance, but Birch couldn't detect anything significant. It was merely a group of young men and women in some relaxed social setting, just a typical group photograph most young people would take with their friends.

"What do you make of it?" Birch asked, handing the picture back to Jane, "and where did you get it?"

"It was in one of the barracks you told me to search over in *Primary Base*, and I don't know quite what to make of it. Maybe if we run it through the computer it'll come up with something."

She moved over to the console, put the picture into the scanner, and tapped a few commands. "Yes," she exclaimed a moment later. "It's working! It's identifying all the subjects in the picture."

Birch was at her side in an instant. A digital copy of the photograph was on the screen and boxes were forming around each face as it flashed up information about them. Birch stared, taking it all in.

"Wait, what was that?" he asked, pointing to a box that had just dissolved from the screen. Jane clicked on the face and the information returned. It was Bruce Marlowe.

"Oh, we've got something here!" Birch enthused. "Look and see if you can find Parsons too."

She did. He was standing near the front, his arm around a young woman and a bottle in his hand. A few other faces in the picture were identified as people who later disappeared. This was significant. The pieces were coming together, but Birch couldn't make any sense of the picture they made.

"What are we seeing here?" he rubbed his chin thought-fully. "What pattern is there with all these people?"

Jane shrugged. "They're all from *Primary Base*, but that's not exactly surprising. Social calls between the bases weren't exactly encouraged. Your research proved that. I'm not sure there's any more to it than that."

"You're almost right," Birch responded, "but let's try him." He pointed to a barely visible form, a fraction of a head mostly hidden by a laughing girl in the foreground. No box had identified him.

Jane touched the screen and the flashing boxes stopped, the icon came to rest finally on the tuft of hair and a quarter of a face. "I'm not sure it'll be enough to ID him," Jane reasoned. "There's not much to go on."

"Let's just try," Birch replied.

The box flashed for a time as the computer calculated the possibilities from its database. Finally, the box glowed yellow and brought up an ID file.

Peter Wagner
Computer/Info tech.
Colony One

"Now that is strange," Jane shook her head. "What would a *Colony One* tech be doing with a bunch of lower level *Primary Base* workers?"

"That's a question worth answering," Birch replied. "Click on his file, and let's find out."

The information flashed up. Birch's eyes narrowed as he

silently read the details.

Wagner's story was a rare example of egalitarianism in the claustrophobic atmosphere of the colony. He had worked in *The Lowers* as a young man, but even in that withering environment his intellect had bloomed. Like a weed it had grown up where it hadn't been planted, and like a weed it had not been welcomed at first. With the limited access to the mainframe granted to a *Lowers* grunge worker (ordering food from a basic menu and unlimited entertainment), he had somehow broken into the system and gained access to the most sensitive material. He had only been detected by a chance inquiry into a slight discrepancy in the coding of his food orders brought about by his activities.

Wagner might have been severely punished. His activity was the very thing that *Colony One* feared the most, yet by dint of his exceptional ability he was rehabilitated and put to useful purpose in the newer colony. He was considered an asset, but because of his background, he was an asset to be watched. He was applauded for his work, but he was never fully trusted.

The files showed no evidence of any further rule infractions by Wagner, but Birch wasn't convinced. On the surface, he seemed to have assimilated into the life of *Colony One*, but was that rebel of *Primary Base* ever really gone? Had he lived a clean life after his transfer, or had he just been good at cleaning up after himself? And how did all of this relate to the 'EVIL' word that pervaded the life of both bases and was written on the back of this very picture? That was the question.

"Bring up the location of Wagner's quarters, Jane," Birch ordered. "I think our little rebel warrants a visit." Jane complied, made a printout and handed it to Birch.

"It doesn't look like he moved up much in the world," Birch observed, scrutinizing the paper. "He's down in the lower section. Looks like a pretty unsavory place for a genius to reside. Well, I guess there must have been a lot of pressure on resources with limited accommodation here. I suppose it would have been hard to fit a newcomer in."

Birch laid the paper aside. "Okay," he said, drawing himself up, "time is short, so we have to be quick. There's two things we need to get done. First and foremost we have to find Pickett's shuttle. We need to get off this rock, but the second part is just as important. We need to find somewhere to go.

"Pickett seemed to think somebody knew more than they were telling; that there was a secret plot by some of the people on this planet to escape to a better place without telling him and all his cronies where it was. That's what I'm counting on. We need to find that place too, and I have a hunch that if anyone knew it, it would have been Wagner. We need to investigate him. He looks like our best chance.

"We'll have to split up," Birch continued. "I'm going to look for the entrance to the secret hangar in Pickett's suite. Jane, I want you and Edwards to investigate Wagner's quarters. Look for any clues to what he did in the last days of the colony, and look for any references to 'EVIL'.

"Lauren," Birch turned to her, "you need to stay here and monitor the base. Until the weather clears you won't be able to see much outside, but keep watching the halls, look out just in case anything from *Primary Base* has braved the weather and snuck over while we can't see them. Warn us at the first sign of anything. Got that?"

She nodded.

"Okay, any questions?" Birch didn't expect any. He started to get up when Jane pulled what looked like a six-inch metal bar from her pocket and slammed it on the table.

"Yeah, I've got a good one," she snapped. Birch only realized now that she hadn't made eye contact with him since their return, but she was glaring at him now, her eyes aflame and boring into him. "How do you explain this?"

FORTY

Birch glanced at the metal bar and then back at Jane. "What do you expect me to say about that?" he asked dismissively.

"I expect you to tell me the truth," Jane hissed.

"We don't have time for this." Birch got up and started putting on his gloves.

"Make time," Jane growled. She rose to her feet, putting her hand on his arm.

Birch hesitated. "So, what do you expect me to tell you?"

"I expect you to tell me why you said that all the seeding supplies were destroyed in the storm when they weren't." She waved the metal bar under his nose. "This is part of the foundation to the quarry conveyor system that we never got time to install before you abandoned the mission. If everything was destroyed like you said, then how exactly did this survive, and how did it get installed, and for that matter how did *Primary Base* get built? If all the automated systems were destroyed in that storm, then how did anything get built?"

"I don't know," Birch shrugged, his eyes cast down. "I can't explain it. That's what I've been trying to figure out."

"Exactly!" Jane thundered. "There's a lot you don't seem to be able to explain. Like how Colonel Ratliff died. Can you explain that to me just one more time because for some reason I still don't quite get it?"

"We're back to that again?" Birch sighed. "I already told everything about it. He went out into the storm. He never came back. What more is there to tell?"

"*THAT'S* what I've been trying to figure out!" Jane snapped. She stood up, clicked her helmet back into place, and shoved her hands into her gloves. "And I will find out." She stormed to the door.

"Oh, and don't bother with Pickett's suite," she shot back as she reached the exit. "I'm checking that myself. You can be the one to hold Edwards' hand this time around. You two go search through the teenage computer geek's bedroom. Just watch out for the dirty socks under the bed."

She threw the metal bar at Birch, "Catch!" she shouted and left.

"You know, I don't think she likes you very much," Edwards observed after a moment's stunned silence.

"Well, I don't think she's your number one fan either," Birch smiled bitterly, "but give me your hand and let's go see if we can find those dirty socks." He rose to his feet, put his helmet on, and walked to the door.

"Wow," Edwards chuckled, fastening his own helmet, "that really does sound fun!"

A few minutes later they were striding through the empty halls toward Wagner's room. It took some time to get there. His quarters were deep down on the cramped lower levels. "From one *Lowers* to another," Birch muttered as they passed through the narrowing corridors.

In the numbing sameness of the gray passages Birch's mind began to wander back to Ratliff, back to his decisions, back to all his decisions. It was strange; the past was a terrible land of comfort. If death was the undiscovered country to be feared, and life was the moment to be endured, then the past should have provided the ballast for the voyage, but the weight was dead. It was dragging him down.

Jane's words echoed in his mind. She was looking for a clear and simple truth, something to answer all of her questions. Birch had given up on that idea long ago. She could look, but things change. Some time ago, back on Earth, he would have fought Jane over the decision to search for Pickett's shuttle, but now it didn't seem to matter. She was just as likely to find it as him, and the information he was searching for in Wagner's quarters was just as important. He had decided to let it go.

They arrived at an unimposing, dirty, dinged up metal door. An eye scanner, like the one at Town Hall, shot out a beam of crimson light. It lingered on Birch's face a moment before clicking off. It seemed satisfied by what it found there. The door hissed open.

They stepped inside. It was a tiny room, similar to the one Birch had slept in when they first arrived at *Colony One*, only it was even smaller. It was a live-in closet. The room was mostly tidy but still cluttered with too many things for such a small space. Books were piled along all four walls. A small bed rested in a narrow space between them, and a stained old model computer rested on a flimsy wire frame desk at the end of the bed. There was hardly enough room for both Birch and Edwards to stand at the same time. Edwards sat down on the bed and a plume of dust rose up from the mattress.

"Oh, nice," Edwards muttered, waving the dust away. "This is a real home-from-home."

Birch didn't take any notice; he was too busy staring up at the walls. They were covered, top-to-bottom, with old posters. Many of them showed advertising from the early days of computers and other basic technology. Clean cut business-men with crisp, white shirts, fancy ties, and winning smiles extolled the virtues of boxy IBM machines. Calculators, digital watches, microwave ovens, and video game systems were all represented here. Happy, smiling people in their Technicolor world all found their joy in what these gadgets could do for them. It was all so simple and undeniably good. Life was better because your Casio watch could tell you the time digit-ally. You didn't have to do the hard math because your Texas Instruments calculator did it for you. And at the end of the day, your family would gather around the faux wood paneled

Atari and, in the warming glow of the TV, you would play and learn the true value of family togetherness.

Birch nudged a few of the books with his foot, glancing at the titles as he moved them. They were mostly technical manuals, but not the sort he expected. The majority of them, like the posters on the walls, related to old outdated technology. They were useless.

"What sort of nut was this kid?" Birch muttered, shaking his head.

"Just the sort of nut I can understand," Edwards replied. "He looks like a pretty classic case from what I'm seeing here."

"Classic case of what, junk hoarding?"

"No, fustalgia."

"Fu-what?"

"Fustalgia," Edwards gestured to the walls around them. "Like nostalgia, but not obsessed with the past, instead it's all about the future. Not the real future of course, but the future that was promised in the past. They yearn for the golden tomorrow that never dawned."

"I know the feeling." Birch sat on the end of the bed, trying to get the computer started. Surprisingly, for a low-level room like this, it seemed to have a backup power source and it was still working. Birch wasn't sure if that was a special dispensation given to Wagner by his new employers in *Colony One*, or if it was the result of his own private enterprise. He would have guessed the latter.

The keys lit up, but the screen remained stubbornly blank.

"Say, that looks familiar," Edwards rose to his feet. Standing on the bed he reached up, pulling down a small poster. "Isn't that the guy we met in the governor's office?" He handed the picture to Birch.

"Yeah," Birch snatched the paper, his hands shaking. It *was* the same man. He had the same smooth, almost metallic look, the same blonde, slicked-back hair, sunglasses, and manic white smile. The name beneath the picture was Max.

Birch turned the paper over. He had been sure already that they were on the right track, but what he found there was the clincher. Written on the blank side were the words,

Go to EVIL!

"I'm not sure I like the sound of that advice," Edwards commented, peering over Birch's shoulder. "What do you suppose it means?"

"That's hard to say," Birch said, turning back to the picture side again, "but the answer's here somewhere. I'm sure of that."

"Maybe it's telling us to go to the source of evil," Edwards reasoned. "I hate to say it, but here on this planet, that would mean *Primary Base*, where all of this started. Maybe there's an answer there that we missed."

"I hope not," Birch answered, scrutinizing Max's leering face. "It's possible, but I don't think so. I think it's a lot more complicated than that. There's so many other factors, strange clues that don't seem to fit. I can't really guess what Wagner's up to. I'm not even sure if he's alive or dead at this point, but the one thing I am sure of is that we can't take anything from him at face value. I get the feeling we're being played."

Birch tried a few more buttons and finally the computer whirred to life. Another red-eye scan ray shot out, confirming his identity before it settled into the startup screen. "Security, security, security," he grumbled, "but it looks like we're finally getting somewhere."

The screen was still black, except for a small icon of a pair of sunglasses. Birch clicked them.

Max's face leapt up and filled the screen. "N-n-n-n-n-ice!" he stuttered mechanically. "But you're going to have to t-t-t-ry a lot harder if you want to get by me!"

The computer switched off and the screen went black.

Birch's fist hit the desk, and the computer wobbled unsteadily on its fragile support. He was leaning over trying to turn the machine on again when Lauren's voice came through his headset.

"Major Birch. I'm not sure if this is anything, but you did say to keep you informed about any developments."

"Go on," Birch demanded.

"Well, I've been having some issues with the cameras around the base. Some have been flashing on and off. They work for a while and then go down. Then they come back on again."

"So?"

"Well, it seems like there's a pattern, like it's following a path."

"A path? To where?"

"It's a little hard to tell." Lauren cleared her throat. "Maybe here, to Main Control. I thought at one point that I caught sight of something, a shadow of something moving on the screen before a camera went out, but I couldn't be sure. I thought I should let you know."

"Yes, you did the right thing," Birch answered. He could hear the concern in Lauren's voice. It must have been bad for her to sound like that. "You need to get out of there. You've done all you can. I want you to meet up with Jane at the governor's suite. Head over there now. Edwards and I are almost finished here. With any luck you two will find the governor's shuttle, we'll find Wagner's information, and then together we can all blast off this rock forever!"

"Alright," Lauren's voice crackled back quietly. "I'm on my way there." She clicked off.

Birch turned his attention back to the computer. The screen was back to what it had been before, black with a single sunglasses icon. He didn't bother clicking on it again. He sent the curser searching around the screen, but there was no indication of any hidden icons. If they were there he had no way of knowing.

An idea came to him. He typed the letters R-o-b-i-n-e-t-t and immediately the screen flashed and a new message appeared.

rObInEtT wAnTs tO pLaY...

Birch whooped, but it didn't take long for his joy to melt back into a confused frustration. A pulsing square cursor winked knowingly at the end of the message, but nothing Birch typed there worked. He tried the obvious 'Robinette', but nothing happened. He tried 'Wagner', 'Marlowe', 'Parsons', 'Parlowe', and many other combinations of words, letters and numbers he could think of, but nothing worked."

Birch leaned back in his chair, frustrated. He was trying to rack his brains for any possible solution. Edwards, still on the bed, was looking at the walls when he suddenly sat up.

"I think we should go!" he stammered.

"Why, what are you scared of now?" Birch responded sourly.

"I'm not scared of anything. Look, what do you think the odds are of you getting the right answer? A million-to-one? It's probably not even that good! But, I've got a better idea. We need to go get the Ares kid!"

"Get the Ares kid?" Birch spat. "Are you crazy? First off, why would I want to bring that little hellcat down here? You don't think we have enough problems with all your space zombies running around? Don't forget, last time he was awake he tried to take over the ship and probably would have killed us all if he'd had the chance. And second, I'm not going to fight my way back up to the ship just to turn around and bring him down here? When I get off this planet I am never coming back!"

"No, listen, it's our best chance. Look," Edwards gestured around the room, "this Wagner kid's a classic fustalgic, and I have no doubt that whatever he's planned for us comes from that background. You and I have no clue about that. We're falling at the first hurdle because we don't think like him. Well, if we want someone who thinks like Wagner we need the kid.

Birch nodded, from what he knew of the Ares that was right. They had an almost religious reverence for the technology and achievements of the past. It was that which had inspired them to attempt kidnapping his crew from Edwards and Konik's convoy back in The Rockies because they were astronauts who represented the hopes of the past.

"Okay," Birch sighed reluctantly. "I guess you're right." He hated the implication of that admission. It meant that even if they did find Pickett's shuttle and make it safely back to the Hypnos their reprieve would only be brief. They had to come back, and there wasn't any way around it. He was never going to guess Wagner's code. If they were going to find out where the escaping colonists had fled to they would have to solve Wagner's clues and the only way to do that was with the Ares kid's help.

They left Wagner's room and strode quickly through the corridors.

"Jane, we're on our way!" Birch barked into his radio as they ran. "What progress have you made with finding the entrance to Pickett's hangar?" There was no answer. He tried again, but the radio remained silent.

"Lauren, have you heard anything from Jane?" Birch asked. She didn't answer either. No one was answering, there was only silence.

FORTY-ONE

"Where are we going?" Edwards puffed as he ran to catch Birch. "Isn't this the opposite way to Pickett's place?"

"Yeah," Birch answered tersely and hurried on.

"So, where are we going?"

"Main Control," he replied. "I've got no reading on where anyone is, and Main Control's the last place we know Lauren was before we lost communication. We need to backtrack and see what happened to her."

"What do you think happened to her?"

Birch shook his head. "That's what we've got to find out."

For a time they kept running. They were about five minutes from Main Control when Birch stopped short, pulling Edwards with him against the wall. He edged along, trying a few doors until one opened and they dove into the darkness.

"What's going on?" Edwards whispered, but Birch only put a hand over his visor, shushing him.

They crouched uncomfortably in the tiny cupboard. Time passed slowly, and when they finally came out Birch had difficulty straightening up. He glanced cautiously up and down the passageway before continuing.

"Someone was coming," he explained, pointing up at the domed mirror at the junction. "Good thing they didn't see us."

"Are you sure it wasn't Lauren," Edwards suggested.

"Absolutely sure," Birch pointed to his chest. "Gold isn't her color."

Edwards shuddered, taking in his meaning. "You're saying they were wearing a badge, that it was one of those constables from *Primary Base*? I thought we'd finished them off!"

"Apparently not."

They hurried on. A few moments later they arrived at Main Control. Birch and Edwards cautiously entered. It was empty. Everything was in order, just as they had left it, except that Lauren was no longer here. Birch hoped that meant she was on her way to the Governor's Suite. They headed that way themselves.

As swiftly as their need for stealth permitted, they made their way toward the center of the base. They didn't encounter anyone else. Birch kept glancing down at his computer readout, but it didn't tell him much. He could see their own location, but as far as he could tell they were completely alone. Jane, Lauren, and whoever else was with them in the base were all invisible.

They were getting close to Pickett's place. The steel floor changed to plush carpeting. The metal walls were covered with a plaster and paint façade. The impression was similar to the rich surroundings of Town Square, only more so. An ornate brass elevator wasn't working, so Birch and Edwards walked to the wide metal staircase. It was reminiscent of something from the Titanic. At the foot of the stairs, a beautiful angel cast in bronze rested atop an iron pedestal. He was clothed in nothing more than a flowing cloth, blowing strategically to cover his modesty. In his hand was a lamp that he held aloft as he ran. Birch wondered if the light bearer was running into the darkness to dispel it, or away from the darkness to escape it. He wasn't sure it was either. The angel was beautiful, but there was something in his expression he didn't like, a knowing smirk that seemed familiar. He wasn't bringing light anywhere, Birch was certain of that, even if it appeared that way.

They climbed the stairs. Reaching the top they came to a foyer with a thick glass wall that split the room in two. Once the glass might have been polished and glistening, giving the appearance of a barrier of light guarding the heavenly places, but now it was smeared and caked with dust. Deep, pitted scars were scattered across it like pockmarked skin. Someone had tried to get in, but they hadn't succeeded.

Birch rubbed his fingers across the glass. There was no obvious way of getting through. He pushed against it, testing it for strength, but there was no give. Judging by the marks a much greater force than he could muster had already failed to gain entry. He was beginning to doubt that there was any way in from here when an eye scanner from the other side of the glass locked in on him. The red beam lingered for only a moment, long enough to confirm his identity, and the outline of a door cut itself into the glass. Birch and Edwards hurried through, and the gap sealed invisibly behind them.

"I guess this place likes me," Birch smiled.

"You have a lot in common," Edwards replied with light-hearted sarcasm, "You're both dark, inhospitable, and without much power."

"Ha," Birch shook his head. "Maybe, but the one difference is that this place is staying right here, and I'm getting away. If you're lucky I might take you with me."

The other side of the glass contained a checkpoint desk and some other security apparatus, but Birch bypassed them. Papers lay strewn across the desk and the floor, but he ignored them too. They were intent on getting into Pickett's private suite.

A couple of doors and passages later they came to the main entrance, a set of steel double doors standing impressively at the far end of the corridor. Birch was looking for an eye scanner, but one wasn't needed. They swung easily aside.

Through the open doorway, he caught his first glimpse of the splendor of the governor's life here. A great glass window dominated the room. It filled the whole wall. Birch was struck by the sense of light and space, but the impression was fleeting. He was immediately distracted by a sound behind him. He spun around, ready to defend himself, but smiled to see Lauren, standing with a chair raised above her, ready to bring it down on his head.

"Put the chair down," Birch chuckled. "I'm really not that tired, thanks anyway."

"I was just making sure you weren't one of them," Lauren gasped. "They were running me pretty close when I got here. It looks like your constables weren't as worried about the weather as you'd hoped."

"I know," Birch replied. "I saw one of them on the way here. Any sign of Jane? I lost contact with both of you at the same time."

"No, I haven't been able to reach her myself. It seems like a lot of the same technical problems you were having over at *Primary Base* have followed you here."

"Yeah," Birch was looking through the window. The governor's personal suite had a panoramic view of *Town Square*. He could see everything. It was rather like living in the executive box at a sports stadium, with all the activity below for your personal observation. There wasn't much to see right now. *Town Square* was empty. Pickett's place took up about a quarter of the upper ring and looking through the curve of the glass Birch could see the clock and most of the street, but there wasn't any sign of movement. Wherever the constables were, they weren't down there.

"It looks like Jane's already been here," Edwards concluded, holding up a yellowed paper he found on a nearby table. Birch snatched it from his hand. The message was brief.

Gone ahead,
Jane

"Gone ahead," Birch wondered aloud, "where?"

The answer came a few moments later when Lauren called him into Pickett's study. Plush, high-backed chairs, walls lined with books, and a decorative globe (not of Earth, but of the gray, pitted orb of R67.3) all gave the impression of a place of quiet study and reflection. A stone fireplace pulled away from the wall made it clear that there was more to this room than initial appearances suggested.

"It looks like this has only been moved recently," Birch observed, picking paint flecks from the carpet. "Let's hope that means Jane was the first one to come through here. Maybe Pickett never made it to his shuttle."

Further examination revealed that the mirror over the fireplace hid another eye scanner. Whoever developed the base's security systems had an unhealthy obsession with eyes, Birch concluded. Hanging beneath the fireplace was an exposed number pad that clicked invisibly back into place when he pushed it. In red digital numbers, it flashed a four digit code that Jane must have typed in,- *1-8-6-3*.

"Ha," Birch smiled, "a security system with a sense of humor." Edwards and Lauren looked blankly at him. "1863," he explained, "*Pickett's Charge*, you know, the retreat that lost the Civil War. Very fitting, I think."

"Yes, very amusing," Lauren nodded thoughtfully. "It seems like a lot of funny things happened around here."

Birch didn't answer. He was already standing above the hole, looking down into the darkness. There was a narrow tunnel with a basic metal ladder stretching down into the void.

"That doesn't look very gubernatorial," Edwards complained wearily. "Shouldn't there be some kind of elevator or something? I could use a rest."

"Just be glad we found it," Birch replied grimly, climbing into the hole without further pause. "Let's go!"

He had expected a long descent, but after little more than fifty meters, they came to a platform. At first, it was dark, but the moment his foot touched the surface a blue strip of light traced the way around its edge, illuminating their surroundings. With every step the light intensified, stretching out further into the horizontal passage. It looked like a subway, but instead of a train, there was a sleek, four seated vehicle resting on shining, metal rails.

Birch took a moment to examine the rails and the car. Everything seemed to check out. "Let's go!" he finally concluded, jumping into the front seat.

"Are you sure it's safe?" Edwards asked, cautiously eyeing the tunnel. "We have no way of knowing this'll still work properly or where exactly it's going to take us."

"There's one way to find out," Birch concluded impatiently, tapping the front seat next to him. "Get in! We don't have time to waste. Besides, Jane's already been through here."

"Yeah, and we haven't heard anything from her since," Edwards concluded, slumping morosely into the back seat. Lauren joined Birch in the front. The moment they were all seated a set of shoulder restraints descended, pinning them in place. The red ray of yet another eye monitor checked each of them. Birch wondered what would happen if they ever failed one of those tests.

The vehicle took off at high velocity. One moment it was still, the next it was hurtling through the tunnel. The blue strip of light around them flashed and then extinguished as they passed swiftly by. They spun and turned in dizzying circles as they sped into the darkness. The g-force was incredible. Birch was pushed right back into his seat, and it was only through gritting determination that he mustered the strength to cast a sideways glance to check on Edwards and Lauren. She was okay, as stony-faced as ever, but Edwards looked bad. His eyes bulged and he was hyperventilating. Birch struggled to turn a little further to face him. "Breathe slowly or you're going to black out!" he shouted over the whooshing howl of the tunnel. Edwards nodded and made a deliberate effort to regulate his respiration.

They sped on. The lights flashed. The same neon blue line

zipped by so quickly that after a while it almost seemed as if they weren't moving at all. It was disorienting to feel the reality of motion pulling on them while remaining unable to see it. His mind grew fuzzy under its influence.

They stopped as quickly as they had started. With a squeal of grinding metal, they came to a skidding halt. An instant later the restraining bars hissed and rose up, but no one got out. They couldn't do any more than pant, gasp, and try to recover from the journey.

Birch was eventually the first out. He lifted himself shakily to his feet and stumbled to the platform, grasping the handrail to stop himself from falling. From here he could see Pickett's private hangar below and in it that the one thing that he had almost feared to hope for- a ship!

Birch let out a whoop and flung himself down the steps three at a time, running to the small, shining craft. He stroked its side, comforting himself with its solidity. Beyond his expectation, it was real.

Edwards followed not far behind, tumbling down the stairs with all the dignity of a child on Christmas morning. Even Lauren wasn't entirely immune to the emotion of the moment. She smiled briefly as she approached the ship, but it didn't last long. She glanced around. "Where's Jane?" she asked.

Birch had been too engrossed with the ship to think of it, but Lauren was right. Where was Jane?

FORTY-TWO

Jane wasn't anywhere- at least she wasn't anywhere nearby. There was evidence that she had been here recently, maybe only a few minutes ago. The computers were still in the early stages of the startup sequence. She had turned them all on, but there was no way of knowing what had happened to her after that. There wasn't any sign of a struggle, so it didn't seem likely that she had been captured, but then, why would she walk away from her one chance to escape from this terrible world?

One possible answer presented itself in the form of a tracking malfunction. The computer wasn't able to get a lock on the location of the Hypnos. That meant one of two things. Either the Hypnos was gone or there was a problem with the tracking system here. It was a chilling thought, but if the Hypnos was gone there wasn't anything he could do about it, so Birch decided not to worry about that possibility. He would assume it was a local technical issue and try to fix it. Perhaps Jane had done the same. The problem would have shown up early, and maybe she had gone out to repair it. Maybe she was out there right now. He would find out soon enough.

It was going to take another outside walk to get it working again. That wasn't an activity Birch relished. The weather was still bad and there were other dangers to consider, like the possibility that Jane had met up with one of the constables. He would have to watch himself out there.

"I'm going up top," he announced nonchalantly. "It looks like I'll need to do a little work to get the launch going, so I'm heading up to fix the problem. You two get things ready down here."

"Okay," Lauren replied without looking up from her console.

"You don't need any help?" Edwards asked dutifully. He didn't seem anxious to go; Birch was amazed he asked at all.

"No, no," Birch shook his head, "piece of cake. It'd be more of a help if you just assist Lauren any way you can. Do whatever she asks."

Edwards looked relieved, nodded and took a step back as Birch climbed the ladder to the surface.

It took a while to get outside. The seals to the doors were tight with age, but eventually, Birch made it through the last of them and was out on the surface. The storm was still in full force, and it didn't take long to feel its effect as the wind slammed into his face. The tap-tap-tap of tiny pebbles and dust hitting his visor was the first indication of the conditions, but as he tried to lift himself from the tunnel he felt the full impact of the howling gale. He had to brace himself just to keep on his feet.

He looked around, searching for any sign of Jane. He couldn't tell if she had been here or not, but there wasn't any sign of her now. Of course, she could have been twenty feet away from his face and he wouldn't have known it. The dust made it impossible to see anything beyond that distance.

Birch fumbled his way toward the base of the tower. The location of Pickett's hangar was disguised as a communication relay station, and the tower here served as an excellent cover for the hidden equipment needed for a launch. The tracking dish would be somewhere at the top.

Birch climbed wearily, hand-over-hand, foot-over-foot, mechanically to his goal. The wind shook the tower. Some day it would bring it down; he hoped it wouldn't be today. As he climbed he tried to use the elevation to get a better look at his surroundings, to see if he could spot Jane, but everything was reduced to the basic elements of dust and dirt. Just once, in a rare moment of clarity, he thought he saw something, a speck of white among the gray somewhere below, but he couldn't be sure.

He finally reached the dish. It didn't take much to see what was wrong. Some wires were unplugged. It was as simple as that and it didn't take long to fix. It was less easy to understand what had caused the problem. Birch had a bad feeling about it. Even in the harsh conditions of R67.3 it was hard to imagine a major connection like that coming loose on its own.

"I've just fixed the link," Birch spoke into his headset, "is there any change on the tracking down there?" No answer came. Birch shook his head, it seemed like the only way to get heard by anyone around here was to be less than five feet away and yell into their face. He sighed, stopped for one last look around, and started his descent.

The tower shook under another heavy gust of wind. Birch didn't even pause to steady himself. He had to get down. He didn't like that he hadn't been able to get a response from Lauren or Edwards. He tried to shrug it off, to remind himself that it was just part of the same communication problem they had been dealing with all along, but he wasn't so sure. Bad things were happening and all he could do was react and run. He hated that. Just once he wanted to make a stand, even if it meant to die, but today wasn't that day. He had people to protect.

Birch reached the surface and quickly opened the hatch to the lower levels. It took him a little while to get through the layers, but when he came out into the hangar he was relieved to see Lauren and Edwards still working there.

"Are we ready?" Birch called out to Lauren as he leaped down the last few rungs of the ladder.

"The tracking is up now," she replied. "We're almost set,

but what about Jane?"

"I couldn't see any sign of her," Birch admitted. "I didn't see any of the constables either. It's a mystery what happened to her."

"And we're still going?"

"We don't have much choice right now."

"Are we really going to do this again?" Lauren asked, looking up from her console. There was more than a hint of emotion in her voice and in her eyes as she looked at him. Lauren was human after all, and Birch might have marveled at that if her words hadn't annoyed him so much.

"No, we're not *'going to do this again!'*" he snapped. Her words stung him. It reflected Jane's accusation (and his own suspicion) that he was a failure- that he always let everyone who counted on him down.

"We have to get that Ares kid down here to help us solve Wagner's puzzle," Birch explained desperately. "Then maybe we'll find out where the survivors of this colony went. We have to do that before things go completely crazy down here. It looks like we woke something up over in *Primary Base* and obviously our time is limited. Some of them are over here already! We'll get the information we need, then find Jane, then get out of this place. It has to be like that or none of us will get out at all. That's the tough choice we have to make."

Lauren nodded. She could always be reached with cold, hard logic, not like Jane who always talked about regulations, but somehow always allowed other concerns to influence her judgment.

"You're right," she finally said, rising to her feet. "We need to launch as soon as possible."

"Then stop talking and get to work!" Birch barked.

It took a few more minutes of preparation, Lauren finished plotting trajectory to the Hypnos while Birch primed the engines, but soon they ready. They clambered aboard the ship, belted, and were ready for launch.

There was a slight possibility that after all this time the

engines would be unstable, that they could explode, but as Birch fired them they responded beautifully. He pulled the control stick and hit the launch button, sending the little craft hurtling down a flashing tunnel, through the open hangar doors, and out onto the surface.

They zoomed into the choking gray dust of the storm. Too long in this environment and the engines would clog, sending them crashing back to the planet in one of the shortest escape flights ever. Already alarms were sounding, warning of the strain. Birch pulled on the stick, pushing the engines hard for escape velocity. The tiny craft shook- juddering and rattling in the turbulence as the rockets roared beneath them.

Dust swirled, covering the ship. The instruments and his innate sense of direction told him they were going up, but in the glass of the window, it was impossible to tell whether they were flying up to safety or down to destruction.

Birch wrestled to keep the ship on course against the bullying wind. They were almost vertical when the smoky monochrome of the dusty air finally transformed into the pure ebony of space as they escaped the atmosphere.

Birch smiled through a grimace. Ahead he could already see the Hypnos. Edwards let out a mighty "whoop!" and pumped his first in the air so hard that the ship shook. "Let's wait until we get there to celebrate," Birch muttered, looking down at his instruments.

The Hypnos was dark. It looked like the ship had gone into hibernation mode, the sort of minimal energy setting you expected when the crew was in stasis. Life support and other regular functions would be off. The computer was in minimal mode because Birch hadn't trusted it enough to leave it alone after the Ares kid had messed with it. That meant not auto-guidance systems to help with the landing. That was a little tricky, but he could handle it.

Birch maneuvered the ship toward the Hypnos docking bay. He typed the code and the doors opened. Nimbly he pulled the shuttle into position; approaching the opening he gently guided the craft, easing through the doors, into the bay, and set her down.

The landing supports sighed, as though in relief, as the ship came to rest on the solid surface of the Hypnos III-A.

"Yes!" Edwards pumped the air again before quickly struggling to get out of his harness to escape the shuttle and the memories of R67.3.

Birch smiled wearily. Even Lauren seemed buoyed by their achievement. It was a rare victory for them. It would be a brief one too. They had to go back. Wagner's riddle had to be solved and Jane had to be found, but for just a second Birch didn't want to think about any of these things. Against the odds they had made it this far; and he was happy with that.

Edwards was fumbling with the door, trying to get out of the back, like a kid who had been stuck in the family car too long on a road trip. Birch wearily pulled the mechanism and the door opened. They all climbed out onto the silent deck.

Everything was dark and still. From here they could see the planet through a large bay window. Birch marveled that such a terrible place could appear so benign from this distance. The gray orb of R67.3 would never seem beautiful to him, he knew it too well, but if you got far enough away from it, even the worst places didn't look half bad.

The planet filled the window. He thought of Jane alone down there, a single white dot in the swirling gray dust, and hurried to the hangar doors.

There was so much they could have done: showering, eating, sleeping- all the things that had been so hard on the planet surface, but they had a job to do. Lauren headed to the flight deck to check on the ship's status. Birch and Edwards had the unenviable task of defrosting their little friend, the Ares kid. If he woke up as angry as he had gone to sleep they were going to have their work cut out for them.

As they entered the cryogenic hall Birch gave a great yawn. His eyes glazed as hours, perhaps days without sleep caught up with him.

It was going to be Birch's pleasure to be the one the Ares kid woke up to. He thought that was the best idea. Edwards would hit the button, starting the waking process, and Birch would be right next to his cryo-chamber, just in case he didn't wake up in a cooperative mood.

The room was dark. Like the rest of the ship it had gone into deep sleep mode, and it wouldn't be up again until Lauren had brought the computer back online. Birch reset the room's life support and a few minutes later took his helmet off, readying himself for the inevitable fight when the kid woke up.

"Okay," Birch said, giving the thumbs up when he was in position, "I'm ready!"

"What number was it again?" Edwards asked, trying to match the code Birch was saying with a number on the control panel. He was struggling to get it right.

"Just hit the red button," Birch replied wearily. "It'll work the same as it only opens the occupied compartments. He's the only one."

Edwards hit the red button, but it wasn't one cryogenic compartment that opened. They all did.

FORTY-THREE

"What are you doing, Edwards?" Birch barked. "I said push the red button, not open every compartment."

"I did push the red button," Edwards responded.

Birch was keeping his eyes on the Ares kid, ready in case he put up a struggle. Everyone was affected by cryogenics differently. Some people were sick for a week; others could come out fit and ready to fight. Birch was betting this Ares kid would be a fighter.

Birch's head suddenly shot up as a thought struck him. He glanced up at the ceiling where plumes of icy cloud were condensing.

"Did you say you pushed the red button?" Birch asked quickly.

"Yes," Edwards nodded, "just like you said."

"Oh..." Birch looked over into another nearby compartment. It was occupied. A sickly white face with a cruel line for a mouth and frowning, closed eyes lay in quiet repose. It looked like a corpse, except not as peaceful.

"Ohhh, you better get that..." Birch had turned to warn Edwards of the importance of pushing the blue (freeze all) button to return all compartments to stasis when a thudding blow from behind sent him sprawling. He landed heavily on the corpselike body, and the Ares kid leaped onto his back, hitting him again and again, pushing his face into the white corpse's chest, only this corpse was breathing and his eyes were open now. Blood red, like angry flames, the corpse's eyes narrowed as he saw Birch and reached for him, choking the air from his windpipe.

Birch now had them coming at him both ways. The Ares pounded the back of his head while the corpse had him by the throat. Birch turned, twisting free of the choking hands; he fell back, sending the Ares smashing into his cryogenic tube as they tumbled backward and fell to the floor.

The kid quickly regained his balance, vaulting the corpse's cryo-chamber; he ran for the door. By now more blanched figures were rising up out of their chambers. Edwards shouted and ran to help Birch but was flattened by one of the intruders rising from his tube.

The kid had reached the door, but it didn't open. He tried all the buttons, but still, it wouldn't open. Birch was back on his feet by now and saw him kicking at the door, trying to get out. For now, it was holding. The safety override wouldn't allow anyone to exit until the halls had been properly oxygenated and heated for habitation. That would change soon, and a whole swarm of trouble was about to break loose on the ship if that door got open and they all got out.

"Listen, Lauren!" Birch shouted into his mouthpiece. "We've got a big problem down here! There's sixty, maybe seventy enemy loose in the cryogenic hall right now, and I need you to keep the doors sealed and go to C-plan 109! Got that? C-plan 109!"

There was a moment's silence. "Are you sure?" Lauren's voice crackled back finally. "That's rather drastic."

"Well, we're rather desperate!" Birch shouted back. He dodged a lunging foe and tried to run to Edwards, who had disappeared under a pack of their newly awakened enemies.

"This may take a few minutes," Lauren's voice came back evenly. "There's a few protocols to get through." Jane would have been a lot quicker Birch thought, desperately fighting his way to Edwards. Lauren handled these things when she needed to, but her expertise wasn't in it. She was just slower.

"We don't have a few minutes!" Birch barked back. "Do it now or there won't be anyone left to save!"

"Hold on, hold on, I'm almost there."

Birch sent another enemy crashing to the floor. He was almost to Edwards when a pair of gnarled hands from a fallen attacker grabbed his ankle and sent him skidding to his knees. Birch didn't stop. He rolled with the momentum, leaped back up before anyone could stop him, and rushed on.

Birch smacked into the scrum, sending two men flying. He grabbed a third by the neck, pulling him off, but immediately another four jumped him. Birch went down hard, his face hit the floor, and he rolled as more attackers piled on top of him.

He was engulfed under a mountain of fighting flesh, surrounded by faces, arms, and legs. Feet were kicking, fists were punching, and the crushing weight was choking him. He couldn't breathe. His lungs heaved, trying to lift the weight above him, to catch a breath, but there was no air for him. He was suffocating, but he wasn't the only one. His attackers had suddenly lost their venom. They were still moving, writhing above him, but their activity was no longer directed at him. They were grabbing their throats, staggering, and falling as the effect of an airless environment took its toll. Lauren had done it- the sucking sound of the vacuum pump confirmed it. She had vented the atmosphere from the cryo-bay and sent them all into a critical status.

Birch saw his chance. Gagging, he quickly brushed aside his suffocating enemies and ran for his helmet. It had fallen on the floor and lay upside down near the Ares' chamber. He snatched it up, put it on, and clicked the seals in place.

The cool air hit him instantly. His lungs were on fire, but he didn't have time to worry about recovering. The Ares kid was lying nearby, clawing at his throat, gasping for air. Birch pulled him up and dragged him to the door. Edwards had already regained his feet. His helmet was still on, and he hadn't been affected by the lack of oxygen.

"The door..." Birch choked the command out to Lauren, "open the door!"

More quickly this time, Lauren followed his command, and it immediately slid aside. Birch dragged the kid through and Edwards followed. The door closed behind them.

"Seal the door," Birch ordered, "and re-oxygenate the room. We'll have to figure out what to do with them later, but that should hold them for now."

"I've got it," Lauren answered and the panel flashed red. "Oxygen levels are up to normal through the rest of the ship now."

"Okay," Birch answered. He tore his helmet off and went down on one knee, examining the Ares kid. He was breathing, but shallowly.

"Let's get him to the med-bay," Birch grunted, pulling the kid onto his shoulder.

They hurried through the halls, up the elevator, and into the med-bay. The kid was starting to come around by the time they got there. It looked like he was going to be alright, but that wasn't Birch's only concern. He threw the kid into a bed and strapped him down.

"Killing two birds with one stone," Birch explained, placing an oxygen mask over the Ares' face. "He looks like he'll be fine. But putting him here helps us monitor his recovery and keep him out of trouble."

"Sounds wonderful," Edwards responded wearily, stretching out on another bed. He pulled his helmet and gloves off and let them drop carelessly to the floor. A moment later he was asleep. Birch shook his head. He knew how he felt.

"Lauren," Birch was blinking hard against an exhaustion that had almost overcome him. "Edwards and I have the Ares down in the med-bay. We're okay. We're going to have some things to discuss: what we're doing next, things like that." His mind was thick with sleepiness. "Get down here, maybe in half an hour or so if you're done with everything by then. I need to rest for a bit."

"Okay," Lauren replied briefly, "I'll be down then."

Birch lay on a bed. He was just going to rest. There was a lot think about, so much to plan, that he couldn't afford the time to sleep. He needed to sleep, but he wouldn't. His mind worked over the options, the way it had to go, but as he mulled it over the details became fuzzy. For the first time in a long time, he was warm, comfortable, and in relative safety. He dozed. He slept.

The line between waking to sleeping blurred. He was sure he was awake, but Birch's senses were jarred when Karla's hand brushed against his face, her soft, white fingers in marked contrast to his rough stubble. He sat up quickly, his reaction a mixture of horror and pleasure.

"Tom..." her voice choked out the last word he had heard her say, but she wasn't there.

No one was there, only emptiness, but he seemed to hear words, snippets of conversations he knew, some recent and others from long ago. The words were all different, but they said the same thing. That he was a coward. That he ran. That he always found a way to make it while others didn't. There was Ratliff, and DeSante, and Karla, and his wife, Sarah, and now Jane's voice was added to the chorus of derision. He had left her down there and done the same to her as he always did. She was probably dead. He knew that, but as usual, it didn't seem that he had had any choice.

It was the usual nightmare, and he would have been glad to wake up from it, but the fact was that it was a nightmare he could never escape. It lived with him as much in the day as it did at night.

Her hand was on him again, only this time the fingers touched his shoulder. He shuddered and awoke. It was Lauren at his side.

"I let you sleep," she said quietly. "You looked like you needed it."

Birch sat up, hastily drawing himself up to his feet. "How long?" he muttered, trying to clear his head.

"About five hours," Lauren replied.

"Five hours?" Birch groaned, air hissing between his teeth. He shook Edwards. "Come on!" he bellowed. "We've got work to do, move it!"

Edwards opened one bleary eye briefly and shut it again. Birch nudged him hard with his foot. It wasn't quite a kick, but it was close. Edwards groaned and rolled over, but Birch pulled him back. "We've got to get down, Edwards. We've been up here way too long already. Come on!" Birch pulled Edwards into a chair, where he sat, dazed.

The Ares kid was awake and had been watching all of this. Birch didn't like the look on his face. There was something too calm, too calculating in his countenance. He knew he had to keep watching him.

"Have you had any ideas about what to do with our little band of guests down in the cryo-room?" Birch asked.

"The problem solved itself," Lauren replied. "They got back into their compartments themselves after the air was put back on. They're all back in stasis right now.

Birch shook his head, puzzling over that one. "You mean to say," he snorted, "that like good little boys and girls, they all went off to bed and tucked themselves in for the night?"

"I wouldn't put it quite that way," responded Lauren, "but I suppose that is essentially it. They are all asleep."

"For how long? Maybe they plan on jumping us in a day or two when we're not looking."

"No," Lauren shook her head. "I checked that. They're all in for the long haul. It's over two years until their wake-up date."

Birch couldn't work it out, but at least it meant that there was one less thing to worry about before he left the Hypnos. He could figure out what to do with their squatters later. For now he would concentrate on his plan.

In theory, it was pretty straightforward. In reality, he

would be lucky to make it work. There were only two simple goals. Get the information and get Jane. He would take the Ares kid down and have him work on Wagner's puzzle (Edwards would come along to help him manage that). After that, they would hopefully know the secret of what happened to the missing colonists. Then, with whatever time they could spare, before things got too hot down there, they would look for Jane. If everything went well in a few hours they would all be back on board and ready to fly wherever the needed go.

Lauren was going to stay on the ship this time, prepare it for the long journey, and keep an eye on their uninvited guests. She hadn't wanted to stay behind, but in the end, she had to agree that the plan was a good one. Edwards had hated it, but the Ares kid, when his role was explained to him, seemed happiest of all. He clapped his hands and smiled, and when he was finally released from his bed he was no longer the dangerous foe he had been hours ago. Instead, he was an eager and compliant helper. Birch didn't like it. He still didn't trust him.

After loading supplies, checking maps, and a final run-through of the plan they were ready to go. Birch, Edwards, and the kid were all strapped into their seats in Pickett's shuttle. The bay doors opened and Birch eased the little craft out into the dark void of space.

FORTY-FOUR

It didn't take long for R67.3 to make its presence felt. Passing into the atmosphere, the shuttle was jostled and shoved by the pounding wind. This storm wasn't going to last much longer, but that hadn't dissipated its power. Birch pulled at the controls, correcting course against it. He had to land soon or the engines would shut down, but he had to be careful how he approached it. He sent the ship into a steep dive, hurtling quickly to the surface before pulling up suddenly and flying fast and low toward *Colony One* on the opposite side to *Primary Base*, trying to avoid the green ray that had brought them down last time.

It worked. A moment later they set down at an airlock entrance on the far side of *Colony One*. Edwards hadn't enjoyed any of these maneuvers. His head was in his hands, and he only looked up when they were finally stationary. The Ares kid, however, wasn't fazed at all. He was unbuckled and out of his seat before Birch could even get his hands off the controls. "Hold it," Birch snapped. "You're not going anywhere until everyone's ready, so just cool it."

The shuttle's doors remained stubbornly locked as the Ares kid paced back and forth. Finally, they were all ready to go. Edwards had been the slowest to prepare. Clearly, he didn't really want to go, that was evident, but there was no way around it. At last, he was ready. "Okay," he sighed, "let's get this over with."

They stepped out into the storm. It was beginning to weaken, a lighter hue of gray was visible on the horizon, but Birch wasn't planning on sticking around to enjoy the view. He set the ship on a shock defense pattern to keep any potential saboteurs away and headed for the entrance.

The door presented the usual problem, it was old, jammed, and wouldn't open, but with a little coaxing they finally got in. The door clanged shut heavily behind them. Inside it was dark and perfectly quiet after the blasting wind. There was still no power in this part of the base, and they would have to spend more time manually opening doors than he would have liked, but by now Birch was pretty adept at the process, and they got through quickly.

Their helmet lights cut through the darkness. All the while they watched for any sign of the constables, but none appeared. *Colony One* seemed as empty and lifeless as it had been when they had first entered.

"Where are they?" Edwards rasped as they descended another level toward Wagner's quarters.

"I'm sure we'll find out soon enough," Birch responded grimly.

"Do you think they had anything to do with those creatures that invaded the Hypnos?"

"Of course," Birch answered simply, glancing up and down the next long corridor. It was empty and they continued following the route plotted on his wrist computer.

"But what are they, and what were they doing on our ship?" Edwards persisted.

"I thought you knew," Birch laughed bitterly. "They're the 'space zombies' you wished for, but what we saw on the ship wasn't the brains of the operation. You saw the way they all meekly climbed back into their chambers. Those are the followers. The real power is down here somewhere."

"We may eventually find out what they want with the ship," Birch continued. "I doubt it'll be good.

Edwards shivered. "I just hope no more of them get up there while Lauren's alone on the Hypnos."

"Don't worry about it," Birch answered. "They got in before because the computer was disabled and there was no one on board to manually seal off the hangar bay. With her up there, no one's getting through."

"But why were they on the ship, and how did they get there without us noticing?" Edwards persisted.

"During the storm, I suppose," Birch sighed impatiently. "Maybe if you and Jane had checked the hangar over at *Primary Base* instead of getting yourselves attacked in *The Lowers* we might have found their ships."

"I seem to remember we had to rescue you!" Edwards shot back hotly.

"I seem to remember that I was only over there because I had to rescue you," Birch replied coolly.

Edwards smiled. "Well, I guess that makes us even."

"Yeah," Birch replied, glancing down at his computer again.

They continued in silence. Lower and lower they traveled until they came to Wagner's door. They came at it from a different direction this time, but the change didn't improve anything. It was still obvious that this was the least attended, most neglected part of the base- the part for those who were needed to make things run, but who didn't really matter.

The same eye scanner popped out and checked Birch's identity before allowing them in. The door opened and they walked into the tiny room.

It had seemed small before, but now, with three of them crowded in, it was impossible. Edwards sat on the front of the bed and Birch pushed himself against the closed door to allow the Ares kid the chance to look around. It amazed Birch to think that anyone as skilled as Wagner would be given such terrible quarters. Still, from his background at *Primary Base*, this squalid little piece of privacy must have seemed like something grand, a great move up in the world. In an unfair world, the beasts of burden always lived in the barn.

Birch started the computer. As it slowly chugged to life he watched the Ares kid spinning around, carefully examining each wall and every picture. His eyes were wide and gleaming and his smile was one of uncomplicated joy. Birch had never seen him like this. He was running up and down, touching the pictures with his fingers, feeling the contours of their shapes. "This is good," the boy murmured reverently, "very good."

Birch shook his head. "If these Ares love technology so much they should try using some of it to improve their lives, instead of living like complete primitives."

"That would break their code," Edwards answered. "Technology has to keep its special status. It's used for sacred purpose, to spare their people. Personal, feckless use of it is almost sacrilegious. They know much more than they use, and they understand much more than they would ever tell, but we may be in luck with this kid. He's an orphan, which means he's grown up outside the code. He'll have gained some knowledge through his peripheral interaction with their society, but as an orphan, he would wander through the forbidden places. He's probably explored the old destroyed cities where tribal Ares would never go. He may know even more than an average Ares would."

"Let's hope so," Birch said. The screen was coming on. "Okay kid," he barked, "you're up. See what you make of this little puzzle." Birch typed in the 'Robinett' word again and the same message came up.

rObInEtT wAnTs tO pLaY…

The young man sat at the screen. He ran his hands gently across the keys. He looked thoughtful for a moment and then smiled. "This is your big puzzle?" he chuckled. "This is very simple. Don't either of you have any idea at all?" Birch and

Edwards shrugged. "The clue's right here," he gestured to the advertisement pasted to the wall. It showed a happy family gathered around an Atari. "Robinett... that's the name of a programmer for Atari back in their glory days, but they never gave their programmers any credit. This Robinett guy fixed that. He made this game called Adventure with all these dragons and stuff, and he got his name in there with some extra coding. He created a secret room where you could find his name. It was the first Easter Egg, the first secret hidden in coding. It started something big."

"That makes sense," Birch reasoned. "There must be some hidden coding in that Robinett program, maybe telling us where everyone went. The problem is figuring out how to get into it."

"That's not much of a problem," the Ares laughed. "Look," he moved the cursor over the screen, "what do you see?"

"Nothing," Birch admitted.

"Exactly," the Ares replied. "That's what you're supposed to see. In the game, you couldn't see the key to the secret room either. It was a hidden invisible dot. Do you see an invisible dot?"

"No, of course not," Birch snapped. "It's invisible."

"Yeah, but do you see anywhere that there should be a dot but there isn't one?"

Birch looked closely at the screen. A black background with small writing in the middle, there wasn't anything remarkable there, except for the font. The alternating of upper and lower case letters was strange. His eyes narrowed as he tried to take it in, to figure out where Wagner had hidden his invisible dot. Then it came to him.

"The 'I'," he exclaimed, pointing at the screen. All those letters should be lower case. If they were the lower case 'I' would have a dot!"

The Ares nodded. "You're not so dumb as I thought." He moved the cursor over the letter. Nothing happened. There was no way of telling that there was anything special about it until he pressed the button. A basic electronic sound effect showed that something had happened. The words faded and the screen went black, then dissolved into a simple gated yellow castle. A yellow dragon (or maybe it was a duck, the graphics made it hard to tell) floated by, and then the screen went blank and a small line of flashing words appeared vertically on the screen.

```
I
n    I
c    n
o    p
r    u
r    t
e    .
c    .
t    n
D    o
e    t
v    .
i    .
c    F
e    o
.    u
.    n
.    d
```

The Ares kid laughed and clapped. "What's so funny?" Birch snapped, squinting at the screen, trying to figure out the message.

"You wouldn't understand," he chuckled.

"'Incorrect device... input... not... found'? What's that supp-osed to mean?" Birch wondered aloud. No one seemed to have an answer. "It's a wall, that's clear. How do we get around it?"

"I think," the Ares answered, "that it's supposed to read,

'*Incorrect input, Device not found.*' This little computer wasn't made to do whatever we're trying to get it to do."

"Okay, I guess that makes sense, but what other computer would Wagner have access to?" The answer came to him a second later. "Of course- his work! Where did he work?" Birch shoved his way into the chair and cleared the screen, bringing up the base mainframe. With his open access he was able to quickly answer that question, but what he found didn't make him happy.

"He worked on the computer systems at *Town Hall*. It looks like we're going back to *Town Square*."

FORTY-FIVE

"Oh wonderful," Edwards groaned. "Wasn't this supposed to be the easy part? Looking on Wagner's computer for five minutes before finding Jane and going home? I wasn't looking for another sightseeing tour of *Town Square*."

"Looking or not, that's what we've got it," Birch snapped, "Let's get going. Sooner we start, sooner we get out of here."

For different reasons, Edwards and the Ares were reluctant to leave. The Ares wanted to stay and soak up the atmosphere of Wagner's fustalgia; Edwards just wanted to stay out of trouble. Birch dragged them both away. Time was short.

They marched through the halls, watching for constables all the way. There wasn't any immediate sign of them. The base was appeared empty. So far, at least, there hadn't been any sign of a mass invasion by the hordes Jane and Edwards had found over at *Primary Base*. Maybe this was going to be easier than he had hoped.

"You know," Birch commented to Edwards as they came to another level, "with all your knowledge of what makes the Ares tick, I'm surprised you didn't figure out the meaning of that Robinett puzzle yourself. The kid seemed to find it pretty straightforward."

"You think so?" Edward replied. "An invisible dot over the

'i', might look obvious to you, but like most Ares stuff, it's only easy when you know what they're referring to. There's only so much pointless trivia you can learn! They value so much garbage: worthless books, forgotten lyrics, empty jingles, you just can't learn them all. I've learned enough to understand where they're coming from, but no one could delve to the bottom of their dumpster of 'knowledge'."

Birch shrugged. "One man's trash is another man's treasure I suppose."

They came to an entrance to *Town Square* but pulled up short before they reached the doors. A constable was there. If Birch wanted to get in without raising the alarm he would have to try somewhere else.

"Let's try another entrance," Birch hissed, backing up the corridor. They made a wide circle around the base and came at *Town Square* from a different direction, but that door was guarded too. They tried a couple more times, but every entrance was blocked. Birch shook his head. "It looks like they know we're trying to get into *Town Square*," Birch muttered. "Maybe there's a better way in."

He set out in a different direction. He tried to be cautious, but even so, his plan for stealth soon fell apart. In one of the corridor's domed mirrors, he caught sight of a group of space suited colonists, like the ones Jane and Edwards had described, coming around the corner. There wasn't any time to hide. They had already seen him.

"Run!" Birch shouted and kept going, rushing past the junction into full view of the approaching enemies. In that brief moment, he saw them clearly, a pack of seven or eight gray-suited figures with a gold-starred constable at their head. They were running at him as he passed, and if their destination hadn't been nearby Birch wouldn't have had much hope of making it at all.

The hard metal floor became plush carpet, stifling the sound of their pounding boots. They were almost there. Edwards and the Ares were right with him, but the clatter of their enemies' feet following behind died out almost as soon as their own did. They were close, but Birch didn't look back. They entered the lower lobby of Pickett's suite with the brass elevator and fancy stairs. He didn't bother trying it this time. He leaped up the steps, taking them three or four at a time.

Edwards stumbled behind him. "Come on!" Birch shouted over his shoulder. The Ares kid was ahead. He was almost at the top by now but turned at the sound of Birch's voice.

Edwards cried out. He was caught, but before Birch could turn or react the Ares kid had jumped onto the ornate wooden banister and, with the easy assurance of a California surfer, slid down in an attempt to rescue Edwards.

With one fluid movement the kid swept down, leaping from the banister, and sending a thudding right foot smashing into the helmet of an attacking colonist. The momentum sent the man flying and pushed another three tumbling after him down the stairs. Immediately another attacker was at them, but the kid saw him coming and rammed him head first in the gut, sending him rolling down after the others.

Birch finally reached the fight and wrestled Edwards free, pulling him, stumbling, up the stairs while the Ares dodged and fought his way up after them. Birch had seen the kid's fighting style before, in the tree back in the Rockies, but that had been at night, and he had been the one struggling to survive then. Now, from this distance, it was a beautiful thing to see as he danced and toyed with his attackers, but even he couldn't hold them off forever.

"Come on, come on!" Birch shouted as he and Edwards reached the top. "Let's go!"

The kid nodded. There was something almost comical about his lank form in a puffy, ill-fitting suit holding his own against a host of attackers. Physically the Ares looked like any other ordinary, skinny teenager, but he knew how to fight.

Birch hurried Edwards toward the clear barrier that divided the upper foyer from Pickett's quarters. The Ares was following quickly now, but his persistent foes weren't far behind.

Edwards hit the glass, but there wasn't an opening yet. The usual eye scanner popped out and shone its probing light into their faces before admitting them. The doorway opened and Edwards and Birch ran through. The Ares dove in a second later as the doorway dissolved behind them, leaving their pursuers stranded on the other side.

The silent colonists advanced as a group toward the transparent wall. Their reflective visors masked their features; Birch could only see his own distorted image shining back at him in their convex surface. They didn't try to get in; perhaps they knew it was useless to try. The red ray of the eye scanner leaped out at them. They stepped back, but one wasn't quick enough and was seized in the crimson beam. It locked on his face, flickered for a moment, illuminating his features in profile behind the mask. The scanner sparked, shooting a jolt of power that flung him against the wall where he lay motionless.

"I guess now we know what happens when you fail the eye test," Birch concluded. None of the other colonists were moving. With the constable at the center, they stood perfectly still, watching and waiting for Birch's next move.

"I guess they know we'll have to come out sometime," Edwards reasoned gloomily.

"They're right," Birch smiled, "just not that way." He was heading for the window. He pulled open a yellow panel and started pushing buttons. "Let's find out just how much this place really likes me. It's given us access to everything else so maybe we'll get away with this." He pushed a few more buttons and slammed the panel shut.

"What is that?" Edwards asked.

"It's a security override, linked into the governor's personal command alone. It'll only obey his direct order. It's a final emergency fallback, in case things ever got out of control. I've just instructed it to help us get into *Town Square*.

"And how exactly is it going to do that?"

Birch gestured to the window, "Watch."

A loud crack, like winter ice shifting in a spring thaw, echoed around them. At first, there was no discernible difference in the glass, then instantly it shattered into a thousand clear pebbles clattering to the floor. Where the window had been a gaping hole now stood, and Edwards took a step back from the edge, away from the sudden drop that now opened up before them.

The constable and his men didn't move. The glass on their side remained intact and there was nowhere for them to go except back down the stairs. They simply stayed and watched; at least Birch imagined they were watching. The faces were still obscured by their helmets and none of them had moved at all in reaction to his movements.

A metal platform slid out from under the hole, crumpling and folding as it went on to form stairs down into the vast chamber below. The Ares kid jumped excitedly about, enjoying the whole process like a wide-eyed toddler at their first fireworks display.

Even before it had finished assembling Birch was pulling Edwards through the hole and beginning their descent into *Town Square*. The Ares followed readily enough and was soon ahead, running almost faster than the stairs could form. Edwards was more reluctant but was soon following close behind. From this height, Birch saw the entire square. Their presence wasn't unknown- that much was clear. Doors were flying open all around the enclosure and from different directions clusters of space-suited figures were swarming out into the dome, running toward them.

Getting to *Town Hall* wasn't going to be easy. Already a crowd of ten to twenty men had come between them and the building. He was hopelessly outnumbered, and that wasn't their only problem. With dread, Birch also noted the changing hue of the sky. It had begun as a standard idyllic blue when they had first entered. Now black clouds were swirling and their edges were slowly reddening.

"Watch the ceiling!" Birch shouted, pointing up. "It looks like we're in for another pounding!"

Edwards nodded. By now they had reached the bottom of the stairs and Birch lead the charge to *Town Square*. It seemed like a futile effort. Another cluster of colonist had joined the first arrivals and there were now at least thirty or forty of them blocking the way.

"Follow me!" Birch shouted, turning away from the obvious paved path to *Town Hall*, heading for the open ground that had once been part of the decorative forest. They ran through the broken stumps of trees toward the empty canal that formed the ornamental water feature that divided *Town Square* in two.

The colonists gathering at the bridge saw the maneuver and rushed to stop their escape. Others hurried to the far side to cut off their path forward.

Birch was the first to reach the canal. He leaped it on the run and kept going. The Ares was right behind him and also jumped it with ease. Edwards was another twenty meters behind, but the colonists were right at him, and as he jumped two of them leaped with him. All three came down together on the other side in a pile of fists and feet as Edwards struggled to get free. He kicked out, sending one toppling over the edge into the empty canal. The second man wasn't so easily disposed of. He grabbed Edwards and held him down. By now another three colonists had made it over and joined him, pinning Edwards in place.

Birch saw all of this and turned back to help, but before he could reach them the crimson clouds that had been slowly building overhead exploded, sending flashing sparks of purple flame streaking everywhere It wasn't like before. When they had dealt with this last time the effect had been like a dangerous electrical storm. This went way beyond that. Booming bursts of lethal power zoomed and sparked across the landscape with a furious frenzy, electrifying and igniting anything they touched.

Birch hit the floor. In the moment before he fell he saw two of Edwards' attackers hit. They lit up in purple flames. One dropped and rolled while the other fell into the canal and disappeared.

Birch struggled to his feet. Everywhere there was falling fire and fleeing colonists dodging, ducking, and running for the nearest exit. It was an apocalyptic scene, but one that Birch and his companions seemed impervious to. None of them had been hit, but Birch wasn't taking any chances. He pulled Edwards up and, half dragging him, ran for *Town Hall*.

They reached its door a few minutes later. Edwards and Birch stood panting. The Ares waited calmly beside them. Glancing back, Birch could see no colonists. They were all gone except for the smoldering remains of a few who hadn't made it out. Already the sky was starting to lighten and return to its perfect blue.

At the door, the customary eye scanner checked Birch before admitting them. Once inside he took the opposite direction to last time and headed for the basement, to the computer administration center. There they navigated their way through the maze of terminals until they came to the little cubical that had belonged to Wagner. There wasn't anything special about it. It was a uniform gray space with nothing to distinguish it from any of the others here- not a single memento, nothing. Birch checked again to make sure it was really his place. It was. All of his personal expression, it seemed, was reserved for home, in his tiny quarters.

They sat down. There wasn't much room, but they all squeezed in. They all wanted to see this. The computer started up easily enough but came immediately to an old password screen. Birch couldn't think of anything else, so he typed in the only idea that came to mind, 'Robinett'.

It worked. The screen melted and brought up the old familiar message he had hoped to see,

rObInEtT wAnTs tO pLaY...

"It looks like we're on the right track," Birch muttered.

"Push the invisible dot!" the Ares urged, but Birch was already on it. He hit the button, but this time instead of an error message the screen display cracked, fragmenting into tiny pieces, white particles that floated, drifting gently down like falling snow.

FORTY-SIX

The snow was falling thickly around them. It was disorienting. At first, the icy blast surrounded their little group, swirling and blowing in their faces, sending a cold chill through their skin. Then it was outside and couldn't reach them as it blew against an invisible barrier. There was a rhythmic, alternating swish-screech sound that Birch recognized and understood once an old cracked windshield formed in front of them. The wipers scraped inadequately against the glass, struggling to clear the accumulating snow.

Birch looked back. Edwards and the Ares were in the back seat. Who was driving? He turned to look but couldn't see anyone. It wasn't that there wasn't anyone there; it was just that they didn't seem to register, like the faceless phantoms of our dreams that are always there but never quite seemed real enough to be noticed.

"Where are we?" Edwards hissed.

Birch shrugged. "Somewhere computer generated I guess. Technically we're still in the basement at *Town Hall*. Mentally we're here, wherever here is."

"We're in The back of a 1977 Chevy Chevette, hatchback, a red one by what I can see through the windshield," the Ares interjected. "Not bad, though a little more cramped than I'd imagined." He adjusted his position uncomfortably on the cold, leatherette seat. Unaccountably they were all still wearing their space suits. It made a rather incongruous picture, Birch thought, to see three space-suited astronauts sitting in a red 1977 Chevette.

"But where are we going?" Edwards persisted.

"That's the real question, isn't it," Birch responded, turning to look through the windshield. The snow was flying at them. Caught in the headlights, the puffy flakes looked like thousands of stars zooming in at light speed. It was impossible to tell where the car was going. He could just see a small patch of the street ahead in the flickering beams of light; glistening white, it didn't even look like a road except that sometimes he caught sight of the faint outline of a sign or the glow of a traffic light in the blizzard.

They were slowing down; the wheels slid slightly as the car eased into the parking lot. To their left, Birch noticed a large lit sign for a chicken restaurant out on its own. Ahead he saw the faint, warm glow of lighted windows from a line of shops huddling against the cold.

The car came to a stop in front of the largest store. "I guess we're here," Birch concluded and got out. He was about to shut the door when he realized that there wasn't another exit and fumbled with the seat's mechanism to let the others out.

They stood in the snow, looking up at the radiant blue and red lettering of the store's sign. "Murphy's Mart," Birch read. "Does that mean anything to either of you?" Even the Ares shrugged at that. Whatever his reasoning, Wagner's illusion was something unique to him. Even the Ares didn't get it.

The Ares kid approached the store, pressing his helmet against the glass, gazing at the wonders inside. One thing, in particular, caught his attention and he excitedly gestured to the others. He pointed to the electronics department where an Atari display had a console running. On the screen was the same game from Wagner's computer, with the same yellow dragon chasing the same yellow dot.

"That's not unexpected," Birch muttered and tried the door, but it didn't open. He was just trying to figure out how they were going to get in when the Ares took off down the sidewalk toward the far end of the strip mall. Birch was about to tell him to stop when he changed his mind and followed instead.

They passed a drug store, a grocery store, and a hair-dresser's, but they didn't stop at any of them. Like Murphy's Mart, they were all lit up, but no one was inside. They kept moving until they reached the second-to-last store. In neon cursive script the single word 'ARCADE' flashed out in the darkness. The Ares pulled the door, and this time it opened. He walked in.

Birch and Edwards quickly followed. Inside they found a small, dimly lit room with a thin, industrial carpet and plain white walls. No thought had been given to decoration. The room's contents were decoration enough. A number of vibrantly colored wooden cabinets lined the walls. Each had a glowing screen, and above it, at head height, an illuminated banner that beckoned players. Birch knew something of these types of places. Arcades, places to waste quarters and time, they had once been popular when electronic technology had first become advanced enough to distract people's attention from the world around them. Birch couldn't see the appeal, but clearly, Wagner's fustalgic bent was at the heart of all this.

There was no one else here. Birch looked around for clues. There was a cracked clock on the wall, stopped at ten-to-seven, and a tear-off calendar behind the main desk that read, December 22, 1982. Flipping through the remaining pages Birch noted that every date read the same. In this arcade, it was destined to forever be December 22, 1982. On the counter of the change booth, on a curled, yellowed piece of paper someone had scrawled a note,

'Save me from the MCP.'

The message meant nothing to him. Birch handed it over to the Ares. He had a better chance of figuring out what was on Wagner's mind than anyone else.

Even the kid seemed stumped for a moment. He tapped the paper, staring at it repeatedly and glancing around the arcade, as though expecting the answer to be somewhere nearby. Birch took off his helmet and waited. Their suits didn't seem to serve anything more than decorative purpose here anyway. He could feel the cold outside, and now the heat in here. He could smell the acrid tang of hot wiring and electricity in the air around him.

The Ares waved the paper and hurried to a sleek black cabinet with black lighting strips and a glowing Joystick. Birch read the name, 'TRON', but it was the screen that the Ares was pointing at.

"Oh yeah," he exclaimed. "This is it! I thought I remembered, but he almost made it too easy!" He was waving at the screen. It displayed the high scores, all in double letter digits except the top score, which had three and read 'MCP'.

"It's the main enemy in this game; there was a movie about it too." He was looking around for a way to start the machine. None of them had any change, but the kid tried the returned coin slot and triumphantly pulled out a game token.

"The MCP is on one of these levels," he put the token in and selected the one player option as jarring electronic music announced the beginning of the game. "There's four parts to each level, the MCP is in there somewhere!"

He moved the icon and selected a game. The first one was a battle between three yellow CPU motorcycles and the Ares' solitary blue one. The bikes sped quickly across the screen, leaving a solid colored wall in their wake. The kid made a quick twist on the joystick and the first enemy cycle crashed into his wall. The other two were swiftly dispatched in the same way, giving him his first easy victory.

In the second game, a swarm of spider-sprites scuttled across the screen, blocking his exit. The Ares fired rapidly and dodged his way through the portal, clearing the screen.

"You played this much before?" Birch asked as the kid guided his icon to the third area.

"Nope," the Ares answered without looking up. He was fighting tanks now. "I got ahold of a book of old technical manuals once. It's all pretty simple coding if you look at it."

He destroyed the last tank and moved on to the final section. Here he was instructed to get into the MCP. The little man on the screen zoomed quickly up toward a colorful barrier that would destroy him. Beyond that was a glittering cone of light, his destination. He shot rapidly at the wall, penetrating just enough to clear a path and secure entry to the computer. The little figure on the screen raised his hands in victory, floated into the light, and disappeared off the edge of the screen before the display went dark.

There was no flash, no thunder or smoke, nothing to indicate that he had achieved anything, only a blank screen flickering silently before them. Birch looked up- nothing had changed- at least nothing noticeable. Turning further around he was startled to see a new occupant in the arcade silently playing the *Space Invaders* machine on the other side of the room.

Birch, Edwards, and the Ares silently approached. In the light of the screen, Birch recognized the same face he had seen in so many pictures. The boyish, plump cheeks, the shock of brown disheveled hair, the wide smile were all there, but there was something hollow about him. Perhaps it was the glow of the arcade lights, but there were dark smudges under his eyes and his smile wasn't an innocent or happy one.

"Funny thing with most of these games," Wagner spoke for the first time without looking up, "you can never win. The invaders just keep coming back." He looked up and smiled. "The only way to win is to cheat, and if that still doesn't work you can always pull the plug. As long as you can pull the plug you can always avoid defeat."

"What do you have to tell us?" Birch asked impatiently.

"You've kept us running around long enough with your stupid games. I have a crewman to save and time is important!"

"Yes, I know, but I can't help being me. You see the real Wagner left me here to protect his secrets, and to that purpose, he created me to be obtuse. I can't break my programming any more you can break free of the upbringing, education, and genetics that have made you the delightful specimen of humanity you are."

Birch's eyes narrowed, but he kept his cool. "Okay," he muttered, "just tell us whatever obtuse thing your programming thinks we need to know then."

"If you understood what you were up against you'd be thankful for these precautions. The enemy is at the gates, beyond the gates even, but I have kept them at bay because they do not understand 'play'. They could have broken any code, understood the deepest reasoning, figured out the wisest conundrums, but they cannot understand play and simplicity. I... Wagner... we have protected everything with our sense of fun and play. Only someone truly human could have figured all this out."

"Where is the real Wagner?" Edwards asked.

"Yeah, well, that's at the heart of it, isn't it?" Wagner's copy responded. "Where is he? He's gone. He left with all the others who were unaffected by the craziness around here, to one of the other colonies. He figured out where its location was through the records. There was a lot of conflicting data from NASA, but there was a plan all along, a way of escape, and he figured it out. He left me behind to point the way to anyone who stumbled through here. This place is all part of that." He gestured around him.

"What is this place?" the Ares asked reverently. "Is this based on somewhere real?"

Wagner turned from his game (which continued happily without him) and put a hand on his shoulder. "You understand this better than most, but you have a lot to learn. It was real, but we have never been here, only in our dreams."

"Wagner read about places like this, about the early days when everything was raw and new. It was his dream to live here; that's why he left me in this place, in his dream world. But like most dreams, it can't last. I've played too many games, had too much fun, gotten all that I've ever wanted, and I can't escape. This is my paradise and my prison. The more I get what I want, the less satisfied I am. It's the one thing the real Wagner never understood, but I've had to learn it over these bitter years. That's why I want to help you, to do something for you and not for me, but it's hard. Wagner's programming is the original sin that infects my mind. I can only help you in the way I'm allowed."

"So where is this colony?" Birch asked bluntly.

"*Tempus Fugit*," Wagner smiled, pointing to the stopped clock. "Hadn't you better go find your crewmate? She's a very foolish woman, treading where angels fear to tread."

"We're not going until you tell us where Wagner went!" Birch snapped impatiently.

"I've told you all I can," Wagner responded, turning his attention back to the game.

"You've told us nothing!" Birch shot back.

"I've told you everything," Wagner replied evenly.

The room fell silent save for the bleeping and blooping of the games and their repetitive little electronic ditties, punctuated by an occasional '*Eight-Ball Deluxe*' announcement from a pinball machine in the corner. Birch fumed, but there didn't seem to be any way he could get anything more out of him.

The silence was broken by the sound of a heavy engine roar and the scrape of metal on the asphalt somewhere outside.

"What's that?" Edwards hissed.

"That was a little sooner than I expected," Wagner admitted, looking up from his game. "What it means is that you don't have any more time for chit-chat. It's those constables and their crazy colonists come to find you. They've known for a long time how to get into the game, but I've always been able to keep them lost in the snowstorm. They must have used your presence to guide them in. They've followed you here, and it's time for you to go!"

"Can they hurt us in here?" Birch asked.

"They can hurt you anywhere they like, but that's not all you have to worry about. They've let things slide with you since you first got into *Colony One* because they thought they could use you to get what they wanted, but that's changed. You've been here, and now you have what they want too. They'll be after you just as much as me now."

The sound outside died down as the engine stopped. Heavy doors creaked opened and banged shut.

"Come on," Edwards urged. "Let's go!"

"Wait, just a second," Wagner was at the Pac-Man machine now and put a token in the slot. "I need to show you something before you go."

"You want us to see your high scores?" Birch muttered, putting his helmet on. "Maybe some other time."

"Come here, now," Wagner demanded firmly. Birch moved over to the machine and saw that the display was not that of a typical game. The maze had been transformed into a layout of *Colony One*, and Wagner was guiding a yellow circle through the dot-lined corridors. "This is the route you'll need to take to avoid trouble and get back to your ship as quickly as possible. In *Town Square*, you'll have to get up to the second level through the balcony here." He pointed to the screen. "From there follow the route you see and you should make it. Your crewmate is over at *Primary Base*, heading for *The Lowers* I believe. She's braver than she is smart. I can't help you with anything over there. It's up to you now."

"What's going to happen to you?" the Ares asked.

"Don't worry. I hardly even exist anyway. Come on now, move it," he pushed them to an emergency exit at the back of the arcade. "They're moving along the line of shops already. They'll be here any second!"

He opened the door and flung them out into the snowy darkness.

FORTY-SEVEN

Birch pulled himself out of the snowdrift, brushed off his visor, and looked around. They were at the back of the strip mall, but it was hard to see much in the dim light of a single lamp at the far side of the building. He pulled Edwards to his feet and the three of them hurried as best they could toward the back of Murphy's Mart.

The snow was still falling, and even this close to the building it was hard to walk quickly through the blowing drifts. Finally, after a few minutes struggle, they made it to the edge of the store and peered around the corner. A rusty truck with big tires and a snowplow attached at the front was parked beside their car, but no one was in it. Probably they were still inside the arcade working on Wagner. Birch hoped he had disappeared again before the constables got in, but he wasn't sure if he'd had the time. It was strange. He was only a computer program (and an annoying one at that!) but somehow Birch felt a responsibility to the faux Wagner. Besides, he had important information that shouldn't fall into the wrong hands. Birch decided to help him if he could.

"Let's go!" Birch hissed and ran for the car. Edwards and the Ares followed. The three astronauts ran full pelt across the empty parking lot. The slick ground made it hard to stop, so that when they reached the car Birch and Edwards skidded into the side of the vehicle, hitting hard against the metal door. The Ares didn't have any trouble and popped right into the passenger seat without any effort.

There wasn't any sign of their mysterious driver and Birch wasn't taking any chances. He would drive himself this time. "Get in!" he barked at Edwards and shoved him into the back seat before jumping in after him.

It took a few coughing attempts, but soon the car roared to life, but instead of pulling away from the strip mall Birch pulled up outside the arcade and, in true teenage fashion, revved his engine provocatively. "Hey fools!" he shouted out the window. "Why don't you all come out and play?"

The Ares kid clapped and then slapped the dashboard in appreciation. He unrolled his window to hurl a few insults of his own.

"Cool it, kid!" Birch barked before he could start. "We're not here to get into a slanging match with the constables. I'm just trying to get their attention."

He had their attention. The door flew open and three of them ran out. Birch gunned the engine while the kid scooped some snow from the windshield and launched a well-aimed snowball into the visor of the lead man.

"Wow, you two are mature," Edwards observed sourly from the back as the car pulled away. "Maybe when we're done here we could all go over and toilet paper their house."

"Not a bad idea," Birch smiled through gritted teeth, "but maybe we should just try surviving first before we think about administering toilet paper justice on the inhabitants of this world."

Edwards didn't answer. He was too busy watching out the back window to respond. "They're coming!" he warned. The constables were already back in their truck and speeding after them. With their better traction, they were right on their tail before they had even made it out of the parking lot.

"Hold on!" Birch shouted, wrenching the wheel, sending the car spinning out onto the street. The constables were one step ahead of him, though; cutting across open ground they pulled ahead, blocking the road before them. Birch pulled the wheel again, pumping the brakes, but too late. The car fishtailed, spun, and smacked into the side of the truck.

The world was spinning, but Birch didn't take long to get his bearings and slam the car into reverse. The wheels spun on in the icy snow, but he managed to slip-slide away from the truck and speed off down the road.

"You're going the wrong way," Edwards informed him from the back seat. "If this is anything like the enviro-dome then there will be set points where we can get out of this illusion. Our best bet would be to go back where we started, the opposite way to where you're headed."

"I know," Birch replied, "but they've got that way blocked. If they're smart they'll keep it blocked, but I'm betting they're desperate enough that they won't risk losing our location in the storm. They'll come after us, just wait and see. That'll be our chance.

They kept going for a few more minutes until Birch finally stopped, turning around at the entrance to an old dilapidated drive-in movie theater. "That should give them long enough to think we're not coming back," Birch muttered. "They'll be panicking about now, wondering if it's too late to find us." He turned off the headlights and revved the engine. "Here we go!" He said and hit the accelerator hard.

The wheels spun and they leaped forward. The little Chevette fairly glided along on the icy surface. Birch barely had control. Any sudden stop at this speed was going to be very unpleasant, but he wasn't planning on stopping.

"You're doing this without headlights?" Edwards spluttered. "Are you nuts?"

"Maybe, but it's the only way," Birch said, hunching over the wheel, pushing the accelerator to the floor. "Either they'll have come after us, in which case without headlights we'll zip right by them before they know it; or they'll be waiting for us back where we left them and I'll detour off the road, and at this speed, we just might get around them anyway."

"Are you kidding?" Edwards spat, clearly unimpressed with the plan. "This is a 1977 Chevette, not some big-wheeled four-wheel-drive. You'll never make it if you try to take this thing off the road!"

"We'll see," Birch answered flatly, staring ahead.

The snow continued to fall, and the wipers continued to scrape, but it was hard to see anything. Without the head-lights, the dashboard lights were out too. The darkness was complete. They couldn't see each other, much less the hood of the car or the road that stretched out beyond them. It was fortunate that the road was so straight and that Birch's sense of direction was so true, or they would have certainly ended up in the ditch.

They sped on through the night, the freshly fallen snow crunching under their wheels. Two smudged orbs of light, like twin moons, appeared suddenly in the darkness. It was the truck. They were coming at them. "Okay," Birch muttered, bearing down on the steering wheel, "here we go!"

The truck's headlights cut through the blizzard, dazzling them in its glowing beams, exposing them to the watchful eyes of the approaching constables. Birch was sure they must have seen them by the time they zoomed past, but for a brief instant, he hoped they hadn't. He caught the outline of a helmeted figure in the driver's seat, staring straight ahead, not looking at them, but the hope was quickly dashed. The truck suddenly turned, clipping the back of their car, sending them both skidding off the road toward the ditch.

Birch wrestled the wheel; pulling hard against the spin he tried to regain control. He almost managed it, but the front end hit the chicken restaurant's signpost, nearly bringing a giant bucket of chicken down on them as it wobbled unstead-ily above their heads.

They were back in the parking lot. Already two constables

were out of the truck and rushing toward them, but before they could make it Birch gunned the engine, sending the car limped away toward the street.

One headlight was broken, the hood was dented, and a wheel was bent, but the valiant little Chevette was still quick enough to outrun the approaching constables and put them back on the road to town.

"Trouble again!" Edwards shouted a moment later. Birch didn't need to be told. Already the blinding lights of the truck were right behind them, blazing in his rear view mirror.

Birch had his foot to the floor, but it wasn't doing much good. The front wheel was badly out of line and smoke was billowing from under the hood. He had to swerve a couple of times to keep ahead of the truck, but he had to be careful not to lose control on the ice.

They were getting close. Birch had his lights back on (though only one worked now) and in its thin beam, he was watching anxiously for the city limit sign. He was just beginning to think they had a chance when a loud clang and scraping sound from behind informed him that the constables had lowered the snowplow.

Ice and snow showered the car, cascading over their windshield. The wipers were barely adequate, but Birch just kept going, straight ahead at the best speed the car could manage.

There was a jolt from behind. They were ramming them with the plow. The car swerved, but Birch kept it under control. The truck came at them again, its plow scraping and its engine roaring throatily. They hit hard and the Chevette's back wheels came off the ground, spinning uselessly as Birch pushed the accelerator, trying to get away. For a moment they sped on like this, but the momentum was still taking them to the city limit and their escape. The truck pulled hard left, trying to bring them off the road, but the car's back end was caught on the plow and the momentum twisted and flipped the Chevette, sending it airborne.

They flew for an instant. It seemed longer than that as they twisted and spun. The kid hadn't bothered with a seatbelt and he smashed against Birch as they tumbled through the air. The car's nose hit the ground and they flipped again. Birch braced for impact, wondering if pain was real in this place when the snow about them froze in mid-air. The flakes came together, reconfiguring, forming into a solid computer screen.

They were back. Birch blinked, his hands tightly clenching an invisible steering wheel. They all shivered as their senses adjusted to the reality around them.

"Wow! That was something!" the Ares kid laughed. He clearly had enjoyed the whole thing a lot more than Birch had.

The screen flashed blue. A message came up,

Tempus Fugit
Game Over

A moment later the display collapsed on itself, shrinking into a single dot of light at the center, and finally disappearing to nothing. The computer hummed and then went dead.

"What happened?" Edwards asked, staring at the blank screen.

"He pulled the plug," Birch muttered sadly and turned away. "Okay," he finally barked, "we've got everything we can here. It's time to go."

They quickly left Wagner's station, climbed the stairs, and exited the building out into *Town Square*. In the main dome, he looked around, glancing up at the clock tower and the word 'EVIL' scrawled there. Something about it struck him for the first time.

"What time does that clock say?" he asked, pointing to the tower.

"Ten-to-seven," Edwards replied.

"Isn't that the same time as in the arcade?" the Ares asked.

"Exactly!" Birch replied, "ten-to-seven, or more succinctly, six-fifty. Now look up there. That's the only side of the tower that shows that time, and it happens to be the same side someone chose to write the word '*EVIL*'."

"So?" Edwards didn't look convinced. "That word's written everywhere around here."

"Yeah," Birch smiled grimly, "hidden in plain sight. Wagner was all about fooling them with humor and simple things. What could be more humorous and simple than leaving the answer dangling right under their noses?"

"I don't know," Edwards shook his head. "That's kind of flimsy. Two clocks stopped at the same time, what does that prove? Maybe the clocks both stopped at the same time."

"Yeah, but there's a lot more than that," Edwards smiled, pointed to the clock tower again. "Look at the word '*EVIL*', now try changing it into Roman numerals."

Edwards looked up, squinting against the glare of the sky. "E- there's no Roman numeral for E. Um... VI- six, L- fifty. Six-fifty. It's the same as the time!"

"Exactly. That's no coincidence, and the real clincher is what Wagner said to us in the arcade. He was telling us exactly what to do. That's why he told us that we already knew everything we needed to know."

"What did he say," Edwards asked. "I don't remember him saying anything that sounded like instructions."

"I didn't think so at the time either, but remember how he pointed at the clock and said '*tempus fugit*'? He was telling us what to do. In Latin tempus fugit means, 'time flies'. He was telling us to use the time as coordinates to fly out of here!"

"That makes sense," Edwards nodded, "but how are we..." He didn't get to finish his sentence.

"Something's happening!" the Ares interrupted, pointing to the ceiling. The sky was reddening again.

Birch looked around the dome. All the entrances had flown open. The colonists were entering again. They were more prepared this time. A few of them had large shoulder mounted weapons that they brandished menacingly as they ran into the dome.

FORTY-EIGHT

The storm clouds were building. Swirling and growing, they gathered strength, preparing to strike, but the colonists weren't running this time.

"What do you think they're doing?" Edwards asked.

"I don't know," Birch said, watching them take up positions around the dome, "but I'm sure we're not going to like it. Let's go." He gestured to the dry, rotted out remains of a tree positioned near the far wall. "That's the escape route Wagner plotted out for us. We have to get up that tree, onto the balcony and out through the executive suite into the main base and then back to the ship."

"Tree climbing?" Edwards shook his head as they ran. "This just keeps getting better and better. Tell me when the cliff diving comes up on your little tour, because I'm really up for that!"

Birch didn't answer. He was watching the colonists. None of them were paying any attention to their escape attempt yet. They seemed to have other things on their mind. They were setting up large weapons, but none of them were pointed in their direction. That at least gave them a chance. Birch hoped that, for now at least, they were too valuable a commodity to kill. They knew Wagner's secret, and he was betting that the colonists didn't. Wagner had terminated his own program rather than give them that chance. The colonists would keep them alive long enough to find out what they wanted to know, but probably not much longer than that.

They reached the tree. The Ares kid was already two-thirds of the way up to the balcony when the colonists launched their first mortar. It hit the ceiling with a thundering boom that shook all of *Town Square*. They were aiming for the weather array, but it was a tough old construction, built to last, and the first impact only fragmented a small section.

"They're trying to disable the defenses," Birch shouted over the sound of another explosion that shook the ceiling above. "Get up that tree, fast!"

Edwards nodded and started to climb, but his progress was painfully slow. He took one branch after another with sloth-like sluggishness.

"Could you hurry it up, please?" Birch snapped, eyeing the ceiling above. Already shards of glass were falling away from the structure and their glowing red clouds were splitting into fractured slithers that sparked and died.

"I'm going as fast as I can," Edwards spat back. "This tree is as brittle as driftwood, and if I put a foot wrong we're both going to fall. I have to be careful."

"Fine, just be careful quickly!"

More sparks were flying from the ceiling. Stray electrical bolts were shooting down. Most were misdirected and hit harmlessly on open ground. One randomly hit a mortar crew and sent them flying. A colonist lit up in flames, but two of his comrades calmly extinguished the fire.

Four more mortars went up, traced lines of smoke exploded into orange conflagration. The roof shook and a steady stream of glass trickled down, but still it was holding.

"These guys are crazy," Edwards shouted, clinging to the tree after the impact of another mortar. "They're destroying their own base!"

"Obviously they think getting us is more important than that," Birch responded grimly. "Keep climbing!" The Ares had disappeared onto the balcony, but they were still only about half way up, and Birch was pretty sure the protection from the ceiling wasn't going to last much longer.

Another mortar hit and a girder broke loose, crashing noisily to the ground. That was the start of it. Another support fell shortly after, and then a sudden torrent of metal and glass showered down around them. The whole dome shook. The tree swayed and toppled, its roots ripped from the ground. It fell against the building, scraping along its marbled side, smashing windows, coming to rest finally against the balcony.

Edwards hung on as the roof collapsed around them, but Birch wasn't so lucky. His branch snapped and he fell, landing heavily at the foot of the tree. The impact winded him and for a moment all he could do was writhe painfully in the dirt. He struggled to get up. Above him, he could see a gaping hole where the roof had once been. A mixture of smoke and the encroaching gray dust of the planet mingled into a hazy smog that was descending upon them all, and the last thing he saw before it engulfed him was the colonists running in his direction.

"Come on!" Edwards' voice shouted to him from the gloom. He had come back down for him. Two pairs of hands hauled Birch to his feet. The Ares kid had come back too, and now together they pulled him to the tree. The climbing was easier this time. Instead of straight up, the trunk now slanted toward the balcony and the three of them swiftly scrambled to the top.

The colonists weren't far behind. Reaching the balcony, Birch looked down into the smoky mist to see their blank, faceless visors just meters away. They were scurrying up the tree, like scavenging insects, crawling out of the darkness toward them.

"Get over here, now!" Birch shouted to the others, trying to push the tree away from the balcony. It was too much for him alone. Even working together it was difficult. They shoved and pushed. The nearest colonist was already level with them before they had budged it. Birch and Edwards tried to beat him back, but the colonist grabbed Birch by the throat and, using his body as support, hauled himself up and over the banister.

He flung Birch aside, but before he could turn his attention to Edwards, the Ares kid rammed him hard, slamming his head into his chest, sending him stumbling backward. The man grabbed the Ares and together they fell back, flipping over the banister. The kid instinctively grabbed a support before they fell and together they dangled as he struggled to hold their weight. The colonist grabbed him around the waist, but with his free arm, the Ares elbowed him in the gut. Kicking and screaming like something wild, the kid tore his attacker's hands free, and pushed him down, sending him falling, tumbling into the darkness below. With a single move, the kid leaped the banister and was up again, ready to fight.

Birch struggled to his feet again. Gasping for air, he rushed to help Edwards, but he hadn't needed it. Edwards had taken up an iron chair and was beating the next ascending colonist repeatedly with it. The attacker had made it to the banister, but he couldn't do anything before Edwards shoved the chair into his face and sent him falling back over the edge.

Now, with less weight at the top, they were finally able to shift the tree. Just a little at first, but soon they had it moving and pushed it away from the balcony, sending it rolling and falling back down into *Town Square*.

Birch glanced down into the smoky darkness. That would keep them off their trail for a few minutes, but he was sure that they were already coming at them from other directions. They had to hurry.

They passed through another spacious well-appointed suite and ran out into the corridor. Birch glanced up and down, but no one was there, yet. He followed the map indicator for the direction to their ship. Wagner had done a good job directing them. From here they were only a few minutes away from the exit they needed.

They ran, following the passages toward their escape. They were nearing the airlock when Edwards, who was dragging at the rear, shouted the warning.

"Here they come again!" he panted. He was right. Another large group of colonists was approaching quickly.

"Go, go, go!" Birch shouted, standing at the airlock door. He ran through last, slamming and sealing it behind him. He quickly worked the mechanism to open the exterior door, and a moment later they were out. Already he could see the blank visors of their pursuers in the glass of the airlock door as they escaped, sealing the final door behind them.

The ship was still there, just as they had left it. Birch switched off the electrical charge and they ran aboard. In the cockpit, he leaped into his seat and flipped buttons preparing for liftoff.

The airlock door opened and the colonists ran out.

"Look what we've got!" Edwards hissed.

"I see," Birch mumbled, toggling a few more settings. "I've put some juice to the hull. I don't have much to spare, but it might convince them to get off if they try it."

They didn't try it. As a group, they simply stood and watched as the engines roared and the ship lifted slowly off the ground. The Ares whooped and waved at them as the ship rose.

Edwards breathed a sigh of relief. "I wonder why they didn't at least try to get on the ship," he pondered aloud.

"Maybe they knew where we were going," Birch responded.

"Not back to the Hypnos?" Edwards concluded gloomily.

"Nope, into the heart of darkness... *The Lowers*, where all of this fun started."

"I can hardly wait," Edwards sighed.

"I feel your enthusiasm," Birch mumbled through gritted teeth, "and I really share it, but first we have to get there." He was looking down at his instruments. "I'll be flying in low, but getting this close it'll still target us. I'm going to need your help with this." He tapped a terrain indicator to his left. *Primary Base* was already coming up on the screen. "I need you to watch that. There should be slight heat trace before the tower lets loose with that beam that brought us down when we first arrived. I'm ready for them this time, I think I can dodge it, but I need you to tell me immediately there's any trace. I can't keep my eyes in two places at once."

Edwards shot a meaningful glance at Birch. "You '*think*' you can dodge it?"

"Just watch the screen," Birch muttered. He had the ship on a holding pattern above *Colony One*, but now gunned the engine and sent them hurtling toward *Primary Base*.

"Don't you think you should take it a little slower if you're not sure about avoiding that green ray," Edwards gasped through chattering teeth.

"Speed's our best chance," Birch shot back. "Now just look at that screen and shout out when you see it!"

Almost immediately Edwards was shouting. "It's there, it's there!"

Birch's eyes narrowed. He was watching the tower. A moment later there was a sharp crackle and the green beam was zooming toward them. Birch was ready and pulled the stick, sending the craft into a roll as the ray passed harmlessly beneath their wings.

"It's heating up again!" Edwards shouted almost immediately after the first shot.

It fired again and again, but Birch was ready now and the ship ducked and weaved through its fire until he pulled close enough to the base to make it impossible for it to fire on them without hitting *Primary Base* itself.

The tower fell silent and Birch brought the ship down near an airlock door. "And now," he sighed as he unstrapped himself from his seat, "the fun really begins."

FORTY-NINE

"You don't really expect us all to go in there again, do you?" Edwards asked gloomily.

"Actually, no I don't," Birch smiled, getting out of his seat. He grabbed the Ares' wrist, tapped a few buttons on his computer and a chip came out. He took it. "You see," he continued, "I'm still not sure I can trust him not to make trouble, and I am absolutely certain that I still can't trust you to stay out of trouble, so I'd feel a whole lot better on my own." He put the Ares' chip into a slot in Edwards' suit and pressed a few buttons on his keypad.

"There," Birch concluded, "now he can't leave the ship unless you give him his control chip back. His life support won't kick in without it. You can both stay here until I return. Can you manage that?"

"Yeah," Edwards' eyes narrowed, "but I'm not so sure. It sounds like another one of your stupid ideas."

"No, it's a great idea," Birch answered shortly.

"You must not go out there alone," the Ares spoke with his hand on Birch's arm, not in a threatening way, but as a gesture of concern. "There are bad things out there, things that cannot and should not be approached alone."

"Sure," Birch laughed it off, "but that's Jane for you! But

seriously, this is the only way. It's all about rescuing Jane, and I know what I'm dealing with. It'll just be easier without any distractions. I know her better than either of you. I know how to bring her back. Trust me."

The Ares shook his head vehemently, but Edwards seemed to be thinking it over. "You see," Birch continued as he edged toward the door, "that's why I put you in charge of the kid's chip. You're the adult here, he's the kid. You know what I'm saying makes sense. I'll be back, watch the ship" He ducked into the airlock and slammed it shut, releasing the mechanism and opening the door to the gray world of R67.3

Of course, it was all a lie. He knew pretty well what Jane's problem was. He didn't know how to bring her back. He didn't know how to bring himself back, but this was the best he could do. At least he wouldn't lose anyone else.

Dust clouded up around him as he walked toward the base's entrance. He didn't bother looking back to see if the others were seeing him off, though he wished they would. He turned the handle, pushed a few buttons, and pulled the old stained metal door aside. It creaked slowly open and his helmet light shone into the gray compartment. He went in and, turning to close the door, saw Edwards and the Ares watching from the cockpit window. He smiled and shut it with a bang.

Already he had lost radio contact with the ship. *Primary Base* was a real dead zone, in more ways than one. He opened the internal airlock door and entered the base. Glancing down at his map he saw that he wasn't too far from *Main Dome* and he started out for there.

His footsteps echoed in the empty corridors. As before, there seemed to be no one in these upper levels. He just hoped *The Lowers* had been emptied out with all the colonists trying to stop them over at *Colony One*. Somehow he doubted it.

He came out into *Main Dome* without having encountered anyone. The world around him was silent and dead. He continued through the dome, watching the windows of the squat, ugly buildings and the walkways between them for any movement, but there was nothing here. He reached the main elevator chamber and found a cage waiting for him. He entered and pressed the button, beginning his descent into the darkness.

He stared down into the abyss, mesmerized by the nothingness he found there. The bare bulb of the elevator shone coldly, casting sharp shadows around him. The battered cage wobbled and groaned its way down and the stark, gray walls passed by with monotonous uniformity.

Birch sighed. This was the one place he had never wanted to be. It was Jane's fault. She had brought them all back to this planet, and now she had brought him here. He should have left her here, but he knew he couldn't. The weight of his sins was upon him and one more would destroy him.

The cage rattled to a stop and Birch got out. He could see from here that this wasn't supposed to be the bottom of the shaft, it had been sealed off, just as Jane and Edwards had described. He got out and started toward the gloomy passages beyond. He wasn't going to try the same way they had gone last time. He wasn't ready for a direct confrontation. He would try another route and hope that he could avoid detection.

Using his map he looked for the least obvious entrance to *The Lowers* and went for that one. It was in a remote corner of the level, but when he got there he found that someone had been there before him. It was a plain metal door without any window, covered with graffiti, big spray painted words, '*DIE! DIE! DIE!*' Birch shivered. The door had been forced off its hinges and pulled back so that the gap now opened the opposite way to normal. Birch wasn't sure if it had been forced recently or not. Some of the scratches looked shiny. Perhaps Jane had come through here.

He peered in through the gap. Stairs stretched out far below. No one was here; there was nothing but dusty emptiness. In some places the dust had been disturbed, but

Birch had no way of knowing if that was anything to do with Jane or whether other colonists had passed through here.

He started down the stairs, his boots echoing on the steel steps. It was strange to think that once this place had been just another access route to the lower levels, nothing special, just a way to get from A to B, but now it was transformed from the mundane to the monstrous. Every abandoned place took on that aspect. He had found that back in Denver, the city he and Karla had explored together. Its ruins had been a tribute to human failure, to the empty hope that they could build something permanent. The settlement on this planet had been the same. Nothing lasted, and that knowledge made Birch wonder why they ever started at all. In every beginning, he could see the end, and he hated it. What was the point in celebrating a birth when it meant death in the end? He had seen too much. Long life wasn't all it was cracked up to be.

Birch kept going. Every shadow and every sound took on an ominous connotation, but as far as he could tell he was the only one here. Step followed step, he lost track of how many levels he had traveled down, but eventually he came to the bottom. There wasn't anything special about it. The stairs just stopped at a blank stone wall. Birch cautiously opened the door and peered out.

Things were different down here. All of *Primary Base* had a rough, unfinished look to it, but nothing at all had been done to humanize the environment here. It was all bare, unshaped rock. Birch stepped out into the tunnel. He could hear the sound of running water somewhere. At this depth, the heat had been sufficient for liquid water. This was the very cradle of the colony's life here. This is what had made everything possible.

Birch followed the sound. He tried looking at his map but it was coming up blank. His locator dot was at the center of the screen, but everything else was empty.

The passage continued for a while. He followed a smooth, beaten path through the rock formations until it opened out into a wide cavern. There a shallow stream splashed and gurgled, zigzagging across the floor of the cave. Birch waded through it.

On the other side, he was puzzled by the appearance of a number of crimson stained stones. At first glance, they seemed to be some sort of unique red rock, but on closer inspection, it wasn't the stones that were red, rather it was a coating that covered them. He reached out to touch it, but quickly pulled back when the goo moved, seemingly in reaction to his approach.

Birch took another step away, stooping down to get a better view of the phenomenon. It looked alive, oozing and shimmering, but perhaps that was a trick of the light. The texture looked soft, like moss, but it didn't look natural. The surface was bobbled, but the components were only loosely connected, circular disks, like enlarged individual cells.

A few meters further along Birch came to a point where the crimson ooze met the water, and the combination was not a pretty one. The lapping stream bathed the red rocks. Their essence seeped and mingled into the liquid, changing the water, transforming the pure flowing current into a scarlet tide that gurgled and frothed deep into the cavern.

He didn't see her at first, but he found Jane behind a rock, face down in the water. He rushed to her side. Pulling her over, he stared anxiously at her, shaking her, trying to get a response. Her visor was fogged up, so he couldn't see her face, but he took that as a good sign. At least she was breathing. He checked her status on her suit's computer. She was alive but not responding.

Birch pulled her out of the stream. Red threads, like tendrils, clung to her suit, solidified like clots around a wound. Birch pulled at them, breaking them off, dragging her to clean water where he bathed her, clearing away as much of the bloody residue as he could.

He wiped her visor, trying to see her face, but the fogging was on the inside. Birch's computer indicated that there was oxygen here. That might have been the result of natural conditions, or maybe the environmental systems were still working down here. It didn't make any difference to him, Birch tore Jane's helmet off. Flinging it aside he held her head in his hands.

She fell limply in his arms. Her hair was matted, and sweat trickled down her chin. Birch touched her forehead; she was hot. "Jane," he murmured softly, "Jane, I'm here. I came to get you."

Her eyes fluttered, moving slightly beneath their closed lids. Her lips parted and a long trail of blood trickled down.

"No!" Birch cried, feeling Jane's pulse again. It was weakening. "No, you don't. You're not doing this!" He pumped her chest, fighting for her life. With every compression a fresh stream of blood gurgled up, flowing from her open mouth.

Jane coughed, her bloody breath spraying into Birch's face. Then she opened her eyes. She looked around, blinking, unable to comprehend her surroundings for a moment before she finally fixed her gaze on Birch.

"You look terrible," she croaked, looking up at his blood-splattered face.

"You don't look much better," Birch responded.

She tried to move but fell back, panting.

"What are you doing here?" she asked.

"Oh, I was just in the neighborhood… I thought I'd drop by and see how you were getting along. What happened to you?"

Jane seemed confused and looked around. "I was… I was coming through here and stopped to examine the stream, you know, where the water turns red. I was doing an analysis, trying to figure out what was causing that effect, and that's the last thing I remember."

"Did you find anything out?"

"Yeah, something." Jane pulled herself up. "It's blood, or at least something very close to it. I'm not sure how it happens. There seems to be a plant element to it, like its growing down here, but in almost every tangible way it is blood." She struggled to her feet. "So, what we have here is literally a river of blood. I don't suggest you go wading."

"I won't." Birch glanced over at the frothing red stream and shook his head. "Anyway, we better hurry. We need to get going." He started back toward the exit.

"Where are you going?" Jane asked.

"Back to the ship," Birch gestured up. "I cracked Wagner's code. 'EVIL' wasn't a word, it was coordinates, E-VI/50. We know where the Hypnos VI went. We can follow them there!"

"Yeah? There's just one problem with that," Jane replied. "Right now we're on R-III/67.3 and we're going to E-VI/50: so what is the final digit? Without that, we don't even know exactly where to look. That's still a huge amount of space to sift through looking for a single planet. You might as well tell me you have a friend living in New York City, and you don't know exactly where they live, but we'll just go look around and see if we can find them somewhere."

"I know," Birch admitted, "but maybe that's all they knew here. That's enough to start with. Come on, let's go."

"No," Jane shook her head. "I'm going to finish what I came here for."

Birch's eyes narrowed. "Are you sure that's a good idea? Remember what happened to you before. Can you really be sure that won't happen again if we try to continue?"

"I was stupid," Jane admitted. "I was worried about my air supply. I wasn't figuring on leaving anytime soon, so when I detected oxygen here I opened my filter vent to supplement my supply. It looks that was a mistake. There's something in the property of that blood that knocked me out I guess," she snatched up her helmet and jammed it on, "but I won't make that mistake again." She walked away, following the arc of the stream further into the cavern.

Birch could have tried to stop her, but what was the point? She was determined, so he followed her.

FIFTY

They followed the course of the stream for some time without speaking. Jane didn't seem to have anything to say and Birch was fine with that. He didn't want to say anything.

They walked on in silence. As they moved deeper into the cavern the color around them gradually began to change. The rocks, reflecting in the cold blue of their helmet lamps, began to warm. An orange glow like an approaching dawn shone ahead. Birch knew what that meant. They were coming to the heart of all operations here, the hydrothermal reservoir. This had been the prerequisite of all successful Hypnos missions- a habitable planet had to have a sustainable power source. This is what had made R67.3 such a good prospect. It had nothing to do with its suitable atmosphere, its balmy weather, or its breathtaking beauty. All of these things had been terrible. It was the available power that made life possible here.

A second, larger stream joined the first, transforming it into a swiftly flowing river, but it wasn't diluted. It stayed as red as ever. Ahead Birch could see an opening growing ever larger as they approached, and he heard the thunder of the water that passed beyond it. It sounded like a waterfall.

Jane ran ahead and Birch followed. They avoided the river, keeping close to the wall, but by the time they came near to the opening there wasn't much space and they had to hug the side to keep from falling in.

Jane gasped as they came to the end of the tunnel. It was impressive. They were standing at the edge of a sheer cliff that dropped hundreds of feet beneath them. The water gushed over, plummeting down into a churning red lake below. The lake itself was clearly not a natural phenomenon. Its shape was uniform and its sides were smooth. It was long and narrow, and surrounding it, clearly visible, was the radiant glow of magma that kept the crimson lake hissing and simmering like an old witch's cauldron.

Spray and steam rose up from the falls, covering everything, making the footing extremely treacherous. Little drops coated Birch's visor, streaming down in red trails that he struggled to wipe clean, but instead smeared into marks that only made it harder to see. He sighed and stepped as carefully as he could. The bloody water was lapping at his feet and one slip would send him over the falls.

He tried to keep close to Jane. Birch knew what she was looking for, the access ramp that would take them over the falls. She found it a moment later, but it wasn't much to look at. It began at the edge of the tunnel, where the waterfall plunged over the edge. There should have been a steel platform attached to it, but that had been eaten away with rust, leaving a stump of decayed metal that Jane was using to get onto the main walkway.

"Are you sure this is a good idea?" Birch yelled over the thundering waterfall.

"Sure," Jane answered lightly taking her first step onto the rusty walkway. It took a noticeable shift to the left. "Of course, I could be wrong," she added nervously, but it didn't slow her down. She was already striding out across the chasm.

Birch shook his head. There was no stopping her. He waited a minute to let her get further ahead. If they kept their distance and evened out their weight then maybe they might get across without bringing the bridge crashing down into the boiling lake below.

He watched Jane. Her white spacesuit smudged in the hazy

heat as she walked away. Finally, Birch followed. The walkway swayed under him with his first few steps, but as he went along things felt more secure. The suspension wires were mostly intact and his confidence grew.

Jane was a distant figure by now. She was walking faster than him, and Birch struggled to keep up. He didn't like the way she was acting. The way she was disregarding danger and making reckless choices worried him. It wasn't like her. She had almost killed herself already, and everything she had done since had the look of a kamikaze mission. It was his job to make sure she didn't succeed.

Birch hurried on. Through gaps in the metal slats, he could see the scarlet lake frothing- beyond that the glowing orange lava was heating it. Everything was bathed in orange and red light. Birch had grown weary of the eternal gray of the surface of R67.3, but he would have given anything to see it right now. Red steam was rising, misting and condensing, making the path ahead slick and dangerous. Far above massive fans were turning. Powered by the heat and steam, they whooshed impressively above them producing electricity. From what he had seen so far the power problems at *Colony One* had nothing to do with the systems installed here. Everything was working perfectly, just as they had planned.

Jane was getting too far ahead again. He hurried to catch her. They were getting close to the center island now. A large jut of solid gray rock in this fiery world, it stood in the center of the lake. Atop it, stretching to the ceiling stood a metal cylinder topped with a pyramid of glass and steel that ended in a sharp metal spike.

In the end, Birch didn't have any trouble catching Jane. When he reached the island she was standing there looking up at the tower. Birch looked up too. Trouble was coming. He could see that. For a time Jane just kept looking up, and all he could do was wait. Finally, she turned on him. In the red glow, her face was startling. Enraged and demonic, her eyes sparked and Birch took a step back.

"That's it!" she spat. "That's exactly what I expected to find." Birch looked up where she pointed. Written along the side of the tower was that familiar name, *Hypnos III*. It was part of the original colonizing equipment they had brought with them, put now to its proper purpose.

"You said all the original equipment was destroyed!" she said, wagging her finger in his face. "You said there was nothing left! Well, where did all of this come from then? This isn't replacement equipment. This is *OUR* equipment! So, how do you explain that all of our equipment that was destroyed in the storm was used to make this place?"

Birch shrugged. There wasn't an answer to that.

"Maybe because it was never destroyed," she answered her own question. "Maybe because you made the whole thing up. Maybe because you wanted to go home and the only way to do that was to take command. Maybe because you killed Colonel Ratliff. Maybe because that was the only way you could get back to your precious home."

"I never wanted to go home," Birch answered. Jane wasn't listening.

"The equipment you said was destroyed," she continued, "maybe you just hid it. Left on its customary settings it could have automatically done all this, so long as there weren't any major breakdowns that required human input. Maybe this whole base has been built on the broken body of your comm.-ander, Colonel Ratliff!"

"Maybe, maybe, maybe!" Birch spat back in exasperation. "You're almost as crazy as that beloved commander of yours. Maybe you don't realize this, but Ratliff was nuts. That last night, in the storm, he and I were alone at the quarry. Things were just normal and then out of nowhere he came at me. He tried to kill me!"

"He... tried to kill you?" Jane gasped, almost unable to get the words out. "What kind of an idiot do you think I am? Why would he do that, and why wouldn't you ever tell me that until right now? Huh? You're pathetic! You're just trying to cover up what you did. Well, I'm not that stupid. You just came up with that story. It makes you sound like a sniveling brat trying to lie your way out of getting caught, and I'm not buying it!"

"Yeah," Birch muttered, "I knew you wouldn't believe me. I knew that then. I knew exactly what to expect if I came back to camp saying, 'Hey, guess what guys. Colonel Ratliff just tried to kill me, and now he's disappeared'.

"Ratliff and I never could get on, and you always took his side. I knew how you'd react. Ratliff had disappeared into the storm and it seemed easier to just leave it that way. When I went out the next day I looked for him and he was gone. When I checked the equipment there wasn't much left. What was there showed obvious signs of tampering. He had destroyed it all, blown it all up. That left us with no other option but to go back home, except you didn't want to go, so I had to convince you."

"That's all lies!" Jane spat, "just like every other lie you've ever told! You never convinced me to leave; you drugged me! And Colonel Ratliff never touched you, and I know how to prove it!" She looked up to the top of the tower. "The complete mission log will be up there, everything to do with building this base, from the first landing to the final completion. Let's see what that has to say about what happened to the equipment that night!" She ran to the tower and disappeared inside.

Birch sighed. This wasn't getting any easier.

FIFTY-ONE

Entering the tower Birch heard the *clang-clang-clang* of Jane's boots pounding on the steel stairs above. She had gotten pretty far ahead, and there wasn't much chance of him catching her now. He wasn't going to try. He climbed wearily after her.

The staircase spiraled up along the center of the metal tower to the top. This whole structure was part of the burrowing technology used to delve deep underground once surface scans had found a suitable location to drill. Geothermal energy wasn't easy to access on a planet like R67.3 where no newer volcanic activity or 'hot spots' occurred. You had to dig for it. This tower had done its job and the rest of the structure had been built up around it by automated systems. Birch understood all of that, but he still couldn't figure out why it was here.

The whirr of turbines thundered in Birch's ears. This part of the power grid, like everything else in this place, was working just fine. He looked up. Jane was further ahead now, almost to the top, and he hurried his steps to try and keep pace.

Birch finally reached the highest level. Jane had been there a while and was already inside. He paused at the door. He wasn't sure he was going to like what he found inside. He shrugged the feeling off, pulled the door aside and strode in.

He was inside the mission command module. Jane already had the main console running, but she wasn't looking at it. She was walking around, running her fingers over the equipment, touching it, as though checking to see that it was real.

She didn't seem to notice him at first. This would have been the very center of their life, or whatever was left of it if they had completed their mission. Jane seemed to be savoring the moment, drinking in the lost possibilities of their time here. Birch shivered like a man walking past his own grave. In truth, that really was what he was doing. This should have been the place he lived and worked, and this should have been the place that he died. They had all been an expendable part of the plan.

The console started bleeping. Jane hurried over and soon had the display up. Birch couldn't see the screen, but he could tell it meant trouble.

"No interruption," Jane hissed. "Nothing reported, no lost equipment, nothing broken, no problems encountered at all. Everything went smoothly. The mission was a complete success. How do you explain that?" she asked, looking accusingly up at Birch.

He shook his head as he looked at the screen. What she said was true, but it didn't make any sense. Then he noticed a discrepancy. It had been deployed early and the start location was all wrong.

"What's this?" he muttered, taking a closer look, but before he could consider it further a loud click and hiss from behind interrupted his thoughts. He spun around in time to see a steel ladder descending from a black hole that had opened in the ceiling above.

Birch and Jane looked at each other. "What do you suppose that is?" he asked, peering up into the darkness. He thought he knew the layout of every piece of Hypnos equipment, but this was new to him.

"I'm not sure," Jane answered. "Let's find out." She moved quickly to the ladder and took three rungs in her first step. A moment later she had disappeared through the hole. Birch wasn't so swift, but he was soon following her into the darkness.

His helmet light clicked on as his head lifted through the gap. Already he could see Jane poking around examining everything. Tutting quietly to herself, she shook her head as she hovered around the equipment. Birch could see why she didn't like what she saw. It was strange. There were five small cryogenic units lining the walls and a sixth one in the center. That didn't make much sense; there were already six cryo-chambers in the Hypnos Lander. Why would they waste the weight doubling up on something they already had? Unless these were later additions, put here by the colonists.

A closer inspection revealed that these were not typical cryogenic units. They had been modified. The changes were peculiar. The five on the walls were all smaller and had less extensive equipment, but the one at the center was larger and had additional dials and gauges that Birch didn't recognize. Strangest of all, however, was the mass of tubes and wires that ran from the center unit into the five smaller chambers. Birch couldn't fathom their purpose. Jane seemed as baffled as he was by all of this, but one important fact became clear to both of them. The five smaller units were empty, but the central chamber was not.

Jane and Birch looked at each other. "There's someone in this one," Jane whispered.

"I know," Birch answered. The stasis field was sealed and all the readings indicated that there was life inside.

"Let's get them out," Jane said, moving to the controls.

"Wait a minute," Birch cautioned, yanking her back. "We don't know what's in there, and from what we've seen so far I'm not exactly anxious to find out either. Just leave it alone"

"No!" Jane pulled away. "This is what I came for... what we all came for, to find out what happened here." She was already back at the control panel, tapping in the opening sequence. Birch tried to grab her, but she was too quick and the panel lit up green as she completed the startup.

The chamber hissed and lights flashed as the lid clicked and opened just a crack. Steam poured out, wafting, drifting up to the glass ceiling. Birch and Jane anxiously peered down, staring through the smoky mist. Birch was ready for the worst. One thought kept running through his mind- they had seen plenty of the five constables and other colonists since their first encounter at *Primary Base*, but one person had been conspicuously absent up to now, Security Chief Miltant.

Birch didn't think it was coincidental that the base's final reports showed that things only really fell apart once Miltant had disappeared. A theory was forming in his mind that explained it all. The way things had begun small and spread out over *Primary Base,* and then finally jumped over to *Colony One* right at the end, it seemed like a virus or an infection of some kind that had spread through the colony. People were disappearing, but others still saw them, not out in the open, but fleeting glimpses on the lower levels. Something bad was happening and it had all started here, down in *The Lowers*. It was clear that whatever had infected the inhabitants of *Primary Base* had also infected the five constables when they came down here; he had seen plenty of evidence of that, but what about Miltant? What had happened to him?

Birch shivered. If it was a virus were they susceptible too? He and Jane were wearing suits, but then the same had been true of the constables. Jane had even opened her vent at one point, and even with filters that was a dangerous thing to have done. Would they both go crazy and betray themselves and their friends?

It seemed pretty clear that this was what had happened here. Birch suspected that the final push against *Colony One* had been an inside job. The fact that it was shortly after Miltant had disappeared that all the weapon stores were emptied was telling, and it was soon after this that the inhabitants of *Primary Base* had launched a large-scale assault. That had been a bold move and nothing like the usual tunnel snatches that had characterized the earlier attacks in *Primary Base*. It seemed pretty clear that everything had changed once Miltant was lost.

The five constables were his henchmen, but Miltant was the brains behind it all. He must have been infected too, and once that had happened he must have become the head of all operations, that's why their tactics had changed. And this place had something to do with that, with these five empty chambers for his constables and the one where he resided now. He wasn't sure how it all fit together, but looking at the cryo-chamber with all its wires, tubes, and complex gadgetry he felt deeply uneasy. There was more to this place than simple cryogenics. He was certain of that.

The dense smoke started to clear. The steel lid was rising, and Birch grabbed a heavy tool from its place on the wall, lifting it up as a weapon. He steeled himself, ready to meet this formidable foe. He was ready.

Jane looked on expectantly; Birch tightened his grip on his makeshift club and clenched his teeth, but what they saw through the thinning cloud made them both gasp. The outline of a body was clearly visible. It was drenched, soaked in the same sort of bloody liquid that had infected the stream further up the cavern. The figure rose, its open eyes aflame like burning suns, but surprisingly it wasn't this that shocked them most. Clearly recognizable beneath a coating of oozing slime was the anguished face of Lt. Colonel John Ratliff.

FIFTY-TWO

"John!" Jane cried, running to his side, snatching him up, pulling him from the sludgy liquid. His eyes were closed and his skin was deathly pale. He showed no sign of life. His head rolled and Jane caught it, cradling him in her arms. "Wake up!" she gasped desperately, pulling him toward her.

Ratliff moaned, finally stirring. A long, slow breath hissed through his teeth. He coughed, doubling over, retching-vomiting out a stream of red bile. Birch took a step back, disgusted, but Jane was unfazed, holding Ratliff's head, lifting him up, cleaning his face as best she could with the sleeve of her suit.

Ratliff's eyes fluttered open. Birch noted their color again-fiery red, like the colonists and other enemies he recalled. There was something in that, but he didn't have time try and figure it out. Ratliff was struggling against Jane, trying to pull away from her as she soothed and clucked, trying to calm him. It wasn't working. She had one of his hands, but his free arm flailed and his wild eyes rolled, darting between him and Jane, staring into their helmet's darkened visors. Birch rushed to her side, pinning him in place.

"He doesn't recognize us," Jane said, letting go of Ratliff's hand long enough to reach for her helmet. Birch saw what she was doing. The readings seemed to indicate that the air was breathable, that she would be safe here, but Birch wasn't so sure. There was still a risk, the possibility that something similar, or perhaps even worse than what had happened earlier could happen again.

"Don't be stupid, Jane!" he snapped, struggling to hold Ratliff down with both hands now that she had let go. Jane ignored his warning and twisted her helmet off. Her long, black hair had been up, but straggling strands fell across her tired face. She smiled. Ratliff looked up, his eyes finally fixed on her. He struggled to get up.

"It's okay," she cooed softly. "We're here. We've come back for you." Her voice was soft and her words soothing, but rather than calm him they only seemed to increase his agitation. He started bucking and rolling, and he slipped from Birch's grasp as he splashed and writhed in the frothy liquid of his cryogenic chamber. An instant later he was up, and he leaped toward Jane, sending them both tumbling and rolling to the floor. Birch scrambled after him, clambering over the chamber, splashing through the bloody contents to reach the struggle. He landed on Ratliff's back, sending three or four swift blows to his head before he was thrown off and sent skidding across the floor.

Ratliff was quickly on his feet again and, ignoring Jane and Birch, he rushed for the ladder. From the floor Birch was able to lunge himself at him as he passed, pulling him down again. He quickly overcame Ratliff, pinning his arms, and Jane assisted with his legs. They had him. He kept fighting for a moment but soon he was exhausted and he fell limp, spitting and biting at the air in protest at his treatment, but there was nothing more he could do, and soon even this ceased.

Ratliff's eyes went back to Jane and then looked up into Birch's blank visor. A single red tear pooled in the corner of his eye. He tried to blink it away, but it escaped leaving a crimson trail on his gaunt cheek. Birch suddenly felt cruel and shifted his knee off Ratliff's chest.

"You can get up if you promise no more crazy stuff," Birch muttered, loosening his grip slightly as a sign of goodwill. Ratliff didn't respond, but he seemed to calm down, so Birch got off.

Ratliff didn't attempt to get up. He pulled his legs in and drew himself up into a fetal ball. Naked and wet, he shivered on the cold, steel floor. Birch found a stiff, white robe in a closet and threw it over him. It covered him like a blanket and the red liquid that clung to his skin oozed through the fabric, leaving moist red patches like bloodstains.

Ratliff didn't move again for a while. He just lay there shivering. Jane was at his side comforting him, stroking his dripping hair, mumbling something inaudible to him. The light suddenly came on in Birch's mind. This was more than professional concern. There was something between these two, something that he had never noticed before, something that Jane's beloved NASA regulations prohibited. They were more than colleagues, they were a couple.

"So, that's it," Birch muttered as Jane lifted Ratliff's head onto her lap. "That explains a lot! Seems like a pretty cozy arrangement, taking your bit of stuff along with you, Colonel. How did you swing it?"

Ratliff didn't answer, he was still shivering, but Jane looked up from her ministrations. "Shut up, Birch!" she snapped. "You know nothing about us." Her voice seemed to bring Ratliff around. His head came up and he looked at them both. For the first time, he seemed to see them with real comprehension, but he didn't seem too happy about it. His shivering increased and he pulled away, trying to escape Jane's grasp.

"You're okay," Jane repeated. "We came back for you," but her words set him off again. He writhed, broke free, and clambered unsteadily to his feet. Birch took a step toward him but stopped when he saw the look of terror on his face. Ratliff recognized them now, there was no doubt about that, but the sight of them didn't bring him any relief. Apparently, it filled him with fear.

"Jane's right," Birch lied soothingly, "everything's okay. We came back for you. You're going to be fine."

Ratliff shook his head. "No," he gasped through gurgling breaths. "No," he paused, hanging his head over the bloody cryogenic compartment, breathing in the wafting steam before slamming the lid shut. "No... can't you get anything right, Birch? I mean, it was a simple job I gave you, and you're simple enough man that I thought I could trust you to do it, even if you didn't know what you did, or why you were doing it. But here you are. Why did you come back?"

"Birch shook his head, but he didn't get the chance to answer. "I did it," Jane announced proudly. "I knew something wasn't right about that crazy story of his about you getting lost in the storm and all that equipment getting destroyed. I had to know what really happened, but Birch wouldn't tell me, so when we left Earth and I saw that this was the only known colony listed in the records it was easy to convince him to come. We're supposed to be looking for life, but all I wanted to find was the truth about you. Now I know why Major Birch wouldn't tell me the truth! He did all this to you!"

Birch turned angrily on Jane, but before he could speak Ratliff answered. "He did nothing. Major Birch doesn't even know the truth about what happened to me." Ratliff paused, catching his breath before continuing. "He was just a tool, a blunt and unwitting instrument at that, but still a tool to get us out of the predicament you had created."

"I created? What predicament did I create?"

"You came."

Jane looked confused and hurt. "You didn't want me to come on the mission?"

"No."

"Because of regulations?"

"Because I didn't want you here."

Jane didn't answer for a moment. When she did reply her voice was tight and cracked with emotion. She blinked back her tears. "You wanted to leave me behind? You were going to just fly off and leave me? Why would you do that? Why would you marry me if that's what you planned? If you cared so little then why did you even make those promises? Did you like the sound they made as you spoke them? Did you like the way I looked when you said them? Was it funny to you?" Her questions came hard and fast, like bullets from a loaded gun, but she didn't wait for answers; she didn't seem to expect any.

"Married?" Birch's single word question hung uncomfortably in the air for a moment. Despite the grave earnestness in Jane and Ratliff's expressions, Birch had a hard time stifling his laughter. These two bastions of regulated legal conduct hadn't just broken the rules, they had shattered them. Any emotional attachment between members of a Hypnos crew had always been frowned upon, but marriage was the ultimate taboo. It had seemed like a ridiculous excess to Birch, but any crewmembers caught trying to sneak that one by NASA faced complete and permanent exclusion from the space program. All of it. You were kicked off the mission, that was obvious, but it went much further than that. You wouldn't even get a place on a satellite repair crew once you had been blacklisted. You were grounded for good, and that was too big a risk to take. Nobody had ever dared to try it, or at least that's what Birch had always thought.

"I just can't believe the regulations would mean more to you than I did," Jane finally continued, ignoring Birch's comment. "I thought I knew you better than that."

"You know me fine," Ratliff responded stiffly. "The regulations were there for a reason."

"We're all here for a reason," Jane snapped back angrily. "And it's for more than just the work. We have to live! You knew that once."

"I still do," Ratliff mumbled, rising slowly to his feet. He pulled his robe around himself, examining the screens that lined the walls as he shuffled from panel to panel, pushing buttons and adjusting settings. "You have to live."

Jane said nothing more. They fell into an uncomfortable silence. Ratliff was still moving around working on something that Birch didn't fully understand. Jane watched silently, holding back, her face expressing the mixture of her emotions- anger, sadness, and confusion. She had been warm and emotional a moment ago, more human than Birch had seen her for a long time, but Ratliff's words threw her back into the darkness she had inhabited since their first failed mission to R67.3.

For a moment nothing more was said. For Birch, this territory was all too familiar. He had abandoned a wife, Sarah, to the cancer he knew would take her life. He had never talked to her about it, he had just left without saying a word, but he hadn't escaped. Though Birch had never given her the chance to say anything, still he could hear her voice accusing him of what he had done, and he couldn't argue with her. She was right. He hadn't loved her enough to stay when things were hard.

Birch finally broke the silence. He had to do it. He hated to speak, he was uncomfortable with the sound of his own voice, but he hated the silence even more. Sarah could speak in the silence, and whenever she stopped it was Karla's turn. Birch's guilt had many faces.

"What exactly is going on here, Ratliff?" Birch asked.

Ratliff didn't look up from his console where dozens of red dots spun and swerved across the display. Birch had the unhappy feeling that they represented something bad. Maybe this place wasn't as empty as he had hoped.

"I'm trying to figure out a way to get you out of here alive," Ratliff answered, pulling up a layout map with more red dots scurrying across it like angry insects on an ant hill.

"That's not what I'm talking about, Ratliff," Birch replied shortly; for once he wasn't interested in the mechanics of survival. This was his chance to do something, to fix something that was broken. For once, he wasn't going to run, even if it killed him.

"What, then?"

"You know what I mean," Birch hissed. "I want to know what happened here, how our mission went so wrong and turned out so right, and just now I'd like you to tell us why you're making out like you couldn't care less about Jane when it's pretty clear that you do."

Colonel Ratliff smiled sadly. His red eyes glanced up at Birch and then across to Jane. "You're not as dumb as they always said," he replied, "but then that's why I chose you. You always had a head full of mud, but you also had a heart, and the heart is where true wisdom lies."

"You chose me?" Birch wondered aloud, ignoring the more obvious jab at his intellect. "My selection had to go through NASA panels and committees, and as I recall, you weren't exactly supportive of me at the time. There's no way *you* chose me!"

"That's how I wanted it to look," Ratliff smiled, "but NASA, like everything else in life, was a multilayered organism honeycombed with conflicting interests that could easily be played against each other if you knew it well enough. I set the wheels in motion. I planted the discrediting information that removed your predecessor from the crew. I steered things toward you being the replacement. The rest was almost automatic. It was easy."

"But, why would you want me? What could you possibly gain by having me on the crew?"

"Yes, that would seem like a mystery," Ratliff agreed. "Your reputation preceded you. I have to tell you that the chance of you getting on a Hypnos mission without my intervention was about zero. Your temperament, your conduct, your questionable family situation, they were all wrong, and according to the textbook, you shouldn't have had a chance for anything more than a simple run to Mars. But I needed you and I knew the buttons to push, so I got you."

Birch thought for a moment. Honestly, he knew Ratliff was right. His application to Hypnos had been an act of desperation, and while he had kidded himself that he deserved it, he knew he didn't.

"Okay," Birch sighed, wearying of Ratliff's rambling explanation. "Just tell me, what was I supposed to do for you?"

"You helped me get Jane back home. You see, Jane knew the NASA system almost as well as I did. In the early planning stages, she wasn't supposed to be on the crew of the Hypnos III. I thought I'd set things up pretty well so that she'd never get on a Hypnos mission at all, but she found a way around my precautions and wangled herself onto the shortlist for my crew. By that time the only way I could stop her natural progress through the system was to do something direct enough that it might spread suspicion and caused an investigation that could have exposed our relationship. Knowledge of our marriage would have ended my mission. I had prepared my whole life for it. I couldn't stop now.

"That's where you came in. I knew what you were like. Your disposition and record spoke volumes. If I put you in an impossible situation, I knew you'd break and run for home, taking Jane with you. So, I used the cover of a storm to achieve my goal. I had to set up the equipment in the distant hemisphere, mess with the computer readings, and leave enough debris around to convince you that it had all been destroyed. The rest was pretty simple. I just had to sit back and watch you follow the course I had set out for you. It worked beautifully.

Birch was silent again. It was a hard thing to have someone so comprehensively quantify your every flaw. He didn't feel like he belonged to himself anymore. He wasn't a person. He was a set of learned and understood responses. He was a rat following the cheese in a maze of someone else's making.

Jane spoke. "You still haven't explained why I couldn't stay with you. Why did you send us home?"

"Because," Ratliff replied, "you weren't my crew, you were food."

FIFTY-THREE

"Food?" Jane gasped. She slumped over, holding her knees in her hands, looking away from Ratliff, hugging herself tightly. She was in shock.

"I suppose that's a crude way to put it," Ratliff admitted, "maybe it would be better to say it was more like you were my batteries, my energy supply to keep me going. It's not like anybody was going to get eaten or anything like that. 'Food' was just the slang term. Everyone lived; it's just that the roles weren't exactly as advertised."

"I'll say!" Birch roared. "'Be a Battery: Join Hypnos' doesn't somehow have quite the same ring to it. Or better still- 'Food Needed: Applications Now Being Accepted'! Honest recruiting like that wouldn't get you too far, would it? It's funny, when people want something from us we get told all the good things that will happen if we go along with them, and then, when bad stuff happens we say, 'I never signed up for this', but we did. We just didn't know it."

Ratliff shrugged. "Truthfully, none of us ever get what we sign up for."

"What did *you* sign up for?" Birch spat the question at him. "I bet it must have been good. At least you knew what you were getting into. That gave you an advantage over the rest of us anyway."

"I signed up for the same thing you did," Ratliff answered, looking over his shoulder at Jane's huddled form. "I just knew a bit more about what form that mission would take. We all wanted to give humanity a chance for a better future, to fulfill our dreams. I had my part to play, you had yours. Yours was the easier part.

"Maybe you've heard of parabiosis," he continued. "At its crudest level, a young person's blood is transfused into an older subject. The result is a moderate rejuvenation and revival of physical aptitude and brain function. The process showed a lot of promise but was eventually banned on the trumped up claim about a link to leukemia. In reality, it was just viewed as too dangerous for the masses. If you doubled the world's life expectancy you doubled its population, and that was something to be feared. This knowledge was too dangerous; it needed to be reserved for a select few."

"And who decided who those few were?" Birch asked angrily.

"People much higher up than you or I," Ratliff replied, "and you'll get no argument from me about what a rotten system it was. I agree, but the Hypnos command missions were based on that and you had to play along if you wanted to be a part of it.

"With further pharmaceutical research ways were found to increase the effectiveness of young blood; life expectancy was greatly increased. It was decided that this was the way forward with the Hypnos project. Expert guidance was needed on these missions, but time was our enemy. The time everything took was prohibitive; by the time anything had been achieved on a planet like this the founders would be dead, and everything would have to start all over again. A new generation would have to be trained, but something is always lost between the generations. The new never remembers the old. The same old lessons have to be learned and then relearned. That's why humanity never makes any real progress. Oh sure, we can make a few more gadgets, but what do we really learn? Ninety percent of our lives are spent trying to figure out what those who have died already knew: how to live and survive in a chaotic universe. Time was our enemy. We had to defeat it."

"Isn't that what cryogenics is for?" Birch remarked. "We sleep out the years and come back when we're needed."

"No," Ratliff replied, "not at all. Cryogenics is far too crude an implement to be of any real use. People aren't a frozen TV dinner to be taken out, heated, used, and refrozen for a future time. A little of that works fine, but for daily operations, it's too harsh a process, the wear on body systems is just too much. Anyone undergoing that repetitively wouldn't last. Besides, cryogenics gains you nothing. You sleep through everything. Your useful life isn't expanded, just paused. Parabiosis increases the actual time we have. So much more can be learned. So much more can be done.

"That's how Hypnos worked. The best officers were made commanders; the rest became 'food'. Their young blood would fuel the mission. Some older crew members were included for show (you're an example of that) so that suspicions wouldn't be aroused. There were many layers of knowledge in NASA. Most did not know how Hypnos really worked."

"Wow," Birch remarked bitterly, shaking his head. "It looks like Edwards was almost right after all, except he was worried about space-zombies when the real danger was from space-vampires all along. You're nothing more than a blood-sucking parasite, Ratliff. You're a leech, bleeding your own crew dry!"

Ratliff nodded. "You're right. Of course, you're right. I'd kidded myself into believing something else, but you're completely right. Having Jane join my crew woke me up to that. You see, before that I could rationalize everything. My crew would be asleep. That was the same as they had expected. They could still be revived when it was necessary, for their area of expertise to be used. Wasn't that what they signed up for? The only difference was that their sleep would not be undisturbed. The cycle of their cryogenic sleep could be altered to allow for fresh blood flow when it was needed. It was unobtrusive. They didn't wake up. It didn't shorten their life. It didn't affect them in any way. The only thing it did was good, so why should I worry about it? It was only the squeamish, petty morality of others that would see any problem in this. But then it was Jane and the petty, squeamish morality was my own."

Birch glanced over at Jane. She had slumped over on her side. Ratliff's eyes followed his gaze. "She's fine," he responded to Birch's worried look. "She isn't accustomed to the gasses down here. It's knocked her out. It's better that way.

"I loved her, you know," he continued. "I still do. I couldn't do that to her, so I sent her away. I'm sorry I used you. There wasn't any other way."

"Seems like you're accustomed to using people," Birch replied angrily. He was thinking of the blood that was supposed to sustain Ratliff's worthless life. The young blood: no blood had been younger than Karla's. That blood that had spilled so worthlessly back on the plains, the blood that had seeped into his uniform as he had held her, the blood that had seeped into his soul, it stung him now. No wonder Ratliff had been so anxious to have her on the crew. Nice fresh blood like that, it could have sustained him forever.

His old accustomed rage was rising. His world was crimson, as red as the blood that he saw in his mind. He took a step toward Ratliff. The colonel was at the computer; his back was to him. He hadn't faced him through his whole discourse. Perhaps he couldn't face him. He wouldn't know what hit him. It would be easy to exact his revenge, or justice, or whatever you wanted to call it.

An escaped sob from Ratliff stopped him. Ratliff's shoulders were shaking. He was crying. Birch waited, caught between his fury and the sudden pang of realization that this monster was a human.

"I suppose I should have ended it all. Really killed myself when I sent you all home, but I couldn't do it. I could complete the mission with the harsh cryogenic method and try to work out an alternative. It seemed to work. I came up with a chemical compound similar to blood and was able to use native resources in replicating it. Perhaps you've seen my river of blood?" Birch nodded that he had. "It's a marvel, isn't it? But it is an imperfect one. It kept me alive, but it didn't keep me satisfied. It was like drinking salt water, the more I consumed the thirstier I became.

"And then the colonists arrived. I had laid the groundwork for them as best I could. Without my crew, there were some gaps, but they managed. They were a marvel to watch. I kept myself hidden from them, sealed up the tunnels, and let them get to work. They did so much. I felt like their god. I had created this world and they populated it, developed what I had started, and grew beyond my original plans under my watchful eye. But there was always the thirst.

"I was sure I had tamed the demon. I was the vegetarian vampire, a benevolent god watching over my people, but when they ventured too far into the depths the temptation grew too great. I was thirsty, so thirsty. Have you ever been thirsty?"

Birch didn't answer, and Ratliff didn't seem to notice.

"Thirsty… thirst, hunger, desire: this is our vernacular, the common language we all speak." Ratliff paused, apparently struggling to regain his train of thought.

"The first time was the hardest. It was messy," he paused again, rubbing his face in his hands. "I didn't plan it. It just happened. I didn't even use the machine. It was sheer, bloody murder, but it felt so good. For once I wasn't thirsty.

"Well, after that it got easier, too easy. Things escalated and my legend began to grow. I had changed from their god to their devil, inhabiting the underworld, destroying them at will. I had my devotees, worshippers of a sort from the local population that aided me after a time. I found later that those who partook in the blood rites were more easily controlled. They came to depend on it just as I did. Their thirst was as great as mine, and that was my mistake. They became greedy, their thirst controlled them and I lost control. I had tried to fight the urges, to overcome the worse part of me. I hated myself, what I had become, but they didn't. Their excesses went beyond what I had ever imagined, and I couldn't fight them. They took over and I was placed here, a prisoner in my own hell."

He glanced over at Jane. "And I wake up to find my own angel fallen into hell with me." He tapped on his screen again. "I need you again, Birch." He brought up a display on the big screen showing the buzzing red dots and a map of the corridors they inhabited. "They know you're here and they aren't going to let you go. I've got a few defense devices at my disposal here, but I can't hold them off forever. I'm trying to clear a path for you now, but I've got to stay here and manage things from this station. They know that. You have to leave, now; they're crazy-thirsty and they'll target me to get to you- dead or alive, they don't care. You're not safe here."

Birch hesitated, glancing down at Jane. "You better come, colonel. We can't leave you here like this. Not again."

Ratliff sighed. "You're not listening. I need you, Birch, like I did before. Last time you did it without knowing. This time it'll be harder. I need you to leave. I need you to choose to leave. I need you to take her, to save Jane for me."

"No," Birch mumbled, shaking his head. "I can't do that again. No more running. No more leaving people. What will it do to Jane to leave you again? How could she live with that? What will she think of me?"

"She'll think you're a monster," Ratliff replied, "but we know who the true monster is. Even now I'm thirsty." He bit his parched lip. "I'm lost, Major Birch. My time has gone, but you can save her, whether she likes it or not. Being a hero isn't heroic: it's just doing the right thing." Ratliff rose from his station and crossed the room to where Jane lay. He bent down, kissing her soft lips lingeringly.

"Goodbye," he whispered. "I loved you." He stroked her hair, running his fingers gently down her cheek, then took her helmet and placed it on her head, resetting her suit to bring her back to consciousness.

"She's ready," Ratliff announced. "She should come back around in a few minutes. You need to be as far from here as possible by then."

Birch nodded and scooped her up into his arms. He walked to the ladder and paused. He wanted to say something, but he didn't know what.

"Colonel..." he stammered, "you didn't... you couldn't stop any of this. If it hadn't been you it would have been someone else. There are bigger forces at work than either of us. We're just small pieces in their game."

"I obeyed orders," Ratliff sighed, "willingly. It takes more bravery than I had to do anything else, despite what others may say. I didn't have it. You did, Major Birch. You didn't obey, but now do me this one last favor and obey this one last order: save her, Major Birch. Save Jane."

Birch nodded, stepped onto the ladder, and descended into the room below.

FIFTY-FOUR

Birch stepped off the ladder into the lower chamber. He paused for a last look up at the lonely trapdoor before heaving Jane onto his shoulder and exiting to the top of the spiral staircase.

He started down immediately. Two or three steps at a time, he took the stairs fast and with little thought for safety or precaution. Ratliff had been right, already Birch could hear the distant rumble of weapons firing. A moment later an explosion nearby rocked the tower, confirming the danger. Briefly, he lost his grip on Jane and she almost slipped over the side. He snatched her legs, pulling her back onto his shoulder, and continued his hurried descent.

Another explosion shook the tower, closer this time, and the stairs groaned and rattled as dust fell from the ceiling. "Where are those defenses you talked about, Colonel Ratliff?" Birch muttered, clinging to the banister as the stairs swayed. Almost in answer, a booming whoosh thundered from above. Birch recognized it as the sound of outgoing mortars. The Colonel was fighting back.

He kept running. Jane was starting to move, and he wanted to get to the bottom before he had to explain any of this to her.

Another, louder, explosion shook the tower. Birch lost his footing and dropped Jane. She fell onto the stairs as he stumbled forward, tumbling head-first, he slipped under the railing and just caught hold of a metal support, saving himself from falling to his death. He dangled there, helpless.

"Jane!" he shouted, trying unsuccessfully to pull himself up. His arm was slipping. "Jane!" he shouted again. She slowly raised her head. "Jane, get over here. I'm falling!" It took a moment, but she started moving, crawling groggily toward him. Almost automatically she extended her hand, helping him lift himself up.

"Thanks," Birch gasped, regaining his feet.

"What are we doing here?" Jane asked, still dazed from the effects of the gas. "Where's John... Colonel Ratliff?"

"He sent us down first," Birch replied. "He had things to finish up and told us to go on ahead. Come on, hurry." Jane nodded and they moved quickly down the stairs. They were near the bottom when a massive explosion shook the tower, sending bricks and metal falling around them. The stairs groaned and toppled sideways, landing crookedly against one wall. The momentum sent both Birch and Jane flying. Birch fell, hitting the ground hard, while Jane caught the handrail and hung on. As soon as the vibrations stopped she hurried down the remaining steps to his side.

"Major," Jane gasped. "Are you okay?"

Birch groaned and did his best to reply, but he was winded and couldn't speak. Jane lifted him gently up, turning him over examining him for obvious signs of injury. "I'm fine," he finally panted. "Let's get out of here."

"What about Colonel Ratliff?" Jane asked. Her mind was clearing now. "He's still got to get down."

Birch shrugged. "Yeah," he answered evasively, glancing up the rickety staircase to the platform far above.

"Oh no!" Jane shrieked, suddenly understanding. "You've done it again, haven't you? You left him up there, didn't you?" She didn't wait for an answer. She was already running for the stairs and had taken the first three when the stairwell groaned and took another sudden shift to the right, throwing her against the railing.

"Get off of there, Jane!' Birch shouted. "It won't hold your weight!" She ignored his voice and the sound of grinding, twisting metal as it swayed beneath her. "Stupid, stupid woman!" Birch growled, following her up the wrecked stairs. He caught up to her a moment later.

"No you don't!" she shouted as he lunged for her. She kicked out, landing a blow to his chest. He fell backward and she used the moment to turn and run again, but the leaning steps made it hard and Birch caught her again seconds later. "No!" she screamed. "No, no, no, no! Don't do this, Birch. Don't leave him up there. Don't leave him alone. Let me go. You can leave if you want to, just walk away. Just let me go to him!"

Birch pulled her down. She kicked and hit him. "No!" she screamed. "Don't do this! Aren't you tired… aren't you tired of leaving people to die alone?"

"Very tired," Birch choked the words out. His grip on her hand almost loosened, but before he could decide what to do the staircase buckled. The top came loose and it shifted, scraping down the wall a few feet before catching on the metal and stopping again. It held, but it wasn't going to last.

He pushed her toward the exit, but they hadn't reached the doorway when the whole staircase began to creak and moaned ominously. It shifted again, grinding, gouging the wall, then cracked, broke in two, and fell down the shaft toward them.

Birch saw the whole thing as if in slow motion. They had to move, now. He shoved Jane through the door, hurling himself after her, and was blasted by a great gust of air and debris that flung him through the opening in a cloud of smoky destruction. He hit the ground face first but quickly regained his feet. The tower swayed under the impact, but it held.

Birch pulled Jane out of the dirt and tried dragging her to the bridge, but she resisted. Pulling herself free, shielding her eyes against the glare, she stared up at the top of the tower.

Birch grabbed her arm again, pulling her so close that their visors clinked. "Look," he spat, "this is what the colonel wanted. He wanted to save you. If you die here he will have failed. All he did for you will have failed. If you want to give him anything then you have got to live."

More mortars were coming in. They landed nearby with thundering explosions, that shook the ground, but Jane didn't flinch. She looked heavenward to the tower, unfazed by the destruction. Finally, her eyes came back to the ground and the world around them. "Alright then," she finally said, her voice dripping with irony, "where exactly were you planning on going?"

"Out," Birch snapped back impatiently, "the way we came, of course." He gestured to the bridge behind him, but as he turned the full meaning of her words struck him. A mob of ten or so space-suited colonists was already storming across the footbridge toward them. The only path of escape was cut off. They were trapped.

The colonists were almost halfway over already. The precarious bridge bounced and swayed under their heavy footsteps. Birch glanced desperately around the small island for another way of escape. There was nothing. Bubbling lava flowed below its steep cliffs. There was no way beyond that. The barren jut of rock was isolated, completely cut off except for the bridge.

He snatched up a metal bar from the pile of debris and ran for the footbridge with the crazy idea of fighting his way to the other side. It was stupid, but it was the only thing he could think of. There didn't seem to be any other way, but as he ran he noticed something unusual. Above all the noise there was a distinctive hum, like electricity, and the further he ran onto the bridge the more pronounced it became. He hadn't gotten too far when the sound intensified and a jolt of energy leaped through his suit, shutting down all functions. It only lasted for a second, but he stopped midstride. The metal bar fell from his hands and he collapsed.

Birch lay gasping. His suit had relit almost an instant later, but the shock left him weak and he couldn't regain his feet. Jane rushed to his side. She hadn't followed him onto the bridge and wasn't affected.

"Get up," she snapped, pulling him to his feet. "We've got to get off this bridge!" She half dragged him, pulling him back to the island. By now the other colonists had regained their feet and were coming toward them again.

The bridge started humming louder than ever. "That was a warning shot," Jane shouted, pointed up to the top of the tower where a green light was flashing. "It's Colonel Ratliff," she smiled bitterly. "You've abandoned him, but he hasn't abandoned us, watch." As they cleared the last section of the bridge the humming intensified and the green light turned red. Instantly the cavern shook and a charge, much fiercer than before, hit.

Jane and Birch were a good ten meters off the footbridge by the time it hit, but the force of the blast slammed into their backs, hurling them both into the dirt twenty feet away.

By the time Birch pulled himself up again the colonists were all either gone or dead. Some had probably fallen into the cauldron; others were lying in heaps on the bridge. Jane was right, Birch was sure that, Colonel Ratliff was responsible for this miracle.

"Come on," Birch shouted, starting toward the Bridge again, "now's our chance."

Jane didn't move. She wavered, glancing back up at the tower, then back down at him. "No," she finally answered shaking her head, "I won't do it. Colonel Ratliff hasn't abandoned us, and I for one won't leave him."

"The whole reason he's helping us," Birch grunted impatiently, "is so we can escape. Your staying here destroys the one thing he's trying to do. Can't you see that?"

"No, I can't," she answered flatly, "and I'd rather stay here with him, even if we both die. We'll still be together. I don't suppose you'd understand that, would you?"

Birch shrugged. Her words stung him, but he wasn't going to let her see the damage. "Fine," he muttered and started back to the bridge. "I'm sure you'll be very happy together."

He sprinted for the bridge and kept running. The humming intensified again. He wondered if Ratliff had seen him leaving without Jane and had decided to zap him as a final act of revenge for his betrayal, but he had done all he could for her. He just couldn't get through. Jane had given up and he had no other option but the one he always had, the one that always saved his life but made it so hard to live. He had to run. He had to leave her behind. He had to get back for the others, for Lauren, Edwards, and the Ares kid. They were depending on him. They needed him to survive. Birch tried to convince himself in this way that running was noble. He knew it wasn't. He just wasn't ready to stay for Jane's doomed love. He hadn't been ready to stay for his own.

The hum grew worse. He could feel the bridge vibrating beneath his feet and his head felt like it was about to split open. A loud boom sounded and Birch's muscles tightened in expectation of a painful death, but he felt nothing. A sudden blast of hot air whooshed by him a moment later and he turned to see the top of the tower in flames.

It didn't make any sense. No mortars had landed, but now in the distance he could see them coming again, more tracer lines burning through the air. They flew in with whistling breath, hitting the island and the lava flowing beneath it. Red, glowing plumes of fire and smoke burst out, shaking the bridge, knocking Birch to his knees.

He leaped up again. Turning, he ran back to the island. He knew just where to look, and quickly he found Jane through the rising smoke and falling ash. She was just where he had expected, at the base of the tower digging vainly, ripping and tearing the rubble from its crushed entrance. Birch pulled her away, and she didn't fight him this time.

"He's gone!" Birch shouted, pointing to the fierce flames flying up from the top of the tower."There's nothing you can do. Come on! The others need you. We all need you!" Her body shook and her knees buckled, but as he held her she nodded slightly. With determined effort, she pulled herself up again and, with one last glance at the tower, followed Birch to the bridge.

They ran. For a short time, the mortar fire continued toward the tower, but soon they changed direction and came down near the bridge. The shots rained down but missed, falling short into the bubbling cauldron below. They exploded, sending up gushing geysers of bloody liquid. Three hit nearby in quick succession, rocking the bridge, pulling it from its support, twisting it almost sideways as one cable snapped. Birch nearly fell, but grabbed the handrail just in time.

"It doesn't look like they want us to leave!" Jane gasped over the booming explosions.

"I'm guessing these must be the guards left to watch over sleeping beauty, to make sure he never woke up" Birch panted, gesturing back to Colonel Ratliff's tower. "I suppose that makes us their enemy too. We woke him up."

"Not for long," Jane mumbled through broken breaths.

Another mortar hit nearby, shaking the bridge, but Birch kept going. "I don't think they're trying to hit us," he shouted, "just slow us down. Keep moving!"

They had to make the last part of their crossing in slow, painful sidesteps as they edged along the last seventy meters of the swaying, leaning footbridge. The waterfall thundered and boomed beneath them, sending up its crimson spray, coating everything with a sludgy mist.

Finally, they made it. Reaching the edge of the footbridge they leaped down from the platform and ran into the darkness of the cave, along the riverbank

Their lights clicked on as they moved further into the

tunnel. Their beams wobbled and swerved drunkenly in the darkness. The footing was slick and treacherous, and running wasn't advisable. One slip could take them over the falls, but they ran anyway. The mortar fire had stopped, but Birch had no doubt that the guards wouldn't let them go that easily. Their blood was too precious for that. His fears were confirmed a moment later when lights appeared in the darkness ahead.

FIFTY-FIVE

The lights were coming slowly down the tunnel. Birch shut off his lamp and gestured for Jane to do the same. They took cover behind a rock and waited for them to pass. He was hoping it would be that easy, that the colonists would walk by and wouldn't notice them, but if they did he was ready. They weren't going to get the jump on him this time.

They waited breathlessly as the lights approached. Twin beams pierced the darkness. Birch was relieved. That was less than he expected, maybe there weren't as many of them as he had feared. Somehow he doubted that. There had been a lot of red dots on Ratliff's screen. The others were probably somewhere nearby.

As the lights approached Birch's headset started catching garbled snippets of speech. He couldn't make out the words but he knew the voices. It was Edwards and the Ares kid. It was them. They had come after them.

"I thought I told you two to stay on the ship," Birch bellowed as he rose from his hiding place. Edwards leaped back, surprised at his sudden appearance, but the Ares kid didn't move. He looked as if he had been expecting to find them exactly where they were.

"That's my fault," Edwards explained sheepishly. "We had some visitors come by the ship, trying to get in, some of the colonists. The charge kept them off but they kept coming back, throwing stuff against the hull, draining the power, so I knew if we didn't deal with them there wouldn't be anything left for the launch, so we went outside."

"You went outside?" Birch shook his head.

"Well, I waited until they were all close enough, then I let them have it with a heavy dose of power, zapped them all unconscious. Once we got outside we figured we should just secure the ship and come get you. Things are getting tricky up there. We need to go."

"What did you do with the colonists?" Birch asked. "Leaving them unconscious by the ship wouldn't exactly stop them for long."

Edwards looked at the kid before answering. "They won't be a problem," he finally answered.

"Yeah, I finished them off," the Ares blurted out.

"Finished them off?" Birch spluttered. "You mean you killed them while they were unconscious, in cold blood?"

Edwards lowered his head. "I was going to try and tie them up or lock them up somewhere, but the kid was at them too quickly, and before I knew what he was doing half of them were gone. It's the Ares' way. That's what I tried to tell you before. You can't change them."

Birch shook his head angrily. Words failed him.

"They were trying to kill us," the kid responded coolly. "I got them first. What's the problem with that?"

"If you need me to tell you then there's no point in me telling you," Birch responded dryly. "But just for once I'd like to know for sure that I was on the side of the angels."

He started back up the tunnel without another word. The others followed. They passed the point where the river narrowed into a stream. They walked beyond the oozing stones, and not a word was spoken. The only sound was the splashing of their boots in the stream as they crossed and the crunch of the gravel underfoot as they made their way through the labyrinth of caves back to the stairs.

Birch was watching for colonists, but all the while his mind kept going back to Ratliff and their futile mission. Hypnos had been one giant lie. Everything had been built on a lie. Their crew had been nothing but a commodity: food and knowledge, to be stored and consumed when needed. But Birch hadn't even been that. He had been a pawn in Ratliff's counter-play to save Jane. It was a strange irony to find that he had abandoned his own wife for the unknown mission of saving Ratliff's wife.

They reached the exit to the stairs. Birch paused long enough to look briefly back for any sign of pursuit before pulling the door open. He squinted up into the darkness. As far as he could tell the stairwell was empty, and he quickly began the long ascent.

With hurried steps, they climbed and made good progress. They were about half way up when Edwards, who was puffing and panting at the rear, let out a cry. Birch looked down. The light from Edwards' helmet shook and swerved wildly a few levels below. There was an impression of movement, but he couldn't see anything more from this angle.

He turned, running to assist him, but Jane and the Ares had already started down, and by the time he reached them the Ares had already sent one colonist over the railing, toppling into the darkness below. Two others were still wrestling with Jane and Edwards. Birch grappled with one, but before he had subdued him the Ares had the other over the banister and came back for the third, and together they sent the last one over the same way as the others.

"Well," Edwards gasped, watching the Ares nimbly bound up the steps a moment later, "sometimes I guess it pays to have a demon on the side of the angels."

Birch didn't answer; he was listening to the sound coming up from below. The colonist attackers had fallen, clattering and smashing all the way down as they hit metal and masonry. The sound had almost disappeared by the time they landed with a faint thud at the bottom, but now something else was happening. Another sound was rising up, louder and nearer than anything he had expected, rhythmic, metallic clangs, soft and slow at first, but growing and intensifying into a pounding, thumping rhythm that shook the air around them.

"What's going on down there?" Birch shouted over the intense noise.

"It sounds like they're beating the railings," Edwards observed. "It could be some sort of rage ritual, a demonstration of their anger over the deaths in their clan." He looked worried. Something about this seemed to register in his mind from his experience with the Ares. "Or maybe it's something worse."

"What could be worse than making them mad?" Jane asked.

"Making them hungry."

Edwards' words sent a chill down Birch's spine.

"The specimens I saw earlier seem far less developed even than the Ares," Edwards continued. "We're talking completely primeval here. They were pure instinct and pure hunger. As primitive as they are, the sight of their comrade's blood could drive them wild. With any luck, that native instinct will kick in and they'll rip their helmets off to feed and suffocate themselves in the low oxygen atmosphere of the base."

"I don't think so," Birch interrupted. He was thinking back to what Colonel Ratliff had told him. "You might be right about the blood making them hungry, or more likely thirsty, but that won't tempt them. Stale, old blood like that wouldn't be so appetizing. I think they'd prefer something fresh, something a little younger."

Jane gasped. "That's not even close to funny!" she snapped.

"It wasn't meant to be," Birch responded. The noise level was growing. They were beating the railings as they climbed and it sounded like they weren't that far below. "We better get out of here," Birch muttered, climbing the stairs more quickly.

They hurried up the remaining steps. All the while the sound intensified. By the time they reached the exit Birch was sure they were right behind them. He was starting to pick up a weird feedback in his headset. It sounded like staticky gibberish at first, but he quickly recognized what it was. The colonists were close enough that he was hearing their transmissions, but what he was hearing wasn't any language. It was more primitive, more guttural than anything human. He thought back to those early reports from *The Lowers*, how they had told of strange animal noises. It must have been this, but he had never imagined he would hear it himself, that he would be the object of their ancient hunger.

They ran through the corridors. All the passages were identical, but Birch remembered the way. They twisted and turned until they came to the room he was looking for. Two caged elevators were there, at the bottom of the long tunnel that led to the surface. Birch flung open the door to the nearest cage, but before anyone else could enter he pushed the button and exited again, sending it clanking up into the darkness. "We don't need anyone following us," he explained, joining the others in the second elevator.

Birch pushed the button again, but they hadn't moved before a swarm of colonists burst into the room. Without a second's pause, they rushed at them, launching themselves at the cage, crashing into it with pounding impact that rocked its wire walls and knocked Birch to the floor.

The elevator started to rise. Eight or nine colonists clung to the sides, like metal to a magnet. As the compartment began its slow ascent they tried to get in, pawing the door, trying to open it. A hand reached in near the floor, grabbing for Jane's ankle. She stomped the fingers, hard. The man pulled back, howling as he fell swiftly into the darkness.

The remaining colonists kept at them, clawing and pulling at the cage. Birch and the others successfully concentrated on keeping them out, but then he saw what they were really up to. While some had been trying the direct approach through the door, others had climbed up, working their way to the top where they now pounded the pulley mechanism that supported the compartment and lifted them to the surface. They were trying to jam the works, and at any moment they would either stop the elevator or send it crashing down the shaft. They didn't seem to care either way. Their thirst made them crazy.

"Trouble!" Birch shouted over the clatter of the machinery and the howls of their attackers. Edwards and Jane were preoccupied with their task of ridding the elevator of its clinging colonists. Edwards had started alone, prizing their fingers from the cage, but had found that every time he loosened one hand, the other was still there supporting them. Jane had come to his aid, and together they brought three down with their combined effort.

That left the Ares, who with Birch had been defending the door. He nodded an acknowledgment and without another word heaved the door open, smacking it into the body of a colonist who lost his grip and fell silently into the yawning chasm.

"Nice shot," Birch commented, but the kid didn't answer. He was already out the door and climbing to the top of the elevator. Birch tried to follow, but another colonist swung down before he could exit and landed a thudding blow into his chest, sending him skidding across the floor. Birch landed with a crunch against the far wall and his attacker followed him in.

Birch lay dazed, unable to move. The colonist came at him, but he did not attack. Falling down at his feet, their helmets almost touched, but still, he didn't attack. He remained perfectly still. It was almost an act of worship, a plea for absolution for sins of the past and those about to be committed. Through the opaque visor Birch imagined he saw the outline of a face, a human face, but mostly he caught the impression of violent movement of the head and flashing teeth. These were the guards Ratliff had warned him about. Driven mad by an eternity of want, they now saw the chance to feed, to finally slake their everlasting thirst.

Frothy droplets of saliva flecked the visor as the rabid colonist forgot his space suit and leaned in to bite Birch, but before he got far enough to discover his mistake Edwards landed a powerful kick to his unsuspecting ribs that sent him crashing to the floor. Birch tried to regain his feet to join the fight but only made it up in time to see Edwards and Jane drag their foe across the floor and push him through the door to a certain death far below.

Birch struggled back to the open door. Another colonist flew by, falling, tumbling helplessly into the darkness. He didn't make a sound. Most of them fell silently, without any struggle, without flailing arms or kicking legs. It was almost as if they embraced their fate. While they were alive they fought and clawed, battling for every breath and any chance to wet their parched tongue and arid souls, but now, as they fell, they were free of all that. They were free to die.

Birch winced. Somehow he almost envied their moment of freedom, but he didn't envy what they would find at the bottom. No one wanted to find what was at the bottom. Jane had tried, but she regretted it now, he was sure of that. The flight was never worth the landing.

Looking up Birch saw that no colonists were left. The Ares gave him a thumbs up and started climbing down to join them in the compartment.

"Well," Birch observe, leaning heavily against the cage, "that was all very interesting. I'm just glad it was only killer-crazed-colonists we had to deal with and not something truly scary like maybe a misplaced spring or a rusted out bolt, right Edwards?" Edwards didn't answer.

It took another twenty long minutes to reach the top. The cage clanked and sighed its way up the long shaft. Birch kept watching, peering into the darkness for any sign of more colonists, but he saw nothing. Every level they passed was empty, and as they finally pulled into an empty chamber on the ground level he actually began to believe that they might escape alive.

FIFTY-SIX

It wasn't until they exited the elevator building and came out into *Main Dome* that Birch's hope for escape finally died. It was impossible. Their way back to the ship was completely blocked. A mass of forty or fifty colonists stood between them and their path of escape. Birch's plan had been to ensure that the ship remained safe, but if they couldn't get back to it that didn't do them any good. These colonists were pure savages, but they were smart enough to know how to secure their next meal. They had prepared for their return, and there was no way back.

"What now, Major Thomas Birch?" Jane asked, noting his hesitation. "Don't tell me for once you came up with a plan and didn't figure out a way to make sure *you* made it back safely."

Birch ignored her barbed comment. His eyes were on the Ares who was running to launch a futile attempt at a frontal assault on the mob. He was a good fighter, but not that good. Birch called him back, gesturing to the main entrance at the front of the dome. It wasn't the right way, but it was clear. "This way!" he shouted. The kid hesitated midway between the opposing groups.

"We're going outside!" Birch shouted again, pulling the others toward the doors. The entryway was wide, ornamental and well preserved. It was one of the few parts of the base that could match *Colony One* for grandeur, but that didn't interest Birch. It was a door and they could get through it. That was all he cared about.

The kid ran double speed and caught them as they entered the airlock. They quickly fled out onto the surface. The colonists chased them, but that didn't bother Birch. That was exactly what he wanted. He was going to draw them off, get them to follow them out of the base. Then he could double back, find another airlock a little further around, and cut through to the ship from there.

It was a simple plan, and simple plans often work, but this one didn't. As soon as he was outside he knew it wasn't going to work. More colonists were already running for them, pouring out from other airlocks around the base. Their path around the *Primary Base* was cut off in both directions. They were surrounded on three sides, and the only way left was forward, the way back to *Colony One*. Without hesitation, Birch bolted for the distant base.

"Well, this isn't exactly going to plan," Edwards panted as they ran. "How exactly are we going to get back to the ship?" Birch didn't have an answer for that and he was too busy running for his life to bother coming up with one. The only thing he cared about right now was surviving for the next five seconds, and anything beyond that wasn't on his horizon.

They all scrambled to escape, fleeing wildly with no plan and no hope, just the wild desire to live. Their need to live was as basic and primeval as the colonist's desire to feed, and it was a race to see which instinct would win out.

There wasn't much doubt in any of their minds who would win. *Colony One* was so far away that there was no hope of reaching it in time. Birch knew that, but even though the base was little more than a gray speck on the gray horizon he made for it and kept running for those five seconds.

The colonists' grunting grew louder than ever behind them, but another sound was added to that, one that quickly drowned out the tumult of their rasping breaths. It was the sound of engines. Birch glanced back then stopped running. His jaw hung loose in surprise. Flying in low and fast above the rocky terrain of R67.3 was their ship, Pickett's shuttle.

The Ares whooped, but the others could only stare in disbelief as the craft approached. It came in fast and low, so low that it cut down a whole host of colonists pursuing them. Birch and the others barely had time to hit the ground before it zoomed over them, convulsing the rock and dust they clung to.

Birch lifted his head first. Before them was the ship, now landed and with its boarding doors open. Glancing behind he saw a whole swath of colonists cut down like timber felled by a mighty storm. Many were dead, but many were not and they rose up again, relentless in their pursuit.

"Come on!" Birch shouted, helping Edwards to his feet. The others were already up and running.

"Who's flying that thing?" Edwards gasped as he struggled to keep up. "Are you sure they're a friend?"

"Who cares!" Birch shouted. The five-second rule continued to apply and if this ship offered him five more seconds of life he would take it.

Birch half pulled Edwards toward the ship. They were the last ones to make it and he slammed the doors shut behind them. They were all safe inside. Birch breathed a sigh of relief, but through the window, he could see the colonists still rushing toward them. The internal airlock door had only just opened, allowing them into the main part of the ship, when the colonists hit against the craft with a crash that sent them flying. Many more hits like that and they would have the shuttle over.

"Let's go," Birch barked, "rushing to the cockpit. There was no time to worry about who was flying this ship or who they would find there, but when they entered they found no one at all. The cockpit was empty.

"H-h-h-hiiiii there!" a familiar, overly pronounced American accent greeted as Birch took the pilot's seat. An image flashed up on the control screen. It was the same computerized man with slicked back hair and sunglasses: Max Headroom.

"Peter... Peter Wagner, is that you?" Birch stammered. I thought you'd switched yourself off."

"Ha... ha, ha, ha," Wagner's Max Headroom persona laughed maniacally and flashed a too perfect smile. "Just my home, Major, that was all I turned off. Now they'll have an even harder time than ever trying to catch me as I run free through their system. But reeeeee-ally," he glitched again, "we have no t-t-t-timeee for such niceties." An outside view of the ship being swarmed by colonists flashed up on the screen.

"I-I-I-I-I... had to f-f-flyyyyy this thing in blind," Wagner continued. "My view of anything outside of C-c-colony One is limited. The only thing I truly p-p-p-picked up was you because of our little vis-s-s-s-s-itttt. I located your ship that way. I g-g-g-guess it worked, b-b-b-b-bu-t-t-t-t the flying is up t-t-t-t-o-o-o-o-ooooo you now Birchy Bab-b-b-b-b-y-y!"

"Okay," Birch sighed, grabbing the stick, "But if you could lose the Max Headroom stutter that would be really great!"

"S-s-s-sor-r-ry," Wagner replied, "but no can do! It's-s-s-s-s the format created to allow me to communicate outside of the c-c-omputer."

"Great," Birch muttered, pulling back on the stick and throttling the engines. Flames burst out, setting some colonists ablaze, but even this was not enough to distract them from their raging thirst, and they continued pounding and clawing at the hull even as they burned.

The ship took off. External cameras showed the colonists trying to hang on to the craft, but Birch shook the wings and they fell to the ground like fleas from a dog.

"Major!" Edwards cried, pointing at a nearby screen. "It's that same heat buildup you told me to warn you about!"

"Great," Birch muttered again, chewing his lower lip in concentration. He held the ship in position for the briefest of moments, before hurtling into a barrel role, pulling up just before impact to avoid a barrage of green rays that shot out from the tower on top of *Primary Base*.

"Remind me to knock that thing down next time I come for a visit," Birch quipped, sending the ship beyond *Colony One* to a safe distance from the ray.

Edwards and the Ares cheered together. Jane showed no joy, but even she seemed relieved to be alive. They had made it. They were finally free of the shadow of this wretched world and its dead colonies. All they had to do was fly away, but Birch didn't leave. He put the ship in a holding pattern for a moment as he turned his attention to the screen and Max's face.

"Wagner," Birch said, "you saved us back there. What can we do for you?"

"Nothing," he replied. The glib smile and the cockiness had vanished from his face. The sunglasses were off and the fake American accent had almost disappeared. "I'm a c-c-computer program. This is my system here, Major Birch. This is where I live. What can you do for me? You might as w-w-well try to rescue a t-t-toaster."

"You're not a toaster."

Max shrugged, or at least he seemed to. It turned into one of his customary glitches. "Do one thing for me though. If you find Peter, the real Peter Wagner, t-t-tell him I did what I was supposed to do, that I helped guide you to him."

Birch smiled sadly. "I'll tell him more than that. I'll tell him heroic tales of the Peter Wagner I met here, the one who outwitted the colonists for all those years and the one who saved our lives. The 'real' Peter Wagner will have an awful lot to live up to."

Max blinked before his mouth curled into a half-hearted perfect smile. "G-g-goodbye," he said, and the screen went blank.

For a while, no one spoke or moved. Eventually, Birch sighed and pushed the thrusters, launching the ship up and out of the atmosphere. Finally, they were escaping, but once again he had left others behind: Wagner and Ratliff. Colonel Ratliff's resurrection had been so brief that it hardly seemed real, but he could see in Jane's face that it was very real. The deepened wounds of the renewed loss were clearly seen there. This wasn't going to be any easier than last time.

The ship was approaching the Hypnos. Birch smiled grimly to himself. At least this place gave him a reason to exist. There was a purpose here. He was going to find the lost colony. He was going to find some place that made living worth the effort.

Birch gently guided the ship into the docking compartment. The pads of Pickett's shuttle landed softly on the hard bay floor and a few moments later they were unbuckling and exiting the ship. It was tempting to bend down and kiss the steel deck as a sign of appreciation for their arrival, but no one did.

Birch exited the hangar bay, heading for the bridge, when strong hands grabbed him from behind and spun him around. There were many faces, but he recognized only one. It was a face that he had never seen in life, but he had seen many times in the video records at *Colony One*. It was Security Chief James Miltant.

"Well, Major Birch, welcome aboard *my* ship," he smiled coldly. "I thought you'd never make it."

Coming Next

Fallout

Planetfall
Book III

Acknowledgments

Our lives are all enriched by the creative imagination of so many people. In my childhood giants like George Lucas and Gene Roddenberry walked large. As I grew older the likes of Charles Dickens and William Shakespeare, or 'Franklin W. Dixon' and Enid Blyton all had their impact. There were many others too, video game programmers, TV producers, and musicians, more than I can mention, who have all inspired me. Some of them, favorites from my formative years, I have referenced in my work here (my own fustalgic urge is hard to resist). I would like to thank them all for the flavor they added to our vanilla lives.

Thank you to my family. It takes a long time to write a book, and you are very patient. I have finished this book. I promise to get off the computer long enough to play and do some useful things for a change!

Thank you to my readers. Time is a valuable thing, and I am humbled that any would spend such a precious commodity on the work of a new author. Your kind words and encouragement mean a lot to me. Thank you so much!

www.ingramcontent.com/pod-product-compliance
Lightning Source LLC
Chambersburg PA
CBHW050900250626
47155CB00001B/39